# THE SILENT BOY

By the same author

*The Scent of Death*
*The Anatomy Of Ghosts*
*Bleeding Heart Square*
*The American Boy*

*A Stain On The Silence*
*The Barred Window*
*The Raven On The Water*

The Roth Trilogy: Fallen Angel
*The Four Last Things*
*The Judgement Of Strangers*
*The Office Of The Dead*

The Lydmouth Series

The Blaines Novels

The Dougal Series

ANDREW
TAYLOR
THE
SILENT
BOY

HarperCollins*Publishers*

HarperCollins*Publishers*
1 London Bridge Street
London SE1 9GF

www.harpercollins.co.uk

Published by HarperCollins*Publishers* 2014
1

A catalogue record for this book
is available from the British Library

ISBN: 978-0-00-813135-7

This novel is entirely a work of fiction.
The names, characters and incidents portrayed in it,
while at times based on historical fact, are
the work of the author's imagination.

Set in Sabon LT Std by Palimpsest Book Production Limited,
Falkirk, Stirlingshire

Printed and bound in the USA

Find out more about HarperCollins and the environment at
**www.harpercollins.co.uk/green**

*For James*

# Chapter One

*Say nothing. Not a word to anyone. Whatever you see. Whatever you hear. Do you understand? Say nothing. Ever.*

*Tip-tap.* Like cracking a walnut.

Now and always Charles sees the blood. It runs down his cheek and soaks into his shirt. He licks his dry lips and tastes it, salty and metallic and forbidden.

He has fallen as he ran down the steep stairs. He's lying on his back. He looks up. It is raining blood from a black sky striped with yellow. Blood glistens in the light of the lantern on the table.

There's shouting and banging outside.

Inside, the blood is crying out. It's screaming and shouting and grunting. The sound twists through his skull. It cuts into bone and splinters into a thousand daggers that draw more blood.

He scrambles to his feet. His shoes are by the door. He slips his feet into them.

There are no words for this, all he has heard and seen. There are no words for anything. There must never be any words.

Awake and asleep, here and anywhere, now and always. Never any words.

Charles lifts the latch and drags open the heavy door. No more words.

*Hush now. Say nothing.*

*Tip-tap.*

Charles darts out of the cottage and pulls the door shut. The cobbled yard is in darkness. So are the workshops and the big house beyond. Above the rooftops, though, the air flickers orange and yellow with the light of torches. The noise is deafening. He wants to cover his ears.

The tocsin is ringing. There are other bells. Their jangling fills the night and mingles with the host of unnatural sounds. The street on the far side of the house is as noisy as by day – much noisier, with shouts and screams, with barks and explosions, with the clatter of hooves and the grating of iron-rimmed wheels.

Someone begins to knock at a door – not with a hand or a knocker. These blows are slow and purposeful. They make the air itself tremble. Glass shatters. Someone is shrieking.

Wood splinters. They are breaking down the door of the main house. In a matter of minutes they will be in the yard.

Charles stumbles towards the big gates beyond the cottage. Two heavy bars hold them shut, sealing the back of the yard. In one leaf is a little low wicket.

At night the wicket is secured by two bolts. He fumbles for them in the darkness, only to find that they are already open.

Of course they are.

He pushes the gate outward. Nothing happens. Locked, not bolted? In desperation he tugs it towards him. The gate slams into him with such force that he falls on the slippery cobbles.

The cottage door is opening.

Panic surges through him. He is on his feet again. The lane

2

outside the gate is in darkness. He leaps through the wicket. The lane beyond runs parallel to the street. The warm air stinks of decay. The city is so hot it has gone mad.

In the confusion, he is dimly aware that the hammering from the house has stopped. There are lights on the other side of the yard. Shutters are flung open. The windows fill with the light of hell.

Chains rattle, bolts slide back. A dog is barking with deep, excited bellows.

Through the open wicket he sees the house door opening. He glimpses the black shape of a huge dog in the doorway.

Charles covers his mouth with his hand to keep the words inside from spilling out. He turns and runs.


There is so much confusion in the world that no one gives Charles a second glance. They push past him. They cuff him out of their way as if swatting a fly.

He is of no interest to them. He is nothing. He is glad to be nothing. He wants to be less than nothing.

He shrinks back into a doorway. He sees blood everywhere, in the gutters, on the faces and clothes of the men and women hurrying past him, daubed on the wall opposite.

At the corner of the street, the crowd has surrounded a coach. They are pulling out the man and the woman inside and throwing out their possessions. A hatbox falls open and the hat rolls out. A man stamps on it.

The woman is crying, great ragged sobs. The gentleman is quite silent. His eyes are closed.

The baker's assistant, who is a burly fellow half a head taller than everyone else, tugs at the woman's dress. He paws at the neck. The thin fabric rips.

Charles slips from the doorway. He does not know where he is going but his feet know the way. He has nothing with him except the shirt he was sleeping in, his breeches and the shoes on his feet.

The sign of the Golden Pheasant hangs above the shop that sells poultry. Someone has draped a petticoat over it.

Old Barbon, the porter of the house five doors down, is lying on the ground. He is pouring wine into his mouth and the liquid runs over his cheeks. Barbon once gave him a plum so sweet and juicy that Marie said it came from the angels.

Madame Pial, who keeps the wine shop in the next street, is dragging a sack along the road. She has lost her hat and her cap. Her grey hair flows in a greasy tide over her shoulders.

The Rue de Richelieu is seething with people. Their faces are twisted out of shape. They are no longer human. They are ghouls in a nightmare. Charles pushes through them in the direction of the river. The street ends at the Rue Saint-Honoré. He means to turn left and cross the river at the Pont Royal. But the crowd is even denser here, clustering around the Tuileries like wasps round a saucer of jam. He will not be able to force his way through.

Besides, lying on the road not three yards away from him is one of the King's Swiss Guards. The man has no head and he has lost his boots and breeches. His entrails coil out of his belly, gleaming in the torchlight, still twitching.

Charles slows. He weaves eastwards towards the Île du Palais. He crosses the river at the Pont Neuf. National Guards are on both sides of the river and also on the Île du Palais itself. But they are taking no notice of the people who stream north over the river towards the Tuileries. He slips among them, against the flow of the tide. He smells sweat and excitement and anger.

There are fewer people on the Rive Gauche. But the noise is almost as bad. The sound of artillery and musket fire near the Tuileries. The screams and shouts. The clatter of wheels and hooves.

On the Quai d'Orsay and the Quai Theatines people are watching the battle on the other side of the river as if it is a firework display.

In the Rue Dauphine, his mind clears, not much but enough to realize where he is going. He has been here only once before, and then it was daylight and everything was normal. It takes him nearly an hour to find his way, casting to and fro in the near darkness, avoiding the crowds, avoiding the people who try to sweep him into their lives.

At last, not far from the Café Corazza, he stumbles on the narrow mouth of the alley. It leads to a paved court. The only light comes from an oil lamp on a second-floor windowsill. The lamp casts a faint dirty-yellow fragrance. The court has trapped the sun's warmth during the day. It is even hotter than the street.

For a moment he listens. He hears nothing nearby except the scramble of rats, a sound grown so familiar he barely notices it.

He finds the door with the help of his fingertips not his eyes.

The wood is old and scarred and as dry as a desert. Charles hammers on it until his knuckles bleed. He hammers on it until it opens.

Marie is not much taller than he is. She is almost as wide as she is tall. She looks like a bull in a faded blue dress and carries with her a smell of sweat, garlic and woodsmoke, mingled with a sour, milky quality that is hers alone. Her smell is as familiar to Charles as anything in the world.

She draws him over the threshold and squeezes him in her arms so tightly that he finds it hard to breathe.

'What happened?' she says. 'Where is Madame?'

She asks him questions over and over again and he cannot answer any of them. In the end she gives up. She brings water and a cloth and rinses the blood from his face and hands.

The only light in the room comes from the stump of a tallow candle and a rushlight on the unlit stove. That is why she does not see the clotted patches of blood in his hair. But

5

her fingers find them. She makes the smacking noise with her lips that signifies her disapproval of something. With sudden violence, she strips off his breeches and his stained shirt. She drags him, white and naked, into the court.

There is a pump in one corner. She holds him under it with one hand and sluices water over him with the other. She runs her fingers through his wet hair, over every surface and into every crack and cranny of his slippery body. She rinses him again. With a hand on his neck, she pushes him in front of her into the room and bars the door behind them.

Despite the heat, Charles is shivering. She wraps him in a blanket, makes him sit on a stool and lean against the wall. She brings him water in a beaker made of wood.

He drinks greedily. She is humming quietly. She often does this, the same three notes, la-la-la, low and soft, over and over again.

He is glad that Luc is not there. Luc is Marie's brother. He is a kitchen porter. He has only one eye, owing to a frightful accident in the slaughterhouse where he used to work. Though she did not witness it herself, Marie has described the accident to him many many times in graphic detail.

Charles's one visit to this house, nearly a year ago, was so that he might see in person the angry red crater that was the site of Luc's lost left eye. It was not as impressive in reality as in imagination. For the sake of his hosts, he acted out a polite pantomime of shock and horror. In truth, however, he was disappointed.

When Marie took him home again, he left a sou on the stove, because he knew that she and Luc were poor. Marie was Charles's nurse when he was very young and later stayed as a maid. But then she was dismissed and the boy cried himself to sleep for nearly a week.

Now the brother and sister live in one room. Their bed is in a curtained alcove by the stove.

When Charles has had all the water he can drink, she brings in the chamber pot and watches him urinate. Afterwards she makes him kneel by the bed. She kneels beside him and says the prayer to the Virgin that she always says before he goes to sleep.

He knows that he is meant to join in. When he does not, she looks sharply at him and pokes him in the ribs. When she begins the prayer again, he moves his lips, mouthing shapes which have no words to them.

She watches him closely but does not seem to mind. Perhaps she does not know the difference between words that have shapes and words that do not.

Marie puts him into bed, blows out the candle and climbs in beside him. The mattress sinks beneath her weight. His body has no choice but to sink towards her and to mould its contours to hers.

It is very hot and it grows hotter. Now he is big he does not care for the way she smells or the way she looms over him like a mountain of flesh.

Soon she drifts into sleep. She snores and twitches.

The snoring stops. 'Tell me,' she whispers. 'What happened? Where is Madame?'

He does not answer. He must never answer. *Say nothing. Not a word.*

Marie prods him again with her finger. 'What happened?'

*Tip-tap.* Like cracking a walnut.

When he does not answer, she sighs noisily and turns her head away.

He listens to her breathing. He closes his eyes but then he sees what he does not wish to see. He opens them again and stares into the night.

Luc does not come back for three days. When he does, he is drunk with blood and brandy. The single eye is bloodshot.

He does not see the boy at first. He calls for wine. He calls for food. Marie tries to press her brother into the chair but he resists.

7

Charles is in the alcove, in the bed. He rolls a little to the left, hoping to conceal himself behind the half-drawn curtains. But Luc's single eye catches the movement.

'What the devil is that?' he says in a voice so hoarse he can barely raise it above a whisper.

'Madame von Streicher's boy. He came the other night.'

'Who brought him?'

'No one.'

Luc advances towards the alcove and stares at Charles, who looks back at him because he doesn't know what else to do.

'Where's your mother?' Luc demands.

The boy says nothing.

'I don't know,' Marie says. 'He was covered with blood.'

'Take him back. We don't want him here.'

'I tried,' Marie says. 'I sent a message to the Rue de Grenelle but Madame isn't there any more. The concierge said she and the boy moved out a month ago.'

'They are traitors,' Luc says suddenly. 'She's been arrested. If we shelter him, they'll arrest us too. You know where that ends.' Luc makes a blade of his right hand and chops it down on the palm of his left.

He means the guillotine. Charles has heard his mother and Dr Gohlis talking about the machine, and Dr Gohlis said that it is a humane way to execute criminals. But, he said, the people do not like it because it is too swift and too clean a way to die. They prefer the old ways – hanging on wooden gallows, or death by sword or breaking on the wheel. They last longer, Dr Gohlis said, and they are more entertaining.

'They've set up the machine at the Tuileries now. At the Place du Carrousel.'

Marie pours her brother wine. She stands, hands on hips, in front of the alcove, with the boy behind her.

Luc takes a long swallow of wine and wipes his mouth on the back of his hand. 'Throw him out. In the gutter. Anywhere.'

'I can't. He's only a child.'

8

'If they find out he's here, it'll be enough to bring us before the Tribunal.'

'But he couldn't hurt a—'

Luc throws the beaker of wine at his sister, catching her on the face. She gives a cry and turns. Charles sees the blood on her cheek.

'You will do as I say,' Luc says. 'Or I'll break every bone in his body, and in yours.'

# Chapter Two

Marie holds tightly to Charles's arm. She pulls him from the shadowy, urine-scented safety of the alleyway leading to the court and into the crowded street.

She tugs him along, jerking his arm to hurry him up. He is a fish on a line, pulled through a river of people.

It is the first time he has been outside since the night he came to Marie's. Everything is brighter, louder and noisier than it should be – the clothes, the cockades, the soldiers, the checkpoints, the swaying, seething parties of men and women. There is urgency in the air, an invisible miasma that touches everyone. He wants to be part of it.

Before they came out, Marie combed his hair. He is wearing his shirt and breeches, which she washed the day before, though her best efforts could not remove all the blood from them. They do not go north towards the river but west. They pass Saint-Sulpice and turn into the Rue du Bac.

Marie drags him across the street, threading their way through the coaches and wagons by force of personality and a steady stream of oaths. She stops outside a great house with black gates, studded with iron.

The black gates are shut. Marie mutters under her breath and tugs on the bell handle with her free hand. She does not let go of Charles with the other hand. She grips his wrist so tightly he fears it will snap.

The bell clangs on the other side of the gates but no one comes. Marie bounces up and down on her little feet. She rings the bell again. A passer-by jostles Charles, wrenching him from Marie's grasp. He sprawls in the gutter and grazes his knees. Marie swears at the man and hauls him to his feet. She pulls the bell a third time, for longer and harder than before.

A shutter slides back in the wicket. A man's eyes and nose are revealed in the small rectangle.

'The house is shut up,' he says. 'Go away.'

'Where's Monsieur the Count?' Marie demands.

'Gone. All gone.'

The shutter slams home. Marie rings the bell again. She hammers on the door. Nothing happens.

She knocks again. By now a crowd has gathered, watchful and silent.

Marie turns from the gates and asks the bystanders what they think they're staring at. Such is the force of her authority, of her anger, that they drift away, shamefaced.

Muttering under her breath, Marie leads Charles away from the gates in the direction of the Grand École. He starts to cry.

A slim gentleman is coming towards them on foot. His left leg drags behind him. He is dressed plainly in a dark green coat. Charles recognizes him and so does Marie.

She leaps forward into the man's path and pushes the boy in front of her. 'Monseigneur!' she cries. 'Monseigneur!'

He stops, frowning, his face suddenly wary. 'Hush, hush – I am plain Monsieur Fournier now. You know that.'

'Monsieur, you came to Madame von Streicher's.'

He frowns at Marie. 'I am sorry. There is nothing I can do for you. Whoever you are.'

'Monsieur.' She shoves the boy forward, so forcefully that he bumps against Monsieur Fournier's arm. 'This is Madame's son. This is Charles. You must remember him.'

11

Monsieur Fournier has large brown eyes that open very wide as if life is a matter of endless astonishment to him.

'This?'

'Yes, monsieur, I swear it. On my life.'

Fournier motions them to move to one side with him. They stand by the outer wall of the great house. The passers-by ebb around them.

Fournier takes Charles's chin in his hand and angles it upwards. 'Yes, by God, you're right.' He bends closer, bringing his head almost on a level with the boy's. 'What happened? Are you hurt?'

Charles says nothing.

'He won't speak, monsieur,' Marie says.

'Of course he can speak.' Monsieur Fournier touches Charles's shoulder with a long white forefinger. 'You know me, don't you?'

'He won't say anything, monsieur. Not since that night.'

'Are you saying he was actually there? When . . .?' His voice tails away, rising into an unspoken question.

'Have you seen Madame?' Marie says. 'Is she . . .?' She runs out of words, too.

Fournier looks at her. 'You weren't there yourself?'

'No, monsieur. I was at my – my brother's house. Charles came to me in the night. He was . . .'

'He was what?' demands Fournier.

'There was blood all over him.' She paws at the faded stains on Charles's shirt. 'See? Everywhere. On his clothes, in his hair.'

'Dear God.'

Her voice rises. 'He won't even tell me what happened. He won't tell me anything. I can't keep him at home. My brother will throw him out.'

'You did well to bring him.' Monsieur Fournier takes out a handkerchief and wipes his face. 'We can't talk here. Follow me.'

He sets off in the direction he came from, walking so rapidly despite his limp that Charles and Marie have to break into a trot to keep up. He takes the next turning, a lane running along the side of the house. There are no windows on the ground floor, only small ones high up in the wall, far above Charles's head. These windows are protected by heavy grilles of iron bars, painted black like the gates.

They turn another corner into a narrow street parallel to the Rue du Bac. Here is another, much smaller gate set in the wall of the house.

Monsieur Fournier looks up and down the lane. There is no one else about. He knocks twice on the gate, pauses, knocks once, pauses again and then knocks twice again.

The shutter slides back. Nobody speaks. On the other side of the gate there is a rattling of bars. The key turns. The gate opens – not to its full extent, merely enough to allow a man to pass through.

Fournier is the first to enter. Marie pushes the boy after him. As she does so she ruffles his hair.

They are in a cobbled yard with a well in one corner. A fat old man in a dirty brown coat stares open-mouthed at them. Fournier limps towards the great grey cliff of the house. The old man jerks with his head towards the house, which means that Charles must follow.

Charles breaks into a run. Behind him, he hears the gate closing.

It is only when he is inside the house, when he is following Monsieur Fournier up a long flight of stone stairs that he realizes Marie is no longer there. She has stayed on the other side of the black gate.

The room is almost as large as a church. Despite the sunshine outside, it is gloomy, for the shutters are still across the windows. Light filters through the cracks. One of the shutters is slightly open and a bar of sunlight streams across the carpet to a huge desk.

13

The desk is made of a dark wood ornamented with gold which sparkles in the sunshine. Its top is as big as his mother's bed and it has many drawers. It is covered in papers – some in piles, some lying loose as if blown by a gust of wind.

Behind the desk, facing into the room, is a stout gentleman whose face is in shadow. He looks up as Monsieur Fournier enters, and Charles recognizes him.

'I thought you'd be halfway to—' The gentleman sees Charles behind Monsieur Fournier. He breaks off what he is saying.

'This is more important,' Fournier says.

'What the devil do you want with that boy?'

Fournier advances into the room with Charles trailing behind him. One of the piles of paper is weighted down with a pistol. Charles wishes that he were back with Marie, lying in her bed against her great flank and smelling her strange, unlovely smell.

'You don't understand. He's Madame von Streicher's son.'

Charles knows that this man is very important. He is Count de Quillon, the owner of this house, the Hotel de Quillon, and so much else. The Minister, Maman says, the godson of the King and once the King's friend. He sometimes came to see Maman, though more often he would send a servant with a message and Maman would put on one of her best gowns and go away in his great coach.

Only now, when the Count rests his elbows on the desk, does the sunlight bring his face alive. He is a broad, heavy man, older than Fournier, with a small chin, a big nose and a high complexion.

'This is Augusta's son?' the Count says. 'This? Are you sure? Absolutely sure?'

'Quite sure, despite the dirt and the rags.'

'How does he come here?'

'He ran away and went to an old servant's. She brought him a moment ago.'

14

'So was he with his mother when—'

Fournier interrupts: 'I don't know. He was covered in blood when he turned up at the old woman's house.'

'It is of the first importance that we discover what happened. Where is the servant? She must know something.'

'She ran off as soon as we came through the gate.'

The men are talking as if Charles is not there. He might be invisible. Or he might not even exist at all. He cannot grasp this idea. Nevertheless, part of him quite likes it.

'Come here, boy,' says the Count.

Charles steps up to the desk. He makes himself stand very straight.

'What happened at your house that night? The – the night you ran away?'

Charles does not speak.

'Don't be shy. I can't abide a timid boy. Answer me. Who else was there? I must know.'

'The woman said he simply won't speak,' says Fournier. 'No reason why he shouldn't, of course – he's perfectly capable of it. I remember him chattering away ten to the dozen.'

'Answer me!' the Count roared, rearing up in his chair. 'You will answer me.'

Tears run down Charles's cheeks. He says nothing.

Fournier shifts his weight from his left leg. 'Give the lad time to get his bearings,' he suggests. 'Gohlis can see him.'

'We don't have time for all that,' the Count says. He adds rather petulantly, 'Anyway, he's not some lad or other – his name is Charles. I should know.' He beckons Charles closer and studies the boy's face. 'Were you there? Did you see what happened to—'

'My friend, I think this—'

The Count waves Fournier away. 'Did you see what happened to your mother? Did you see who came?'

Charles stares at the pistol on the pile of papers. Is it loaded? If you cocked it and put it to your head and pulled the trigger, then would everything stop, just like that? Everything, including himself?

'It is most important that you tell us,' the Count says, raising his voice. 'A matter of life and death. Answer me, Charles. Who was there?'

But Charles is still thinking about the pistol. If he shot himself, would St Peter take one look at him and send him down to the fires of hell? Or would there simply be nothing at all, a great emptiness with no people in it, living or dead?

'Oh for God's sake!' the Count snaps.

The boy recoils as if he has been slapped.

'Very well, then.' The Count tugs the bell pull behind him. 'We'll talk to him when he's past his absurd shyness. Someone will look after him and give him some food.'

Fournier rests a hand on Charles's shoulder. 'But what about later? If we leave?'

'Then he comes with us.' Monsieur de Quillon bends his great head over his papers. 'Naturally.'

# Chapter Three

Charles is placed in the care of an elderly, half-blind woman. She lives in a room under the roof over the kitchen wing. Opening out of her chamber is a smaller one, which has a barred window. This is where Charles sleeps.

On the second night, he has bad dreams and he wets the bed.

On the third day, Monsieur Fournier summons him. He is in a salon overlooking the great courtyard at the heart of the Hotel de Quillon.

He is not alone. Dr Gohlis is there. He is another gentleman who used to call on Maman in the old days. He is young and stooping, a German from Hanover. He has cold hands.

In heavily accented French, the doctor asks Charles his name, and Charles does not answer. He asks Charles how old he is. Then he asks exactly the same questions in English and German, and all the while Charles stares out of the window at the weeds in the courtyard and imagines the words rising into the sky like startled birds.

Dr Gohlis examines him, looking at his teeth and poking at his belly with his forefinger. He walks behind Charles and claps his hands, making Charles twitch.

'There is no physical cause for his silence that I can see.

Everything is perfectly normal,' he says. 'You tell me he eats and moves his bowels. I could try purging or bleeding, but I doubt it would answer.'

'He has sustained a great shock,' Fournier says, throwing an unexpected smile at Charles. 'Could that have disturbed his faculties and made him mute?'

'Indeed, sir – that may very well be the case. If the hypothesis is correct, then it follows that the best course of treatment may be another shock. If one shock has removed his powers of speech, then a second may restore them.'

'They say he wet the bed the other night.'

'Really? Was he beaten for it?'

'I do not know.'

'If it happens again, I would advise it, for his own good. He will achieve nothing without discipline.'

'Thank you, Doctor,' Monsieur Fournier says after a moment. 'I won't detain you any longer.'

Dr Gohlis bows and leaves the room. He does not look at Charles, who is still standing by the window.

As the door closes, Fournier opens a bureau. He takes a sheet of paper from one of its drawers and a quill from another. He puts them on the flap and uncovers the inkstand. He places a gilt chair in front of the bureau.

'Sit, dear boy. Take the quill.'

Charles obeys. He dips the pen in the ink without being asked.

'Good,' says Fournier. 'Your mother told me that you are an apt student. Pray begin by writing your name.'

Charles bends his head. He writes. The quill scratches on the heavy paper.

'Now write my name.'

Charles writes.

'Excellent. And now – write the names of those who visited your mother in your cottage in the Rue de Richelieu.'

The pen moves again. The tip of the feather brushes Charles's chin.

Monsieur Fournier comes to stand at his shoulder. 'Let me see what you have written.'

Charles hands him the sheet of paper, the ink still glistening. He has answered each question with lines that go up and down, across and diagonally. They are black marks on white paper. They reveal nothing other than themselves.

The following morning, Charles wakes with the light.

Before he opens his eyes, he is aware of rustles and small movements which he thinks must be rats and mice, which come and go at will and treat the place as their own. He opens his eyes.

Without warning, his stomach gives a painful twitch as if someone has punched him there. He gasps and sits up in bed.

A boy is standing beside the window, his outline clearly visible in the light filtering through the cracks of the shutters. He is smaller than Charles and he is very still. He has his back to the room. He stands upright, his shoulders squared like a soldier on parade.

Just for an instant – for a hundredth of a second – Charles feels joy. He is not alone.

His feelings are no sooner there than they are gone. His lips move. They form the words: Who are you? But the words have no sound so the boy cannot hear them.

Charles is afraid as much as excited now. He swings his legs out of bed.

The boy does not move.

The boards are cold. Draughts swirl around Charles's ankles and rise up his legs under his nightshirt. He shivers, partly from fear.

He takes a step nearer the window, nearer the boy. Then another, and another. Between each step he pauses. It is like the game he used to play with his mother when he was very, very young.

The strange boy does not even twitch. Step by step, Charles

draws nearer to him. Still the boy does not move. He has been turned to stone, Charles thinks, he is a statue. He feels pity, though he knows the boy cannot really be like this; but, if he were, surely that would be even worse than losing your voice?

Charles takes a deep breath, stretches out a hand and touches the boy's shoulder. It is cold, a little damp and hard – hard like wood, not stone. Charles walks around him and opens one of the shutters. The light from the window falls on the boy's face.

Or rather – the light falls on the place where the face should have been.

The boy's eye sockets are empty. There is nothing but a hole where the nose should be. The cheeks are sunken. The lips are almost gone. He still has some of his teeth. He is grinning. He will always grin because he can do nothing else.

Charles draws in a long, shuddering breath. His face contorted, he breathes out: a silent scream.

The door creaks. A current of cold air sweeps into the room.

Dr Gohlis is on the threshold.

'I see you have found my little friend,' he says in his strange, thick voice. 'His name is Louis.'

As he speaks, he comes closer. Charles cannot move.

'Who knows who this boy was?' the doctor says. 'Were you aware that before the Revolution, the poor were so desperate that they sent their children to prison – they sold them on the streets – they disposed of them like unwanted kittens?'

Charles stares at Dr Gohlis over the boy's shoulder. He wishes with all his heart that the boy was still alive, that he was not alone with the doctor.

'But even dead boys may be worth a few sous. In life they were quite useless to society. But in death, the lucky ones are granted the chance to serve a higher good.'

Dr Gohlis is standing by Louis's shoulder now. He throws back the second shutter. More light floods over the boy. Charles covers his mouth with his hands when he sees what has been done.

'So their parents take the money and drink themselves senseless in the nearest wine shop,' the doctor continues. 'And a man of science takes the boy.' He stretches out a surprisingly long arm and grips the right wrist of the figure. 'The dead boy. The man of science conveys the boy to another man, a man skilled in the art of flaying skin from a body. Believe me, it is not easy to do it properly, to do it well. It is one thing to remove the skin. It is quite another thing to do it without harming what lies beneath.'

The doctor releases the wrist. His fingertips play on the arm of the boy, patting it gently, rising from the wrist up to the elbow up to the shoulder and then to the neck. He points at a place on the neck.

'See? This is the line of the great artery which carries blood to the heart. This is bone, here, and here the humerus, and here we have the scapula.' The hand flutters higher. 'Note the cheekbone. Do you see how some of the skin is still attached? The man who did this was truly an artist.'

The doctor's hand sweeps down and grips Charles's neck. Charles tries to pull away but Dr Gohlis tightens his hold. His hand is as cold as a dead thing, colder than the flayed boy.

'After this boy was flayed, shall I tell you what happened then? He was covered in plaster, every inch of him. When the plaster was dry, they cut it open – and there is a mould of the dead boy. When you have a mould, you can make many copies. The copies are painted, in this case by another artist who is trained in the work of portraying what lies beneath, the inner mysteries under the skin. See how the muscle and tendon and bone stand out in their proper colours. Is it not a marvel?'

His grip is painfully tight. He forces Charles to move around the boy and to come closer. Now he is looking at the boy's back.

'These poor simulacra of humanity are called *écorchés*,' Dr Gohlis says, 'the flayed ones. Isn't that droll? They assist in the instruction of students of medicine and drawing who are obliged to learn about the inward architecture of the human body. Observe.'

He picks up Charles's right hand with his own left hand. Charles wills himself not to resist, not to pull away. The doctor forces him to extend his index finger. He runs the finger down the spine of the *écorché*.

'Here are the cervical vertebrae,' the doctor announces. 'And below, in the middle of the spine, here are the thoracic ones. See the natural curve of the spine. Is it not elegant? And further below still, here are the lumbar vertebrae. They are much larger than the cervical ones, are they not? That is because they need to be, for they carry a greater burden.'

The doctor lowers his head to the same level as Charles's.

'You see?' he says. 'You will never forget this lesson, will you? Not while you live and breathe. You will always remember what lies beneath.'

He stares into Charles's face. Charles stares back and thinks of nothing but the blank grey sky beyond the window.

'Above all, you should draw this conclusion from it. You should remember that a boy who is useless in life may at least be useful in death.' Dr Gohlis releases Charles's neck and pushes him against the *écorché* boy. 'You are no use at all to us if you will not talk.'

As he is speaking, Dr Gohlis moves towards the door. He pauses on the threshold.

'I should examine him carefully if I were you. If you do not find your voice, you may be like that yourself one day.'

# Chapter Four

On the very night before the letter arrived, Savill thought of Augusta. He had not thought of her for months, perhaps years. These were the dog days of the summer. Perhaps that had something to do with it, for the heat bred unhealthy desires. The long scar on his right cheek itched.

Before getting into bed, he had tied back the curtains and opened the window as wide as it would go. The smell from the cesspit wafted up from the yard beneath. These houses in Nightingale Lane were as old as Good Queen Bess, and so was their sanitation.

It was not the heat alone that kept him awake. He had the toothache, a savage sensation that drilled into the right-hand side of his jaw and sent tendrils of discomfort among the roots of the surrounding teeth. He had taken drops that had blunted the pain. But they did not send him to a comfortable oblivion: instead, they pinned his body to the bed while leaving his mind free and restless, skimming above the surface of sleep.

London was never quiet, even on the darkest night. He heard the watch calling the hours, the cries of drunken passers-by, the hammer-blows of hooves and the rumble of distant wagons bringing their loads through the night to Smithfield and Covent Garden.

The heat warmed the fancies of his brain to an unhealthy temperature and stirred into life the half-buried memory of another hot night. He had supped with fellow clerks at the American Department and returned late to the lodgings on the wrong side of Hill Street. It was their first married home. The apartments were too expensive for them but the address was genteel and Augusta had argued that a man did not rise in the world without seeming worthy to rise; and nor did his wife.

He found her sitting on the ottoman at the foot of the bed. There were two tall candles on the mantel. The edges of the room were dark, the corners populated with shifting shadows. But Augusta herself was coated with a soft golden glow.

She wore a simple white nightgown, so loose at the neck that it revealed most of her smooth shoulders. Her hair was down. She smiled up at him and held up her hand. The movement dislodged her gown and he glimpsed the swell of her breasts and the darkness between them.

This was how it had been in the beginning of their marriage: Savill had revelled in the contrast between Augusta by day and Augusta by night – the one icily elegant, ambitious to the point of ruthlessness, calculating yet so strangely foolish; and the other, everything a man could desire to find in his bed, and more. Even when he grew to dislike her, which did not take long, she retained her ability to excite him.

'I have an appetite,' she said that night as she sat astride him, her belly already swollen with Lizzie. 'And you shall feed me.'

The excitement drained away from him, leaving a residue of bitterness, of regret, that mingled with the dreary ache of his tooth. The drops were making his head swim and they had given him a pain in his stomach. His eyes were full of sand. He felt nauseous but lacked the strength to roll out of bed and find the chamber pot.

At times like this, in these long, sleepless nights, Savill wondered whether he, too, had been to blame for what had happened. But that was folly. Memories are not real, he told himself, they are little more than waking dreams; and there is no guilt in dreams, neither hers nor mine, and no betrayals, either.

For are we not innocent when we dream?

The next morning, the servant brought up the letter when Savill was at breakfast with his sister and Lizzie. He noticed it had been franked by an obliging Member of Parliament in lieu of postage. He broke the heavy seal. As soon as he unfolded the letter he recognized the handwriting as that of a man who no doubt included many Members of Parliament among his intimate acquaintance.

The women were watching him. He read the letter twice. The questions crowded into his mind but he had long ago schooled his face not to betray his feelings.

Savill looked up. 'I shall not dine with you today after all. I am obliged to go out of town on business.' He registered the disappointment spreading over Lizzie's face, then watched her instantly suppressing it. 'Tomorrow,' he said. 'There's always tomorrow.'

Why now? he wondered. Why a summons to Vardells, not Westminster? And again, and above all, why should Rampton want to see me now?

'She is dead.'

Twelve feet above Savill's head, plaster putti writhed, a pair of them in each corner of the salon. Each set of twins were shackled together with garlands. The infant boys had short, stubby limbs and plump, inflated bodies. Their eyes were sightless blanks, their lips slightly parted.

Give it time, Savill thought. He imagined the gilt and the whitewash fading and cracking, staining with candle grease, and the plaster crumbling and flaking from the ceiling: plaster snow.

'Did you hear me, sir?' Mr Rampton said.

25

The grandfather clock chimed. Savill counted the quarters and then the stroke of the hour: five.

'Dead,' Mr Rampton repeated, this time more loudly. 'Augusta is dead.'

Savill's eyes dropped slowly to the marble chimney piece. On one side of the fireplace was a bronze man with bulging muscles restraining a rearing horse with one arm while waving to something or someone with the other. What in heaven's name was it all for?

Mr Rampton coughed. 'Augusta. My niece, sir.'

Savill looked at him. 'My wife, sir.'

Silence settled like dust in the air. Savill looked across the room at Rampton, who was sitting in the big wing armchair on the left of the fireplace. The chair was angled to catch the light from the two tall windows. Beside the chair was a lectern on wheels with candles on either side of the slope and a sturdy quarto, the pages held open with clips.

Rampton scratched the fingertips of his left hand on the arm of the chair. His face was wrinkled but still ruddy with the impression of good health. He looked smaller than he had been. Perhaps age was shrinking him as his fortune increased. The Lord giveth, as Savill's father used to say with a certain grim satisfaction, and the Lord taketh away.

'Of course,' Rampton was saying, 'your unhappy wife, Mr Savill, despite everything. And it is a cause for sorrow that the unfortunate woman is dead at last. We must not judge her. We may safely leave that to a higher power.'

Rampton was not a big man but he made good use of what he had. He wore a sober grey coat and very fine linen. His hair was his own but he still wore it powdered, a political statement in these changing times: a public demonstration of his attachment to old virtues and old loyalties. The heels of his shoes were higher than was usual for gentlemen's shoes. He looked every inch a statesman, albeit a smallish one, which was a pretty fair description of what he was.

26

'The poor woman,' he went on. 'Alas, she paid the price for flouting the laws of God and man.'

The rectangle of sky outside the nearer window was cloudless, a deep rich blue. Against this backdrop danced black specks, sweeping, diving and climbing with extraordinary rapidity. The swallows and the martins had begun their evening exercise. They would be vanishing soon as they did every year, though where they went, no man knew.

'Those confounded swallows,' Rampton said. 'You cannot begin to comprehend the mess they make on the terrace.' He too was staring out of the window; he too was glad of an excuse to think of something other than Augusta. 'They nest under the eaves of the house or in the stables – I've tried for three years to get rid of them. But wherever they nest, they use my terrace as their privy.'

'Where?' Savill said.

'What?' Rampton turned from the window, away from the swallows, from one annoyance to another. 'Paris. The foolish, foolish girl.'

'How did you hear, sir?'

'Through the Embassy. It happened just over a week ago.'

'When the mob stormed the Tuileries?'

'Yes. By all accounts the whole of Paris was delivered up to them. Riot, carnage, chaos. It beggars comprehension, sir, that such a civilized city should sink so low. The poor King and his family are prisoners. Tell me, when did you last hear from her?'

'Five years ago,' Savill said. 'A little more. She wrote for money.'

'And you sent it?'

'Yes.'

Rampton grunted. 'There was no necessity for you to do that.'

'Perhaps not. But I did.'

'On the other hand,' Rampton said, 'perhaps it was for the

best. If you hadn't, she might have been obliged to return to England.'

'You mean she might still be alive?'

'Would that really have been better? For her or for anyone else? For Elizabeth? After all, you could not have taken her in, even if you desired to, and she could not have been received anywhere.'

Rampton had lost all his teeth. As a result his voice had changed. Once it had been precise and hard edged, with every consonant squared off like a block of ashlar. Now the words emerged in a soft slurry of sound. No doubt he had a set of teeth, but he had not troubled to put them in for Savill.

Savill said, 'She was in Geneva when she last wrote. She had parted from von Streicher, though she kept his name for appearance's sake.' The words still hurt when he said them aloud, but only his pride. 'She said she had set up house with an Irish lady and they planned to take in pupils.'

'Pupils? You did not believe her?'

'I didn't know what to believe. In any case, it didn't signify. All that mattered was that she was in Geneva and she needed money.'

'If she did not apply to you again, that suggests that she found it elsewhere.'

'What were the circumstances of her death?' Savill asked, his voice harsher than before. 'Had she been in Paris for long? Who was she with?'

'She had been there for several years. I believe she had granted her favours to a number of gentlemen since von Streicher's departure. But I have not been able to ascertain whether she was under anyone's protection at the time of her death. I'm afraid she was killed during the riots. I understand that a band of sans-culottes attacked her in the house where she had taken refuge.'

'Was she alone?'

'I believe so.' Rampton took his spectacles from the lectern

28

and turned them slowly in his hands. 'Despite the German name she bore, you see, she was known to be British. It was said that she was a spy and she had been forced to leave her former lodgings for fear the mob would find her, or the police.'

'Was she?'

'A spy?' Rampton shrugged. 'Not as far as I know. Does it matter now?'

The frame of the glasses snapped between the lenses. Rampton stared at the wreckage in his hands. For a moment neither man spoke.

'She was stabbed, I understand,' Rampton went on in a rush. 'It must have been a quick death, at least. And the place was ransacked.'

Savill turned his head so Rampton could not see his face. He thought of Augusta as she had been when he had first seen her: at Mr Rampton's house in Westminster. Seventeen, coolly beautiful even then, with a way of looking at you that would heat the blood of any man. Ice and fire.

'We must look ahead,' Rampton said. 'Sad though this occasion is, sir, I believe I should congratulate you.'

Savill stared at him. 'What?'

'You are free at last, sir. Should you wish to marry again, there is now no impediment to your doing so. Your unhappy condition, this limbo you have been in, cannot have been easy for you.'

That was true enough. Augusta had given Savill ample grounds for divorce when she eloped so publicly with her German lover to the Continent, while he himself had been three thousand miles away in America. But divorce was a rich man's luxury, even when the husband was so clearly the injured party.

'This will draw a line under the whole sad affair,' Mr Rampton went on.

'She was my wife, sir,' Savill said. 'Not an affair.'

Rampton spread his hands. 'My dear sir, I intended no disrespect to the dead.' He folded his hands on his lap. 'I fear

I have been clumsy. You have had a shock. Will you take a glass of wine? A cup of tea?'

'Thank you, no. Tell me the rest.'

'I do not yet know the whole of it. But I am told that someone informed a friend of hers, a Monsieur Fournier, and he communicated with the Embassy. Everything was done as it should be, which must be a great comfort. There was a doctor in attendance to certify the death. A notary took down a statement concerning the circumstances of her demise, and it was signed by witnesses.'

Savill gazed out of the window. The swallows were still there but they had moved further away. Like charred leaves above a bonfire, he thought. A pyre.

Rampton cleared his throat. 'It would give me great pleasure if you would stay and dine.'

'Thank you, but I believe I shall ride back to London.'

'There's plenty of time yet,' Rampton said. 'And there is something else that we need to discuss which may perhaps take a while.'

Rampton paused. Savill said nothing.

'There are the documents I mentioned,' Rampton said. 'The notary's statement and the death certificate.'

'If you have them, sir, I shall take them now,' Savill said. 'If not, then perhaps you would send them to me. You know my direction. Nightingale Lane, near Bedford Square.'

'I don't have them. They are in the possession of Monsieur Fournier. And he has something else of hers that may interest you.'

'I doubt it,' Savill said, rising from his chair. 'There is nothing of my late wife's that interests me.'

'The matter is more delicate than it first might appear,' Mr Rampton said. 'And that is why I asked you to wait on me here at Vardells and not in town.' He smiled up at Savill with unexpected sweetness. 'Augusta had a son.'

# Chapter Five

'That scar on your cheek from New York,' Rampton said when they were at table. 'I had expected the wound to have healed better over the years. Does it pain you?'

'Not at all,' Savill said. 'Why should it, after all this time?'

'I'm rejoiced to hear it, sir.'

Rampton had ordered the curtains drawn and the candles lit, shutting out the blue sky and the swallows. Even in the country, he lived in some state. There were two manservants to wait at table. The food was good and the wine was better. The presence of the servants kept the conversation on general topics.

'And how is your little daughter?' he asked as Savill was helping himself to a delicately flavoured fricassee of chicken.

'Lizzie?' Savill glanced down the table. 'Your goddaughter is in good health, sir, but she is not so little now.'

'Good, good.' Rampton nodded and looked pleased: it was as if the excellence of Lizzie's health was something he himself had worked towards, something for which he could take credit, had he not modestly waived his right to it. 'Is she like her mother?'

'Yes. In appearance. Her face is softer, perhaps, gentler.'

'As long as her character does not resemble her mother's. Let us pray it does not.'

Savill said nothing.

'Her mother was very beautiful at her age. If Elizabeth takes after her, she will have plenty of suitors. I dare say she will soon be of an age to marry.'

'Should she wish to, sir, yes. If she finds a man who pleases her.'

'If you take my advice, sir, you will encourage her to do so as soon as possible.' Rampton dabbed his lips with his napkin. 'Though it's an expensive business, of course. Marriage, I mean. However one looks at it.' He applied himself to a dish of lamb cutlets.

Savill sensed something unsaid here; he caught the ghost of its absence. 'Is this your main residence now, sir?' he asked.

'Alas, no – I am much at Westminster. I must own I wish it were otherwise. I find I have a taste for country life. Of course this is little more than a cottage, and there's barely fifty acres with it. But it's enough for my simple wants. I'm building a wing to accommodate my library with bedrooms above, with a fine prospect over the garden. In the spring, I shall improve the prospect still further by sweeping away those old hedgerows and farm buildings to the west of the drive. Then it will be perfection.'

If this is a cottage, Savill thought, then I am a unicorn. The house had been refurbished since he had last been here. It now sat in grounds that were in the process of being newly laid out; on the east side of the drive, a great expanse of grass swept towards a small lake that had not been there before. As for the house, the new wing would increase its volume almost by half as much again. The work was nearly finished. Earlier in the day, carpenters had been fitting the French windows that would open from the library to the terrace.

'Will you retire here, sir?'

'Retire?' Rampton smiled. 'I doubt my masters would permit me to do that, not while this crisis continues in France. And

God knows how long that will last. I tell you frankly, sir, I see no sign of its ending.'

'You do not think that the King and the National Convention will come to an accommodation?'

Rampton's smile did not waver. 'That is for wiser heads than yours or mine to decide.' He turned the subject smoothly. 'But when I do retire, it will be delightful to be here.'

'Will you not find it sadly dull?'

'Not in the slightest. I shall have my books, of course, and I have a mind to turn farmer.' Rampton crooked his finger at the servant who sprang from the shadows to refill Savill's glass. 'I have bought two or three tenanted farms nearby. I may take them into my own hands. A toast, sir – to your Elizabeth. May she find herself a husband that suits you both.'

Savill drank. He had once been a civil servant, and in those days he had known Mr Rampton's ways as a dog knows his master's. Rampton had not been talking idly during the meal. He had been making sure that Savill understood him.

'I am rich,' he was saying, 'and I have the ear of powerful men, so you would be wise to oblige me. For your daughter's sake as well as your own.'

With unnatural reverence, the servants removed the cloth and set out the wine, the nuts and the fruit. Rampton signalled for them to withdraw. The two men were sitting side by side now.

Savill bit down on a walnut and a stab of pain drove into his jaw. He twitched on his chair but managed to avoid crying out. He must find time to have the offending tooth pulled out. The truth was, he told himself, he was a coward where his teeth were concerned.

'A toast, sir,' Rampton said.

Savill pushed aside his plate and took up his glass with relief. They drank His Majesty's health. Avoiding each other's eyes, they drank to Augusta's memory. Then the conversation faltered.

'His name is Charles,' Rampton snapped, as if Savill had said it was something quite different. 'He must be about ten or eleven years old. Thereabouts.'

'Do you know who his father is?'

Rampton cracked his knuckles, in the old days a sign of calculation; his clerks had mocked him for it, but only when they were safely out of his way. 'I have not been able to ascertain that. I believe Augusta had left the Bavarian gentleman by then and was living in Rome, but my information is not exact.'

'Does Charles speak English?' Savill said.

'The question had not occurred to me. I suppose, if he was born in Italy and he has spent the last few years in France . . .' Rampton turned away and stared up at a portrait of himself. 'Still,' he went on in a quieter voice, 'at his age it hardly signifies. The mind of a child is as porous as a sponge. It soaks up whatever you pour into it with extraordinary rapidity.'

'If his father cannot be found, no doubt his mother's friends will care for him. Where is he staying?'

'The Embassy will let me know as soon as they hear.'

'He's nothing to do with me,' Savill said, more loudly than he had intended. 'He's Augusta's bastard.'

'Pray moderate your voice, sir. You do not want the world to know your business.'

'But it is not my business, sir. That's my point.'

Rampton refilled their glasses. 'The law would say otherwise. Augusta was still your wife at the time of her death. You and she were not divorced. I understand that she did not even leave a will, which makes you her heir. The child's paternity is not established, and probably never will be. In sum, this is one of those cases where the law and common sense point in the same direction as a man's duty as a Christian. The boy is your responsibility.'

'Nonsense.'

To Savill's surprise, Rampton smiled. 'I thought you would

34

say that. And, that being the case, my dear sir, let me propose a solution.'

'You may propose what you wish, sir. It is nothing to do with me.'

Rampton leaned closer. 'What if I take the boy myself?'

# Chapter Six

Charles dreams of the boy called Louis.

He, Charles, is lying on his bed and Louis is standing by the window. This is similar to what actually happened when Dr Gohlis came at dawn that morning. But, in the dream, Charles already knows Louis's name. He also knows that Louis is alone and naked in the world.

In the dream the light is much stronger than it was in real life. It floods over the doubly naked body of Louis. The colours glow like the stained glass in Notre Dame. Who would have thought there would be so many colours under a boy's skin?

Charles glances down at his own body. He discovers that, though it is daytime, he is not wearing any clothes. Nor is he lying under the bedclothes. Like Louis, he has lost most of his skin. He sees rope-like arteries, the blue filigree of veins, the slabs of muscle, the shiny white knobs of bone. He too has become doubly naked.

He too has become beautiful.

Louis stares out of the window. But now he turns, his head leading his body. Charles sees his ruined face. Louis smiles, though of course it is not easy to tell that he is smiling because his lips and skin are gone and so has most of his facial tissue.

Louis holds out his right hand towards Charles. The gesture is unmistakably friendly. Charles tries to smile in return. That is, he thinks a smile, but he knows that he too lacks lips and skin so the smile may not be obvious.

He raises his right hand. It looks webbed, like a duck's foot or the ribbed leaf of a cabbage.

'Hello, Louis,' he says.

Day by day, the house in the Rue du Bac empties itself of people and things. It also empties itself of its invisible contents, its rules, its habits, its regime. Charles does almost as he pleases now. He is under no restraint as long as he does not try to leave.

The servants are slipping away, despite the guards at the gates and doors leading to the outer world. They leave their tasks half-done – a mop standing in a pail of dirty water in a corner of the grand staircase; a drawing room with only a third of the furniture covered up and the pictures and ornaments ranged along one wall on the floor with the packing materials beside them.

The house is sliding into an unknown, unpredictable future, just as Charles is. He wanders from room to room, from salon to hall, from attic to cellar, frequently losing his way. The old woman who was meant to be looking after him is hardly ever there. He realizes after a while that he has not seen her for days. Perhaps she is dead.

Time itself loses its familiar markers, the hours of the day, the days of the week. There are many clocks in this house but no one troubles to wind them now or to set their hands. So time disintegrates into a variety of smaller times: and soon there will be no time at all.

Now that the old woman no longer brings him food, he is obliged to forage for it himself. He finds his way to the vaulted kitchens whose cellars run under the street.

In the city outside, people are starving. Here there is more food than anyone could ever eat. There are vegetables rotting down to brown mush; joints of meat turning grey and breeding maggots; and bins of flour that feed a shifting population of insects and small animals.

There are still people who cook and serve food, however, and their leftovers lie around the kitchens. There is water from the pump that serves the scullery tap. On one occasion he drinks a pot of cold coffee. On another he finds a bottle of wine nearly half full. The wine is golden and silky sweet. It cloys in his mouth. He drinks it all. It makes him sick and then sends him to sleep: he has a bad dream in which blood drips on him from a black sky streaked with flickering yellow; and he wakes with a headache.

He spends hours watching the Rue du Bac through the cracks in the shutters in what used to be the steward's room. He stares down at the hats and heads bobbing to and fro and listens to the grinding roar of wheels and the shouting. Sometimes he hears a popping sound in the distance which he thinks is musketry.

Charles encounters the Abbé Viré. The old man wanders restlessly about the halls and stairs, his slippers shuffling like falling plaster on the marble and the stone. His cassock is stained with old food.

In the old days, Maman would take him to the Abbé for instruction in religion and tuition in mathematics and the classical authors. When Charles was very young, he believed Father Viré to be the earthly form of God.

All this makes the priest's present conduct unsettling in the extreme. The Abbé does not appear to recognize Charles. He usually ignores him completely. He carries a breviary as he walks and reads from it, muttering to himself.

Once, Father Viré comes across Charles trying to read a ten-day-old newspaper in a disused powder-closet. The old priest raises his hand and sketches a blessing over Charles's head, murmuring the familiar words into the dusty air.

As for the Count de Quillon, he stays in his suite of private apartments beyond the grand salon. Monsieur Fournier comes and goes. When he sees Charles, he often stops to ask how he does and whether he needs anything. Charles does not answer.

'All will be well soon,' he says one morning. 'You'll see.'

But Charles knows that nothing will ever be well and that the only thing he will see is more of what he sees now. Still, it is good of Monsieur Fournier to tell kind lies.

Sometimes they ask him the questions again – Fournier, the Count and Dr Gohlis. Always the same ones. What happened on the night your mother died? Did you see who was there? What was said?

*Say nothing. Not a word to anyone.*

One day, a wagon comes into the main courtyard, where the weeds are advancing in ragged green lines along the cracks between the flagstones. Men bring packing cases and begin to put things in them – pictures, statues, clocks and carpets. Some of the clocks are still ticking. They are nailed up alive in their coffins.

The remaining servants, working in relays, bring trunks and valises from the attics. They fill them with books, papers and clothes. Two more wagons come down the lane at the back of the house with a guard of armed men. They are loaded with the heavier items. They go away during the night. So do more of the servants, and then the house is emptier than ever.

As the people and the objects seep away from the Hotel de Quillon, Charles notices how shabby everything is – the damp patches on the plaster in the grand salon where the old tapestries used to hang; the cracks that snake across the ornate ceiling of the ladies' withdrawing room; the leak in the roof of the room next to his which, one rainy night, brings down the whole ceiling.

Charles does not like the nighttimes because sometimes he wets the bed. This often happens on the nights after they have asked him the questions.

39

When he wets the bed, he is beaten the following morning. He understands this. He has done wrong. Since the old woman disappeared, no one notices if he wets the bed so it no longer matters.

One night, Dr Gohlis comes into Charles's room and wakes him from a deep sleep. He squeezes the boy's chin between finger and thumb. He holds the candle so Charles can see his face, orange and gold in the light of the flame.

'Remember my *écorché* boy?' he says. 'Are you going to be like him one day?'

Charles knows that the *écorché* boy is called Louis. He is kept in the sitting room that has been set aside for the doctor's use at the Hotel de Quillon. The door is locked when the doctor is not there.

One morning, Charles watches the doctor leave. He sees him hide the key on the ledge of the lintel above the door. Now Charles can visit Louis.

Often he chooses the very early morning when few people are stirring and the doctor is unlikely to be there. The *écorché* boy stands beside the doctor's desk. Charles examines him carefully and presses his own body to see if he is the same underneath, under all that skin. He thinks of conversations they might have and games they might play. He likes to touch Louis and wishes that Louis could touch him. Once he kisses Louis's cheek and he has the impression that Louis's face is slightly wet, as if he has been crying.

One day the key is not on the lintel. The door is locked. Dr Gohlis is not there.

Who is left? Charles thinks there are perhaps half a dozen servants, the old abbé and himself. He cannot remember when he last saw the Count or Monsieur Fournier or Louis.

What will happen to me, Charles wonders. Will they leave me quite alone?

\*     \*     \*

Then comes the night when everything changes. Just before dawn, Dr Gohlis wakes Charles, makes him dress and takes him downstairs. An old servant waits with two small valises in the hall.

Charles wants to say: 'Where are we going?' He also wants to ask Dr Gohlis what has happened to Louis.

But of course he cannot speak. He must not speak.

*Not a word to anyone.*

# Chapter Seven

'Mr Savill – may I make known Mr Malbourne, my clerk?'
Rampton said, enunciating the words with precision because he
was wearing a set of ivory teeth. 'Mr Malbourne – Mr Savill.'

They bowed to each other. Malbourne was a slender man
with delicate, well-formed features and the address of a
gentleman. Savill had found him and Rampton at work in
the study when he arrived. The clerk's right arm was in a
black-silk sling, though he removed it when it was necessary
for him to write.

This was Savill's second visit to Vardells, nearly a month
after his first, prompted by a letter from Rampton. It was late
September now, and the leaves were turning on the lime trees
beside the drive.

'Mr Malbourne has intelligence that relates to Mrs Savill's
son,' Rampton said. 'It appears that Charles has been brought
to England.' He gestured to his clerk that he should continue.

'Charles is living in the country with a party of newly
arrived émigrés,' Malbourne said. 'Fleeing the massacres. There
has been quite a flood of them.'

'Where are they?'

'They have taken a house in Somersetshire a few miles beyond
Bath. Charnwood Court in the village of Norbury. The émigrés

are people of some position in the world. Have you heard of the Count de Quillon?'

'The late minister?'

'Precisely. Though he held the seals of office for no more than three or four weeks before he was forced to resign.'

'He was the old king's godson,' Rampton said. 'Some say it was a nearer connection still, through his mother, and that was why he was in such favour at Versailles when he was a young man. This king made him a Chevalier of St Louis. Not that it stopped him from dabbling with the Revolution when it suited his purpose.'

'The point is, sir,' Malbourne went on, 'Monsieur de Quillon is altogether the grand gentleman. He is not an easy man to deal with. He is accustomed to having his own way, to moving in the great world.'

'Then why has he buried himself in the country?' Savill asked.

'Because his resources are limited,' Malbourne said. 'Most of his fortune is in France, and it has been seized. His estates have been sequestered. Also he and his allies have not many friends in London. After all, they are dangerous revolutionaries themselves: they tried to manipulate their king to their own advantage.'

'Their chickens have come home to roost,' Rampton observed.

'Indeed, sir,' Malbourne continued. 'Moreover, they are detested by those of their fellow countrymen already in London, who have never wavered from their old allegiance to King Louis and never compromised their principles.'

'Very true,' Rampton said. 'And, to speak plainly, my dear Savill, the Count and his friends have such a history of fomenting sedition, of flirting with the mob, that we ourselves have little desire to play host to them.'

'Yet you let them come here.'

'Unfortunately we lack the legal instruments to prevent it,' Malbourne said.

'For the time being,' Rampton said. 'But that is neither here nor there. Tell him about Fournier.'

'Fournier?' Savill said. 'The man who dealt with the funeral arrangements?'

Malbourne bowed. 'Yes, sir. He is the Count's principal ally. Fournier preceded Monsieur de Quillon to England. Indeed, I believe Charnwood is leased to him, not the Count. He is a younger son of the Marquis de St Étienne and was the Bishop of Lodève under the old regime. But he has resigned his orders and now prefers to be known simply as Fournier.' He smiled. 'Citizen Fournier, no doubt.'

'An atheist, they say,' Rampton said sourly. 'The worst of men.'

'Mind you keep your seat this time,' Rampton said as Malbourne was leaving.

Malbourne saluted them with his whip. 'I'll do my best, sir.'

He rode down the drive, urging his horse to a trot and then to a canter.

'Foolish young man,' Rampton said fondly. 'He sprained his arm last month when he had a tumble. Hence the sling. It cannot be denied that there's a reckless streak to Horace.' He smiled. 'Just as there was to his grandfather. That's where the money went, you know, and the estates. He gambled as if his life depended on it – Vingt-et-un.'

Horse and rider were out of sight now but Savill heard the drumming of the hooves accelerate to a gallop.

Rampton stared along the terrace, at the far end of which two workmen were building a low wall. 'Look, sir. Those damned swallows. They are already smearing their filth on my new library.'

'Is Mr Malbourne in a hurry or does he always ride like that?' Savill said.

'He is expected at the Woorgreens' this evening and he will not wish to be late.' Rampton glanced at Savill and decided to enlighten his ignorance. 'Mr Woorgreen, the East India Nabob. He is betrothed to the younger Miss Woorgreen. He will have twelve hundred a year by it, I believe. There's also the consideration that her mother's brother is a friend of Mr Pitt's.'

They went into the house. Savill was engaged to dine and spend the night.

'Horace Malbourne is a man of parts,' Rampton said, leading the way into the study. 'Well connected too. But if he wishes to get on in the world, he knows he must set aside his wild oats and marry money. If all goes well, we shall see him in Parliament in a year or two.'

How very agreeable it must be, Savill thought, to have one's life mapped out like that: a comfortable place in a government office, a rich wife, a seat in Parliament.

'He was my ward, you know – his poor mama entrusted him to me when she died.' Rampton rang the bell and sat down before the fire. 'But he has amply repaid my care and now he is most valuable to me. When he marries, though, he will spread his wings and fly away.'

Like a swallow, Savill thought, when winter comes.

The manservant came and Rampton gave orders for dinner. Savill wondered whether the introduction of Mr Malbourne had been designed to serve a secondary purpose: to show Savill that Rampton was worthy to stand in the place of a father; that he might safely be entrusted with the care of Augusta's son.

'By the way,' Rampton went on, 'I have not confided in him that I may adopt Charles.'

'Because that has not been settled, sir.'

'Quite so. But in any case I think it better that Malbourne believes that I'm assisting you to win control of the boy solely in view of our family connection. Also, of course, it's in the Government's interest to know more about the household at Charnwood and what they are doing.'

Soon afterwards, they went into dinner. Savill had not

accepted Rampton's proposition, but the very fact of his being here was significant, and they both knew it. Rampton had the sense not to press home his advantage. Instead he talked with an appearance of frankness about the situation in France and the Government's policy towards it.

It was almost enjoyable, Savill found, to talk with Rampton on a footing that, if not precisely equal, was at least one of independence. Once upon a time, Rampton had been his unwilling patron because Savill had married his niece. He, Savill, had served as one of his clerks in the American Department during the late war, though he had never been in such high favour as the elegant Mr Malbourne.

Despite himself, he was impressed by his host. Rampton's career had collapsed near the end of the war, when the King had dismissed the American secretary and closed down the entire department. Yet, somehow, he had clawed his way back.

But to what, exactly? When Savill had tried to probe further, all he could discover was that Rampton now worked in some capacity for the Post Office, and also advised the Secretary of State for the Home Department on regulations for the government of Ireland. He let slip that he held a sinecure, too, Clerk of the Peace and Chief Clerk of the Supreme Court in Jamaica, which must provide him with a substantial income. All this suggested that the Government now held him in considerable esteem.

After dinner, Rampton showed Savill his new library, where they inspected the fireplace he had imported from Italy. They took a light supper in the salon next door at about eleven o'clock. They drank each other's health in an atmosphere that might almost have been described as cordial.

Rampton sat back in his chair. 'Well,' he said. 'Have we an agreement? In principle, if not in detail.'

'Are we not ahead of ourselves, sir? The boy's still in Somersetshire, still in the care of his friends.'

'You have the power to change that, sir.' Rampton took up

an apple and began to peel it with a silver knife. 'It's in the best interests of everyone concerned.'

'We don't know what the boy would wish.'

Rampton waved the knife. 'That's neither here nor there. He is only a boy, after all. He is not legally of an age where he may control his own destiny. We may safely leave his opinions out of it.'

Savill said nothing.

'Well?' Rampton said, setting down his glass more forcibly than was necessary.

'I reserve the right to defer my final decision until I have met the boy.'

There was silence, which grew uncomfortable.

'You have changed, haven't you, Mr Savill?' Rampton said.

'Time does alter a man, sir.'

'True – and that scar, too. And, if I were to hazard a guess, I should say that you are not as comfortably situated as perhaps you might have wished to be at this time of life.'

'You suggest I am a poor man.' Savill's tooth began to throb.

'Not at all, sir. I merely meant to imply that perhaps, like most of us, you would prefer to be a little more comfortable than you are.'

Savill bowed.

'I'm told that you act as the English agent of several Americans who have property in this country and you under-take a variety of commissions for them. And sometimes also for gentlemen of the law.'

Rampton paused. He sat back in his chair and smiled at Savill, who said nothing.

'That's all very well, I'm sure,' Rampton went on, 'But in this unsettled world of ours, there is much to be said for the tranquillity of mind that a fixed salary brings, is there not?' Frowning, he massaged his fingers. 'I might possibly be able to put you in the way of a position, which would provide a modest competence paid quarterly. A clerkship in the Colonies, perhaps, you know the sort of thing. You would be able to appoint a deputy to do the work so you would not find it inconvenient or unduly onerous.'

A bribe, Savill thought. He is offering me a bribe if I do as he wishes. He took out a pair of dice he kept in his waistcoat pocket and rolled them from one hand to the other. A seven.

'I had not put you down as a gambler, sir,' Rampton said.

'I'm not. The dice remind me that chance plays its part in all our actions.'

'You are grown quite philosophical.'

Savill shrugged. In truth, he kept the dice in his pocket because they reminded him that nothing should be taken for granted, that the Wheel of Fortune might spin at any moment, that everything was precarious. He had learned that long ago in another country.

'Permit me to tell you why I want the boy,' the old man said.

'Charles, sir,' Savill said. 'His name is Charles.'

'Indeed, sir. But pray hear me out. You have had a month to grow accustomed to my proposal. You see this?' He waved his hand about the room. 'This house of mine, the gardens, the farms, the house in Westminster. All this, and indeed there's more. But I have no children of my own – no one to leave this to. Nor do I have any close relations left alive, no one to carry my name into the future. That is why I want Charles. He is Augusta's son, therefore he is my own kin, my own great-nephew. I wish him to bear the name of Rampton. And is this not the happiest outcome for all concerned? After all, I am his nearest relation, in blood if not in law.'

'No, sir, you are not.' Savill took up his glass. 'My daughter Lizzie is his nearest relation. She's his half-sister.'

'A quibble, my dear sir. She does not even know of the boy's existence. She cannot miss what she has never had. Nor is she in a position to do anything for him.'

Rampton placed his hand on Savill's arm. 'So perhaps we can come to an arrangement?'

48

'You cannot buy him, sir, if that's what you mean.'

'I would make him my heir. My adopted son.'

'Then I am surprised you have not brought him here already,' Savill said. 'Rather than leave him in such evil company.'

Rampton took a deep breath and tried the effect of a smile. 'You must understand that my position makes it quite impossible for me to be seen as a principal in this affair. As one of His Majesty's civil servants, it would not be fitting for me to have private business with the Count de Quillon and his friends, whose reputations are irrevocably stained by their political and moral degeneracy. For the same reason, I cannot send Malbourne. Besides, the press of business is such that I do not believe I could spare him.'

'I see that no such scruples need restrain me,' Savill said, resisting a sudden urge to laugh.

'Indeed – as a private citizen and Augusta's husband, you have every right to claim the boy. My name need not appear in the matter at all. There is another consideration which may sway you – Monsieur de Quillon and Monsieur Fournier hold the papers attesting to Augusta's death and burial. You must have these. You will need them, not least if you should ever wish to marry again . . . after all, my dear sir, you are still in the prime of life. And then – what if the Count should refuse to surrender Charles? Only you are in a position to force his hand. Indeed, it is your duty.'

'But why the devil should Monsieur de Quillon wish to retain him?' Savill said.

Rampton cracked his knuckles. 'Oh, as to that – that is part of the difficulty; the Count has a foolish fancy that Charles is his son.'

# Chapter Eight

Charnwood is an old house where nothing is correct. All the lines are crooked – the walls, the roofs, the chimneystacks. It stands in a muddy place where it is always cold and raining. At night it is so dark and quiet that if a person screamed only the stars would hear him.

We are quite safe here, Fournier tells Charles. No one can harm us.

But nobody is happy here, Charles thinks, even Fournier and the Count, who talk endlessly about King Louis and the poor royal family, captives in the Temple, and about their own unhappy plight.

'We are in exile,' the Count says one morning when Charles is in the room. 'No one will visit us here. I declare I shall die of boredom.'

It is settled that Dr Gohlis will join the party, though Charles understands that he is not so much a visitor as a superior sort of servant who is permitted to dine with his masters. Fournier gives him permission to use a room over the stables for his experiments.

'Monsieur de Quillon and I do not want you pursuing your studies in the house,' Fournier says to the doctor by way of pleasantry. 'It would not be agreeable to hear the screams of your victims.'

Charles listens to the servants' conversation. The servants talk quite freely when he is among them. He learns that, in their eyes, his inability to speak makes him an idiot or a dumb animal. He also eavesdrops on the Count, which is not diffi-cult because he rarely moderates the volume of his voice.

So Charles soon learns the reason why nobody comes to call on them. It is a fact to be recorded in his memory and relied on. The Vicar of Norbury, Mr Horton, does not approve of the Count and Monsieur Fournier. Their politics, their lack of religion and their amoral conduct put them beyond the pale.

The local gentry, such as they are – 'Jumped-up farmers,' says the Count, 'clodhopping peasants with turnips under their fingernails' – take their lead from Mr Horton. The King of England does not like them either, so no one is allowed to come down from London.

Mrs West, who lives at Norbury Park, is their friend, but she cannot call at Charnwood because there is no lady in the house to receive her. Sometimes the gentlemen call on her and she asks them to dine. But Charles always stays at Charnwood.

The Count summons Charles. The grown-ups are dining so they are all there around the table. The room with its peeling wallpaper smells of gravy and wine and perfume as well as of damp.

'You went outside today,' the Count says. 'Saul saw you in the stableyard.'

Saul is Monsieur de Quillon's valet, who has come with him from France.

The Count leans his elbow on the table and brings his great head almost to the level of Charles's. 'That's all right. When you are at liberty, you may go there. And you may go into the gardens. But that is all. You must not go into the woods, or the fields, or into the village. Is that understood?'

Charles stares at him.

'Well?' the Count says. 'You understand? Why the devil will you not speak?'

'We must see what we can contrive,' Gohlis says, putting his head on one side and studying Charles. 'He can do better than this.'

Fournier says, 'Yes, he does understand. You can see it in his eyes.'

'It is most interesting,' the doctor says to the Count. 'Considered philosophically and scientifically. You must permit me to try an experiment, sir.'

'You can do as you like, as long as you make him speak.'

In the last week of September, the doctor's luggage arrives – two trunks and three wooden boxes.

One of the boxes contains the figure of Louis, wrapped in a cotton shroud and floating in a cloud of wood shavings. Dr Gohlis himself unpacks him. Charles watches the disinterment from the second-floor landing, where his room is. He peers through the balustrade, down the well through the middle of the house to the floor of the hall where the doctor is at work.

He is like a gravedigger, Charles thinks, bringing out the dead.

The contents of the boxes, including Louis, are transferred to the room in the stables. Gohlis calls the room his laboratory.

Next morning Charles rises very early. Only the servants are downstairs. He goes out to the stableyard. The doctor's room is at one end of the loft over the looseboxes, where there is now only a solitary horse.

The door is locked. Charles cannot find the key.

Beside the stable is the coach house. It is possible, Charles finds, to scramble on to a water butt in the yard and climb into the lead-lined gully at the foot of the sloping roof of the coach house. If he walks along the gully, and climbs up the slope of the tiled roof, he can look through the dusty window of the laboratory.

Charles feels a surge of relief when he sees Louis standing at the end of the table on the other side of the window. He is looking across the table and keeping his own counsel.

If, as is possible, there is still someone there, a living boy locked in the prison made from the mould of his own mutilated body, then he must be able to see the window from the corner of his eye.

Charles thinks of the saints in Notre-Dame on the Île de la Cité. You may pray to the statue of a saint and the saint hears your prayer and will answer you, if he or she pleases. What is prayer but conversation in church? Why should Louis be any different from an image of the Virgin?

Charles taps the glass. Louis, he thinks as hard as he can, it's me.

At first he thinks it in French. Then, to be on the safe side, he thinks it in English.

Next day, Thursday, the Charnwood laundry comes back. The washerwoman has a dark, wrinkled face. Her name is Mrs White, and she lives in the cottage at the end of the drive and opens the gate to visitors. (These are all facts, and may be relied upon.)

Mrs White is fat, deaf and very small. She is like a hedgehog in a dirty brown dress. She comes up the back drive in a cart drawn by a donkey with the scars of old sores and old beatings on its flanks.

The clean linen is in three wicker baskets, on one of which she sits. Charles wonders how many shirts and sheets and pairs of stockings have been squeezed into them.

The gardener's boy leads the donkey. He holds the bridle in one hand and a stick in the other. The stick is for beating the donkey. The boy is a year or two older than Charles and has red hair. According to one of the maids, he is Mrs White's grandson.

Charnwood is surrounded by a small park. Charles shelters in a clump of trees and watches them coming up the drive. He likes to know who comes and goes. In this strange place among strange and half-strange people, he does not know very much yet. But gradually he accumulates information. It is not much but it is something. Facts are solid things. You may trust them, unlike people.

The old woman in the cart stares straight ahead. She does not move at all. Perhaps she is asleep. The boy trudges up the drive, occasionally glancing at the donkey and prodding or hitting it with his stick.

The cart passes within twenty or thirty yards of the trees where Charles is standing. He is not exactly hiding, but he does not wish to be seen so he stands well back, partly concealed by the trunk of a cedar tree.

At the nearest point between them, the red-headed boy looks at the trees, looks directly at Charles.

The donkey plods on. The cart rattles. The boy glances at the donkey and hits it very hard with the stick.

That's all it takes. Charles knows from that moment that the gardener's boy hates him. If you can have love at first sight, then why not hate? You do not need a reason to love and you do not need a reason to hate.

Later he encounters the gardener's boy again. It is in the stableyard. Charles has gone there because Dr Gohlis is paying an afternoon call on Mrs West, so he will not be in the laboratory. Charles plans to search for the key to the door. Even if he doesn't find it, he will be able to peer through the window at Louis and greet him.

To his horror, though, he finds the red-headed boy is in the yard. He is shortening the donkey's reins.

There is no time to retreat. The boy abandons the donkey. He comes up to Charles, herding him like a dog with a sheep into the corner where the mounting block stands by the door to the house.

He prods Charles with his forefinger. 'Cat got your tongue, then?'

He is a head taller and his accent is as dense as mud. Charles stares at the ground. There's a hole in the sole and the upper of the boy's right shoe. His big toe pokes through.

'You're an idiot.'

The boy comes closer and blows a raspberry. His spittle sprays over Charles's face.

'Little baby. Look at you – dribbling all over your baby face.' The boy smiles. 'You can't even speak. So I can do whatever I like to you. Can't tell no one, can you?'

He sucks in air, ready for another raspberry. But suddenly the door bangs against the wall and the Count himself is there. He grabs the boy by the scruff of his neck and flings him down on the cobbles.

The Count is dressed for riding. He is carrying a crop. He beats the boy to the ground. The whip slashes this way and that. Charles watches.

The boy squirms like a worm. He cries for mercy. He cries for his mother.

Charles puts his hands over his ears in an attempt to block out the screams. There is blood on the boy's shirt, so bright that for a moment Charles has to close his eyes.

# Chapter Nine

At first, Charles cannot make out much of what the English say. Their words collide and mingle with one another in a babble of sound, like water running over pebbles.

He thought he would be able to understand everything because Maman taught English to him at home, as far back as he can remember. But perhaps Maman spoke a different sort of English.

Gradually, however, as the long days pass, Charles learns to understand more and more of what he hears. Sometimes he even dreams in English.

He wishes there were only one language in the world. He speaks – or rather used to speak, French, Maman's special sort of English and – left over from when he was very small – some Italian and even a little German. Oh, and there is yet another language – the Latin the priests use, the language of church and lessons.

Often he does not know where one language ends and another begins. In his head they bleed into one another like watercolour paints when you splash water on them.

Why are there so many words? And why can he say none of them?

\*   \*   \*

Early in the afternoon on the first day of October, the sun comes out for a short while and Charles goes to the Garden of Neptune. This is higher up the valley than the house, where the pleasure grounds give way to meadow and woodland.

It is a garden within the garden, enclosed by walls and tall hedges. In the middle is a pond with a stone statue, discoloured by age and lichen. The god has lost his trident. He looks stunted because he has disproportionally short legs and arms, like a dwarf that Charles and Maman used to see begging on the Rue Saint-Honoré, near the Palais Royale.

The other night, Charles had a nightmare about Neptune. The sea god found his trident in the water. He waded across to the wall surrounding the pool and began stabbing Charles with his weapon. In the dream, Neptune's body was dripping and hung with weeds. His legs had scales like a fish. But as the god stabbed and stabbed, the blood poured from Charles's body in great gouts. Soon it was raining bright blood and Neptune himself turned red.

Blood spurts from people like water from a pump. Charles knows that. (It is a fact.)

He has made himself return to the garden. For, if Neptune has not found his trident, then everything Charles remembers from the dream has never happened.

It never rained blood. Not really. Never, never, never. It is important to be sure of these things.

Neptune has not found his trident.

Afterwards Charles decides to measure the garden. A network of paths connects the gates and runs between the beds where small bushes grow. He walks up and down, counting.

The path parallel to the wall is fifty-two paces on its two long sides. It is thirty-four paces on one of the shorter ones, and thirty-two paces on the other – which worries Charles because it means that the garden cannot be a perfect rectangle and he will find it hard to calculate its area. He knows how to calculate areas, but only if they form exact squares and rectangles. A further complication is that he does not know exactly how long his paces are.

He has all these numbers in his head, and he scratches them on the gravel to help him remember. But they are just that – numbers. They don't tell him other things. They float like clouds, unattached to anything solid.

In his frustration, Charles kicks the low wall around the pool and hurts his foot. The water is green and covered with weeds and insects that play on the surface as if it were a sheet of glass. Neptune is reflected in the water, sneering up at him.

Charles picks up a handful of gravel and throws it into the pond. The smooth glass shatters. The reflection of Neptune disintegrates.

There, he thinks, that will teach you to hurt me.

That is when he hears the footsteps.

Charles turns. The gardener's boy has come into the garden. He walks slowly along the wide alley that runs down the middle of the garden towards Neptune and his pond.

The gardener's boy stares at Charles. His face is very serious. His lips are moving slightly. Charles wonders if he is trying to multiply big numbers in his head, perhaps calculating the number of stockings and shirts in his baskets. There are still red weals on his cheek from the beating.

The boy stops just before he would bump into Charles. He scuffs at the numbers in the gravel, obliterating the facts they record. His face is dirty. He has freckles that make it look dirtier. Words pour out of his mouth in his thick, soft, shapeless voice.

'Goddamned foreigner, you can't even speak, you're a baby, you piss in your bed, you're a windy great looby, you skinny ballocks, you stinking Frog noodle . . .'

He says the words over and again, like a prayer. The more he says, the angrier he becomes.

He takes Charles's left ear by the lobe. He pinches it. Charles opens his mouth and a scream comes out, a high, wordless sound like a small animal in pain. The boy does not let go. Charles tries to hit and kick him but the boy holds him at arm's length.

There is a spark in the boy's green eyes. He drags Charles's head backwards. With his other hand he turns Charles around. He forces him to his knees. He bends him over the parapet of the pool.

The stone coping digs into Charles's ribs. The gardener's boy pushes Charles's head slowly towards the water.

The sun is reflected in its surface. He closes his eyes. The pain in his ear fills his head with white noise.

With his free hand the gardener's boy pins Charles's body to the parapet.

The water is cool and as soft as a silk dress. Charles opens his eyes. A fish slips away into the murky depths. He opens his mouth to scream. He swallows water.

The grip on his ear drags him down and down. His legs flail. The pain in his chest is now worse than the pain in his ear. Then pain has no borders. It goes everywhere.

In an instant Charles remembers how he saw a man drown a litter of kittens in the yard when he was very small. The man put them one by one into the bucket of water and held them under the surface. The kittens' legs kicked. The bodies writhed. When there was no more movement, the man took each scrap of dripping fur from the water and laid it on the ground where it lay perfectly still. Then he reached for another kitten, and soon they were all dead. Sodden scraps of flesh and fur.

While Charles is drowning, in the middle of all the pain, he sees this bucket quite clearly. He sees the man's hand and remembers how the back of it was covered with black hairs. He sees the head of a drowning kitten between his fingers.

Then, as suddenly as it began, it is over. Charles is dragged out of the water and thrown to the ground, where he lies, panting and dribbling.

Slowly the white noise and the pain diminish. Charles coughs. He hears the boy's running footsteps.

Charles retches – at first weakly and then with increasing violence. Dirty water spews out of his mouth and splashes on his face and hands.

That night Charles wets the bed again.

He doesn't know why this shameful and babyish thing should happen: it just does. This is the first time that he has been caught wetting the bed since they came to England.

When the maid discovers that he has wet the bed, she calls the housekeeper, who is very stern, very English. Her name is Mrs Cox and she has a voice that sounds like chalk scratching on a slate.

Mrs Cox shakes her head and says to the maid that the boy is a dirty, devilish imp, and what can you expect of these foreigners? This one can't even speak his own language.

The maid says maybe he's a simpleton, like the girl in the village who looks like a monkey and cannot keep herself clean.

Mrs Cox replies that in any case the boy should be whipped to beat the nonsense out of him.

For some reason Charles thinks of the way Marie used to beat the dust from the carpets in the backyard of their lodgings in Paris. In the middle of his fear, he has a picture in his head of himself draped over a fence, with Mrs Cox and the maid on either side of him, beating him with carpet beaters so that the wickedness flies out of him in puffs of evil. He thinks Mrs Cox would enjoy that, and probably the maid too.

But the housekeeper is not quite sure of her powers. She says she will speak to Monsieur de Quillon's valet, who has some English, and ask him to speak to his master.

Charles waits all day for the blow to fall. But nothing happens. Not that day, nor the next, nor the one after.

Every night he prays on his knees to God that he will not wet the bed again.

Sometimes God listens. Sometimes he doesn't.

# Chapter Ten

Savill's daughter, Lizzie, had lived with her aunt and uncle in Shepperton, on the Thames, from the time that she was little more than a baby until the death of her uncle.

That melancholy event had been two years ago. Afterwards, Savill had brought his sister and his daughter to Nightingale Lane. The freeholds belonged to a widow in New York, who stubbornly refused to sell them, though he had forwarded several offers to her. There were four houses in the lane, and he had the largest, which had a garden with a small orchard.

The builders were at work all around, raising new houses in new, neatly proportioned streets. Most of the land around was owned by the Duke of Bedford, apart from a rectangular enclave north of Great Store Street where the City of London held the freeholds.

Nightingale Lane was squeezed between the Duke's estate and the City's land, a tiny kink in the pattern, an outrage against the principles of rational design and commercial good sense. But sometimes, early in the morning, before the builders started work and the streets filled with traffic, Savill heard the birds singing their laments in his garden, singing for lost fields and ruined hedgerows.

It was the first time that he and Lizzie had lived under the same roof for more than a few months. It healed a wound he hardly knew he had until it began to scab over.

In the past, he had missed his daughter more than he cared to admit, even to himself. When she was seven, he had commissioned an artist to paint a miniature of her, which he had had framed and enclosed in a square case, bound in green leather, now faded and much worn. He had kept it on his table or by his bed, standing open. It had been a poor substitute for a flesh-and-blood child, but it had been better than nothing.

On the last Saturday in September, more than a week after Savill's second visit to Mr Rampton's house in Stanmore, he came home from the City to find Lizzie in the parlour, waiting to preside over the tea table.

'You look fatigued,' she said in a severe voice.

He kissed her. 'Where is your aunt?'

'Drinking tea with Mrs Foster and admiring her grandchildren, especially the new one. But why are you looking so stern, sir?'

'I shall tell you directly.'

'You shall tell me nothing until you have sat down in your armchair and we have rung for hot water.'

She would not let him say what he wished to say until the water had been brought, the tea measured out, and the infusion was brewing.

'Well, sir, you may speak,' she said, folding her hands in her lap and looking at him with a sort of mock gravity that usually made him laugh.

'I was obliged to go out of town the other day and see your Uncle Rampton,' he said.

She made a face. 'Nothing disagreeable?'

'Not for you, I hope.'

'I think he must be an odious man. He does nothing for you.'

'My dear,' he said. 'I'm afraid there's news of your mother.'

At once the cheerfulness left Lizzie's face. She raised her hand to her mouth as if holding back the words that were trying to get out. Savill knew that she barely remembered her mother, who had absconded when she was very young; and, even before that, she had seen little of her, for in those days Augusta had not been much troubled by maternal feelings.

'She's not here?' Lizzie blurted out, the colour rushing to her cheeks. 'Not in London?'

'No. My dear, you must prepare yourself for a shock. I am sorry to say that your mother is dead.'

Lizzie's face puckered, as if age had prematurely withered it. 'Oh. I – I see.'

'She died in Paris.' Savill leaned forward and took his daughter's hand, which lay limp and warm in his. 'Mr Rampton said it was very sudden. I do not know the details yet, but I shall in a week or two.'

'I don't know what to say, Papa.'

'You don't have to say anything. Nothing is changed – not for you – not for me.'

She raised her head suddenly. 'But it has. For you, at least. You can marry again.' Her colour deepened. 'That is to say, should you wish to.' She sat up very straight and turned away to busy herself with the tea.

Savill was seized by a desire to laugh. He said gravely, 'I have no intention of marrying at present. Besides, you must not worry about me. Or about your mother.'

'But I don't know what to feel,' she said in a voice that was almost a child's wail.

'You don't have to feel anything, my love.'

'Will we go into mourning?'

'Perhaps not, in the circumstances.' He rubbed his scar, which had begun to itch. 'I will consult your aunt – she will know what is proper. But first there is one other thing you must know.'

She looked down at her lap and did not speak.

'After she went away, your mother had a child. A son. He is still alive.'

Her head jerked up. 'I have a brother?'

'Yes. A half-brother.'

'Why did you not tell me before?'

'Because I did not know myself until I saw your uncle Rampton.'

'How old is he?'

'Ten or eleven, I believe,' Savill said.

'A half-brother,' she repeated. He watched her calculating the arithmetic. 'So – who was his father? I – I'm sorry, perhaps it is indelicate of me to—'

'It is natural that you should ask. But I'm afraid I cannot tell you that either, because I do not know. Perhaps I will find out when I see him.'

'Is he here? In England?'

'Yes. Not in London, though.'

'When shall we see him? Where will he live? Will he live with us here?'

'I expect you will see him at some point, but I do not know quite when. As for where he will live, Mr Rampton has a fancy to adopt him. If he does that, I dare say the boy would live with him, except when he is at school, and so on.'

'But he should live with us, Papa.' Colour flooded over her face. 'If he's my brother, I'm nearer kin to him than Mr Rampton.'

'True. But Mr Rampton can give him things that we cannot give him.'

She forced him to stop again. 'It is not that you don't want him, is it? Because he – he's not your son?'

'No . . .' Savill hesitated. 'Or rather, I do not think so.'

'What is his name?'

'Charles.'

'Charles,' she repeated, as if turning the name over in her mind and examining it from every angle. 'Charles. Where is he living now? Who is looking after him?'

'In England, at the house of a French gentleman, the Count de Quillon, who was obliged to leave his country because of the Revolution. Which is another complication. The Count had a kindness for your mother and, for her sake, he wishes to keep Charles with him and remain his guardian.'

'But surely you would not let them take him from us? Either this Count or my uncle Rampton?'

'The poor boy is alone in the world, and orphaned. He does not know us at all. I wish to do what is best for him, not for us.'

There was a silence.

'Will you pour the tea?' he said.

She obeyed mechanically. But as she passed him his cup she looked directly at him.

'Will you ask him about my mother?' she said. 'Will he tell you who his father is? Do you think he knows?'

'I don't know,' Savill said. 'I don't know anything except that he's your mother's son and his name is Charles. And I shall go down to Somersetshire next week to fetch him.'

# Chapter Eleven

The house in Crown Street was one of a gently curving terrace. The building had been newly refaced and refurbished. It must once have been a private residence but, like so many of its neighbours in the vicinity of the Palace of Westminster, it had gradually become a government office.

Savill mounted the three shallow steps up to the front door. At his knock, a shutter in one of the door's upper panels slid open. Savill glimpsed a fat finger that lacked a nail. He gave his name and asked for Mr Rampton.

After a pause, he heard the rattle of a chain within and the grating of bolts. The door opened, revealing a vast porter whose bulk filled most of the height and width of the narrow hallway. He was as tall as a Potsdam grenadier but far wider. His barrel of a body balanced on tapering legs that seemed too thin and fragile to bear its weight.

Beyond him was an inner door. Breathing heavily through his mouth, for his nose was a flattened ruin, he studied Savill and then consulted a sheet of paper in his hand. He looked up. 'You're to go in,' he said in a combative tone, as though Savill had expressed a wish to do otherwise.

The porter rapped twice on the inner door. As he did so,

Savill glimpsed the palm of his right hand, which was disfigured by a broad welt or burn.

There was the rattle of another bolt. The inner door opened. A grizzled, whippet-thin clerk took Savill's name and business without comment. He waved him into a room on the left of the passage, where two other clerks were at work. The office was divided by a tall wooden partition into unequal parts. In the larger part, nearer the fire and the window, were the clerks' high desks. In the smaller part were four dirty wooden chairs for visitors and a row of hooks.

'I dare say Mr Rampton will see you shortly,' the clerk muttered.

He retired behind the partition, where he pulled a handle in the wall by the fireplace and clambered on to his stool. Savill heard the ping of a distant bell. He sat, his face impassive, while the three clerks took turns to peer over the partition at the visitor. As soon as he met their eyes, they looked away.

Five minutes passed, perhaps ten. There were footsteps on the stairs and Malbourne came into the office. He was no longer wearing the black-silk sling.

'Mr Savill, sir, your servant. I beg your pardon for keeping you waiting. Mr Rampton's quite at leisure now and begs you to step up.'

'What is this place?' Savill asked as he climbed the stairs.

Malbourne glanced over his shoulder. 'We are part of the Post Office, sir.'

A clock ticked on the first-floor landing and the brass door furniture shone. Malbourne led him into an office overlooking the street and tapped on an inner door. Rampton's voice cried 'Enter'.

The room beyond was large, airy and comfortably furnished. Only a large table set along one wall hinted that business was transacted here. It held bundles of letters tied with pink ribbon, some of them sorted into flat, rectangular baskets.

Savill bowed to Mr Rampton who, with great condescension, rose from his chair behind his desk and inclined his head in return.

'How obliging of you to call,' Mr Rampton said, as if this was no more than a casual meeting. 'Shall Malbourne send out for something? Is it too early for a glass of sherry?'

'Not for me, sir, thank you.'

'You may leave us, Horace. Close the door, but hold yourself at readiness in case I need you.'

Malbourne bowed and withdrew. He closed the door but Savill did not hear the snick of the catch engaging.

Rampton waved Savill to a chair beside his desk. 'Tell me, how does Miss Elizabeth do this morning?'

Savill said she was very well and added that his daughter would be most gratified to hear that her uncle Rampton had been enquiring after her.

Rampton nodded impatiently. 'I take it that you have not had second thoughts about our agreement?'

'No, sir. As you may recall, I have committed myself merely to—'

'Yes, to be sure we are quite clear about where we both stand.' Rampton opened a drawer and took out a small packet. 'For my part, I have not been idle since we last met. I directed my attorney to write on your behalf to the Count, informing him that you, as my poor niece's husband, propose to call on him at Charnwood to collect the boy and the necessary papers. My name does not appear, of course. The Count should have received the letter by now.'

The top of Rampton's desk was almost empty – it was a fad of his, Savill remembered, to keep the desk he worked on as clear as possible. He broke the seal that secured the outer wrapping of the packet. He took out two sheets of paper.

'This one confirms who you are,' he said, 'and this one is an attested copy of the marriage certificate of my poor niece and yourself.' He put down the papers and took up a third.

'Are you familiar with the terms of the new Police Act? No? Well, I suppose there's no reason that a law-abiding citizen need be. One of the provisions of the act was to set up police offices and appoint stipendiary magistrates. Foolish people always assume that such measures constitute a mechanism for government to suppress the liberties of individual citizens . . .'

'Are they wrong?'

'Of course they are. Our police have a particular task, and only one: to prevent revolution. One of their magistrates, Mr Ford, has provided you with this warrant: it gives you the authority to enter Charnwood Court and remove the boy Charles into your keep. I hope it will not be necessary for you to use it, but there is no harm in your being prepared.'

Savill watched the papers multiplying on the desk. He felt stirrings of alarm. Attorneys? Magistrates? Police offices?

Rampton picked up another document. 'Now, you should not need this but it will serve to introduce you to a local justice as a representative of the police office. Mr Ford requires him to give you any assistance you may need. In case of emergency, he appoints you under the Police Act as his agent or deputy, which gives you temporary powers of inquiry, arrest and detention, subject of course to his confirmation.' He looked at Savill and his hand fluttered as if shaking drops of water from his fingers. 'Again, just in case.'

'Surely this is quite unnecessary, sir?'

'Almost certainly it is,' Rampton said. 'But the Government believes these are dangerous people. One should take nothing for granted.' The fingers fluttered to alight upon another sheet of paper. 'Say, for example, you should desire to communicate with me while you are at Charnwood. Do not write to me here or at Vardells. Address the letter to Frederick Brown, Esquire, at the White Horse Cellar in Piccadilly, to await collection. I have made a memorandum here.'

Savill said, 'Who is Mr Brown?'

'There is no Mr Brown, as such. He is a convenient fiction.

70

I must emphasize that my name must not appear in this in any way. It would be prejudicial to the Government.'

'Why, sir?'

'I'm afraid I am not at liberty to say.' Rampton smiled across the desk. 'Now – this is an inside ticket to Bath, on the mail diligence. I understand that Charnwood is fifteen or twenty miles from the city. You will have to hire a conveyance to take you on to Charnwood. And perhaps on your way back with the boy, you will find it easier to hire a chaise at Bath and travel post up to London.'

Rampton unlocked another drawer and took out a small canvas roll. He placed it on the desk, where it lay like a grey sausage.

'Fifty guineas in gold,' he said. 'You must sign for it, of course, and we will require a full account of any monies you disperse. The sum should be ample, but in case of emergency here is a letter to Mr Green of Green's Bank in Bath. It will authorize you to withdraw further funds. But I do not think you will need to trouble him.'

Savill took the papers and looked through them. Rampton pushed pen and ink towards him. Savill signed receipts for the money and the papers. He stowed them both in an inner pocket. He felt the weight of the gold dragging him down.

'There's more to this than the boy,' he said.

'I beg your pardon?' Rampton said. 'I don't follow you.'

'All this. The money. This deed. The warrant. Your Mr Brown.'

'My dear sir, you are allowing your fancies to run away with you.' Rampton sat back and stared at Savill. Then, unexpectedly, he smiled. 'I have been quite candid with you. I want to restore Charles to his family. I want to bring him up as my heir. All these precautions are necessary solely because of the peculiar nature of his present guardians – and, indeed, the delicate nature of my own employment. Is all this so very strange?'

'Pray, sir,' Savill said, 'what exactly is the business of this office?'

'What? Oh, there's no mystery about that. We are a sub-department of the Post Office. We are known as the Foreign Office, or the Black Letter Office, because we handle the foreign mails.' Rampton rang a bell on his desk. 'While you are here, it may be helpful for you to hear a little more about Charnwood.'

Malbourne entered the room. He inclined his head. 'Sir?'

'Charnwood Court, Malbourne – who owns the freehold?'

'A lady named Mrs West, sir, the widow of the brewer. She resides at Norbury Park, I believe, when she is in the country. Charnwood is a house on the Norbury estate.' Malbourne cleared his throat. 'When she was in town in the spring, she was often seen in the company of Monsieur Fournier. In fact, I believe it was he who arranged the tenancy, and it is his name on the lease.'

'That backsliding priest,' Rampton said. 'A traitor to his God as well as to his king.'

'Yes, sir. He arrived in England after the massacres in September. I believe he took the lease for Charnwood in the spring, which suggests he is remarkably far-sighted. He declines to call himself an émigré, however.'

'In other words, he's sitting on the fence,' Rampton said. 'Waiting to see what happens with the King. Besides, most of his wealth is in France and he doesn't want to lose it if he can help it. But he's a clever devil, Savill – if he's at Charnwood, he's a man to watch.'

Malbourne cleared his throat. 'And a charming devil, sir, as well. Monsieur Fournier is a man of great address and he is very adroit at worming his way into intimacy with those who he believes may further his interests.'

'What if Mr Savill needs to summon a magistrate to enforce his claim?'

'He should communicate with Mr Horton, sir, the Vicar of Norbury. He is the nearest Justice now. The village is less than a mile from Charnwood.'

Rampton turned to Savill. 'The coach leaves tomorrow. You should be back with Charles by Saturday at the latest.'

Malbourne showed Savill out. The porter in the outer hall did not move from his stool when the inner door opened. His eyes were closed.

Malbourne stopped. 'Jarsdel!'

The eyes snapped open. 'Sir?'

'Stand up and make your obedience, damn you.'

The porter rose from his stool with the caution of a snail emerging from his shell. He bowed ponderously.

'This gentleman is Mr Savill,' Malbourne told him. 'He is a particular friend of Mr Rampton's. If he calls again, you are to admit him directly and show him every courtesy. Is that understood?'

Malbourne followed Savill down the steps and on to the pavement.

'I beg your pardon, sir,' he said. 'Jarsdel's an insolent fellow. It amuses Mr Rampton to make a pet of him, and he's inclined to give himself airs in consequence. If we do not bring him up occasionally, he grows intolerable.'

Savill smiled and nodded, but said nothing.

'I hope your journey prospers,' Malbourne went on.

All that money, Savill thought, all those papers – and all this for a little boy.

'I wonder what it is you really do here, sir,' he said.

Malbourne glanced back at the house and smiled: and that was all the answer he gave. 'I wish you a safe journey, sir,' he said. 'And a happy return.'

# Chapter Twelve

It took Savill over twelve hours to travel by the mail coach from London to Bath. Most of that time it rained.

He spent the night in Bath at the Three Tuns inn. It was still raining in the morning, when he hired a gig to take him to Norbury, with a groom to drive him. The owner of the livery stable told him that the village's situation was remote, far from the nearest post road.

The chaise was open to the elements. Savill sat behind the driver. Despite his great coat, a travelling cloak, top boots and a broad-brimmed hat, the rain found ways to reach his skin.

Their road was narrow and winding; the rain filled the ruts with puddles and turned the higher parts to mud. The country was generously provided with hills, which no doubt would have afforded a variety of fine prospects if the rain and the mist had permitted Savill to see them.

As the day passed, they laboured on, mile after mile. The driver muttered under his breath. The horse was a tired, broken-down creature that seemed incapable of going much beyond a foot-pace. They stopped twice, ostensibly to rest the unhappy animal but really for the groom to dose himself against rheumatic fever with gin and hot water.

There was said to be an inn at Norbury. Savill had intended to put up there, order his dinner and then call at Charnwood Court to make the necessary arrangements to take the boy away in the morning. But he realized that he had been too optimistic before they had covered half their distance. They would be lucky to reach the village before evening.

The light was already beginning to fade when they came to a small but swollen river that surged between high green banks, its surface mottled with muddy froth. The lane passed over the river by a wooden bridge resting on stone piers that were coated on their upstream side with green slime.

The two men climbed down. The groom led the horse and chaise across the bridge, with Savill behind. The wood was slippery with moisture and in places had rotted away.

'How far is it now?'

'A mile, sir. Maybe.'

After another mile, by Savill's reckoning, they were still no nearer the village. The lane narrowed again and began to twist and climb. They came to a sharp bend with a partly open field-gate on its outer edge. As they rounded the bend, they found themselves face to face with a bull.

It was a large brown animal that to Savill's eyes seemed the size of a small cottage. The horse came to an abrupt halt, straining against the harness of the chaise. The bull had its back to them. For a moment no one moved. Then the great beast slowly turned round. It examined them with sad, incurious eyes. Its legs were coated with pale mud, which gave it the appearance of wearing stockings.

The groom stared open-mouthed at the bull. There was no room to turn in the narrow lane even if there had been time to do it. But the horse did not wait to be told what to do. It twitched violently and bolted to the right toward the field-gate. It blundered through the opening. The chaise followed. For an instant the right wheel caught on the gatepost. The horse strained forward. Suddenly they were through.

75

Just inside the gate, however, sheltering beneath the branches of an ash tree, were half a dozen cows, the bull's harem. These came as a second, equally unwelcome surprise to the horse, which veered to the left, pulling the chaise after it.

It was unfortunate that at this point the field sloped steeply towards a hedgerow running from the lane. The chaise bumped down the incline, its wheels swaying and skidding. The horse stumbled as a hoof sank into the ground. Its momentum carried it forward but sharply sideways, dragging the chaise after it. The hoof came free.

The vehicle fell on its side, tipping out the two men. Wood splintered. The groom shouted an oath. The horse whinnied. Savill felt a stab of pain in his jaw. The impact had set off his toothache, which had been grumbling steadily since his departure from London.

When the pain subsided, he found he was lying on his side in the sloping field. He stared at the sky. Rain fell on his upturned face. The grass beneath him was soggy. Moisture seeped into his clothes. He heard the groom's voice, swearing, a steady stream of obscenities.

Savill sat up and then rose unsteadily to his feet. The groom was on his back a few yards away. The horse was on its feet, though entangled with its traces, which still attached it to the chaise.

Savill looked up the field. The cows hadn't moved. They were staring at the visitors with mild curiosity. The bull, however, was taking a more active interest. He had come through the gateway and advanced a few yards into the field. His head swayed from side to side.

'Get up, you fool,' Savill roared at the groom.

'It'll kill us, sir, I know it—'

'Be quiet.' Savill eyed the bull. 'Free the horse.'

The groom stood up. 'If that poor beast has to be shot, sir, the master will—'

'Stop talking. Free the horse. Then we'll find help.'

76

'Help?' the groom said. 'Where?'

It was a reasonable question. They were in the middle of a field. Apart from the bull and the cows, there were no signs of life, nor any trace of human habitation. The hedge at the bottom of the field was a dense green wall.

'The village can't be far,' Savill said.

The groom jerked his thumb towards the gateway. 'I'm not going near that thing.'

Suddenly, the hedge spoke up. 'Good afternoon,' it said in a crisp, ladylike voice. 'Are you in need of assistance?'

The young lady had a sunburned face and was dressed for walking. Her cloak was spattered with mud. She wore heavy winter pattens that squelched across the field as she approached. The town-bred groom stared at her, as well he might, to see a lady walking alone.

'You've met with an accident, sir.'

'You are quite right, madam,' Savill said. 'I am obliged to you for pointing it out.'

'And I don't much like the look of that bull.'

'Nor do I.'

'Is there a stile there, ma'am, or a gate?' the groom burst out.

'Of course there is. I didn't get here by magic.' She was still looking at Savill. 'Just beyond that chestnut tree. Can't you see it? There is a path along the field boundary.'

'I think that animal's coming,' the groom said.

'Unharness the horse,' the lady told him. 'What are you waiting for? Quick! Cut the traces if necessary.'

Her brisk tone freed the groom from his trance-like state. He unharnessed the horse with remarkable speed and led it limping down the field. It was fortunate that it hadn't broken a leg.

Savill picked up his portmanteau and offered the lady his arm. The bull watched the proceedings.

'It's Farmer Bradshaw's bull,' the lady told him. 'We shall send a message to Mr Bradshaw and have the animal safely confined. No doubt he will have your chaise brought up to the village.'

'What's left of it,' Savill said. The chaise had a broken wheel and the end of the axle had splintered.

As they passed through the gate, he glanced back at the field. The bull had lost interest in them and was grazing beside his harem.

Savill felt ridiculous, even cheated. A crisis was one thing but an anticlimax was quite another, particularly one which must lead to so much inconvenience.

He walked with the lady along a narrow path, strewn with rocks, that ran between hedges. The groom followed, muttering under his breath, with the horse plodding after him.

'It was most obliging of you to come to our assistance,' Savill said, breaking the silence long after it had become awkward.

'I don't think I've provided much of that, sir.'

'At least you had the kindness to come and share our fate.'

'Don't be too sure of that, sir.' She smiled up at him, revealing very white teeth. She was older than he had thought, perhaps in her thirties. 'I should have run off directly the bull began his charge.'

'I hope we are not taking you out of your way.'

'Not at all. Where are you going, sir?'

'Charnwood Court.' Savill flicked water away from his face. 'Is it far?'

'The other side of the village. I thought you might be going there.'

'And why is that?'

'You weren't coming from the village or you couldn't have got the chaise into the field, not with the gate at that angle. I suppose you might have been going somewhere in the village, but I can't think where. I know you're not expected at Norbury

Park or the Vicarage. So that only leaves Charnwood, really. There's nowhere else, you see. You can't get any sort of vehicle much beyond Charnwood.'

There was a silence. The rain continued to fall steadily from a soft grey sky. Savill glanced at the lady. She had dark curls between the top of her collar and the brim of her hat.

He cleared his throat. 'My name is Savill, ma'am. I have business with Count de Quillon at Charnwood. Perhaps you know the gentleman?'

'Yes,' she said. 'That is to say, I have been introduced to him. Have you come far, sir?'

'London, ma'am.'

'It won't help,' the lady said.

Savill stared at her. 'I beg your pardon. What won't help?'

She glanced up at his face. 'Brooding on your troubles, sir. It never answers.'

Norbury lay at the bottom of a dark, steep-sided coomb. Dilapidated cottages faced each other across the single street. The church was set back above the road among a huddle of gravestones. Chickens pecked the dirt and squabbled with one another.

At the upper end of the village was the inn where Savill had intended to dine and spend the night. The lady introduced him to the landlord, Mr Roach, a brisk, efficient man with bright eyes.

'Mr Savill, sir, is it? Good day to you – we've been expecting you.'

'Really? You surprise me.'

'Yes, sir – they sent down from Charnwood two or three days ago to say you'd be coming. I'm to send you up to the house directly.'

'I was intending to put up here.'

'No, sir. Mr Fournier was most insistent, you are to go up to the house. But what's happened?'

'There has been an accident, Roach,' the lady said. 'We must send a message to Mr Bradshaw that his bull is loose. This poor gentleman's chaise had a smash in Parker's field because of it.'

It was arranged that the remains of the chaise would be brought to Mr Roach's barn. The groom would stay the night at the alehouse and return with the horse to Bath the following morning to consult with the proprietor of the livery stables about what should be done and about the thorny question of obtaining compensation from Farmer Bradshaw. Savill, having left a sum of money to defray the immediate cost of this, would travel to Charnwood in a vehicle that Mr Roach had in his stable.

'An admirable plan,' the lady said. 'Now my father will be wanting his tea, and you must excuse me.'

None of the men spoke as she walked away, lifting her feet high above the mud of the village street. She crossed the road and took a narrow path that ran between two stone walls. It led to the churchyard, higher up the slope of the valley. Beyond the church were the roofs of a house that looked more substantial than the cottages in the village.

'Ah well,' said Mr Roach. He squinted up at the sky. 'We better get you up to Charnwood, sir, before it starts raining again.'

Twenty minutes later, a boy led out a small, sad pony attached to a two-wheeled vehicle that was the next best thing to a cart. Savill scrambled up to the seat beside Mr Roach. In the interim, they had become the focus of attention for a small but growing crowd that watched their every move with great interest. Some of the younger ones followed the chaise. Their comments floated up to him like a chorus of Somersetshire voices commenting on the action of a Greek tragedy.

'Looks a cross one, don't he? . . . Wish I'd seen him rolling in the mud . . . That bull wouldn't hurt a fly. Reckon he's scared of cows.'

As the road left the village, it turned and climbed. One by one, the followers dropped away.

'Who is the lady, by the by?' Savill said. 'I didn't catch her name.'

'Vicar's daughter, sir; Miss Horton.' Mr Roach pointed to the right with his whip. 'See that, sir? That's Norbury Park. She'll have been on her way home from there.'

In the distance, partly concealed in a fold of the hills, was a plain stone house of some size. Savill dredged a name from his memory. 'Mrs West's house?'

'Yes, sir.'

'Hardly the weather for a lady to walk out in.'

'Lord bless you, sir, Miss Harriet don't mind a bit of rain, no more than a duck does.'

They pulled up in front of a pair of gates set in a wall with a small cottage beside them. Mr Roach leaned out of the cart, rattled his whip on the bars of the gates, and shouted: 'Hey, there!' in a voice that was possibly audible in the village.

'Deaf,' he explained to Savill, lowering his voice to a normal volume. 'I don't know why Mrs West lets her stay there. The lady's too soft-hearted, and that's a fact.'

An old woman shuffled out of the cottage.

'Good afternoon, Mrs White,' Mr Roach shouted. 'How's your boy doing in the Dragoons? Keeping well, I hope?'

She appeared not to hear him.

'Leave the gates open, will you? I shan't be long.' Mr Roach dropped a copper into Mrs White's outstretched hand before passing into the drive. She nodded to him. She paid no attention whatsoever to Savill.

'Poor woman,' Mr Roach said to Savill as they rattled slowly up the drive. 'Lost her husband last winter, one son went off to be a soldier and the other one fell under a wagon when he was drunk. Grandson works in the gardens here but he's always in mischief. Maybe the good Lord knows what He's about, but damned if I do.'

81

The light was already fading from the sky. Dead leaves on the ground muffled the sound of their wheels. The drive sloped steadily downwards.

'Gloomy old place, eh, sir?' Mr Roach said. 'Wouldn't want to live here myself. Dreadful damp. That's why Mr West built the new house higher up on the other side of the valley.' He grinned. 'Still – better than living in France or heathen parts like that.'

Savill's discomfort was steadily increasing. His clothes were soaked through. He had missed his dinner and he was ravenously hungry. Worst of all was the damage to his pride: he was aware how forlorn he must look. His arrival in this wretched chaise would hardly improve matters.

'Sorry about the bumps, sir,' Mr Roach said. 'The back drive is even worse. That's the one I generally use. But I reckon having you here turns this into a gentleman's chaise.'

He burst out laughing. Savill bared his teeth in what he hoped might resemble an answering smile. The drive followed a bend and suddenly reached its destination. Now they were clear of the protection of the overhanging trees, Savill became aware of how hard the rain was falling.

'Well, this is it, sir,' Mr Roach said, raising his whip in a sort of salute. 'Charnwood. Not to everyone's taste, perhaps, but you know what the sailors say: any port in a storm.'

# Chapter Thirteen

It is growing dark when Charles is summoned. Mrs Cox sends a maid to tell him that he must go at once to the library.

Monsieur de Quillon is seated in his armchair, his legs wide, stretched towards the fire. Dr Gohlis is in the shadows, idly turning a great globe that stands in the corner.

The Count beckons Charles towards him. 'What's this I hear?' he says in his deep, hoarse voice. 'You've fouled your bed again? It won't do, do you hear? Not for someone like you.'

Charles wonders whether it would be different if he were like someone else.

'I was going to have them thrash the nonsense out of you. But the doctor suggests we give you a chance to make amends.'

Charles glances at Dr Gohlis. He is surprised, and made wary, by the kindness.

The Count massages his temples with his fingers. 'So if you start talking again, we'll say no more about it. You won't be beaten. The matter will be closed.' He looks directly at Charles and says, almost as if they were equals, one man to another: 'Well? What do you think?'

Charles would like to say, 'Thank you, sir,' but he can say nothing. He does not even bow.

The Count sighs and throws himself back in his chair.

'It's merely a matter of will,' the doctor says, abandoning the revolving world and coming toward the fireplace. 'There's nothing wrong with you, my boy. Nothing at all.' He takes Charles's chin and tilts it so Charles is forced to look directly up at him. 'Open your mouth.'

Dr Gohlis prods Charles's lips with his forefinger, forcing the mouth open. He pushes the lower jaw further down.

'You see, my lord,' he says, looking from Charles to Monsieur de Quillon, 'the tongue, the vocal cords – everything is there for the production of speech, nothing is damaged.' He releases Charles's chin. 'I am demonstrating to him that there is absolutely no medical reason why he cannot speak. The argument is addressed to his intellect – for, though he is still young, he has a rudimentary rational faculty, and we must make this our ally.'

'I dare say, Doctor.' Monsieur de Quillon takes up a paper from the table beside him. 'But I don't want to hear your lecture on the subject. Get on with it, man, will you?'

Charles glimpses a flicker of anger in the doctor's face as the Count bends his great head over the paper. He is surprised to find himself entertaining the notion that grown-ups can like or dislike other grown-ups.

Gohlis brings his head down to Charles's. 'No one likes pain, do they, my boy? It is abhorrent to any rational being. And you, being human, are capable of reason, *capax rationis*. You will have enough Latinity for that. In other words, to put it as plainly as I can, this means that, if you have any choice in the matter, you will strive to avoid pain.'

Charles stares at the globe, which is no longer turning. He hears the rustle of paper and Monsieur de Quillon's laboured breathing.

'I intend to beat you for fouling your bed like a baby,' Dr Gohlis says. 'Unless – and listen carefully now – unless you say to Monsieur de Quillon, "I ask your pardon, monseigneur."'

The words float into the air. There are black, buzzing insects, swirling, darting, following their own secret paths.

'That is the rational thing to do, Charles. Your intellect knows that pain is not agreeable, and that it should be avoided if at all possible. You may do this very easily, simply by saying five words.'

Charles has not wronged Monsieur de Quillon. Or Dr Gohlis. He has wronged no one except perhaps the maid who changed his bed, the old woman who will wash his sheet, and the red-headed gardener's boy who leads the donkey and the laundry cart up and down the back drive. But they would do all these things in any case; they are paid to do these tasks, so he cannot be said to have wronged even them.

'You must understand what I am saying. I have already demonstrated to you that there is no reason, no physiological reason, for your silence.'

Surely you cannot apologize for something that does not deserve an apology to someone whom you have not harmed? It is not a rational thing to do. Why does the doctor not see that? Perhaps it is the doctor who is not a rational being.

'Remember, my boy – you are *capax rationis*.'

Charles knows what the phrase means because the Abbé Viré, the priest who used to give him lessons, explained it to him long ago before he lost his wits. Man is a reasoning being, the old man told him, and that is why Charles is obliged to love God. Reason offers no other choice.

'Will you speak?' Dr Gohlis asks. 'Will you?'

Charles says nothing.

There are footsteps in the hall. Monsieur Fournier enters the library. The doctor clicks his tongue on the roof of his mouth and goes to stand by the window to look at the rain. Charles shrinks away from him, knocking against the globe.

Fournier's eyebrows rise at the sight of the boy. His eyebrows are unusual because they have a kink in them in the outer edges. This makes him look elegantly surprised all the time.

85

Charles thinks this may be misleading. Nothing really seems to surprise Fournier at all.

'Still silent?' he says.

'It's quite ridiculous,' says the Count.

Fournier smiles and the crooked eyebrows ride even higher. 'Mum's the word,' he says in English, though they have been talking in French until now. 'That's what the English say. Is it not droll?'

'I confess the humour escapes me at present.'

Monsieur Fournier cocks his head. 'It may have to escape you for longer. You remember the gardener's boy?'

'No,' the Count said. 'Why the devil should I?'

'The one you thrashed the other day.'

'Oh yes – what of him?'

'His grandmother has been to see the Vicar, who is also the magistrate here. There is talk of an action for assault.'

'Oh, for God's sake – he's only a peasant, and our own servant too. What is the difficulty?'

'This is England,' Fournier says.

'Do they not beat their servants here?'

'Yes, of course. But not as we do. You know the English – they do things differently. When it suits them.'

'More fool them.'

'Besides, in theory he's in the employ of Mrs West. I think a few shillings should resolve it, as far as the boy and his grandmother are concerned. But it will be inconvenient if we upset Mr Horton any more than we already have.'

'A village curé?' the Count says. 'What a country this is! What an absurd country.'

'Yes, indeed. But Mr Horton is a gentleman, and a man of much influence in his own parish.' Fournier smiled. 'We would do well to make him obliged to us. And, fortunately, there is a solution to hand: Charles.'

'Dear God, you speak in riddles this afternoon.'

'It's quite simple. Mr Horton believes in the power of prayer.'

86

'Superstitious nonsense,' Gohlis muttered.

'That's neither here nor there,' Fournier says. 'I shall write to Mr Horton before dinner. And you would do well—' He breaks off and cocks his head. 'What's that?'

'Someone coming up the drive, sir,' Gohlis said. 'We have a visitor. In a cart, of all things.'

'Who?'

'I don't know.'

Fournier glances at the Count. For a moment the men do not move or speak. Everyone is listening. Rain patters on the long windows at the end of the room. Dr Gohlis laughs, a high, nervous giggle. Monsieur de Quillon scowls at him.

'Charles,' the Count says, 'go upstairs. Go to your room and stay there until you are summoned.'

Fournier says nothing. He watches them with his bright eyes.

Someone knocks on the front door.

'Use the main stairs,' Monsieur de Quillon says to Charles. 'Go. Go now.'

Fournier accompanies Charles into the hall. Joseph the footman is moving towards the front door.

'Just a minute,' Fournier says to the servant in English. 'Who is it? Do you know?'

The footman changes course. He goes to a small window that commands a view of the forecourt in front of the house.

Charles climbs the stairs. He turns at the half-landing and continues up the next flight.

'It's Mr Roach's cart, sir,' he hears Joseph say. 'And there's a man sitting beside him. Don't know him from Adam.'

'You may open the door now,' Monsieur Fournier says.

Charles hears the click of the library door closing. He glances down the stairs but he can see little of the hall below. What he can see, however, is the great mirror that hangs at the turn of the stairs so that the ladies and gentlemen may look at themselves as they go to dinner. The mirror is set in a gilt frame that is no longer golden but a dirty yellow brown. The glass is spotted with damp. The silvering near the bottom has quite worn away. Charles has hardly noticed the mirror's existence before because usually he uses the back stairs.

In the foggy world of the reflection, a boy wavers in the depths of the mirror. Ignoring the voices in the hall below, Charles steps up to it and stretches out his right hand towards the boy he sees there. In the mirror the reflected boy mimics his action.

Charles's right hand almost touches the boy's left hand. The mirror glass is all that divides them, that and the layer of candle grease and dust that has settled along the bottom rail of the frame and spread slowly higher over the years.

'Gentleman's had a mishap on his way here,' he hears a man say below in the rolling, comfortable voice that the peasants use in this place. 'His chaise turned over in Parker's field.'

Charles wonders whether he has lost his reflection as well as his voice. He does not recognize the boy's face, his ragged clothes or his untidy hair – he is a stranger. Yet it is he, Charles. But he looks like someone else, not the boy who used to examine himself in Maman's looking glass.

'My name is Savill,' says another voice, a man's. 'The Count de Quillon is expecting me.'

Charles turns and runs up the stairs.

# Chapter Fourteen

Two manservants, a French valet smelling of scent and an English footman smelling of sweat, converged on Savill. At a nod from Monsieur de Quillon, the valet peeled away his outer garments.

'My dear sir, you are soaked,' the Count said in French. He glanced at his valet. 'Make sure they've lit the fire in Mr Savill's room.'

'You are most kind, sir, but I cannot possibly—'

'Nonsense, sir. You will stay with us.'

Fournier smiled at Savill. 'Monsieur de Quillon is right,' he said in English. 'You will be doing us a kindness, sir – indeed, we have been counting the hours since your attorney's letter arrived. We see very little company. Besides, the inn is quite intolerable.'

The two Frenchmen were both richly dressed but it was their manner rather than their clothes that proclaimed their station. Monsieur de Quillon was the elder of the two. His features were too irregular, and his face too marked by good living, for him to be accounted handsome. His German physician, Dr Gohlis, had been introduced but kept himself in the background.

'Do you have a man with you?' Fournier asked.

'No,' Savill said. 'My chaise was hired in Bath and the groom will return there.'

'No matter. We will find someone to look after you.'

'Were you injured in the accident? I cannot help noticing . . .'

His voice tailed away, but his fingers fluttered, indicating the streaks of mud and cow-pat on the left side of Savill's greatcoat and breeches.

'It is nothing, sir. No more than mud and a few bruises.'

The footman brought in Savill's portmanteau and set it down near the stairs.

Fournier glanced at it. 'I see you are an old campaigner, and do not encumber yourself with baggage. Joseph will show you to your room.'

'Yes, yes,' the Count said. 'So we shall meet again at dinner.'

He and Fournier retreated without further ceremony, and Gohlis trailed after them with the air of a dog uncertain of his welcome. Joseph the footman conducted Savill to a bedchamber on the first floor. According to the clock on the landing, it was nearly half-past five.

'His Lordship and Mr Fournier dine at six, sir,' Joseph said, as he laid the portmanteau on the bed. 'I'll fetch a jug of hot water for you after I've unpacked.'

Savill unlocked the portmanteau. The émigrés dined at a fashionably late hour which, in view of his late arrival, was fortunate. Joseph laid out a pair of darned stockings, a clean shirt and a black-silk stock. Apart from a pair of light shoes and the clothes he stood up in, Savill had nothing else to wear.

Joseph brushed and aired Savill's breeches and then helped him to wash and dress. By the time they had finished, it still wanted ten minutes to dinner. Savill told the man to bring him the leather portfolio from his bag.

The footman obeyed and then left the room with the cloak and greatcoat over his arm and the muddy boots in his hand.

Savill sat by the fire and opened the portfolio. Here were the papers that Mr Rampton had provided him with.

Only now, as he glanced through them again, did it strike him as strange that no one at Charnwood had yet mentioned Charles. The boy was Savill's reason for coming here. The two Frenchmen and the German doctor must have known that as well as he did. But none of them had said a word about Charles. Nor had the servants.

Nor, for that matter, had he. It was as if the boy did not exist.

During dinner, which was long and elaborate in the French fashion, Savill's toothache returned. The pain caught him unawares on several occasions, and once he could not avoid making a sound of discomfort. He noticed Fournier glancing at him, though there was no break in his conversation.

Afterwards, when the servants had left them, Savill introduced his reason for being here, since no one else was in any hurry to do so.

'Pray, my lord,' he said to the Count, 'when may I expect to see Charles? After dinner, perhaps?'

'He will be in bed by then,' Fournier said. 'We keep country hours at Charnwood. He'll soon be sleeping the sleep of the just. Isn't that what you English say? The sleep of the just?'

'Quite so, sir. But is he in good health?'

The Count reared up in his chair. 'Perfectly. He is my own son, after all, and I would not see him go lacking for anything.'

Savill bowed. 'Naturally.' The Count's remark had not been tactful, since it served to remind Savill that he had been cuckolded. 'But after the loss of his mother and the trials he has gone through . . .'

'There is one thing you should know, sir,' Fournier put in. 'Since the death of his mother, Charles has lost his voice.'

'I'm sorry to hear that. An infection of the throat?'

'No, not exactly. Dr Gohlis will explain. He has been treating him for over a month now.'

The doctor glanced up the table at Monsieur de Quillon, who gave an almost imperceptible nod. 'It is a very unusual case, sir,' he said, speaking in fluent but accented English. 'There is no sign of infection. There is nothing wrong with him physiologically. Everything we know about him indicates that until recently he was fully capable of speech, and indeed showed a lively intelligence. But now he will say nothing at all. Moreover, his behaviour has become furtive. And at night he sometimes loses control of his bladder.'

'What is your diagnosis, Doctor?'

'I have constructed a hypothesis that the symptoms he displays are an extreme manifestation of a form of hysteria. This was obviously caused by the shock he received when his mother was murdered in such terrible circumstances. It follows that—'

'He witnessed what happened that night?' Savill said, his voice rising. 'Is that what you're saying?'

Gohlis nodded. 'We cannot know for certain, sir, but it is a reasonable assumption. We believe he was in the house at the time.'

'It is borne out by the fact that there were bloodstains on his clothes when he came to us,' Fournier put in. 'The old woman who brought him had tried to wash them out, but they were unmistakable.'

'The poor boy.'

'Indeed, sir. The heart weeps for him.'

'Ah!' Savill said.

'What is it, sir?' Fournier asked.

'I beg your pardon, sir. A touch of toothache.'

The Count waved at the doctor. 'Have Gohlis make you up a dose before you go to bed.'

'Of course, my lord,' Gohlis said, and swiftly lowered his eyes. A moment later he begged permission to withdraw, so that he might make up the medicine.

When the three of them were alone, Savill said, 'Forgive me for raising the subject, my lord, but we have business to discuss.'

'Of course we do.' Both the words and the tone were obliging but somehow the Count contrived to suggest that Savill had committed a breach of good manners, for which of course he was forgiven. 'But it's growing late,' he went on, 'and we're all tired. You especially, sir, no doubt after your terrible journey. We shall leave it until the morning when we are fresh.'

He spoke pleasantly enough but he left no room for manoeuvre.

At that moment there was a knock on the door. Joseph entered with a letter on a salver, which he handed to Fournier with a murmur of apology.

The latter broke the seal and skimmed its contents. With a snicker of laughter he tossed the letter on the table.

'Something amusing?' the Count asked. 'Can it be shared? Or is it a private pleasure?'

'The letter is from the Vicar – Mr Horton.'

'He will not call on us,' the Count said to Savill. 'I fear he disapproves of us.'

Fournier smiled. 'But this is different. It is by way of a professional matter.'

During the evening, the wind freshened, bringing draughts throughout the old house with its warped doors and creaking floorboards, and sending flurries of rain to beat against the windows.

They met again for supper. Afterwards the Count retired early to write letters. Savill sat with Fournier and Gohlis in a small parlour with a smoking fire.

The doctor had given Savill a dose of medicine – four drops in a glass of warmed water flavoured with brandy. Within half an hour, he felt better than he had for weeks. The toothache subsided and a sense of well-being spread throughout his mind and body. The medicine's benevolent glow allowed him to ignore the faint – and surely unjustified – fear that he might have been unwise to trust himself to the ministrations of the Count's personal physician.

'The man who understands pharmacology,' Gohlis said when Savill thanked him, 'understands human happiness.'

'Then it's regrettable that pharmacology does not provide a drug to cure the dumb,' Fournier said.

'Not yet, sir,' the doctor said eagerly. 'But we make great strides every day. We have come a long way since poor Dr Ammam, who ministered to the dumb in the last century. He believed that to be mute was to be spiritually null, since man needs to be able to speak, for otherwise he does not resemble God the creator and God the son.'

'It's curious that the Ancients touch so rarely on the subject,' Fournier said. 'The affliction of being dumb, that is. The blind often have a heroic stature ascribed to them – consider Oedipus, for example. Or they have a peculiar wisdom, as Tiresias does. Even Samson, one might argue, does not attain his full moral stature until he has been blinded.'

'Perhaps the Ancients sensed a truth that Science is now confirming,' Gohlis said. 'Mutes are often brutish creatures, less than human. Buffon mentions a case in his *Histoire Naturelle* of a young man born mute who learned to speak suddenly when he was twenty-four years of age. Despite having been trained in the outward observances of religion, he was found to have no conception of the soul or of salvation.'

Fournier smiled. 'Is having no conception of the soul necessarily a sign of being less than human? One might even say it is a sign of a superior type of humanity. A type that transcends a need for a personal god.'

'Indeed, sir.' Gohlis was growing heated. 'But in this case, it seems, the young man's external piety concealed the mental faculties of a mere animal. And this is but one case among many. Herder records the story of a dumb boy who watched a butcher killing a pig and then promptly killed his brother, in the same way, for the simple pleasure of imitation. He felt no remorse whatsoever.'

'But surely Charles has not always been dumb?' Savill said. 'Only for a few weeks.'

'True, sir. But how long will the condition last, that is the question, and what will be its effects? Speech, it seems, is the wellspring of civilization, of our moral and intellectual life. Why, when I was last in Königsberg, I heard Professor Kant remark that the dumb can never attain the faculty of Reason itself, but at best a mere analogy of it.'

'Then what treatment do you recommend, sir?' Savill asked.

'The continuation of what we have been following: a strict regimen, together with the occasional short, sharp shock to the system.'

'Why?'

'The shock, sir?' Gohlis said. 'Because it was the shock of his mother's death that rendered him mute. Consider the mind and body as a complex mechanism – a sort of clock, if you will. Just as a clock may stop if it receives a jar or knock, so it may start again if it suffers another.'

'But now,' Fournier said, almost purring with pleasure, 'just by way of contrast, we shall see how the Vicar proposes to treat it.'

'The Vicar, sir,' Savill said, more loudly than he had intended. 'What has he to do with this?'

Fournier smiled. 'You recall the letter I received while we were at table? Mr Horton is a clergyman who tends towards the Evangelical persuasion. He has a charming faith in the simple power of prayer to make the dumb burst into speech. In short, my dear sir, he desires to cure Charles with a miracle.'

# Chapter Fifteen

From the safety of the darkened second-floor landing, Charles watches the gentlemen leaving the dining room. Their shadows leap across the floor. One of the gentlemen is the stranger.

Charles knows that the visitor is English; his name is Savill and he is come on business. The servants don't like him being here because it means more work for them.

It is completely dark now. Charles crosses the landing and goes down the back stairs, which come out between the kitchen and the servants' hall. He knows these stairs well. He has counted them many times, so the number of stairs is a fact that can never be doubted. He does not need to take a candle but feels his way with his hands.

The corridor at the bottom is dimly lit. The door of the servants' hall is open. Standing at the foot of the stairs, Charles listens.

Joseph is talking to one of the maids. Charles understands most words he hears in English now.

'That man,' the footman is saying, 'grim-faced devil, ain't he, with that scar? Like walking death.'

'Oh, Joseph,' says Mary Ann. 'Get on with you.'

'Know what I think? He's come for the Frog bastard.'

Sometimes they stare warily at Charles as if fearing that he

96

might bite them if they let their guard down. He doesn't belong with them, he doesn't belong with the gentry, he doesn't belong with the animals. He doesn't belong with anyone. He belongs in a category all of his own.

'What's he want him for?' Mary Ann says in her slow, thick voice like the cream in the dairy. 'The boy's an idiot.'

'Damned if I know,' Joseph says. 'But that's gentry for you. And foreigners makes it worse.'

When Charles sleeps at last, the nightmares come, as he knew they would. He sees the blood dripping like gentle red rain.

*Say nothing.*

The whisper sounds in his head like the wind under the door.

And then he hears it again. *Tip-tap.* Like cracking a walnut. *Not a word.*

Nightmares have this to be said for them: they wake you up.

He's screaming but nobody comes. But at least he is awake. The nightmare is reluctant to leave him. Gradually its hold on him loosens. He cries for a while, almost for the sake of something to do, something to fill the silent darkness.

At last the pressure on his bladder forces him to leave the warmth of the bed and pull out the chamber pot from under the bed where, when he was a baby, he had believed that nightmares lived.

So this nightmare has a silver lining of sorts. The bed stays dry.

This is the best time. Shortly after dawn, before anyone else is up except the servants.

The air is very clear, the colours of the distant hills are crisp and clean. The shadows are long and cold.

His footprints make ragged marks in the scythed grass, darker patches on the shining patina of moisture. In the pleasure grounds, he has to be wary, but it is easy to slip about unnoticed now he knows his way. He stays within the paling that encircles them – it would not do to risk the unknown terrors of the village and the fields around. He has never lived much in the country and he is afraid of cows, pigs, donkeys, dogs and much else he might reasonably expect to find there.

The gardener and his boy are cutting down a dead tree at the other end of the drive. So it is safe to go to the Garden of Neptune. The dew is heavier here because the garden is below the level of the surrounding land. The walls around it retain the cold and damp rather than the warmth.

Charles walks the paths, counting his steps. Counting fills his mind and quietens it. Moreover, in this world where so much has changed, and is changing, it is important to make sure that at least something remains unaltered: and the length and breadth of this garden is as good a place to start as any.

When he has finished his counting, he says to Louis, who has been pacing beside him, 'See, it is just the same as it was before.' And Louis agrees with him, for he was counting too.

They sit on the wall that surrounds the pool at the centre of the garden. Neptune stands above them. If only he had had his trident when the gardener's boy tried to drown him. The sea god could have dropped it on the boy's head and the prongs would have dug into his brain.

Charles imagines how the gardener's boy would look if his face were covered with blood. His mouth would be open and gushing more blood like a fountain. His hair would then be the colour of blood rather than the colour of rust.

The creak of the gate.

Joseph is coming into the garden from the side nearest the house. 'Why the devil are you hiding away here?' the footman says.

Louis has gone.

'You are wanted in the dining room. Look sharp.'

98

Charles follows Joseph, avoiding his footsteps in the dew but counting them as he walks.

'It's that Mr Savill,' Joseph says over his shoulder, talking to himself as much as to Charles. 'They want to show you to him. Give him a laugh, eh? Looks like he needs it. Mr Fournier's been telling him all about you.'

The footman makes a patriotic point of anglicizing the names of all the foreigners. It is always Mr Fournier or Mr Saul, never some mangled form of Monsieur.

'Maybe he'll take you away. After all, you're not much use to man or beast here. Or maybe he'll just tan your hide hard enough to make you speak. That's what I'd do, given half a chance.'

Charles wonders why the visitor should want to see him, why there is even a possibility that he might take Charles away.

A dark tide of panic rises, filling his throat, making it hard to breathe. Here there is at least something that belongs to his old life, that belongs to the old days when everything was all right, when his mother was alive and they lived in the apartment in the Rue de Grenelle.

Monsieur Fournier and the Englishman are still sitting at the dining-room table, though all trace of their breakfast has been cleared away. Mr Savill looks cross. Something has irritated him. Perhaps it is Charles.

Mr Savill is solidly built and has strongly marked features. But what you really notice is the long scar from the corner of his eye to the corner of his mouth.

'Ah, my boy,' says Fournier in French. 'Good morning. Come here.' He dismisses Joseph with a nod and turns to the Englishman. 'And now, sir, allow me to present Charles.' He turns back and smiles, for Fournier smiles a great deal, even at Charles. 'This is Mr Savill.'

Charles takes a step backwards. Mr Savill stares at him. Charles shrivels under the gaze.

'Come, Charles,' Fournier says, in English this time. 'Make your bow.'

Charles bows as his mother taught him, low and sweeping as she said the gentlemen did at Versailles as the King passed by. When he was little and he bowed to her like that, his mother would clap her hands. Once she gave him a grape coated with sugar.

Mr Savill inclines his head in acknowledgement. Charles thinks his manner lacks entirely the distinction of a French gentleman. He is rough and clumsy. He is dressed like a tradesman or a lawyer.

'Oh!' his mother would say when talking of men like this, 'but he is such an oaf!'

'I am part of your English family,' Mr Savill says slowly, also in English. He pauses. 'Do you understand what I say?'

Charles stares at the wall behind Mr Savill's head at a particular stripe in the wallpaper that runs through a small brown stain where the damp comes through the wall.

'Do you understand?' Mr Savill repeats. 'Nod your head if you do.'

Mr Savill waits a moment and then repeats the question in French, which is perfectly comprehensible though his accent is quite barbarous, worse than Dr Gohlis's.

'Nod if you understand me,' Mr Savill says once more.

Charles sees the trap before him: he knows that it is possible to coax answers without words, and that these may do just as much harm as answers with words. He lets his eyes drift up to the cornice of the room. He senses the attention of the two men on him, feels the weight of it, feels the pressure of their impatience.

Time passes. The weight lifts, the pressure relaxes.

'So,' Fournier says in his normal voice. 'There you have it, sir. A neat philosophical conundrum, as the doctor puts it. But undeniably inconvenient for the rest of us.'

'And indeed for Charles himself,' says Mr Savill, his face twisting, as if with pain.

'Let us have fresh coffee,' Fournier says. 'Ring for the

servant, Charles. Then you may leave us, but do not go far away.'

The boy does as he is told. As he is leaving the room, he looks back. They are watching him, Monsieur Fournier and Mr Savill, and he wonders what they see.

'You see?' Fournier says. 'He understands simple instructions and sometimes will execute them.'

Mr Savill nods. For a moment, he stops frowning. He turns his head and looks straight at Charles. The scar crinkles. He is smiling.

# Chapter Sixteen

As Charles closed the door, Savill stood up and walked to the window, as if by doing so he could walk away from the pain. He rubbed the condensation on the glass with the heel of his hand to make a peephole. The world outside sharpened and came into partial focus, streaked and distorted by trails of moisture.

The rain had stopped. The sky was a pale, duck-egg blue. The dining room overlooked a lawn silvered with a coating of dew. Beyond the grass was the darker green of shrubberies and trees that marched up the slope of the valley towards wooded hills. Further still, another line of hills smudged the horizon.

Usually the pain was deep, chronic and continuous. But sometimes there were acute and penetrating additions, like flashes of lightning, of something far worse.

Today, Savill thought, seizing on another subject that might distract him from the pain, I have seen Augusta's son.

He wished Lizzie had been here. He had not known that his daughter wanted a brother. Why had he never thought to ask?

He had brought the miniature of Lizzie. Perhaps he would show Charles what his sister had looked like when she was a child. Not at once, of course. He must wait until they had grown accustomed to one another's company.

What would Charles say if he could speak? Had he been there when his mother was murdered? Had he seen her killed?

The lightning returned.

'Ah!' Savill said.

'You must see Gohlis immediately,' Fournier said behind him.

'Later.'

'No, no. Now. One cannot trifle with pain, sir.'

'Indeed.' Savill drew a deep breath. The lightning had receded for the moment. 'Tell me, can Charles read and write?'

Fournier raised his face. In the clear light of morning, the eyes beneath the crooked eyebrows were a shade of brown that merged imperceptibly with green, like pond water. 'Oh yes.'

'So one may converse with him on paper?'

'I'm afraid not. He used to be an apt scholar, but if you ask him to write anything now – anything at all – he will give the appearance of applying himself to the task with great industry. But the result of his labours is merely scratchings and scribblings. From a distance they mimic the look of handwriting. But when you try to read them all you see is a tangle of impenetrable marks.' Fournier paused and his murky eyes seemed larger than ever. 'The servants think he is either an idiot or possessed by the devil. If not both.'

'And what do you think, sir?'

'I am aware merely of my own ignorance.' Fournier smiled, inviting complicity in a shared superior understanding. 'Poor Charles almost certainly witnessed the murder of his mother. How can one predict or even understand the effect of such a shock on the delicate sensibilities of a child? He was always inclined to be highly strung and full of fancies.'

'When will the Count be downstairs, sir? There are papers that—'

'My dear sir, permit me to be frank: you are not well.'

Savill rubbed his forehead, and found it hot and damp to

103

the touch. The pain was even there now, dull and throbbing. It had spread all over the head and even to the neck.

'I must take Charles to London.'

'Yes, of course,' Fournier said. 'Now pray sit down a moment. Your pacing is making me feel quite dizzy. You cannot take Charles to London now, not for a day or two.'

'I can, sir.' Savill sank into a chair. 'I have full authority—'

Fournier flapped his napkin in mild reproof. 'I know, sir, I know. I do not dispute that. All I am saying is that it is not practicable for you to travel. Your chaise is a wreck, I understand, and I hear this morning that the groom who brought you has taken your horse back to Bath. There is neither horse nor chaise for hire in Norbury. And I regret to say that our establishment at Charnwood is so limited that we cannot even send you to Bath in our own coach because we simply do not have one.'

'There must be a way.'

'Unless you wish to walk, sir, I'm afraid that you must send to Bath for a chaise to fetch you. And that will take at least two days. In which case, you might as well put the delay to good use by allowing Gohlis to deal with your tooth.'

'A horse,' Savill said. 'Ah!'

Another blinding flash of pain destroyed everything but itself. As it receded, he became aware that Fournier was speaking.

'. . . So, in the circumstances, perhaps it's a blessing in disguise.'

'I beg your pardon, sir. What is a blessing?'

Fournier smiled. 'I was saying that, since today is Friday, and since the postboy has already called, it is unlikely that a letter could reach Bath until tomorrow evening. And I doubt a livery stable would wish to act on your instructions until Monday.'

'I could not impose on you so long,' Savill said, but feebly.

'Nonsense, my dear sir.' Fournier stood up and rang the

bell. 'Now – we shall find Gohlis, and he will deal with your tooth. And tomorrow morning our good Vicar will try his hand at a miracle with Charles. Who knows? One must always keep an open mind. Faith may succeed where science has failed.'

'If I had a free hand, sir,' Dr Gohlis said, opening the side door of the house, 'I have no doubt that the boy would be speaking within days. More than that, I would most certainly have succeeded in eradicating his other undesirable habits.'

Savill winced as the rush of fresh cool air sent a needle of pain into his jaw. 'Surely, sir, you have been in a position to treat him for nearly two months?'

'That is precisely what I have not been able to do.' The doctor glanced at him. He wore steel-rimmed glasses that magnified his eyes into gleaming blue pools. 'Once or twice I have been able to test the theory on him for an hour or two but that is all. But, in a case of this nature, it is imperative that a physician should have unfettered access to his patient and complete responsibility for his care. The Count refuses to surrender Charles to my control.'

For a moment they walked in silence down the flagged path beside the house.

'I am afraid that he places too great a reliance on the theories of Rousseau,' Gohlis continued. 'Nature is a wonderful guide in the management of children, but it must not be our only one.'

'What course of treatment would you recommend?'

The doctor's lips moved silently as he considered the question. 'If I were all-powerful, I should wish to know a great deal about the boy and his upbringing. Have you read Dr Gregory's *Comparative View of the State and Faculties of Man with Those of the Animal World*? It is most instructive. I wonder, for example, whether Charles was fed at his mother's breast or whether his parents hired a wet nurse.'

'I cannot understand why that should be of any importance,' Savill said.

'That is because you are a layman, sir. A mother's milk does more than nourish the body of an infant. It also imparts sentiments of virtue, even morality. If a woman feeds another's child purely for mercenary reasons, then what nourishes the body does not nourish the soul as well, or not in the same way.'

'His mother's milk won't cure him now.' Savill spoke roughly, the toothache affecting his manners. 'The boy has been mute for nearly two months.'

'I agree, sir, it is very curious.' The doctor was unruffled by Savill's tone. 'It's a most unusual case, quite fascinating. And I believe our best chance of curing the patient is to rely not on the nostrums of the past, but on the philosophy of the future. Tell me, are you aware of the work of Karl Philipp Moritz? He edits a journal on what we physicians call *Erfahrungsseelenkunde*.'

'And what does that mean?'

'I suppose one might translate the term as the empirical science of the soul. It is an inductive science above all. Facts should be the building blocks for theory, not the other way round. Moritz encourages his readers to write down their childhood memories, and to use them for self-analysis.'

'Ow!' said Savill. 'I – I beg your pardon, Doctor.'

'Not at all. My own view, sir, is this: the human mind is a complicated matter but there are always causes for any effects we perceive. Reason tells us that and natural philosophy confirms it at every turn. Somewhere there is a key to Charles's silence. If we can find that key we may turn the lock and he will speak again.'

'I wonder—' Savill broke off as another exquisitely refined pain streaked along the side of his jaw.

Dr Gohlis looked at him with mild interest. 'My dear sir. We shall soon make you more comfortable.'

They passed through a gate in a wall and left the pleasure

106

grounds behind. The doctor walked briskly towards the stableyard, which was entered by an archway, and led the way to a door between the coach house and the loose boxes. The two men climbed a narrow flight of stairs to another door, which Gohlis unlocked.

'My laboratory,' he said, glancing back at Savill. 'A poor place compared with what I had in Paris.'

The room was long and thin, with the door at one end and a solitary window at the other. Once it had been a loft. Now, boarded and freshly whitewashed, it resembled the inside of a tent. The air was very cold. The doctor's possessions were drawn up in two lines against the longer walls, which left a narrow corridor to the window.

'First I must examine you,' the doctor announced. 'Be so good as to sit.'

The only chair in the room was by the table underneath the window. Savill walked towards it but stopped halfway and gave a muffled exclamation.

'What the devil?'

Gohlis laughed. 'It is only my *écorché* figure.'

'I thought for a moment—'

'That it was Charles? How amusing. This is smaller, of course.'

Savill sat. 'I have heard of these figures,' he said. 'I have never seen one.'

'They are invaluable to students of anatomy and musculature. When I was a student I would not have been without it for the world.'

'It was once a real child?'

The doctor had opened a chest and was rummaging through its contents. 'Well, to be precise, sir, it was taken from a mould made with a child's corpse. Did you see a dentist in London?'

'Yes, in the summer. He assured me that there was no need for the tooth to come out, and that the pain would deal with itself in a day or two.'

107

'Clearly the diagnosis has not answered.' Gohlis approached. 'It does not surprise me. Most of the so-called dentists I have come across are mere quacks or charlatans. Pray allow me to examine your mouth.'

With a sense of surrendering to the inevitable, Savill leaned back in his chair and tilted his head.

'Towards the light if you please, sir.'

The doctor's head was now within a foot of Savill's own. His eyes were magnified by his spectacles, giving him the appearance of a large, pale insect crouching over his prey. He tilted Savill's head slightly and poked inside with a thin steel instrument.

'Yes,' he said, 'I see. Oh dear.'

Savill closed his own eyes, unable to look at Gohlis any longer.

'I see the problem. A molar at the back is decayed, and the gum around it is badly inflamed. I suspect the root is infected. I believe I see a trace of lead. Did some clumsy fool once try to fill it?'

Savill cried out as the tip of the steel touched the area of gum next to the afflicted tooth.

Gohlis had already supplied his own answer: 'They clearly botched the job to a quite remarkable degree.' He took out a handkerchief and polished his glasses on it.

Savill swallowed and cleared his throat. 'What's to be done, sir?'

'The tooth can give you nothing but discomfort. It must be extracted. Otherwise the discomfort will continue and quite possibly grow worse. I will remove it myself. It is a simple mechanical operation, and I have the necessary tool.'

There was something deeply unpleasant about the idea of allowing Gohlis to rip a tooth from his mouth. Besides, it would weaken him just when he needed all his wits about him for the negotiations with the Count, and all his strength for the rigours of the journey up to London. And would it not be better to have his London dentist, a man who knew him, do the job?

Somewhere deep inside himself, Savill knew the truth of his own hesitation: he was afraid.

'I must consider it carefully,' he said. 'I am deeply sensible of your kindness.'

'It must come out!' the doctor exclaimed. 'I will give you another dose of my mixture, a larger one than last night, and we shall do it now.'

As if to underline the wisdom of this, Savill suffered another flash of pure agony, which made him cry out and left him breathless. Gohlis took no notice whatsoever. He filled a wine glass with water from a carafe that stood on the table and measured into it ten drops of dark brown liquid from a flask. He stirred the mixture vigorously with the steel probe and handed the glass to Savill.

'Drink,' he said. And Savill drank.

Afterwards, he sat back in the chair, longing for the mixture to take effect.

'Allow me to show you a model of the mouth,' Gohlis said. 'It will deepen your understanding of your condition.'

The doctor took up a plaster of Paris model from a shelf. It was a cast of a set of teeth, together with their gums. He opened and closed the jaw. The plaster teeth clicked together.

'Look!' he cried, as gleeful as a child. 'They move! They bite!'

Gohlis lectured him on the construction of the jaw, the architecture of the mouth and the behaviour of roots, both healthy and diseased, with particular reference to his own decayed molar.

Savill's mind drifted away, lulled by the German's monotonous voice. He stared at the *écorché* figure. He had often seen masks of the dead – but those were very different, being replicas of what had been in life, dignified in appearance and respectful in purpose. Here there was neither dignity nor respect. Everything that had made the child himself had been stripped away, even his name.

'He fascinates people,' the doctor said in a voice that had suddenly grown harsher. 'I used it in an experiment with Charles when we were staying in Paris, but it did not answer.'

'What was the experiment?'

'The effect of a shock. I showed him the figure without any notice at all as he woke from sleep. This, I told him, was what happened to boys who are no use to society or themselves. This was what he might one day become.'

'But the tactic failed to work?'

Gohlis shrugged. 'The boy seemed fascinated with the figure. Obsessed, even. I have made a note of it in case I can use it. Charles is so purged of both sentiment and intellect that any exception to the rule must be interesting to his physician. I am convinced that one day he will furnish me with materials for a paper. There is such a very simple question at the heart of it, simple yet profound: why does he not speak?'

The pain and perhaps the medicine were making Savill light-headed. He forgot for a moment where he was and who he was speaking to. He said, 'I suppose you have considered the simplest answer, sir: that Charles is afraid of what he might say if he did?'

# Chapter Seventeen

In his garden, Neptune is still staring down at the water. Perhaps he is looking for his trident.

Charles and Louis walk over to the steps that cut through the wall at the far end of the enclosure. There are six of them. They count them again to make quite sure.

At the top of the steps is a gate of wrought iron. Beyond it, the path winds up a grassy slope towards a stile leading to a wood. This marks the point where the pleasure grounds of Charnwood give way to a scattering of paddocks, meadows and copses.

The two boys are together, side by side. Their shoulders touch. They look at the woods and the fields and the hills beyond.

'One day,' Charles says.

'One day,' Louis says.

They walk back to the garden and measure the paths, pacing up and down. The numbers are the same as they were before. Facts are facts. Nothing has changed, though it is a different time of day and fewer birds are singing.

The Englishman, Mr Savill, walks into the garden.

Louis slips away to his flayed shell in Dr Gohlis's laboratory.

Mr Savill sits on the low wall that surrounds Neptune's pond.

'Come here,' he says in English.

For a moment, neither of them moves. They might be made of stone like Neptune himself. Mr Savill wears a scarf around his neck that covers the lower part of his face and makes his voice sound muffled.

'Come here,' he says again, this time in French.

Charles comes forward. He stops ten yards away, out of reach of the Englishman's arm or his stick.

'I tried to find you earlier,' Mr Savill says. 'You like to hide away, don't you?'

His shoes are worn, Charles sees, the leather muddy and scuffed. Mr Savill cannot be a rich man.

'I dare say you feel safer that way. What were you doing just then? Your lips were moving.' There is a pause while Charles's eyes rise slowly to Mr Savill's face. 'Were you talking to someone?'

*Say nothing. Not a word to anyone.*

Louis is different.

Charles looks over the Englishman's head at Neptune without his trident. Neptune could dash out Mr Savill's brains with one blow of his stone fist; he wouldn't need to use his trident because he is a god and gods have magical powers. But he, Charles, will permit Mr Savill to live. For the time being.

'You look like your mother,' Mr Savill says. 'Not always – sometimes. You must feel her loss.'

Charles feels the loss of everything – his mother, their old life in Paris, all the certainties of existence that no one ever questioned until suddenly they were not certain any more.

'I'm sure they wish you nothing but good,' Mr Savill says.

Surprised, Charles stares at him.

'The Count, I mean, Monsieur Fournier and the doctor.'

Charles examines the man's face, as far as he can see it with the scarf covering so much. The skin of the scar tissue is paler and shinier than the rest of his face. His eyes seem very blue because the pupils have shrunk to small black dots.

'There is much I don't know,' Mr Savill says. 'But I believe you hear me and you understand what is said.'

The Englishman has not shaved for a day or two, Charles notes, which adds to his uncouth air. The material of his coat is coarse and stiff. Charles's mother would have said that he lacked address, lacked distinction.

'What do you do all day? This want of occupation cannot be good for you.' A spasm passes like a wave across Mr Savill's face. 'Damnation,' he says in an altered voice, 'and the devil take this toothache. The doctor has given me a draught but it has done nothing for me yet.'

It is very strange. Mr Savill speaks almost as if Charles were someone he knew well or as if he were talking to himself.

'I've come to take you to London, to your mother's family. You'll be safe. No one will harm you. I promise.'

Charles's mother said that. *No one will harm you.* She was wrong. No one can be trusted except Louis.

*Tip-tap.* Like cracking a walnut.

Mr Savill fumbles in his waistcoat pocket and takes out two ivory dice. He shakes them in the palm of his hand and throws them on the parapet beside him.

A two and five.

That makes seven, Charles thinks. Mr Savill repeats the process. This time he throws a four and three: another seven.

He throws again, and the dice make a six and a one.

A third seven. Does it mean something, the coincidence of the three sevens? Or is it just a matter of chance, unpredictable, and therefore terrifying?

Three sevens are twenty-one. That is a fact.

Mr Savill points to the dice. 'Your turn. See if you can throw a double.'

Charles takes them up. They are warm in his hand. He shakes them. He casts them on the parapet. Double six.

That is a fact.

'Bravo,' says Mr Savill. '*Bravissimo.*' He stands. 'They are yours now,' he says. 'If you want them. The dice, that is.'

# Chapter Eighteen

The medicine had at last begun to do its work. Savill's mind was clearer than usual, capable of remarkable clarity of vision and enormous leaps of understanding.

Dr Gohlis's mixture did not deaden the pain, however, let alone remove it. Rather, the draught served as a distraction, steering Savill's attention towards other things while leaving the pain to pursue its vicious career unchecked – but in remote parts of his mind where it was much less noticeable than before.

Nothing, he reminded himself, can be taken for granted. It was clear that the boy did not want to come with him. That was understandable enough. Savill was a stranger who proposed to take him away from what little remained of his mother and his old life, and to place him among strangers who spoke an unfamiliar language.

He contemplated the difficulty from all angles. It no longer seemed to matter very much. He also considered the dice, which he had given to Charles on a whim. Now the action seemed a philosophical curiosity of enormous interest.

Savill's mind considered another question with the same Olympian detachment. Had he perhaps been foolish to agree to the doctor's offer of treatment? The people of Charnwood had no reason to wish him well, and the Count had a positive motive to wish him harm. The question was fascinating rather than disturbing, however, and soon gave way to an intense consideration of the remarkable greenness of the grass of the parkland.

Time passed, or rather floated agreeably away in the manner of the clouds that were now scudding across the sky as the afternoon moved towards evening.

Savill walked back to the house. He went up to his chamber and wrote two letters. The words flowed fluently, the pen skimmed across the paper and the wet ink gleamed, making delightfully elegant patterns.

His first letter was to the livery stables in Bath, requesting that another private chaise should be sent to Charnwood no later than Monday.

The second letter was addressed to Mr Rampton, or rather to Frederick Brown, Esquire, at the White Horse Cellar in Piccadilly, to await collection. The precaution of addressing letters care of a coaching inn, which had seemed so absurd in London, now proved its value. It would not be wise for Fournier or the Count to learn of Mr Rampton's connection with the matter. Savill did not trust them and he had no faith that they would respect the sanctity of the mails.

*Dear Sir,*

*I regret that I am delayed in the country and cannot have the pleasure of dining with you on Monday after all. But I hope to be in London later in the week and do myself the honour of calling on you as soon as possible.*

*The matter of my late wife's son is proving more difficult to resolve than I had apprehended. Charles has entirely lost the faculty of speech. He refuses even to communicate by writing. The Count's physician believes the cause may be that he was a witness to his mother's death, which occurred in peculiarly distressing circumstances.*

116

*I am uncertain how best to proceed, both now and when Charles returns with me to London.*

*I am, Sir, etc.*

*E. Savill*

He sealed both letters. He floated down to the hall and dropped them into the postbag. Joseph was passing.

'Doctor was asking for you, sir,' the footman said with gloomy satisfaction. 'He said to tell cook you won't be down for dinner.'

Gohlis did not waste time in social exchanges. Savill's chamber would be the best place for the extraction, he said, because it faced west and the light was better than in his own laboratory. Besides, Savill might find it convenient to have his bed so close to him.

The doctor ordered the fire to be lit in the chamber and a sturdy chair, high and equipped with arms, to be brought up, as well as a bottle of brandy. He set his case of instruments on the dressing table.

'Remove your coat and cravat, sir. Sit down. Loosen your shirt. Put your head back and open the mouth.'

Gohlis tilted Savill's head towards the light from the window and examined the mouth's interior with the aid of his forefinger and his steel rod. He took an instrument with an ivory handle from the case.

'Is that a corkscrew?' Savill said, his mind turning to the brandy.

'No, sir. It is a tooth key, for the removal of teeth.' He prised open Savill's mouth. 'One inserts it horizontally. So. At the end is a piece of metal padded with chamois leather for the patient's comfort; it rests against the gum of the diseased tooth and provides a—'

'Ah—' Savill twisted in the chair and jerked his head away.

'A little tender?' said Gohlis, showing himself a master of

117

understatement. 'I am not surprised. The gum is remarkably swollen. Indeed, I do not recollect having seen a—'

'For God's sake, sir. Let us leave the tooth where it is.'

'That is not possible. Perhaps we need assistance. It will not take a moment, sir, once we proceed.'

The doctor gave Savill a bumper of brandy and told Joseph, who was hovering by the door, to fetch the gardener. In the end, even with Savill's arms strapped to the chair, it took the two servants to hold down the patient while Gohlis went about his work. Joseph tried with partial success to keep the body from moving, while the gardener, breathing heavily and scenting the air with onions, cradled Savill's head under his arm and came near to throttling him.

'At the end of the key,' Gohlis said, thrusting the instrument into Savill's mouth again, 'is a hook that clamps over the crown of the tooth. This is held in place by a spring clip. Then all one has to do is twist it, as if turning a key. Simplicity itself. So.'

Savill's body bucked and twisted. The gardener tightened his grip. The chair shifted an inch on the floorboards. Gohlis wrenched the tooth again and this time it shattered.

There followed a nightmarish time of blood and pain. When the key could do no more, Dr Gohlis extracted fragments of tooth with a pair of curving pincers. The medicine seemed to intensify the nightmare rather than mask it. Savill heard repeated groaning, which he eventually realized came from his own wrecked mouth.

'Ah. Observe the root! It is cracked! If you permit my joke, sir, I fancy that this is the root of the problem.'

Savill lost not only his tooth but also the rest of the day; he remembered only fragments of it, confused in their sequence and entangled so closely with his dreams that the one could not be distinguished from the other.

At one point, during a lull in the proceedings, he opened his eyes for a moment. The chamber door was ajar. It seemed to him that Charles was staring at him through the crack between door and jamb. He tried to alert the doctor to this but Gohlis did not understand his mumbles and, when he looked again, the boy had vanished. Perhaps he had not been there in the first place.

Afterwards they put Savill into his bed and Dr Gohlis spooned more of his mixture into the wounded mouth and made him wash it down with a few more mouthfuls of brandy. The spirit stung so much he cried aloud again. Afterwards it spread a fiery anaesthetic glow through the affected parts.

Later – it must have been later, for candles were burning on the dressing table – he woke from a doze to hear voices.

'I have not extracted a tooth since I was at the university,' Gohlis was saying. 'And this one was not easy. But, though I say it myself, no one could have done it more neatly.'

'No doubt, Doctor.' This was Fournier's voice. 'Now you must be exhausted. There are sandwiches and wine in the dining room. I will sit with Mr Savill in case he needs anything.'

Savill dozed again. Later – minutes? hours? – his eyes opened. The room was swaying, with light slopping to and fro like water in a bucket. Or perhaps it was merely that someone was carrying a candle about. He heard a rustle of dead leaves. But there were no trees in his chamber. Only papers.

He opened his mouth to ask who was there and what they were doing with his papers. But it was too much effort to speak. His mouth closed, and then his eyes. He slept.

# Chapter Nineteen

Later, when the candles are lit and the other men are lingering in the dining room, Charles returns. He climbs the back stairs, passes along the dimly lit landing and hesitates by the partly open door of Mr Savill's chamber.

A single candle burns on the night table by the bed, whose curtains are still open on that side. Mr Savill lies in the bed. His mouth is open. He is snoring.

So he isn't dead. Despite all the blood. And his face is no longer a gaping, bloody mouth.

No one else is in the room, even a servant. Charles tiptoes inside and slowly approaches the bed. A fire is dwindling in the grate. Mr Savill swallows noisily. He snorts and snuffles like a hog. His breathing resumes its slow, regular, rasping rhythm, and Charles comes closer and closer.

The light of the candle turns the man's face into a place of sharp rocks and pitch-black hollows. The interior of his mouth is as dark as the bottom of the well in the stableyard. He does not look human at all.

Charles pushes his hand in his pocket and touches the two dice. Two sixes make twelve. That is a fact.

*    *    *

In the first few days at Charnwood, nobody told him to go to bed and he lingered within sight of a candle or a lamp for as long as possible. But the housekeeper, Mrs Cox, finding him kicking his heels on the landing at nearly midnight, informed him that if he wasn't in bed by eight o'clock each night like a good Christian boy, and with his candle extinguished, he must face the consequences.

Charles does not know what these consequences might be, but he is sure that he does not want to face them. So, every night, he is in his room by eight o'clock and usually in bed.

His bedroom is at the back of the house on the second floor. It is a small room with a casement window that doesn't close properly because the catch is broken. He has tried to wedge it with a scrap of newspaper but sometimes the paper falls out and the window blows open.

Outside the window is an ash tree, which Joseph says should be cut down because it is far too close to the house: its roots threaten the foundations and, besides, it makes the servants' hall dark and gloomy.

Charles does not care about this but he does care that, when the wind is in the wrong direction, the branches of the tree tap like fingers on the window. The ash tree is trying to get in. When it does, he knows that something horrible will happen, something perhaps worse than what has gone before.

So the window is where the evening ritual starts. First, Charles makes sure that it is still wedged shut. Unfortunately there are no shutters, but he closes the curtains instead to stop the tree looking in. Next he does the counting, to make sure nothing has changed since the morning. The room is six and a third paces long and four and a half wide, not counting the alcoves on either side of the fireplace, one of which has been boxed in to form a cupboard. These measurements make a fortress of facts that protects him as he sleeps.

The cupboard itself comes next: Charles must check that it is as it was this morning. There are five shelves from floor to ceiling, and also three hooks on the back of the door. His spare shirt is on one shelf, with his hat beside it. He takes off his coat and hangs it on one of the hooks. Next comes the wooden box at the end of the bed. There is nothing to count inside it. It is still as empty as it was when he last looked inside it. Nor is there anything under the bed except the chamber pot with a chip in its rim and a rat-trap that still contains the dusty bones of a small rat.

Only after he has made sure that everything is as it was does he permit himself to undress down to his shirt and scramble into the cold bed.

The bed is in one corner of the room. Its curtains are thin and worn, designed for hot summers long ago. He lies on his side, shivering, curled into a ball.

The tree scratches on the window, so faintly that the sound seems both there and not there. He pushes the heels of his hands against his ears to block the tree that is or isn't there: and instead he hears the roar of a distant ocean.

He makes himself think of a blue, endless sea beside a broiling sun. He has never seen a warm blue sea, only the grey English Channel that made him seasick for what seemed like weeks.

One day, he and Louis will voyage to the Indies and find a remote island. On an island, silence will not matter because they will speak to each other as they always do, without words. They will be there for ever and ever.

By degrees, Charles glides into sleep, his mind wandering this way and that, seemingly under the direction of someone other than himself. His sleep is light and fitful at first; then, as he warms up, he plunges down and down into the darkness.

Charles does not know how long this continues. Suddenly, though, he is no longer asleep. He wakes abruptly, without passing through the usual transition that is neither one thing nor the other.

The bed-curtains are so thin that the material does not keep out light. The room should be completely dark, filled with a soft blackness without boundaries. But it is not. There is murky yellow radiance beyond the curtains.

He does not move. His own breathing is deafening so he holds his breath. It is then that he hears, or thinks he hears, that someone else is breathing: so faintly and slowly that it lies on the very edge of sound.

Minutes pass, perhaps hours. He cannot pace out the length and breadth of time. In a few places, the radiance shifts. It grows less dense, its power no longer absolute. Charles listens and listens, imagining his ears are on slender, supple stalks that probe like green suckers into the loamy darkness.

The house is not quiet, nor is the night. He hears, far away, a sort of creaking sigh deep in the bowels of the building, like a dog settling to sleep.

The tree scratches on the window, still trying to get in. He wishes it would give up and go away.

Then, much nearer, in the room with him: a footstep. Another. A third. A breath of air touches Charles's cheek as the curtains sway.

Then: a click. The metallic click of the latch. The sigh of a hinge. A floorboard groans. Another click. Another current of air touches his cheek, this one a cold caress.

Then it is gone, whatever it was. Charles is left with the creaking house, the scratching tree and the thudding of his own blood. There is a sour tang of sweat and brandy in the air.

This has happened before, more than once.

Charles trembles. His teeth chatter. He is so very cold.

Worse than cold.

He discovers that he has wet the bed again.

# Chapter Twenty

When Savill woke, slowly and painfully, he forced himself out of bed to use the chamber pot. Movement made him dizzy and slightly nauseous; but that was scarcely to be wondered at.

He rang the bell and slumped into the chair by the dead fire. He pulled a blanket over his knees. The chair still had the straps attached to the arms. There was a spot of dried blood on the floor. He probed the crater in his mouth with the tip of his tongue. The hole was the size of a small country.

There was a knock and Joseph entered the room with a jug of hot water.

'Tea,' Savill croaked.

Joseph hesitated. 'Doctor said you should stay in bed.'

'Tea.'

'He wants to bleed you before—'

'Tea, damn you,' Savill said. 'But stay – has the postboy collected the letters?'

'Yes, sir.'

He scowled at Joseph, who took this as a signal to leave the room.

The time had come, Savill thought while he waited, to put an end to this catalogue of disasters, irritations and difficulties that had afflicted him since leaving Bath. He would insist on an interview with the Count this very day and retrieve the necessary papers from him. If the livery stable failed to send another chaise by Monday, he would use to the full the powers that Mr Rampton had given him. He would require the Vicar, as the nearest Justice of the Peace to assist him, and he would commandeer whatever horses and conveyance the village had to offer. If necessary, he would settle even for Mr Roach's cart.

Savill took up his waistcoat, neatly folded with the rest of his clothes, and found the key to the portmanteau. He fetched the case, stumbling across the room like a drunkard to the cupboard where he had told Joseph to put it.

As he turned the key in the lock, something niggled in the back of his mind, demanding attention. He opened the bag and took out the folder. It was then he remembered that he was in the habit of leaving the key in the right-hand pocket of his waistcoat; but he had found it in the pocket on the left.

The niggle pushed its way to the front of his mind: from the depths of his clouded memories of yesterday evening came the light that had slopped to and fro like water in a bucket and the rustle of leaves.

But there was no tree in his chamber and the only water was in the carafe on the dressing table.

Someone in this house had been looking through his private papers.

His mind groped towards the implications, one by one. If Fournier and the Count knew about the warrant, they knew that Savill had the legal power to force them to give up Charles.

More than that, they must know that he was suspiciously well prepared. The question was, would they also realize the significance of a warrant signed by one of Westminster's stipendiary police magistrates?

'In case of emergency,' Rampton had said, 'he appoints you under the Police Act as his agent or deputy, which gives you temporary powers of inquiry, arrest and detention.'

If they had seen that, they would know that Savill could be no ordinary private citizen. They must infer that behind him was someone infinitely more powerful.

Alarm spread through him. What a fool he had been to trust his hosts. Had the Count ordered Gohlis to drug him? Had the tooth even needed extraction?

Joseph returned with the tea. By this time, Savill was back in the chair, with the portmanteau on the floor beside him and the portfolio of papers on his lap.

'Is His Lordship downstairs yet?' he demanded. 'And Monsieur Fournier?'

'His Lordship doesn't come down before twelve, sir.' Joseph sounded scandalized by the possibility that Savill might have thought otherwise. 'And Mr Fournier's walking over to Norbury Park. He said he might dine there.'

'Send Master Charles to me then.'

'He's not here either, sir. Vicar's praying over him this morning.'

'Oh, for God's sake, you blockhead,' Savill said. 'Give me the tea.'

# Chapter Twenty-One

'What are you doing in there?' Mrs Cox cries, her voice shrill with anger and perhaps fear. There is a terrible knocking. 'Open the door at once.'

Charles wakes in a damp bed. The door is banging against a box that stands in its way.

The housekeeper continues to rattle the door handle as he pads across the floor and pulls aside the box. He dragged it from the end of the bed to the door last night. It was Louis's idea, not his, to keep him safe from whoever might come in the night.

Whoever or whatever might come back.

Mrs Cox pushes open the door and slaps him.

'Don't do that again, you wicked boy. Do you hear?'

She gives him a clean shirt and stockings, and a freshly pressed stock. 'Put these on,' she tells him. 'But not until you've had your breakfast. And I need to sponge your coat and breeches.' She catches sight of his shoes. 'You can't go out in those.'

He realizes that she is not, for once, angry with him. If she's angry with anyone, it is with her masters, the Count and Monsieur Fournier, for failing to tell her that Charles would be appearing in public today. It is one thing for him to look no better than a beggar's boy in the privacy of Charnwood but quite another for him to venture into the village like that. It would reflect badly, in some obscure but powerful way, on Mrs Cox herself.

She gives him an old coat and a pair of slippers to wear while he has his breakfast. The coat hangs from his shoulders like a cloak, and the cuffs reach his knuckles. While he eats bread and milk in the housekeeper's room, Martha, one of the maids, does what she can to improve the appearance of his coat and shoes. After he has eaten, Mrs Cox herself brushes his hair so hard it brings tears to his eyes. She trims it with a pair of scissors and ties it with a black ribbon.

She sends him away to dress himself in the clean clothes. On his return, she makes him stand before her. She examines him front and back. She clicks her teeth as she straightens his stock. Finally she gives him his newly brushed hat.

'You'll do,' she says. 'You look almost fit for decent company.'

There is a note of pride in her voice, the pride of a creator. For a moment she looks at him with a slight smile, as if she does not really hate him after all.

Mrs Cox takes him through to the gentlemen, who are still at breakfast in the dining room. Fournier and Dr Gohlis are there. Fournier stares and the crooked eyebrows rise.

'Well, well. I congratulate you, Mrs Cox.'

'I could have done better with more warning, sir, and really he needs another suit of clothes. He's grown out of these, you can see for yourself, sir, and there's a hole in—'

'You have done admirably,' Fournier interrupts. 'You may leave him here now. We will send him to the Vicarage, by and by.'

'Will his lordship be down today, sir?'

'I believe so. But it seems that Mr Savill is unwell, and he may not be able to leave his room. He is having trouble with his teeth. You may leave us now.'

When the housekeeper has withdrawn, Fournier tells Charles to sit. He gives him a roll to eat and pours him a cup of coffee mixed with cream and sugar.

'This is quite like old times,' Fournier says. 'We must enjoy it while we can.'

Old times: Charles knows that he means the apartment in the Rue de Grenelle. Fournier would often drop in, sometimes alone and sometimes with another gentleman, and he would sit at table with Charles and Maman. They would fuss over Charles, play with him and drop morsels of food in his mouth as if he was a pet bird. And Maman would laugh and look so pretty and happy.

His eyes fill with tears.

'Eat your roll,' Fournier says gently. 'You must leave in a moment.'

The gardener takes him to the Vicarage. He is a burly, middle-aged man called Jevons with skin like the shell of an old walnut engrained with dirt. They go on foot, walking in silence side by side down the drive, with Charles breaking into a trot every few yards to match the man's longer strides.

The red-headed boy is sweeping leaves. He makes a face at Charles as they pass. You can still see the mark on his cheek, the faded red weal, the last trace of the whipping that the Count gave him.

'Enough of your nonsense, George,' Jevons roars. 'You're paid to work, not make a fool of yourself.'

Charles has not seen the village since the day that he arrived at Charnwood. As they pass through the outskirts, they attract the attention of a few boys, younger than Charles. Jevons snarls like a dog at them but, jeering and sniggering, the boys follow them up the lane to the church and as far as Mr Horton's gates.

At the Vicarage, they go to a side door, not the front. A manservant answers Jevons's knock. He stares with both

129

curiosity and apprehension at Charles, as if he were an odd and potentially dangerous monstrosity.

'Is he safe?' he asks Jevons. 'In the village they say he has fits. Is it true he bites people?'

'Only if you let him see you're scared of him,' Jevons says.

The servant's colour rises. He says in a haughty voice that Jevons is to wait in the kitchen until he is summoned.

A spaniel with a curly liver-and-white coat appears, her nose cocked in curiosity, her paws pattering on the gravel. She ignores the servant and Jevons but sniffs Charles's hands and allows him to scratch her head. He feels a rush of uncomplicated affection towards this animal. He would like to kneel and throw his arms around her neck.

'Go away, Bessie,' the servant says. 'Drat the dog. Always in the way, always trying to get into the house.' He looks at Jevons. 'Go on round to the kitchen. She'll follow you.'

The servant takes Charles by the shoulder, gingerly as if he fears Charles might explode if handled incautiously, and draws him inside. He pushes the door shut with his foot.

The hall is clean and airy. It smells of lemon and beeswax. Charles hears the sound of a woman's voice. A door opens, and a young woman appears with a book in her hand.

'Thomas – is this Charles?'

'Yes, ma'am.'

She looks at the boy and smiles. 'Come in here and wait with us. The Vicar was obliged to go out but he will be back directly.' She glances at the servant. 'Ask cook for a jug of lemonade and some biscuits.'

Thomas bows, a token nod, and withdraws.

'I'm Miss Horton,' the woman says to Charles. 'Come along.'

He follows her into a drawing room. A square-faced, vigorous old woman is sitting by the fire.

'This is Charles,' Miss Horton says. 'The boy from Charnwood. Charles, allow me to present Mrs West of Norbury Park.'

130

Habit does its work: he bows as his mother would have wished, as if the King himself were passing by at Versailles.

Mrs West claps her hands. 'How pretty!' Her voice is harsh and carrying. 'Come here, child. Let me look at you.'

He stands by her chair and she examines him. 'How do you like England?' When Charles does not reply, she repeats the question in French.

Charles stares at her.

'You know he does not speak, ma'am,' Miss Horton says.

'I like to examine these things for myself, my dear. He needs a new suit of clothes. I shall talk to Monsieur Fournier about it.' She nods at Charles. 'Sit down, child. There on the fender where I can see you.' She smiles at Miss Horton. 'Intriguing, is it not? It reminds me of those wild boys the French and Germans find in their woods. Noble savages. Except they rarely seem to be noble, do they? They show Monsieur Rousseau to be quite wrong, on that head at least. It seems to me that, without the society of human kind, they can be scarcely human.'

'This does not apply in Charles's case, ma'am,' Miss Horton says. 'One can see at a glance that he is entirely civilized.'

There is a tap at the door and the manservant enters with a tray. He is not alone – Bessie pushes between his legs, nearly oversetting him, and hurls herself into the room. The stump of her tail wags vigorously, waving a ghostly plume.

'Bessie, you wicked girl,' Miss Horton says.

The dog makes a rapid circuit of the room and comes to Charles. She sits on his foot and gazes into his face.

'My father dotes on the wretched animal,' Harriet says to Mrs West. She leans across and gently tugs one of the dog's ears. 'I truly believe he cares more for Bessie than he does for me.'

Bessie ignores her. She licks Charles's cheek.

'Take her away, Thomas, and shut her in the stables.'

The servant seizes Bessie and backs out of the room. Bessie

131

whines and, Charles thinks, looks straight at him, imploring help.

'She likes you, Charles,' Miss Horton says. 'You're honoured indeed. She is most particular about where she bestows her favours.'

'I can't abide a dog that comes into the house,' Mrs West says. 'Nasty dirty creatures. But go on about the other day, my dear. Was it a terrible smash?'

Charles sips lemonade and listens to Miss Horton telling the story of Mr Savill's unlucky arrival in Norbury.

'But what is he *like*?' Mrs West says.

'He has a scar on his face and a most sarcastic turn of phrase. On the other hand, he was provoked. He was as wet as a sponge and covered in mud. I dare say he was bruised all over as well.'

'Men never like to look ridiculous. Poor Mr West couldn't bear it when I laughed at him.'

Miss Horton cocks her head. 'There's a horse on the lane.'

Mrs West looks at Charles. 'Perhaps Miss Horton would bring you to see me at my house,' she said. 'You might take a boat out on the lake.'

'What a charming idea,' Miss Horton says. 'I should like it above all things.'

The horse is on the drive now.

'Is the Vicar really going to . . .?'

'Pray with Charles?' Miss Horton says. 'Yes, ma'am, he is.'

'How very odd,' Mrs West says. She smiles, perhaps sensing that she has not been polite. 'But I'm sure dear Mr Horton knows his business better than I do.'

# Chapter Twenty-Two

The Vicar is a stout, red-faced gentleman. He peers through thick spectacles at Charles and wrinkles his nose as if there was a bad smell in the air. 'Take him to the Justice Room,' he tells the servant. 'That will do very well. I will join him there in a moment.'

'Pray be gentle with him, sir,' says Miss Horton.

Mr Horton snorts, bows to Mrs West and marches away to the back of the house with the heavy tread and silent determination of a man in need of his privy.

Miss Horton smiles at Charles, and Thomas the manservant leads him along a passage. He hears the two ladies talking, the volume diminishing, and wishes he was with them.

The servant shows Charles into an apartment at the side of the house. It is plainly furnished with a scratched mahogany table, four hard chairs and a high clerk's desk. The walls are lined with shelves and cupboards. There are few books on the shelves – only bundles of paper, tied with ribbons, and japanned metal boxes with labels attached to their handles. The room is gloomy, even in the morning, because the dripping leaves of a bush press up against the window.

Left alone, Charles does not dare to sit. He tries to read the labels on the boxes but finds they say only names, dates and incomprehensible combinations of letters. His head feels as though someone is squeezing it in a vice. He makes a survey of the room. It is slightly more than eight paces long by six paces wide.

This knowledge makes him feel somewhat better. He commits the measurements to memory, where they jostle with all the other measurements that lie there. In a perfect world, he would like a memorandum book in which to record all the figures. It would be agreeable to look at those columns of numbers, those neatly arranged and incontrovertible facts.

'What are you doing?'

Charles turns so sharply that he bangs his thigh on the corner of the table. Mr Horton is standing in the doorway.

'I've been watching you. Are you playing a game? Or is it the devil's work? Eh?'

Charles stares up at him. He has heard the servants saying that the Vicar does not call at Charnwood for fear of moral contamination. Charles does not know what this is but he suspects it is something to do with the drains.

'Either way, you should be able to answer a plain question. This silence of yours won't do.' Mr Horton advances into the room. 'Pasty little thing, aren't you? And thin as a rake. It's all that foreign muck they make you eat. You need some English food.'

He pulls out a chair from the table and sits. He inflates his cheeks and lets the air out in a rush. His pink jowls quiver and his wig is slightly awry. He has three white crumbs on the lapel of his black coat, arranged like the points of an isosceles triangle.

'Come here.' He beckons Charles towards him. 'I assume you speak English like a Christian? Or rather understand it, in your case? Your mother was English, after all – not that it signifies, necessarily. You could know Hottentot and nothing else – it would come to the same thing.' He thrusts his face close to Charles's. 'The material point is that God will understand you, whatever language you speak. That's all that matters.'

Charles feels the soft touch of Mr Horton's spittle on his cheek. He turns his head away.

The Vicar's voice sharpens, becomes peremptory. 'Kneel, sir! Kneel, I say!'

Charles does not move. Mr Horton seizes him by the neck, spins him about and pushes at the back of his knees to make them bend. Charles kneels. When he shows a tendency to slump on his heels, the Vicar seizes his hair and tugs him upwards, compelling him to kneel erect.

'That's better, my boy,' Mr Horton says. 'We are praying to Almighty God, you see, and we must show Him respect. Even a boy like you must understand that. It is no more than common sense, after all.'

Huffing and puffing, he wriggles from his chair and lowers himself to his knees in front of Charles.

'The Gospel of St Mark,' he says, his voice slipping into the declamatory rhythms of the pulpit and the lectern. 'Chapter seven, verse thirty-one: the miracle of the deaf-mute of Decapolis. "And they bring unto him one that was deaf, and had an impediment in his speech. And he took him aside from the multitude, and put his fingers in his ears, and he spit, and he touched his tongue." Are you listening, my boy? You must lift up your soul unto God, even as a burnt offering unto his altars.'

Charles sways on his knees.

The Vicar pats him on the side of his head. 'Stay still. Do me the courtesy of remembering that we are doing this for your sake. Now' – he resumes his pulpit tone – '"And, looking up to heaven, he sighed and saith unto him, Ephphatha, that is, Be opened. And straightway his ears were opened and the string of his tongue was loosed, and he spake plain . . ."'

Having established the scriptural authority for miracles involving mutes, Mr Horton sets to work in pursuit of his own miracle. He prays aloud, extempore and with much spittle

135

and great enthusiasm. As the minutes pass and the Vicar continues with no sign of abating his fervour, and no suggestion that the flow of his eloquence will ever come to an end, Charles ceases to grapple with the meaning of the words. Even the sound of them blurs and recedes. Mr Horton's voice roars like the wind and the waves in the English Channel, the volume rising and falling. Charles feels seasick now just as he had then.

Later, as the words continue, he loses awareness even of their sound and, at last, even of himself.

Everything changes.

Charles finds himself lying on the floor. The Vicar and Miss Horton are kneeling beside him, one on either side. Charles's nostrils are tingling and his lungs smart. Miss Horton holds an open bottle of hartshorn in her hand. Mrs West, her face alive with interest, is behind her.

'The swoon's passing,' Miss Horton says. 'Thank God.'

'This is quite in order,' the Vicar announces, wiping his forehead with a snuff-stained handkerchief. 'The blessing of the Holy Spirit falls like a jolt of lightning on our weak mortal frames and prostrates us with its benevolent power. It would indeed be strange if it were otherwise.'

Miss Horton presses Charles down. 'Lie still,' she says. 'You need to get your breath, and then we'll send for the chaise to take you home.'

Home? Charles wonders. Where is home?

'My carriage!' Mrs West exclaims. 'We shall take him back to Charnwood in that.'

The Vicar waves his hand impatiently. 'We have been privileged to witness the power of prayer,' he tells the ladies sternly. 'And now behold a miracle.' He prods Charles in the chest. 'In the name of Christ Jesus,' he cries. 'Speak!'

Charles clenches his teeth to make a wall against the words. He stares at Mr Horton.

Miss Horton pushes the cork into the bottle of smelling

salts. 'I'm afraid the miracle hasn't worked, Papa,' she says. 'Or not quite yet.'

There's a pattering in the passage. Bessie noses open the door, slides between the Vicar and his daughter and sniffs Charles's face.

# Chapter Twenty-Three

'The boy is mine,' the Count said. 'And that is all that matters.'

Savill felt a twinge of pity for Monsieur de Quillon. Here was a man who was used to being the master, whose health, birth and abilities had set him apart and above most of the human race. But now he was diminished: he retained the habits of grandeur but not its substance.

They were in the room the English servants called the library, though there were few books in the two glass-fronted bookcases. Apart from a large table and a few chairs, there was no other furniture. Despite the fire, the air was chill and damp.

The Count leaned back in his chair, which creaked beneath his weight. 'I do not wish to cause you pain, sir. But you must realize that your wife was your wife only in name.'

'Thank you, sir – I am perfectly aware of that,' Savill said.

'So you have no connection with the boy whatsoever – apart from in a narrowly legal way. Whereas I – well, sir, you leave me no choice: I must speak frankly – my blood runs in his veins. I am the boy's father, with all that means in the way of natural affection and moral duty.'

'Moral duty, sir?' Savill said. The throbbing in his jaw acted as a goad to his temper. 'Is that quite what you mean?'

'I had the honour to enjoy the favours of the lady who was your wife at the time that he was conceived. There – I cannot put it more plainly than that.'

'The lady was married to me, sir. She was married to me when the boy was conceived and born, and she was married to me at the time of her death. I have a right to the boy. I also have a responsibility for him.'

'I doubt a court of law would agree with you, sir,' the Count snapped. 'The claim is against nature – it is against common sense.'

'That is neither here nor there.' Savill heard his own voice rising in volume to match the Count's. 'What matters is that it is the law. And, even if it weren't, I've seen no evidence that the boy is in fact your son. Besides, even if you could prove that, which you can't, it would not give you the right to dispose of the boy as you wish.'

The Count pushed back his chair and stood up. He leaned heavily on the desk, his face flaming with anger. 'You don't know who you're talking to, sir. I shall write to Mr Pitt – I shall write to the King – I shall—'

'This is England, sir. Not France.'

'You shall find that I am still capable of keeping my own son. You would do well to remember that—'

The sound of a carriage on the drive brought him up short. Breathing hard, he walked to the window. There were voices in the hall and then outside. He bowed curtly to Savill and walked out of the room without another word.

Savill stood up and stretched. The exertion made him feel dizzy and he clung to the back of his chair for support. His limbs still ached and the crater where the tooth had been was a place of pain. He wondered whether his letters to Rampton and the livery stable in Bath had really gone out this morning. He had seen the Count in a new light. He had glimpsed the strength of his determination to keep Charles, which confirmed how right Savill had been earlier to suspect

Dr Gohlis's motives. The question was, how ruthless was Monsieur de Quillon prepared to be in order to achieve his desire?

The door opened, and Fournier came into the room.

'Good morning, sir,' he said. 'I'm rejoiced to see you downstairs. I had not dared to hope you would be able to leave your chamber today. Have you heard? Charles is returned from the Vicarage.'

'In the carriage?'

'Yes – Mrs West was so good as to bring him back. She desires to meet you. Would the fresh air distress you? She does not wish to come into the house. Miss Horton is with her. No doubt you will wish to thank your fair rescuer as well.'

Savill followed Fournier to the library door. 'And Charles?' he said.

Fournier shrugged. 'Mr Horton's miracle? Alas, his prayers failed to answer.'

The sun was out and the ladies had climbed from the carriage and were talking to the Count, who stood with his hand resting on Charles's shoulder. They turned as Fournier and Savill descended the shallow steps from the door.

Fournier approached the elder of the two ladies, a stout woman with a weathered face. 'Madam, permit me to introduce Mr Savill from London.'

'An encounter with Mr Bradshaw's bull!' she said in a harsh, carrying voice. 'And a ride in Mr Roach's cart. What a welcome Norbury has given you, sir.'

Savill bowed to her. 'I shall cherish the memory for the rest of my life, madam.'

She laughed. 'And you have met Miss Horton, of course.'

'Good morning, sir,' she said, coming forward to greet him. 'I hope I find you a little more comfortable than you were on Thursday?'

She was older than he had thought – well past thirty, probably, though the years sat lightly on her because of her unlined face and the vivacity of her manner.

'Pray excuse me,' the Count said, in a manner that made it sound like an order. He bowed to the ladies and went into the house, pushing Charles before him.

'Will you come inside a moment?' Fournier asked.

'I think not.' Mrs West looked at Fournier for an instant, and Savill was aware of words unsaid between them. 'But a walk in the garden would be delightful. Harriet has never seen the statue of Neptune there. I remember Mr West telling me that it is of Roman manufacture, and it was brought from Bath.' She touched Fournier's arm playfully, almost flirtatiously. 'But you will be able to advise us whether it is a real antiquity or a mere copy.'

So, Savill thought, is that how the land lies? He remembered the hint about Fournier and Mrs West that Malbourne had dropped in London. There was a disparity in age between them – Mrs West was perhaps a dozen years older than Fournier, but that signified no more than the fact that Fournier was lame. The only thing that mattered was that each of them had something the other wanted. That was always the only thing that mattered in affairs of this nature.

Arm in arm, Mrs West and Fournier strolled away. Savill felt weak and light-headed. He gave Miss Horton his arm but he was uncertain which of them was really supporting the other. They followed the others towards the Garden of Neptune.

'I'm sorry your father's experiment proved fruitless,' he said.

'It's a pity, certainly.' Miss Horton's fingers tightened on his arm. 'I feel so sad for him. Charles, that is. You should have seen him with Bessie, my father's dog. He must have been starved of affection since his mother died.'

'Yes.'

'Not that I mean to imply that the Count and Monsieur Fournier do not do everything that is proper. But . . .'

'A child needs more than what is proper,' Savill said.

141

'Precisely. Which is why I wondered whether you or anyone else would object if I tried an experiment of my own.' She looked up at him. 'Simply to spend a little time with him. To read him a story, perhaps, or play a game.'

'You're too kind,' Savill said stiffly. 'But unfortunately it will not be possible. I shall take him to London with me on Monday.'

'Oh.'

'I'm sorry,' he said, seeing the disappointment in her face.

'Not at all, sir. It was merely a whim. Do you reside in London?'

'Yes, madam.' He felt a need to provide more information, if only to compensate for his curtness. 'In Nightingale Lane.'

'How charming. Is it "a green and grassy shrine, With myrtle bower'd and jessamine?"'

He knew by her tone that she was quoting some wretched poem or another. She was mocking him. 'It is hard by Bedford Square,' he said. 'We are bowered with new houses and roads and shops.'

They fell silent and walked on. Twenty yards in front of them, Fournier and Mrs West were deep in conversation, their heads very close together.

Savill seized on a change of subject. 'Norbury seems an agreeable spot.'

'It is the most tedious place imaginable,' Miss Horton said sharply. 'If it were not for Mrs West's society, I believe it would drive me mad.'

'Have you always lived here, ma'am?'

'Since I was fifteen, when we came here from Bristol. Mr West and Papa were at Oxford together, and he presented Papa with the living when it became vacant.'

They came to the garden, where the four of them lined up in front of the statue and solemnly inspected it.

'It is sadly battered,' Mrs West said. 'I'm afraid it is not as impressive as I remembered.'

'One must always inspect antiquities with the eye of the

imagination, dear madam,' Fournier said, gazing raptly at the statue. 'Think what dramatic scenes must have unfolded before its unseeing eyes.'

Mrs West had lost interest in Neptune. 'Mr Savill, pray show me the view from the further gate. I have quite forgotten what it looks like.'

She took Savill's arm and drew him away from the others. 'I understand that you are come to take Charles away.' The old lady's curiosity was naked. 'Do you represent his family, sir?'

'Yes. His late mother was my wife.'

Mrs West's mouth hung open for a moment. There was a burst of laughter from Fournier.

'You must forgive me, sir,' she said. 'I had no idea.'

'Pray do not give it another thought, ma'am.' Savill glanced back at Harriet, who was smiling at Fournier.

'Has Charles much family in England, sir?' Mrs West said.

'My daughter, my sister and myself – and my wife's uncle.'

'It must be a great consolation for the boy to know he is not alone in the world. Is he to live with you?'

'I do not know, ma'am.' Savill stumbled but regained his balance. 'I beg your pardon. You see, there is a good deal to be settled.'

'Has he met his English relations before?'

'No.'

'Well then,' said Mrs West, 'if you ask me, sir – and I know it is none of my business – there is much to be said for leaving him at Charnwood for the time being. Here at least he is surrounded by familiar faces. And of course there's his condition to consider. It must be accounted a considerable advantage that the Count has his own physician. Dr Gohlis is a very superior man. He has studied all over Europe and is entirely *au fait* in all the modern developments of his profession.'

'No doubt.' Savill wondered if Fournier had put her up to this. 'But I believe Charles will do better in the long run with

143

his own kin. I would have left with him already if it had not been for the accident to my chaise.'

'And a troublesome tooth, I hear?'

'Yes.'

She peered up at his face. It seemed to him that her own face shimmered as if under water.

'Forgive me, sir,' she said, 'but you are not well. I do not like the look of your pallor. Charles may not need the doctor, but I'm quite sure that you do.'

# Chapter Twenty-Four

The Count steers Charles into the house. In the hall, he lifts his heavy hand from Charles's shoulder. He stares down at him and shakes his head. He goes into the library, closing the door.

Charles does not know what to do. Given a choice, he would stay with Miss Horton but the Count has clearly decided otherwise. No one takes any notice of him. He sidles away towards the servants' quarters.

Two of the maids are whispering in the passage leading to the kitchen.

'Turned my blood cold as ice,' Martha says. She's carrying a bowl covered with a cloth.

'I'll have them screams ringing in my ears till the day I die,' says Susan. 'You just see if I don't.' She catches sight of Charles. 'Has Parson done it?' she demands. 'Can you talk now, lad?'

While they wait for an answer, they stare at him with huge eyes, hoping for wonders and miracles. He stares back.

'He'd not talk English, would he?' Martha says. 'Not like a Christian. He'd talk French.' She nods at him. 'Parley voo? Eh? Parley voo?'

Joseph comes up behind the women. 'He won't parley anything. Jevons said that Parson prayed so hard he had steam coming out of him, and the boy just fell down in a swoon, like he was dead. And all for nothing. He's got the devil in him, that one has.' He points at the basin. 'What's all this then?'

'Mr Savill's mess from yesterday, from when doctor pulled his tooth out. Screaming fit to burst, he was. Found this by the washstand.'

Martha twitches the cloth aside. Charles glimpses the bloody rags in the bowl. He shuts his eyes and leans against the wall. He pants for breath.

'Bellowed like a stuck pig. Didn't have him down as a coward,' Joseph says. 'I thought he'd bear it like a man.'

'Tooth was rotten and it broke up when doctor pulled it out,' Martha says. 'That's why it was so bad.'

'Happened to my auntie,' puts in the other maid. 'They could hear her shrieking all the way from here to Bath.'

'But I blame the doctor too,' Martha says, pursing her lips. 'He's not used to pulling teeth. Not like the blacksmith.'

'So much blood,' says Susan. 'You just wouldn't believe.'

Charles opens his eyes, just a crack, so he can see through the blurred veil of his lashes. Martha has pulled the cloth over the bowl, hiding its contents. Charles finds he can breathe properly again.

'More work,' Joseph says. 'More inconvenience. That's what it means, you mark my words. It's bad enough having all this up-and-down to His Lordship's chamber. Now we've got another damned invalid in the house.' He tweaks Charles's ear. 'As well as Idiot Boy here.'

Charles stares at the open kitchen door and contemplates his own evil with what amounts to a sense of relief. It is something to have it so firmly established. It may be considered a fact now, a fixed point in the shifting confusion, like the length and breadth of Mr Horton's Justice Room. In time he may find ways to chart its outlines and measure its dimensions.

Charles knows that he must be very evil indeed if God Himself cannot cure him. The Vicar was talking to God, and God would not listen. It must make it worse that Charles clings to his evil, that he does not want to be cured.

*Say nothing. Not a word to anyone. Whatever you see. Whatever you hear. Do you understand? Say nothing.*

Even to God? Even to Louis?

Dr Gohlis appears. Charles lifts up his eyes and there he is, just for a second or two, hurrying down the path from the stables to the side door, with Jevons just behind him. There are noises in the main part of the house, and a bell rings long and hard.

Joseph swears under his breath, straightens his coat and smooths the expression from his face. He marches into the hall.

Jevons comes into the kitchen. 'Mr Savill's took ill again,' he says cheerfully. 'Mortal bad. Looks like he needs Parson, not doctor.'

In the stableyard, the shadows are beginning to lengthen. No one is about. A chicken has escaped from its place of imprisonment and is pecking the dirt by the horse trough.

Charles ducks into the stable and climbs the steep stairs. The door at the top is locked. He returns to the ground floor, where there are six loose boxes, only one of which is ever occupied.

His presence startles a pigeon that has found its way in here. It flies to the doorway in a flutter of clumsy panic and swoops up into the sky.

The sudden movement makes Charles glance upwards. The floor above is of rough boards supported by crudely cut beams. Between two of the beams, above the manger of the nearest loose box, is a trapdoor.

Charles scrambles into the manger and reaches upwards.

147

He presses the hatch. It shifts. A draught of air tickles the skin of his hands. He pushes the trapdoor harder. It's heavier than he expects. Steadying himself on the side of the hatchway, he climbs on to the rim of the manger and pushes harder. Suddenly the trapdoor rises and falls backwards, clattering on to the floor above. He wriggles into the laboratory. The hatch is under the big table in the middle of the room, concealed from view.

The light is fading, but Charles is able to make out the figure of Louis beside the smaller table at the window. He crosses the room and lays a hand on Louis's arm. He touches muscle, tendon and bone.

Charles tells him about the priest's attempt to perform a miracle.

'I don't believe in miracles,' Louis says.

'Nor do I,' Charles replies. 'They aren't real. Not facts.'

'Stupid people believe in miracles because it makes them feel better.'

'Mr Horton has a dog,' Charles says. 'She's called Bessie.'

Louis does not comment.

'Look.' Charles holds out the dice. 'Mr Savill gave me them.' He turns them in the palm of his hand until the two sixes are uppermost.

'Six and six are twelve,' Louis says. 'That is a fact.'

'I wish we could be together all the time.'

Louis does not reply. But he stares towards the door. It occurs to Charles that perhaps Louis is saying something – after all, the two of them say things without words and sometimes, as with spoken words, you do not quite catch what is being said.

'Yes,' Charles says, suddenly grasping what Louis is thinking. 'We must escape.'

'Well done,' Louis says. 'I knew you'd understand.'

In his happiness, Charles does what he has never done before: he embraces Louis. Louis responds as best he can,

148

which is to rock slightly towards Charles; and that is enough to complete Charles's happiness.

Their faces are together. Louis's of course is terribly damaged – the skin flayed, teeth and muscle, bone and flesh, exposed for anyone to see. But the roughness is endearing, a shared intimacy and a shared secret, and his touch is not cold either.

Charles tightens his embrace and Louis shifts under the pressure, rocking slightly on his pedestal. 'But we can't escape. They wouldn't let us.'

'We shall run away.' Louis shifts again and Charles realizes that Louis is much lighter than he looks, a shell. 'Hide from them.'

'In the woods?' Charles remembers Monsieur Fournier and Dr Gohlis talking of the wild boys who lived in solitude in the depths of the forest, and how nobody knew they were there. 'We'd be together, always. We could do whatever we wanted. We'd eat berries and roots and leaves like they do in the stories.'

Charles squeezes Louis's arm and climbs through the hatch. Louis watches him. Standing on the manger, Charles draws the trapdoor towards him. He pauses.

'Louis?' he says, though his lips do not move. 'They tried to make me speak this morning. They sent me to the priest in the village. But I won't speak. I mustn't.'

He hovers on the edge of telling Louis the reason. But there must be some secrets, even among friends.


Charles has left not a moment too soon. As he jumps down from the manger, the door to the yard opens.

Dr Gohlis stops short, framed in the doorway. His hand flies up to his throat at the sight of Charles in the empty loose box.

Charles knows, for he has grown an expert in this, that the doctor is scared. He has seen a boy in the gloom of the stable, where he expected to see none. Worse than that—

149

*He thinks I'm Louis.*

The enchantment breaks. 'You stupid boy,' Gohlis snaps. 'You're not allowed here. What the devil do you think you're doing?'

The doctor pauses, as if waiting for a reply. For an instant, it has slipped his memory that Charles is mute. Charles will never answer questions because both science and religion have failed to restore his power of speech.

150

# Chapter Twenty-Five

After breakfast on Monday, Mrs Cox says that Mr Savill is still lying ill in bed and that Charles must stay here in her room; he must not go anywhere else in the house and he must not go outside. She does not say why.

At first Charles does not mind. He has not been sleeping well, partly because of the dreams and partly because he is afraid that someone or something will come for him in the night. He feels grey with weariness.

Mrs Cox has left him with nothing to do, so he occupies himself by pacing the room to measure it. He commits its dimensions to memory. Afterwards he sits down and thinks about Bessie, Mr Horton's dog.

There are footsteps in the passage. The housekeeper returns. To Charles's surprise, she brings Miss Horton from the Vicarage, who is carrying a book and what looks like a chess set.

'Charles!' Mrs Cox says sternly. Her thin, scratchy voice makes him shiver. 'To your feet, sir. Make your bow to Miss Horton.'

He rises. He bows elaborately.

'He sits there or moons around the garden,' Mrs Cox says. 'Like a ghost. Day in, day out. You wonder what he thinks about.'

'Thoughts are private,' Miss Horton says. 'Which I suppose is just as well, ma'am, in many ways.'

'You won't get a word out of him, ma'am. Mind you' – Mrs Cox lowers her voice to a perfectly audible whisper – 'he's not had an easy time, by all accounts, especially on the Continent with all those French devils on the loose.'

'Thank you, Mrs Cox. Pray sit, Charles.'

The housekeeper lingers. 'Shall I stay, ma'am? Is there anything they can bring you?'

'We'll do very well as we are, thank you.'

The door closes.

'Pray sit,' Miss Horton says again.

Charles does not move. He wonders what she will do now, how she will force him to do what she wants.

To his surprise, she ignores him entirely. She sits at the table, choosing a chair that faces towards him.

He braces himself for questions, for yet another method of treatment designed to make him speak. From the corner of his eye he sees Miss Horton draw the book towards her and open it, running her finger down the page. She does not look up.

She begins to read in English: 'I was born in the year 1632, in the city of York, of a good family, though not of that country, my father being a foreigner of Bremen, who settled first at Hull. He got a good estate by merchandise, and leaving off his trade, lived afterwards at York, from whence he married my mother, whose relations were named Robinson . . .'

Miss Horton's voice is pitched so low that Charles has to strain to hear what she is saying. By degrees, however, he is drawn into the remarkable story that unfolds, though he continues to stand and stare at the wall.

It seems that the narrator is a young man who does not want to settle down to learn a trade or profession: he craves adventure. Ignoring the advice of his aged parents, he takes ship on a whim at Hull, wherever that is, on a vessel bound for London. There is a terrible storm on the way, and the ship founders.

Charles's limbs grow stiff and weary from standing in one place. Moreover, as Miss Horton speaks so low, it is not always easy to distinguish her words.

Gradually, he edges closer to the table where Miss Horton sits. She appears not to notice, for the flow of her words does not alter in any way.

The narrator of the story survives the shipwreck by the grace of God. Instead of returning home, however, he journeys on to London, despite the stern warnings of the ship's master. There, to make matters even worse, he boards a ship bound for Africa in the rash and foolish hope of making his fortune.

At this interesting juncture, Miss Horton breaks off. 'I beg your pardon, Charles,' she says in tolerable French. 'I have been reading in English. Perhaps you would prefer me to read in French?'

He does not reply. But he cannot prevent his eyes drifting to the open book.

'Very well then,' she says as if he has answered. 'I shall continue in English. To be frank, I find it easier.'

The story continues. Almost without noticing, Charles sits. He rests his chin on his hands. His eyes close. In no time at all, it seems, the narrator acquires a small fortune but then, on his next voyage, has the misfortune to be captured by pirates and sold into slavery. Naturally he escapes. After shooting a lion and a tiger, and also dealing with naked African savages, he is taken by a Portuguese ship en route to Brazil. Whereupon—

There is a knock on the door and Mrs Cox enters with the news that their dinner is ready. By orders of Monsieur Fournier, a table has been laid for Miss Horton in a small parlour at the other end of the house from the dining room; it seems that Miss Horton prefers not to dine with the rest of the Charnwood party.

Charles eats with the servants. Afterwards, he is allowed

to go outside for twenty minutes, which is until the stable clock strikes the hour.

He goes to the stable yard, drawn by the presence of Louis there. But he does not linger. The red-headed gardener's boy is chopping logs in the coach house that no longer contains a coach. He sees Charles coming into the yard. He spits on the ground and then makes an elaborate show of grinding the spittle with his heel.

Miss Horton is waiting for him. He hopes she will read more of the story. Instead, she has opened the board and is drawing up the black pieces in their two ranks.

She glances up as he comes in. She pushes the white pieces across the table towards him.

He sits and stares at a horse.

'Do you play?' she asks.

He ignores the question. The horse is a strange, deformed piece – the animal's head and shoulders perched on a pedestal. He likes the horse because it is different from the others.

'That is a knight,' Miss Horton says. 'Each side has two of them.'

He picks it up and puts it down on the board. Glancing across the table, he sees that the two black knights are already standing on the back rank of the board. He has a memory of the two lines drawn up at each end of the board, ready for battle. He places his white knight directly opposite one of Miss Horton's.

'Good,' she says, and places a piece resembling a tower in the corner of the board.

He finds a similar piece among the whites. He puts it in one of his corners.

Miss Horton puts her head to one side, considering. 'You see, they are like an army facing itself in the mirror,' she says. 'But the mirror reverses them, as mirrors do. White becomes black and black becomes white.'

154

She sets up the rest of her army. He imitates her, piece by piece, safe on the other side of the mirror. There is a pleasure in this, he discovers, for there are eight squares along each side of the board, which makes sixty-four altogether, which is a comforting, secure sort of number.

When all the pieces are in their pre-ordained places, he admires the neatness and regularity of the display. The pattern they make is fixed in his memory.

'I have not played chess for years,' Miss Horton says. 'Not since my brother was home.'

She speaks even more quietly than before. Perhaps she is thinking aloud. She is not looking at him but at the board.

'He laughed at me because at first I could never remember the different moves the pieces make. But I think I have them by heart now. John – my brother – used to say that chess follows patterns and laws, however random it seems to someone who does not know the rules. He said it was like navigation, which depends on the patterns made in the sky by heavenly bodies, which are always fixed. He was a sailor, you see, so he knew all about navigation. Once you know the patterns, you can depend on them for ever. You can use them to find your way.'

Miss Horton blows her nose while Charles wonders what happened to John and whether he is still a sailor. But she changes the subject directly and picks up each sort of piece, one after the other, and names it and describes how it moves.

This is interesting in itself, as is the fact that one piece can take another. The most interesting piece of all is the king, which can only move one square at a time, though in any direction. But an army cannot fight without it. The two kings are the reason for the battle. When one of the kings is held in check by enemy pieces, when it cannot move at all, then the battle is over.

To remind herself of the game, Miss Horton says, she begins to play against herself. Charles watches. After the first

155

half-dozen moves, she asks him to save her the trouble of advancing the black pawn on his left by two squares. He cannot see a reason not to do this. Besides, he wants to see where she will move next.

The game continues in this manner for some time. Charles soon realizes that the actual disposition of pieces on the board is only part of it. Each arrangement carries within it a multitude of possibilities. It is necessary to keep in mind hundreds if not thousands of possible outcomes for each move. To make matters even more complicated, the other player might see other possibilities. Best of all, everything follows the rules: if only one had a big enough brain, Charles thinks, it should be perfectly possible to calculate the outcome from the very first move.

There comes a moment when Charles not only moves the piece but also suggests the move itself – the capture of a white castle by a black bishop that is able to swoop almost the length of the board in an elegant diagonal.

'Huzza!' Miss Horton says.

Then she captures the gallant bishop with a flank attack from her queen, whose presence Charles has failed to note. But this, it seems, is not a fault after all.

'Losing your bishop was a price worth paying, you see, because you captured a castle. John used to say that you must always take the long view in chess. A castle is worth much more than a bishop.'

The game ends in what Miss Horton says was a draw, though Charles is not quite able to understand how this has been achieved.

By now, the light is beginning to fade. Miss Horton rings for candles. The maid brings tea as well. While they drink it, Miss Horton takes up the book again and continues reading from where she left off.

On reaching Brazil, the narrator becomes a tobacco planter. After a year or two, however, he sets sail for Africa to buy slaves, having determined that this trade would be more profitable. Unfortunately, he is shipwrecked in the course of the most terrible storm, during which the vessel sinks and all his shipmates perish.

He finds himself quite alone on a desert island.

By this time Charles is leaning over the table so that he may hear every word that Miss Horton says in her low voice. He starts violently at a knock on the door. The maid brings news that the Vicar's pony chaise has come to collect her.

Miss Horton closes the book and rises. 'Thank you, Charles,' she says, quite as if he has done her a favour. 'I must say goodbye. I hope to return tomorrow in the afternoon.'

She nods to the maid, who picks up the book and the chess set. At the door, Miss Horton pauses and looks back at him.

Without thinking, Charles has risen to his feet. Automatically, without being told to do so, he bows. She smiles at him.

A moment later he is alone, as solitary as Mr Crusoe on his desert island.

# Chapter Twenty-Six

The forbidden woods occupy a wedge of land that tapers to a tip to the south. To the north, however, where the land rises, the wedge broadens. The trees flow on, climbing steadily, widening their territory as they go, until they merge with the hills beyond Charnwood.

After breakfast, Charles goes into the Garden of Neptune. When he is sure there is no one to observe his disobedience, he slips through the gate and up the path to the woods.

It is cool and damp under the trees – there has been more rain in the night. Charles walks over a carpet of sodden leaves that muffle sound.

The project of running away does not seem quite so straight-forward now. He realizes that he and Louis will need a shelter to protect them from the wind and rain. He walks further and further but does not find anywhere that would be suitable.

'Trust me,' Louis says in Charles's mind. 'It's all right. We'll find somewhere soon.'

Woods can be as hard to navigate as oceans. In the absence of landmarks Charles loses his sense of direction. To his left he sees that the trees are thinning. He changes course.

'Trust me,' says Louis. 'Trust me.'

The land rises. There are fewer trees but the undergrowth is thicker, catching at his legs so that he stumbles, nearly falls and is forced to walk.

Suddenly Charles can walk no further.

'You see,' Louis says. 'I brought you here.'

The incline has led him to the top of a knoll. A stream runs around most of it so it is nearly an island. A old beech tree dominates the little hill. One of its lower branches has broken off. The bough lies like a ship abandoned on land by the tide. Beside it is a yew so old that the parent trunk is dying but the roots around it have sent up a grove of saplings beside the fallen branch of the beech. The tops of the saplings are entangled with the branches of a young birch tree that spreads above it.

The mingled branches make a green cave. Charles stoops and touches the ground. It is nearly dry. Or at least not very damp.

'We've found it,' Louis says, deep in Charles's mind. 'This is our place.'

Everything is right. They have found their secret place. Shelter. An almost complete moat to protect them and to provide drinking water. This is their castle. This is their desert island.

'Trust me,' Louis says, and the thought of his voice fills Charles's chest with a surge of joy. 'Here we shall be free.'

Charles is lucky that day. Nobody catches him outside the grounds of Charnwood.

He has returned to the Garden of Neptune. He is pacing the length of the garden. It is a day or two since he has measured the garden, apart from the pool's circumference, and it would not be wise to leave it any longer.

Charles is only halfway along the path, the numbers tumbling obediently over one another in his head, following their unchanging sequence, when the further gate, the one nearer the house, swings open.

159

Joseph comes through it. He strides into the garden, his face a rigid, righteous mask. He seizes Charles by the hair and shakes him.

'Devil take you – look at the state you're in.'

The pain makes Charles's eyes fill with tears. For the first time he realizes that he is not as clean and tidy as he was. Long streaks of mud decorate one side of his coat and breeches. One of his stockings is around his ankle. Probably, he thinks gloomily, the parts of him he cannot see are just as bad or even worse.

Joseph boxes Charles's ears. 'You'll catch it.'

He escorts Charles to the house's back door in the service yard near the stables. Mrs Cox is in her room with an account book open before her.

'What is it now?' Then she sees Charles. 'Gracious heaven! What has he been doing?'

'His Lordship wants him,' Joseph says. 'Half an hour ago.'

'Take his coat off,' Mrs Cox commands. 'Fetch damp cloths.'

While Joseph is gone, she tells Charles to pull up his stockings and straighten his breeches. She brushes and sponges him. She reties his cravat so tightly he thinks for a moment she means to strangle him.

A few minutes later, Joseph takes Charles to the library and nudges him through the doorway.

The Count is not alone. Dr Gohlis is with him. The doctor's mask slips and he cannot prevent his face from wrinkling with disgust.

The Count beckons him closer. For the first time, he embraces him. He does it clumsily for want of practice. He smells of pomade with a sour tang of brandy.

He pushes the boy away. 'He is filthy. Why's he so dirty?'

'He was playing in the garden, my lord. It's boys, my lord, they're all the same. He was much worse when I found him, though – me and Mrs Cox cleaned him up.'

'A child of nature,' Dr Gohlis says, seeing the matter from

another angle, as he often does. 'The savage coexists, at least in theory, with the most refined and delicate sensibilities. Or rather not, in this case? That is the question, is it not? I must make a note of it before it slips my mind.'

'What?'

'The human boy, my lord. I was merely observing—'

'Yes, yes. You may return to your studies, Doctor.' The Count's eyes flick towards Joseph and his hand waves him out of the room after Gohlis.

The Count sighs. For a moment his eyes meet Charles's. A tiny and wholly unexpected spark of communication leaps between them. Sympathy? Mirth? Whatever it is, it's gone before the door has closed behind the doctor and footman.

'Sit on the chair by the window. I wish to have you with me. Take that book on the table. It has pictures.'

Charles does as he is told while the Count turns to his desk and picks up his pen. The book is in French, an account of Switzerland with many views of lakes and mountains. Charles does not find it amusing. He turns the pages slowly and thinks about the castle that he and Louis will share. What will they eat, he wonders.

In a while, he grows bored so he counts instead – the panes in the window, the books on the shelves; whatever is available.

There is a tap on the door and another person enters. Charles cannot see who it is – the chair is angled towards the window and its back blocks out half the room – but he recognizes Monsieur Fournier's voice.

'I have been thinking,' he says.

'You always do,' says the Count. 'What about?'

'About Savill. About those papers in his bag.'

There is a silence. 'He has a warrant from a magistrate,' the Count says in a harsher voice. 'But he also has a wedding certificate, and there's no reason to doubt it. That's what concerns me.'

161

'There's more. I looked at the warrant again this morning while he was sleeping. It's signed by one of the new stipendiary magistrates. I hadn't noticed that before. They are the ones who watch for sedition. And it grants him sweeping powers if he needs to use them. He's carrying a fair sum in gold as well. This can't be merely a family matter. The long and the short of it is that Savill must be a police informer.'

'So are you saying that he has no claim on the boy after all?'

'No, no – unfortunately that part is true enough. But not the whole truth. He's no ordinary spy to come so well prepared. The question is, who's behind him?'

'God damn him,' the Count says, his voice a low growl. 'Charles is over there, by the way.'

'What?'

There are footsteps. Fournier stares down at Charles, who shrinks back into the chair, holding the book to his chest like a breastplate.

'I have decided to have him in my company more often,' the Count says. 'He must learn to know his father. He must learn how a man of honour behaves, and he can only do that by living with one.'

Fournier's crooked eyebrows wrinkle together. 'I wish you'd told me he was here.'

'Why? What does it matter?' The Count's voice sounds as if he is smiling. 'If we can be sure of nothing else about Charles, he is at least discreet.'

The rest of the week passes in this manner. Mr Savill lies in bed upstairs, the subject of whispered conversations among the servants. Miss Horton comes to see Charles on most days, if only for half an hour, and Robinson Crusoe's story unfolds.

On Friday, Miss Horton comes in Mrs West's carriage, and he is allowed to drive out with her. The coachman takes them into the village, where the countryfolk watch them pass by. They travel very slowly on the rutted lanes between the high hedges, the machine swaying like a ship on the ocean.

When they come to the long, smooth drive of Norbury Park, however, the coachman urges the horses to a canter. The trees on either side flicker as if alive as the carriage whirrs past them. The horses' hooves and the remorseless grinding of the carriage's iron-rimmed wheels become deafening. It is all Charles can do to prevent himself from crying out in excitement.

They stop outside the house where Mrs West lives. It is a big stone box with large windows. They do not go inside but a servant brings out lemonade and biscuits.

While they eat and drink, Miss Horton points out the beauties of the park, gives the servant a message for Mrs West and praises the lemonade. Everything is natural and easy. Miss Horton makes so much conversation that it does not matter at all that Charles says nothing. She talks for both of them.

Once or twice she touches his arm and asks, 'Do you not agree, Charles?' but she takes his answer for granted. It is almost as if she hears the words he does not speak.

Charles visits the castle in the woods again, first on Wednesday and then very early on Friday morning. The second time he takes an earthenware mug stolen from the scullery and half a loaf of yesterday's bread that he found among the scraps set aside for Mrs White's pig. He hides them behind the fallen branch and covers them with leaves.

'Now we have provisions,' he tells Louis, proud of the word which he learned from *Robinson Crusoe*, and proud of his own foresight.

For a time, he is almost happy.

On the way back, Charles loses his way, for this is not a wood with many paths. At last he reaches the edge of the wood but it is not in the same place as usual. He cannot see the gate to the Garden of Neptune. Instead there is a muddy lane strewn with stones. It comes from the hills and goes towards a farm, a huddle of roofs in the distance. It winds through scrubland with a few stunted trees bowed by the wind. Somewhere a cock is crowing, over and over again.

There is a horseman in a blue coat on the lane. He is several hundred yards away and he is riding in the direction of Norbury.

Charles retreats into the safety of the trees. He sets off in another direction, deeper into the wood. He is warier now and less optimistic.

He walks faster and faster, careless of the mud that splashes his legs and the branches that reach out to poke and slap and scratch him. He believes he hears sounds behind him and for a moment he is convinced that the rider is following him.

But that is foolish, and he dismisses the idea. The fear that grows inside him is because he will be missed if he doesn't reach Charnwood before everyone else is stirring.

He breaks into a stumbling run. A stitch drives deep into his side. His breath is a fugitive's, ragged and urgent, but he is fleeing towards what he fears, not away from it.

The nights are worse than ever.

The autumn winds are rising, and the trees are swaying like dancers in the grounds. They are beginning to scatter their leaves. Charles does what he can to protect himself – counting and measuring, stuffing rags into his ears to block out the sounds. He would like to block the door with the box but he is too afraid of what Mrs Cox might do.

But how does one block the dreams?

As the winds grow wilder, so does the ash tree that taps on the window. *Tip-tap*.

The tapping brings the blood, dribbling from the ceiling, oozing between bare boards.

Twice he wakes up. The second time, he finds that he has wet the bed. Mrs Cox reports the sin to Monsieur Fournier, who orders Joseph to beat Charles.

'It is for your own good,' Monsieur Fournier says.

# Chapter Twenty-Seven

As well as the pain, the heat was unbearable, driving him to and fro in search of coolness. There were dreams of dead women and old wounds. The old question returned: are we innocent when we dream?

People gave him liquids. They sponged him.

The Count appeared, looming over the bed like an angry red cloud, though perhaps that too was a dream.

Savill's face was swollen on the side where the tooth had been, and the swelling ran up to his brain and down to his neck. If only someone would chop off his head, he thought, he might be tolerably comfortable again.

Sometimes he talked; sometimes others talked; but he could not remember what was said.

Slowly the fever receded and the swelling subsided. He was very weak and slept for most of the time.

There were patches of lucidity, however, and of a blessed absence from pain, which he learned to connect with the glasses of Dr Gohlis's mixture. Whether it was the same mixture as before he neither knew nor cared. Sometimes it brought relief, and that was all that mattered. What did it matter if they were poisoning him? Only pain mattered. All he desired was its absence.

166

One morning he was woken by the sound of the fire irons rattling in the grate. Savill pushed the bed-curtain aside. The fabric seemed heavier than usual.

'Who's there?' he said, and his voice sounded dry and feeble; it belonged to a stranger.

'Me, sir.' Mary Ann appeared, a pair of tongs in her hand and a smut on her cheek.

Savill swallowed. 'What day is it?'

She looked strangely at him. 'Saturday, sir.'

'What? Still? It can't be.'

'No, sir. You were taken queer last Saturday.'

'So I've been here for' – he struggled with the arithmetic – 'a week?'

'Yes, sir.'

He stared at her, as the information seeped slowly into his mind. 'A week,' he repeated, and the very words were wearisome. 'A week.'


Dr Gohlis came in, rubbing his hands. 'Ah, that is better, sir. I knew the treatment would answer in the end.'

'I must get up. I must—'

'You must do no such thing. The fever is down, and so is the swelling. I believe we have at last expelled the poison that caused your tooth to rot and gave you so much pain. But if you over-tire yourself, there is a danger that you will have a relapse.'

'I cannot afford to lie here.'

'You have no choice, sir. And you must not have too much society, either. That will tire you as much as exercise.'

Savill sank back on the pillow. 'I must speak to Monsieur Fournier. Allow me that, at least.'

His eyelids were very heavy. He closed his eyes.

'You see?' Gohlis said, remorseless in his authority. 'It is better to let nature take its course. You may speak to Monsieur Fournier later.'

\* \* \*

167

Fournier came in the afternoon and drank tea with Savill. After the conventional enquiries, he picked up the miniature of Lizzie, which stood open on the night table by the bed. His eyebrows rose and made Gothic arches.

'A pretty child,' he said. 'Your daughter, sir?'

'Yes. When she was much younger.'

'There is a resemblance, you know.'

'To Charles?'

'Yes. Not as he is now, of course, but when he was younger. Does she know she has a half-brother?'

'Yes, but not that he does not speak.' Savill was so weak that his eyes filled with tears.

Fournier sipped his tea. He looked at Savill over the rim of his cup. 'And does Charles know about her?'

'Not yet. Only that he has family in London.'

'Family? Besides yourself and your daughter? I did not realize.'

Savill saw the trap in time. In his way, Rampton was a public figure. If Fournier did not know of him already, he would make it his business to enquire.

'My sister keeps house for us.' Savill allowed a pettish note proper to an invalid to enter his voice. 'The chaise I ordered from Bath – pray, sir, has it arrived?'

'Alas, it has come and gone. A groom brought it on Monday evening, a loutish fellow, but he would not stay when he heard you were ill.'

'I will write again directly.'

'The doctor says you must leave it two or three days. At least. Preferably a week. And even then you must travel by easy stages.'

A silence fell, oddly restful. Savill's mind began to drift. With an effort he dragged it back to the present.

'How is Charles?' he said.

Fournier set down his cup. 'Ah, yes. Miss Horton is visiting him again this afternoon.'

168

'Miss Horton? But what has she to do with Charles?'

'A good question, sir. She is evidently a woman of some determination. One might almost say that she makes her own reasons.'

'What do they do?'

'She reads to him, I'm told. And tries to play games, as far as that is possible. Once they went out for a drive in Mrs West's carriage. I cannot see the harm in it. She is a member of the gentler sex and partakes of its virtues.'

'No doubt, sir.' Savill hesitated. 'But . . . does the Vicar permit her to call at Charnwood?'

'Mrs West tells me that he considers it in the nature of visiting the sick, a duty she practises in the village twice a week in the normal run of things. She has no intercourse with anyone here except Charles and Mrs Cox. Looked at in that light, her calling at Charnwood does not imply that Mr Horton approves of the house's inhabitants. It is a matter of Christian charity, and therefore entirely respectable.'

'That alters the case entirely, sir,' Savill said, his head drooping on the pillow. 'Let us be respectable above all.'

Savill thought about the key in the wrong waistcoat pocket.

By Sunday, he was well enough to leave his bed for a few hours. He sat in an armchair by the window, covered with a blanket, and stared over the untidy garden to the hills beyond. The woods were a darker green and above them was a heavy grey sky. Once he saw the foreshortened figure of Charles hurrying across the grass in the direction of the Garden of Neptune.

The key fitted Savill's portmanteau, at the bottom of which was the portfolio that held his warrant and other papers, together with the heavy canvas roll that still contained almost fifty guineas in gold.

If Savill was right about the key having been moved, then his possessions had been searched even before he took to his bed. Moreover, he had been lying here for days in a condition that could scarcely have been more vulnerable. He had been entirely in the power of his hosts and at their mercy. The Count in particular had no reason to love him. They could have searched his belongings a hundred times without his knowing anything about it.

He called for pen and ink and wrote a letter addressed to Frederick Brown, to await collection at the White Horse Cellar in Piccadilly. He wrote that illness had kept him in the country but he hoped to be well enough to leave in a day or two.

Yet, Savill thought as he sealed the letter, he had survived the infection. If their motives were sinister, surely Gohlis could have ensured that the infection became fatal, as so many did? It followed that either his hosts were to be trusted, despite appearances, despite the fact that the Count was determined to keep Charles; or they had discovered the powers Savill held from the Westminster magistrate and had inferred from these that he was a man of greater significance than in fact he was.

The spy for a police magistrate? The secret agent of the Black Letter Office?

His head swam. When it cleared again, he realized his logic was not impeccable. Perhaps his hosts had merely wanted to immobilize him for a while for a purpose he did not understand. His attempts to guess what this might be made his head swim again, and in a moment he fell into a fitful sleep.

By Monday, the pain had subsided. Savill was still weak; but he was well enough for Joseph to shave and dress him, and for him to spend much of the day in the armchair.

In the afternoon, Fournier came to see him, bringing the news that he and Charles were to pass a few hours at Norbury Park on Wednesday, and that Mrs West had promised to send her carriage for them.

'Mrs West has a desire to improve her acquaintance with

him. He is become quite a lion in this village of ours. I understand that Miss Horton will be there as well, so he will not be dull. And she writes that, if you were well enough, it would give her much pleasure if you were to join us. Her carriage is most comfortable, and when you were there you might have a sofa to yourself. Dr Gohlis says the excursion would raise your spirits. I have promised that we shall not allow you to overexert yourself.'

'But I would take another's place in the carriage, surely?'

'Not at all, sir. Monsieur de Quillon and Dr Gohlis are detained by their work. Only Charles and I will be going.'

As Fournier was leaving, Savill asked to see Charles. Twenty minutes later, Joseph brought the boy up to Savill's bedchamber. He sidled into the room and made his bow. Savill told him to sit opposite him.

There was a forlorn quality about him. He sat very still. Only his eyes were restless: his gaze darted over the room, out of the window, towards Savill, though he did not look up at Savill's face.

Someone, probably Mrs Cox, had supervised his toilette. His black clothes were threadbare but perfectly clean, as were his face and hands. His hair had been brushed back and tied with a ribbon. But his wrists poked from the cuffs of his coat and shirt, and his hair needed cutting.

'I hear Miss Horton has been reading to you,' Savill said. 'That must be pleasant.'

Charles showed no sign of having heard him.

'Your sister Lizzie is fond of reading too. Perhaps she will read to you as well, if you wish it.' The lack of response had an oddly wearying effect but Savill persevered. 'I shall tell you about where we shall live when I take you away from here.'

At last there was a flicker in the eyes, a sudden intake of breath.

'I shall take you back to London. Your sister is your nearest relation, and so you will live with us, at least for a while. My

171

own sister, who is a widow, keeps house for us. Your mother's uncle will want to see you too, but he lives elsewhere.'

Charles's eyes flicked towards Savill's face for an instant.

'I live in Nightingale Lane, which is on the northern edge of London, near some grand houses they have built in a place called Bedford Square. Nightingale Lane sounds rustic, does it not? Perhaps it was once, but the town has grown up around it. There are four small houses in the lane and they all have gardens and old trees, where birds nest.' Savill paused, suddenly homesick. 'Sometimes it isn't like living in the town at all. I have a walnut tree so at this time of year we eat a vast deal of walnuts.'

Charles stared at him.

'I have heard a nightingale singing in the garden,' Savill said. 'So the name is still apt. I was with Lizzie, your sister, and she was transported by it. Myself, I think the nightingale's song is overrated. Lizzie says I am too plain and prosaic.' He smiled at Charles and listened to himself babbling on like a lunatic. 'There is an alehouse in the little road beyond the lane, and their garden backs on to mine. The establishment is called the Royal Oak, which sounds rural as well. Sometimes we hear the coachmen and hackney drivers singing there, and to my mind their songs are more agreeable than the nightingale's, at least at the start of the evening. Besides, their songs are much better than the noises of the builders and the passing traffic that we hear in the day.'

Savill ran out of things to say. The boy's silence was like a wall. Savill's words bounced off it and fell to the ground.

'Pray pass me that little case on the table by the bed,' he said.

At first, Charles gave no sign that he had heard. Then he turned and looked towards the bed. Like a sleepwalker he moved across the chamber, picked up the miniature and brought it to Savill. He dropped it on the outstretched palm of Savill's hand, taking great care that their two hands should not touch.

Savill opened the case. 'This is your sister,' he said, angling the portrait towards Charles. 'The likeness was taken when she was younger than you are now. You may hold it if you wish, and look at her more closely.'

Charles stared at the miniature. Slowly he backed away, inch by inch, foot by foot. He swallowed. His eyes were very bright. As Savill watched, still holding out the picture of Lizzie to him, the boy's mouth trembled and he bit his lower lip.

'Yes,' Savill said. 'There is a similarity, is there not? I believe your mama must have looked much the same when she was a girl.'

# Chapter Twenty-Eight

The following day, Tuesday, it is raining. Miss Horton comes in the morning.

'I'm rejoiced that Mr Savill is so much better,' she says to Charles as she removes her bonnet. 'But saddened too – I suppose it must mean that you will soon be leaving?'

He watches her nimble fingers. She has bitten one of the nails to the quick.

'I shall miss our times together,' she goes on. 'Shall we read some more?'

Robinson Crusoe is progressing most satisfactorily. With the help of the items he has salvaged from the ship, he does his best to construct a life for himself on the island. First, to protect himself from possible savages, he makes a fortress where he stores his goods.

Charles cannot help thinking of his own castle in the woods. He and Crusoe are similar, for each of them has been imprisoned by solitude, Crusoe by being shipwrecked on a desert island and Charles by the loss of his voice. God has locked them into themselves and thrown away the keys.

Crusoe finds wild goats, which he kills and eats, which is just what Charles would like to do, though he is uncertain about how one would kill, cut up and cook a goat in the middle of a wood where it is nearly always raining.

The likeness between the two of them increases when Crusoe erects a wooden cross, into which he cuts a notch to mark every passing day of his captivity. Charles imagines the castaway staring at the notches and counting them, first from left to right and then top to bottom, and later in reverse, to make sure the total is the same in both directions. In that way, he contrives to count time itself, despite the fact this is an invisible thing.

The excitement becomes unbearable when Mr Crusoe discovers the imprint of a naked foot in the sand. It implies, of course, that he is not alone, locked in his solitude. Another human being is on the island.

At this very moment, when the thoughts are bubbling through Charles's mind at a furious rate, Miss Horton closes the book. She looks at Charles.

'We shall read some more later,' she says.

How can she be so sure, Charles wonders? So many things might prevent her from continuing.

For once Charles wishes desperately that he could speak, that he could express his enthusiasm to hear more of the story. Instead he looks at Miss Horton and hopes that his face will say it all.

If it does, she appears not to notice. She is absorbed in arranging her shawl around her shoulders, standing on tiptoe to see part of her reflection in the mirror that hangs above Mrs Cox's table.

'Will you walk with me? It is a shame to frowst indoors.'

Charles, still sitting at the table, touches the book's cover.

Miss Horton glances down at him. 'Not now, Charles. Another day. You will need your hat. Where did Mrs Cox put it?'

His hat is hanging on the back of the door. He glances in its direction. She's still looking at him expectantly. He lifts his hand from the book and points at the hat.

'Don't point, my dear,' Miss Horton says. 'It's rude.'

He obeys. Miss Horton bids farewell to Mrs Cox and then the two of them walk into the garden.

It is only then that Charles realizes what has happened. The knowledge brings with it a lurching sense of fear that makes his stomach feel as if it has lost its moorings and is sinking rapidly like Mr Crusoe's wreck.

He has had the nearest approach to a conversation that he has had since that hot August night in Paris when blood rained from the ceiling and the world came to an end.


They stroll to the Garden of Neptune. Charles tries to count the length of the paths but it is difficult with Miss Horton beside him.

The years drop away from her in the garden. She steps on to the parapet around the pool and walks around it with exaggerated care, as if she were on a tightrope high above a crowd.

She returns to where Charles is standing, having walked entirely around Neptune. She extends her hand to him.

'Come,' she says. 'We shall do this together.'

He will not take her hand but he steps on to the low parapet. She sets off again, not looking behind her. This time she executes a series of bows and curtseys to Neptune. Charles follows, as does his blurred and shifting reflection in the water.

Miss Horton begins to sing, clapping time to the tune of a jig.

Round and round they go. It is the strangest dance in the world, Charles thinks, glad there is no one to see it but himself. But a dance is a dance and a tune is a tune.

His body responds without asking permission. He steps in time with Miss Horton, and his limbs sway from side to side, and a bubble of laughter threatens to erupt from him if he does not exercise the greatest caution.

Charles glances up at Neptune. For an instant, it seems as if the god is smiling down at them.

When the dance is over, they walk to the gate at the far end of the garden. Both of them are breathless.

Miss Horton presses her hand to her side. 'Oh, I have a stitch. I must rest a moment.'

She stops at the gate. She smiles at Charles, showing her very white teeth. The smile vanishes almost at once.

'Who's that?' she says. 'Over there, talking to George White.'

Charles follows the direction of her gaze. The grass beyond the gate is strewn with dead leaves. The path leads his eyes up to the stile into the woods. The red-headed boy is standing there, talking to a man on the other side of the stile. The man wears a blue coat and a dark, broad-brimmed hat. He is standing among the trees. His face is in shadow.

'George!' calls Miss Horton.

The gardener's boy looks up. Even at this distance he looks guilty.

'Come here. Who are you talking to?'

But there is no longer anyone there.

# Chapter Twenty-Nine

As they entered the village, the temperature dropped and Charles shivered. The day was fine but the single street was set too low in the valley to catch much sun for most of the year.

Fournier rapped on the roof of the carriage with the head of his stick. The coachman pulled up.

'No, my dear sir,' Fournier said to Savill. 'I insist – you must not move. I shall enquire for you.'

The footman let down the steps. Fournier clambered awkwardly out and limped towards the alehouse, picking his way among the puddles.

No one was in sight. A dog sidled out of an alley, its belly close to the ground. Snarling, it circled Fournier, barking furiously, and then scurried forward to nip at his ankles. Fournier brought down his stick on the animal's back. There was a dull crack like a snapping twig on a wet day. The dog collapsed, half in and half out of a puddle.

The door opened, and Mr Roach rushed into the yard. His coat was off and his face was lathered for the barber.

The dog lay twitching and whimpering. Charles stared at the animal, shifting along the seat so that he had a better view of it. Savill watched Fournier talking to the landlord without being able to hear what was said. A group of boys gathered, their attention ranging from the carriage to the dog, from Fournier to Roach. Mrs West's footman surveyed the scene with an absence of curiosity that was almost insulting.

At length, Fournier returned, seating himself beside Charles. The carriage moved on.

'Bad news, I'm afraid,' he said. 'It appears that your original chaise has gone. A man came down from Bath and managed to contrive a repair, enough to take it away. And there's worse – the man told Roach that his master was outraged about the wasted journey last week and declines to serve you any further. He will recover his costs from your deposit, his man said, and you will have to apply to him for any balance due to you. What can one do with such people?'

They drove in silence through the village. At the forge, a man was waiting for his horse to be shoed. He spat on the ground and turned his back on them.

Fournier turned to Savill. 'You see? They have no love for us here.'

'Even the dogs.'

'I cannot abide curs.' Fournier paused, smiling, perhaps aware that he had spoken with unusual warmth. 'Whether they come on two legs or four. But I should not take much credit for dealing with this one. A lead-weighted stick will do a good deal of damage wherever it falls.'

'You came prepared.'

'I always come prepared.'

They stared out of their windows for a few moments as the carriage jolted along the rutted street. Then Fournier turned back to Savill.

'Did you hear about the stranger?' he said.

'No. Where?'

'In the woods beyond the Garden of Neptune. Yesterday afternoon. Miss Horton and Charles saw him in the distance, talking to the gardener's boy, Mrs White's grandson. She questioned the boy afterwards, and so did Jevons. It appears that it was a traveller who had lost his way. He asked what the village was, and where the principal houses of the place were. A gentleman, the boy says, though I doubt he's a fine judge of the matter.'

'What was he doing here?' Savill asked.

'I don't know. It was curious, though – the man must have seen Miss Horton and Charles, but he went away at once. Perhaps he was reluctant to approach a young lady without an introduction. But such niceties are not usual in such a retired and rustic spot as this.'

'I dare say there is a perfectly innocent explanation. Perhaps it was the obvious one: that a stranger had lost his way, and the gardener's boy put him right.'

Fournier lowered his voice, though there was no one to hear except Charles. 'I would have thought it most unusual for a stranger to stumble on Charnwood. I don't suppose you are expecting a visitor?'

'No,' Savill said. 'Are you?'

Once they were clear of the village, the coachman turned into a lane to the left of the road to Bath. The lane was part of the Norbury Park estate, and its surface was almost as good as a post road's. They picked up speed and were soon whirling along, with the trees and hedges flickering past on either side.

Fournier leaned forward. 'If you look to your right, over the hedge, you will see the field where your chaise had such a smash.'

'I had not realized it was so close,' Savill said.

'Everything seems nearer when one knows the way. Don't you find that?'

The horses slowed as the lane began to run uphill along a park paling. Within a hundred yards they came to a lodge gate and turned into a drive lined with saplings.

'The lime avenue will be a fine sight in fifty years when we are all dead and gone,' Fournier said. 'I find it hard to understand

180

the English mania for planting trees. There is no present benefit, only a deal of expense.'

'It is something for future generations to enjoy.'

'But in this case there are none. Mrs West has not been blessed with children. I believe the estate will pass on her death to a nephew of her late husband, a man she has never even met.'

The drive wound its way through open parkland, newly laid out in the modern style. Here and there, an old tree had been permitted to remain. The drive crossed a small lake by a handsome stone bridge. At the end of the water was a grotto of rustic stone with a plantation of young trees behind it.

'It will be charming,' Fournier predicted. 'Modest, I grant you, but everything as it should be in your natural English style. Mrs West has considerable taste in these matters.'

The house itself came into sight, a gentleman's residence built of stone and flanked by small pavilions.

Fournier gestured towards it. 'After that dreadful village – not to mention dreary Charnwood and the domain of mud and weeds that surrounds it: why, this looks like paradise, does it not? Not a large paradise, perhaps, or a very grand one, but paradise nonetheless.'

Savill glanced at him, catching what for once might have been a hint of sincerity in the Frenchman's voice. 'These things are relative, I suppose, sir. Even paradise.'

The moment dissolved. 'How delightful,' Fournier said, laughing. 'Added to your other virtues, sir, you have a turn for philosophy.'

The carriage drew up outside the house. The footman jumped down and lowered the steps. The three passengers descended from the carriage and looked about them, Charles standing apart from the others.

The front door opened, and there was Miss Horton smiling at them.

'Look!' cried Fournier, bowing to her. 'We were talking of paradise. And here is an angel!'

'You are talking nonsense again, sir. You are making fun of me, and I will not allow it.'

'My dear Miss Harriet, nothing could be further from the truth. Our discourse had turned to theology, and suddenly you appeared most opportunely, as if heaven-sent to exemplify a point I was making. But pray put a shawl around your shoulders – this autumn weather often causes chills.'

'If you come inside, sir,' she said, 'I shall close the door directly and retain my health a little longer.' She touched Charles's shoulder and smiled at him before turning to Savill. 'How do you do, sir, and are you quite recovered?'

The four of them mounted the shallow flight of steps and entered the house. Another footman moved across the hall to take their coats.

'Mrs West and I are in the morning room. She saw you from the window and sent me to bring you in at once. I have been wearying her with my conversation all morning and she is in great need of diversion.'

Mrs West welcomed them with enthusiasm, especially, Savill thought, Monsieur Fournier. The footman brought wine and biscuits. Miss Horton beckoned Charles to sit beside her on the sofa, where he sat upright, staring into space.

'Now you are better, sir,' Mrs West said to Savill, 'no doubt you will soon be leaving us.'

'That may be easier said than done,' he replied.

'The hired chaise is the difficulty, madam,' Fournier said. 'Its owner has lost patience and declines to serve Mr Savill any further.'

'Charles and I must reach Bath by some means or other,' Savill said. 'If necessary we shall travel in Mr Roach's cart.'

'Dear me,' Mrs West said. 'That would never do. Poor Mr West's phaeton is still in the stables. You shall have that. And the horses to go with it, of course – they are eating their heads off, and the exercise will do them good.'

'But, madam, I cannot possibly—'

'It is quite settled, sir. My groom shall drive you, and I shall give him a list of errands as long as my arm.'

Savill smiled at her. 'You're very kind, ma'am.'

'When do you wish to leave?'

'Perhaps the day after tomorrow, if that would be convenient for you.'

'It's all the same to me.' Her voice hardened. 'But you must not infer that I approve of your taking the boy away.'

'Pardon me, ma'am,' Miss Horton said, 'but I think Mr Savill is in the right of it. Charles should be with his English family.' She turned to Fournier. 'Of course, my opinion is immaterial.'

He bowed. 'On the contrary. You must know him as well as any of us does by now.'

Beside her, Charles stared at nothing.

Later, Mrs West suggested that Miss Horton should show Savill and Charles the pictures in the dining room. 'Particularly Mr Zoffany's portrait of Mr West with his mother, my dear. It is generally reckoned to be very like. The detail is exceptionally fine. It repays careful inspection.'

It was a transparent excuse for Mrs West to have a tête-à-tête with Monsieur Fournier. Miss Horton led Savill and Charles into the dining room, where they examined a portrait showing a very old lady with a curious resemblance to the present Mrs West, attended by an anxious-looking middle-aged man with a receding chin.

'Poor Mr West,' Miss Horton said.

'Were you acquainted with him?' Savill asked.

'Oh yes. He would often seek refuge at the Vicarage when he desired masculine company.' She swallowed. 'He was very kind to us when John died. My brother John.'

'I'm sorry. Is the loss a recent one?'

'Three years ago. John was in the Navy, you see, and his ship was ordered to the West India station. Yellow Fever. My father has never been quite the same.'

Miss Horton fell silent. She was looking at Charles, who was standing at the far end of the room with his back to them, apparently rapt in contemplation of a portrait of Mrs West attired as Minerva, the goddess of wisdom.

After a moment, Savill said, 'It was kind of you to say what you did to Mrs West.'

'About taking Charles to London?' She glanced at him. 'To Nightingale Lane.'

He remembered her touch of poetic mockery the other day. Perhaps she had intended a form of apology by mentioning the name. He smiled at her. 'What was it? Something about "a green and grassy shrine, With myrtle bower'd?"'

'"And jessamine", sir.' She gave him an answering smile. 'We must not forget that. But to return to Charles, if I were being selfish, I would keep him in Norbury. We are so dull here. And I like to be useful. I think he is beginning to show signs of improvement. I am reading *Robinson Crusoe* to him and he is sometimes on the edge of his seat with excitement. Quite literally. If I may be so bold to advise you, sir, you must keep talking to him, trying to draw him into books or games. Otherwise he will retreat into his silence.'

'Thank you. I shall do what I can. And so will my daughter and my sister.'

'I had not realized you had a daughter. How old is she?'

'Lizzie is nineteen. She has her head full of foolish notions, like all girls of her age.'

'Has she a beau yet?'

'Not that I'm aware of. Tell me, ma'am, do you ever come to London?'

'Oh yes,' she said. 'Sometimes Mrs West is so kind as to invite me. She has taken apartments in Green Street. We are to go up to town in a week or two, I believe, before the weather worsens.'

'Perhaps you would permit me to call on you? If Mrs West would not object. I should bring Charles, of course, so you might renew your acquaintance with him and see how he does.'

184

She coloured like a girl at a compliment. 'Yes,' she said. 'By all means. I know I can answer for Mrs West too. And bring Miss Elizabeth as well, if you wish. I should like that.'

A movement caught Savill's attention. Charles was watching them intently. His face was pale, with bluish bruises under the eyes. He opened his mouth and drew breath as if about to say something. Then he turned back to Mrs West as Minerva.

# Chapter Thirty

Monsieur de Quillon was not alone, which disconcerted Savill – Fournier was with him, standing by the window and looking out at the garden at the dark smudge of woodland higher up the valley.

'Well, sir?' the Count said, without the usual courteous preamble. 'What is it now?'

'I wished you to know of my plans as soon as possible.' Savill was equally brusque; he knew by the Count's tone that Fournier had already told him the news. 'Mrs West has offered me the loan of her phaeton. I intend to leave with Charles on Friday.'

The Count threw himself into a chair, which creaked under his weight and skidded an inch on the floorboard. 'You cannot snatch my son away from me.'

'First, sir, we cannot be sure he is your son. In the second place, the law has placed him in my care as a child of my late wife: and as far as the law is concerned, he is my son, not yours. Thirdly, if necessary I shall obtain an order from Mr Horton. I warn you, my lord, if you put obstacles in my way, you will find yourself in court.'

The Count's face was even redder than usual. 'I will not be lectured like that in my own house. I warn you, sir, I—'

Fournier laid a hand on his arm. 'My friend, calm yourself.'

'The boy is my son,' the Count said. 'My *son*. He stays with me.'

'I'm afraid that is not possible.'

'What? You would deny the ties of natural affection? Only a monster would—'

'Forgive me,' Savill snapped, 'but we cannot be sure that such a tie even exists.'

'Nonsense. You have only to look at Charles to see the resemblance. Besides, a father knows.' The Count pounded his chest. 'He knows here.'

'All we can be sure of is that the boy is his mother's son and that the law requires him to be placed under my guardianship. I know you have received a letter from my attorney explaining why you must release the boy into my custody. If you refuse to comply, I am in a position to enforce my right to him. I have a magistrate's order here. I also have a letter that obliges Mr Horton to afford me any assistance I require on the authority of His Majesty's Government. And if you compel me to use it, my lord, the matter will inevitably become public knowledge.'

Savill paused to allow the implications to sink in. The émigrés at Charnwood were unpopular enough, here and in London. It would do none of them any good if it became known that the Count de Quillon was flouting the law by refusing to release an English boy into the care of his English family.

The Count stared fixedly at the fire, breathing rapidly and heavily. He looked like a sulky bear that might at any moment erupt into violence, albeit a bear that wore a sombrely magnificent dark brown coat.

'I need time to consider,' he said at last, not looking at Savill. 'Time to consult my advisers.' He waved towards the door as if indicating the approximate whereabouts of a flock of secretaries, lawyers, equerries and aides-de-camp.

'I myself am pressed for time,' Savill said. 'We leave on Friday morning. And may I remind you that I shall require the papers relating to my wife's death?'

'What papers?' demanded the Count.

'You know very well, my lord. The certificate of death. The notary's statement.'

'I shall write to Mrs West,' the Count said, changing his line of attack. 'I shall forbid the foolish woman to help you.'

Fournier said nothing. Nor did Savill. The threat fell into the silence. The Count's words vanished like a handful of stones dropped in a pond.

The Count shook himself like a wet dog emerging from water. 'Well, sir. You have had your say.' His voice was low and quiet, almost gentle. 'But I tell you this: Charles is mine, and one way or another I shall keep him.'

There was no going back now that Savill had set his will so openly against the Count's. The conventions of hospitality, of host and guest, had broken down.

When he left the library, Savill stood in the hall for a moment, listening to the rise and fall of voices on the other side of the door – the Count's growling bass and Fournier's higher-pitched, nimbler chatter.

No one else was about. Savill rang for Joseph and desired him to ask the housekeeper to wait on him in the drawing room. Joseph did not trouble to conceal his surprise at the request.

Mrs Cox arrived moments later, keys jingling and skirts rustling.

'Madam,' Savill said without preamble, 'I am obliged to leave Charnwood on Friday, at about nine o'clock. Master Charles will accompany me. Mrs West's phaeton will collect us.'

Her tongue appeared between her lips. 'His Lordship hasn't mentioned it, sir. Or Monsieur Fournier.'

'I am just come from them. I would like you to ensure

that Master Charles is ready to go. He will not be returning here.'

Her face was sulky now. 'Very well, sir. If His Lordship says—'

'Does he have many possessions? If necessary, perhaps you would arrange for them to be sent on.'

'Master Charles doesn't have much more than the clothes he stands up in. Left them all behind in France, I dare say. Or had them stolen, more likely.'

'Charles,' Savill said. 'Do you understand? We shall leave here on Friday, you and I.'

The boy lowered the spoon to the bowl. He did not look at what he was doing. The spoon overbalanced and spilled its load of bread and milk on Mrs Cox's table.

'You heard what Mrs West said, no doubt. We shall drive to Bath in her phaeton. It will be quite an adventure.'

Charles stared at him. He licked the white line from his upper lip. It occurred to Savill that perhaps the boy did not want any more adventures.

'If all goes well,' he went on, 'we shall reach Bath in a few hours, though it will depend on the state of the roads. We shall go to an inn and I shall hire a chaise to take us to London after we have dined.'

The boy lowered his eyes. Savill came closer, drew out a chair and sat down beside him. He took Charles's hand, which lay limp and unresponsive in his own.

'I know this is hard,' he said gently. 'And you cannot want to venture among strangers. But I promise you this: once this is over, once we reach London, your life will be more settled. You will be with your own family.'

As he heard himself saying this, Savill wondered if he was misleading the boy, lying to him even. He did not know what would happen to Charles in London, whether in the end he would go to his uncle Rampton or stay with Savill.

But would Rampton want a mute boy as his heir? What would Lizzie do with a silent half-brother?

Beneath this was another, darker question: was the muteness merely a symptom of some deeper and more dangerous disorder that unfitted Charles for life in a private family?

'I will make sure you are quite happy and comfortable,' Savill said, knowing it was a promise no man could make.

Charles slowly turned his head away and stared at the wall.

That evening, Joseph brought Savill a packet of papers tied with a blue ribbon and sealed with the Count's seal. It contained the papers that recorded Augusta's death and burial, together with the statement from the notary. Nothing else was enclosed. Savill examined them carefully. The papers seemed entirely in order.

Now, at last, he told himself, Augusta is dead and here is the proof in my hand.

He knew he should feel happy. The day after tomorrow he would travel home, a free man in the eyes of himself and the world. He would see Lizzie again and introduce her silent brother to her.

But happiness proved fugitive. His spirits were depressed. He had a great desire to drink until he had driven away the memories and arrived at peaceful oblivion. Moreover, he could not quite believe that the Count would let them leave Charnwood. There was more going on in this house than Savill understood.

Supper that evening was an awkward occasion despite Fournier's attempts to lighten the tone. If the Count had been a small boy and not a former minister of state and peer of France, Savill would have said he was sulking.

Afterwards, the Count retired at once. Dr Gohlis, who had been sitting apart from the others and eating with silent efficiency, moved closer to Fournier and Savill.

'Your departure will leave quite a vacancy at our table,'

Fournier said, turning to Savill. 'Have I phrased that idiomatically? No matter – the sense is clear.'

'You have been kindness itself,' Savill said stiffly. 'And the good doctor here, who has dealt with my wretched tooth. I wish I were leaving on a happier note.'

Fournier took up an apple and began to peel it. A coil of skin slipped from the knife and fell to the plate beneath.

'We all do,' he said. 'And permit me to express the hope that our paths will cross again, perhaps in London. I have enjoyed our conversations so much.'

'I fear His Lordship would not say the same.'

'Come, let us not quarrel about what cannot be mended.' Fournier cut a slice of apple. 'I am afraid that the Count is not a man to give up his son without a struggle.'

'A boy he *believes* to be his son.'

'Faith is always stronger than reason, as any bishop will tell you. I was once a bishop myself, of course, so I speak with confidence on the matter.' Fournier smiled, and for an instant malice flickered over his smooth, agreeable face. 'But in this case, sir, it is not only the Count who is unwilling to compromise. Is it?'

# Chapter Thirty-One

'Listen,' Charles whispers. 'Can you hear me?'

Louis is still near the window. The day has only just begun. In the pale grey light, Charles can see only part of him, from the waist down. This is because he, Charles, is standing on the manger in the stable below. He has raised the trapdoor less than a foot above the floor of Dr Gohlis's laboratory. His view of Louis is limited by the legs and the top of the table.

'It's tomorrow,' Charles says. 'He's taking me to London tomorrow.'

'You won't leave me behind?' Louis says. 'Please don't.'

'Of course I won't. Trust me.'

'Oh, Charles – thank God you are my friend.'

'I'll come for you very early in the morning, before anyone is about. But I must get the back door key tonight.'

'You think of everything,' Louis says. 'Where would I be without you?'

It is still early in the morning on this, Charles's last day at Charnwood.

His preparations are already well advanced. Yesterday, he took more scraps from the pig bucket to the castle in the woods. A few days earlier, he stole a tinderbox and a broken knife from the scullery.

Today, when he sets off towards the Garden of Neptune and the woods beyond, he is carrying a bundle in his arms. There are two moth-eaten travelling cloaks, relics of previous tenants, which he discovered in a closet in the side hall. The nights are growing colder and they will need the warmth. Inside them, wrapped in an old newspaper, is a large slice of veal-and-ham pie that Charles found in the larder. His mouth waters at the very thought of it.

As he reaches the trees, a momentary doubt touches him. He clambers over the stile and pauses, peering into the gloom ahead. The ground is sodden with dew and yesterday's rain. It is colder and greyer than in the garden. He screws up his courage and plods on, reminding himself that it will be worth it in the end, when he and Louis are living together, wild boys in the woods, talking to each other with silent words.

Charles reaches the castle, the mound among the trees that is almost entirely surrounded by the stream. This will be their desert island, he reminds himself, and when they are living here he will tell Louis the story of Robinson Crusoe.

He drapes the cloaks over a branch. He adds the veal-and-ham pie to the items concealed in the hollow in the yew tree which has become his cupboard. As a reward, he allows himself to break off a fragment of pastry. It dissolves in a moment, adding to his hunger rather than diminishing it.

Everything is orderly, Charles thinks, everything is planned, everything is known. Mr Crusoe would approve.

He makes his way back to Charnwood. As he is running down the path from the woods to the Garden of Neptune, he hears the sound of hooves. He stops, resting his hand on the gate into the garden.

His eyes drift over the trees to the hills beyond the wood, which at this time of day are grey smudges against the paler

193

grey of the sky. From here one can see a stretch of the track that crosses into the next valley. A rider is approaching. He is too far away for Charles to be able to distinguish anything about him, beyond the fact that he wears a blue coat.

He passes into the garden. The stable clock is striking eight. Charles's breakfast is waiting for him in the housekeeper's room. Mrs Cox isn't there.

She does not like to watch him eating, and nor do the other servants. They treat him as if he was a wild animal, he thinks, dirty and unwanted. They are afraid, perhaps, afraid that the terrible thing locked up inside him might somehow be infectious, that the thing is catching, like measles.

Perhaps it is.

The long day passes. At last it is evening, and Charles is alone in Mrs Cox's room, eating bread and cheese by the light of a single candle. There was also a slice of cold beef rimmed with yellow fat on the plate, but he has put that in the pocket of his breeches for tomorrow.

When he has finished, he eases his chair away from the table. There is a spare key to the back door hidden behind the clock. He is about to dart across the room and take it when he hears footsteps. The door handle rattles. Mrs Cox bustles into the room.

'You've had your supper,' she says in her creaky voice. 'Why are you sitting there like a great lump?'

It is an accusation, not a question.

'You're wanted in the library,' she says. Candle in hand, she comes closer and stares down at him. 'Look at the state of you. Come with me.'

He follows her into the kitchen and then out into the scullery, where the dirty plates are piled high from dinner. The kitchen maid scrubs his face and hands at the sink and wipes his coat with a damp cloth.

When Mrs Cox is satisfied, she herself runs a comb through

his hair, tugging the tines through the tangles so forcefully that he cries out and the tears come again to his eyes.

'He can squeal, ma'am,' the maid says to Mrs Cox. 'I never knew that. Sounds like a piglet, doesn't he?'

Mrs Cox stands back, hands on hips, and stares at him. 'I wish he was a piglet. Pigs are useful.'

Charles feels the eyes of the adults on him. He looks at the fire. The flames are slipping and sliding like tongues through the gaps in the bars of the log basket. The fire is talking fire language.

Monsieur de Quillon is there and Monsieur Fournier. The Count's voice booms and crashes at Mr Savill, who sits by the fire and says little in reply. As the Count talks, his great red face twitches. Cracks and craters appear in the skin.

Sometimes Monsieur Fournier speaks, and his voice is soft and high, almost like a woman's. Dr Gohlis sits on a chair by the door and does not say anything at all.

Charles does not bother to listen to the conversation of the grown-ups. He has heard what they have to say to each other so often before. All it comes down to is this: that Mr Savill wants him, and so does the Count. Charles has no more interest in the outcome of the discussion than the rope has in the outcome of a tug of war.

Instead he watches the shadows that the fire and the candles throw on the walls. He talks in his mind to Louis.

At long last they ring for Mrs Cox. Mr Savill says that Charles must retire, for he will have a long day tomorrow.

The great difficulty is the spare key to the back door. In an hour or two, Mrs Cox will lock the door of her room and retire to bed. The key will be inaccessible until morning. But by then it will be too late.

Charles asks Louis for advice. But Louis only says that Charles must be bold and resolute, which is true but not useful.

195

So he must do it all himself.

In his chamber he undresses down to his shirt and climbs into bed. He waits for half an hour, measured by the chimes of the stable clock. He leaves his bed and tiptoes from his chamber to the head of the back staircase.

He stands and listens to the sounds below, funnelling up from the service wing of the house. Draughts swirl around his ankles.

Downstairs they are preparing for supper. He hears footsteps passing along the passage, a clattering of plates and pans and once, quite distinctly, Joseph swearing at Susan for getting in his way and making him spill the soup.

Charles knows that he must not rush. He goes back to his bedroom and waits. Later, when he returns to his post at the head of the stairs, it is quieter below. He guesses that they are now serving supper. The cook and the kitchen maid will be in the kitchen.

And Mrs Cox?

He slips down the stairs. He goes slowly, testing every step before he puts his weight on it. He cannot risk a candle.

The door at the bottom of the stairs is ajar. The passage beyond is empty. Mrs Cox's voice is raised in anger, upbraiding someone in the kitchen.

Charles emerges into the passage. His bare feet make no sound. They are now so cold he can hardly feel them.

Mrs Cox's door is unlocked. Inside the room, it is almost dark. The only light comes from a dying fire. He crosses to the fireplace and takes the key, which has a head like a three-leafed clover. He slips it through the neck of the shirt and holds it under his left arm.

As he is leaving the room, Mary Ann rushes through the kitchen doorway with a dish in her hands. When she sees Charles, she shrieks, drops it and cowers against the wall. The dish shatters and syllabub spatters the flagstones.

Immediately there are footsteps and voices. The passage fills with servants.

196

Charles remembers a girl from the country who helped Jeanne when he was a very little boy. The girl was strange in the head, Jeanne said, and had to be sent away, though she was quite harmless. He imitates her in one of her strange times.

He ignores everyone. His face blank, both arms clamped against his body, he walks slowly and stiffly towards the door to the stairs. His eyes are wide open and fixed straight ahead.

The servants fall back.

'Will you look at him, ma'am?' Susan says in a hushed voice. 'He's like a ghost.'

'Charles!' Mrs Cox says. 'Master Charles! What do you think you're doing?'

He ignores her. Slowly and deliberately, he climbs the stairs.

'Come here at once, you wicked boy.'

Charles continues to climb. He senses the servants clustering at the foot of the stairs.

'He's bewitched!' Mary Ann shrieks.

'Don't be foolish, girl,' Mrs Cox says. 'Hold your tongue.'

'He's sleepwalking,' Joseph says suddenly. 'You can see it in his face. My brother used to do it.'

Charles hears someone gasp.

'He don't know we're here, ma'am. He's in another place.'

'That's all very well,' says Mrs Cox in a voice that lacks its usual assurance. 'But he's also on the back stairs.'

'Leave him be,' Joseph advises. 'If you wake him now, he could run amok. That's what my granny said.'

Mrs Cox and Joseph follow at a safe distance. The light from Joseph's candle runs ahead, showing Charles the steps before him. He walks slowly along the landing and turns into his own chamber.

He does not close the door. He climbs awkwardly into bed and allows the key to slip away from him, under his body. He draws the tails of his shirt around him. He is so cold his teeth begin to chatter. He clenches them to keep them quiet. He closes his eyes and breathes evenly.

Mrs Cox and Joseph linger in the doorway with the candle.

'He'll sleep now,' Joseph says. 'In the morning he won't remember anything. That's what always happens.'

'Mad,' Mrs Cox says. 'Quite mad. I always thought so. He could murder us in our beds. Thank God he's going in the morning.'

When they have left him alone, Charles hides the key under his pillow. He is obliged to leave his bed again because tonight of all nights it is important that he does the counting and checking with particular care.

The window, Charles knows, is a particularly weak spot in his defences. There is nothing he can do about the ash tree if it starts tapping on the glass again and trying to get in.

*Tip-tap.*

When the job is done, Charles scrambles into bed, curls himself into a ball with his knees up to his chest. He shuts his eyes but that is no use for instead he sees blood-red curtains behind his eyelids.

He summons Louis, and talks to him. He makes Louis say that there will be no blood in their castle in the woods. Louis says this so often that Charles almost believes him.

Gradually the sounds of the house diminish. Charles cannot afford to fall asleep because he might not wake up early enough.

Then, just as his eyelids are growing heavy and his mind is wandering, someone walks along the landing and stops at his door.

The door creaks as it opens. Charles holds his breath and opens his eyes. The light from a candle streams across the floor, dazzling him. Behind the flame is a great shadow.

Slowly the footsteps approach, bringing the shadow with it and the faintest odour of brandy. From the darkness comes a great, gusty sigh.

'Oh, my son,' whispers the Count. 'Oh, my son.'

# Chapter Thirty-Two

Despite his intention to stay awake, Charles falls asleep. The night is crowded with dreams of monsters and blood, of Marie, his old nurse who has lost her comforting smell, and the great house in the Rue du Bac.

Words drift in and out of his mind: *Oh, my son. Oh, my son.*
*Say nothing. Not a word to anyone. Whatever you see. Whatever you hear.*

Other sounds too.

*Tip-tap.*

Then, once again, he's half awake: the branches are scratching on the windowpane, it's raining blood, and the blood falls on him like red rain. The blood is screaming just as it always does.

*Do you understand? Say nothing. Ever.*

Quite suddenly Charles is fully awake. It is dark but there is a hint of grey, a faint glimmering pallor that takes the edge from the night. He feels perfectly refreshed.

He discovers that he has not wet the bed. A good omen.

He dresses in the dark. He puts on all his clothes, including three shirts and three pairs of stockings. The key is heavy in the pocket of his breeches.

Carrying his shoes, he slips out of the room. Memory and touch guide him along the landing and down the back stairs.

The kitchen is a damp cavern. The fire is out. He has never seen the room without people.

It is so dark that Charles knocks his leg against the table as he crosses to the door. He cries out. In a sudden panic – what if the kitchen maid is stirring? – he fumbles for the bolts for nearly half a minute before he finds them. They screech as he pulls them back.

The chill of the outside air makes him gasp. He walks to the stables, which are in complete darkness like the house itself. Fortunately there are no dogs at Charnwood. In the yard, there's no sign of movement from the donkey's shed in the corner. But the old mare hears him when he opens the stable door: she shifts in her stall at the far end of the row.

Charles climbs into the empty manger and pushes up the trapdoor. 'I'm coming,' he calls softly, 'I'm coming.'

Louis says: 'At last.'

Charles wriggles into the laboratory and crawls from beneath the table. Louis is a shadow by the window. Charles hugs him.

Then comes the first great difficulty. Charles lifts Louis. He discovers that an *écorché* figure – or this one, at least – is far heavier than he expected, partly because the base on which it stands is weighted for stability.

He drags Louis towards the table. The base bangs against the leg of a chair. He pauses to take stock. Their escape will take far longer than Charles hoped. They will have to adapt the plan.

He drags aside the table. Holding Louis under the arms, he draws him to the open trap, nudges him, feet first, into the void and lowers him towards the manger.

Louis's weight again takes him by surprise. Charles loses his balance. To save himself, he lets go of Louis, who plunges the last few inches to the manger and almost topples out.

200

The mare whinnies and shifts in her stall. Charles panics. He scrambles into the manger and tries to find out if Louis is damaged.

There is a cracking sound. The manger disintegrates. Louis and Charles fall with a crash to the floor, with Louis on top, his shoulder digging into Charles's face. Wooden slats clatter around and on top of them. Charles cries out. The mare whinnies more loudly.

Charles forces himself to his hands and knees and then to his feet. 'Come on,' he says. 'Come on.'

He wraps his arms around Louis and lifts him a few inches from the ground. Charles staggers across the stable to the door.

'You're so heavy,' he mutters. 'I wish you'd help.'

'It's not my fault I can't,' Louis says.

For a moment they are on the verge of their first quarrel. Charles apologizes. Tears prick against his eyelids.

Weighed down by his burden, he leaves the stable and crosses the yard. The sky is much lighter now. He fancies he sees a wisp of smoke rising from the kitchen chimney. If the kitchen maid is downstairs, the other servants will soon be about, and Charles's particular enemy, the red-headed gardener's boy, will come up the drive from Mrs White's cottage at the gates.

He takes the path to the Garden of Neptune. The world fills with soft grey light, cold as charity (a favourite phrase of Mrs Cox's). The birds have come alive and their conversations fill the air. A cock crows higher up the valley.

Neptune looks sternly at them as they pass. Charles had imagined this encounter, how he would pause a moment and show Louis the sea god and point out the very spot where the red-headed boy nearly drowned him. But time is running out.

At the end of the garden, the boys go up the steps, through the gate and along the path into the wood. The leaves are

201

dripping with dew and the ground is soggy. Within moments, both of them are covered with a chilly sheen of moisture.

Charles discovers that he is hungry. It occurs to him that there is one advantage to the fact that Louis is an *écorché* figure and is not flesh and blood: he will not want any food.

It's the thought of food that makes it possible to move forward, half dragging, half carrying Louis. They are not far from their destination when Charles trips. The impetus of the fall throws both of them into a patch of brambles. A thorn cuts open Charles's cheek. Even Louis looks scratched and muddy.

'How can we go on from the castle tomorrow?' Charles demands. 'You're so heavy.'

Their whole plan is in ruins. They had decided to rest at the castle and, as soon as possible, press on into the depths of the woods, to a place so remote that even hermits and wolves never went there. But how can they go anywhere if Louis is like this?

'Well? How are we going to manage?'

Louis stares straight ahead, his expression unchanging and unyielding.

Something, Charles thinks, has broken. It is not even a proper quarrel. A quarrel needs two people, and Louis says nothing. He can't or won't. When Charles tries to speak to him in his mind, Louis refuses to come to life. He has dwindled to an object, a thing without words.

What is the point of bringing Louis now?

Nevertheless, Charles struggles onwards through the wood with him, with it. He doesn't know what else to do except to follow the plan.

Brambles scourge his face and hands. Branches poke and slap him. Nettles sting his skin. By the time he reaches the castle, the secret place, Charles is exhausted.

The cloaks are still draped over the branch, black with rain and dew. He stands Louis in the green cave by the fallen branch.

Charles sits down on the branch and feels in his pocket for the beef he kept back from his supper. It is gone.

The meat must have fallen from his pocket as they stumbled through the wood, perhaps when they fell into the bramble bush. He looks up at Louis, hoping against hope for help or at least sympathy. But Louis is staring ahead at nothing in particular. His ruined face is wet with rain.

Charles reaches into the hollow in the yew tree. He finds nothing but damp leaves and twigs.

With increasing desperation, he searches the hollow. It is no use. The veal-and-ham pie has gone and so has the stale bread. So has the tinderbox, and so has the knife.

A snake writhes in Charles's belly. He puts his head in his hands and weeps.

At present he does not much mind the prospect of dying. But he minds very much the process that will take him there because it must involve him growing hungrier and hungrier. He wants to scream from lack of food. He has nothing left except hunger.

He knows now that the dream is over, that he and Louis will not live together for ever as wild boys in the woods. Louis is not his friend, not now. He is nothing but an *écorché* figure, nothing but a thing.

Charles picks up Louis and pushes him over the fallen branch, rolling him over and laying him flat behind it. In this abandoned state, Louis loses his last vestige of humanity and becomes what he truly is: a thing of paint and plaster of Paris.

Charles stoops over Louis and spits on him. The spittle slides down the exposed bones of Louis's shoulder. What does it matter? Louis is not a person. He is a wordless thing who has never spoken or even made a sound.

Charles snatches up a fallen branch. He grasps it in both hands and pounds it on the thing that was Louis.

The anger's bitterness has the effect of lessening Charles's hunger but increasing the stomach ache. He gathers up an armful of damp, dead leaves and throws them on top of the figure.

He stumbles down the slope of the hillock. He does not go back the way he came but blunders towards the stream.

At this point, the water runs clear and cold over a bottom of silt strewn with fragments of rock. It is too wide to leap but it is only a few inches deep.

Jesus, Father Viré had said long ago in that lost life, Jesus walked on the water not because He wanted to, but to show others that He could. To prove beyond doubt that He was different from the foolish ones who doubted Him. To demonstrate His divinity to those of little faith.

Perhaps, Charles thinks, I too am different. Perhaps that is the reason for all this. Perhaps I am divine.

On the face of it, the idea is no more unlikely than the idea that an *écorché* figure speaks and lives.

Charles steps from the muddy ground on to the surface of the water. The surface will not hold his weight. His foot descends to the bed of the stream so quickly that he almost falls forward into the water. He steadies himself.

To make quite sure, he puts his other foot on the water. It sinks to the bottom. He stands in the stream, feeling the current brush his knees. The water is surprisingly cold, almost icy.

So. He is not divine. He cannot work a miracle. That is a fact.

He allows the current to direct him downstream. He walks slowly, enjoying the fierce distraction of the cold on his skin and the silky touch of the water. One step follows another. He is shivering but it does not matter.

The stream winds according to its own incomprehensible whims. He loses all sense of direction. Sometimes the banks are clear on either side. Sometimes branches meet overhead and the water draws him through a green tunnel.

Nothing else exists except the quiet agony of the cold and

the gentle but remorseless thrust of the water. His mind is as numb as his feet. He does not bother to look from side to side. What is the point? He stares at the water. No birds sing. The wood is silent.

A fish darts away from him. It is four or five inches long, as swift and unpredictable as quicksilver. Charles realizes with a sense of wonder that it is probably terrified of him, an alien giant invading the fish's world. As he marches slowly on, he stares at the place where he last saw it, willing it to reappear.

Perhaps the fish lives in a hole in the bank, which is very close. Perhaps it will come out again and Charles, if he is very quick, can snatch it from the water and take it back to the castle. Perhaps by then he will be hungry enough to eat it raw for breakfast.

Charles lets his eyes drift along the side of the stream, searching for the fish's home. He does not find the fish. But he does find the reason why no birds sing.

Standing on the bank is a swarthy-complexioned man in a long, blue travelling coat.

# Chapter Thirty-Three

'Where is Charles?' the Count bellowed.

Like his physique and his position in the old pre-Revolutionary world of France, Monsieur de Quillon's emotions were on the grand scale, designed for a larger stage than Charnwood afforded. He had come downstairs far earlier than usual in order, he said, to take his leave of Charles before the boy was torn from his bosom.

'Where is my son? Bring him to me.'

Mrs Cox backed away. 'My lord, I'm sure I—'

'One moment.' Fournier's voice was sharper and louder than usual. He put down his cup and wiped his lips with a napkin. 'Have you looked for him, Mrs Cox?'

'He's not in the house, sir, we're sure of that. And he's not in the garden, either.'

'When did he go?' Savill said. His mind was still clouded with wisps of fog, the dangerous legacy of Dr Gohlis's sleeping draught.

'I don't know, sir. I thought Martha had roused him, you see, and she thought Joseph was—'

'Did he take anything?'

'Only the clothes he stood in. Not that he's got much else.' She hesitated, biting her lip. 'He maybe took a bit of yesterday's pie. Unless the cat had it.'

The Count turned to Savill. 'Is this some devilish plot of yours?'

'No, my lord. What possible purpose would it serve?'

'At least Charles won't starve if he has some food,' Fournier said. 'He'll be back in a moment or two, you may depend on it. Perhaps he's saying goodbye to his favourite haunts.'

'In that case they would have seen him in the garden,' Savill said. 'Unless he's broken bounds.'

Fournier frowned. 'Does he do that? Break bounds?'

'He's a boy like any other boy, for all he's mute,' Savill said. 'It would not surprise me in the least.'

'We must send out a search party.' Fournier pushed back his chair. 'How very tiresome. He is probably immersed in some game or other.'

'It is hardly the weather for playing outside,' Savill said.

'Boys are hardy creatures. Not that I was myself, but then, I was always an exception.'

The Count stared at Savill. 'Charles would never run away from his father,' he said with slow, cold anger. 'It's because you are trying to take him away from me. I blame you for this.'

The crisis gave the Count a vigour that Savill had never seen in him before. Breathing heavily, he wandered at random about the house and garden, leaning on a cane with a golden head and sometimes poking it into shrubs and bushes. He left Fournier to arrange a more methodical search of the house and grounds, as he left Fournier to do so much.

Almost everyone was pressed into service. They began with the house. Mrs Cox led Fournier and Savill up the back stairs, which Savill had never seen before. Charnwood as a whole was a cheerless place, damp and in poor repair, but the servants' quarters were much worse than the rooms the gentlemen used, with crumbling plaster and discoloured whitewash on the walls. The air smelled musty.

Charles's meanly furnished chamber had clearly been a servant's room in other times. A tree too near to the window stole most of the light. The covers had been thrown off the bed.

While they were searching the house, Dr Gohlis came downstairs; he had slept badly, he said, and had been obliged to dose himself in the early hours of the morning. He seemed as surprised by the news as any of them.

In the stable, Fournier was the first to notice the remains of the manger. 'When did that happen?'

'It was on the wall yesterday afternoon,' Gohlis said. 'I'd take my oath on it, sir.' He turned over some of the debris. 'Riddled with woodworm.'

Savill glanced up. Between two of the joists was the oblong outline of a trapdoor. He touched Fournier's sleeve and pointed.

'You have your key, Doctor?' Fournier asked. 'We shall look in your laboratory now.'

'Of course, sir.' Gohlis searched in the pocket of his breeches. 'But I changed the lock myself. I have the only keys, and I keep them safe.'

Fournier and Savill followed him up the stairs. Gohlis unlocked the door.

'You see?' he said. 'All is as it should be.'

Fournier ignored him. He limped to the table that ran down the centre of the room and lifted one edge of the cloth that covered it. Savill stooped beside him. The upper side of the trapdoor did not quite sit in its frame.

'Marks in the dust,' Fournier said. 'You see? Just there.'

'You think he came in here?' Gohlis said. 'But why?'

'The boy's gone,' Savill said.

'Of course he has,' the doctor's voice rose in pitch. 'That's why we—'

'No. *Your* boy. The *écorché* figure.'

'Two lost boys,' Fournier said. 'Not one.'

*       *       *

208

Mrs West's groom had brought the phaeton when they returned to the house. They questioned him but he had not seen a boy as he came up from the village.

'Not that I would have done, your honours,' he said. 'Not necessarily. Especially if he didn't want to be seen.'

'We need dogs,' Savill said.

'We don't have any,' Fournier said.

The groom coughed. 'Beg pardon, sir. Maybe Parson would lend you Bessie. If the lad's left a scent, she can follow it, if any dog can.'

The Count clicked his fingers. 'Fetch her.'

The Vicar arrived with Bessie within the half-hour. In the excitement of the moment he seemed entirely to have forgotten his disapproval of the gentlemen of Charnwood. The dog had been trained for rough shooting, he said as he clambered down from the phaeton, and the animal had no equal in the entire county for following a scent. She was notably sagacious as well.

'If there's the ghost of a scent,' he said, 'Bessie will follow it for you. She is a canine marvel, sirs – I would not take twenty guineas for her.'

Joseph brought a sheet from Charles's bed. The dog picked up the scent at the kitchen door. Nose to the ground, she towed Mr Horton away, with the rest of the party trailing after them.

Bessie led them to the Garden of Neptune. The Count, panting with exertion, sank down on the parapet around the pool and propped his chin on his stick.

'I'll rest for a moment. Go on without me.'

'He's making for the wood,' Mr Horton said, bouncing up and down from heel to toe in his excitement. 'We'll soon flush him out. I hope so, indeed – I have a christening later this morning.'

Fournier, Gohlis and Savill hurried after the clergyman, who had a surprising turn of speed for such a portly gentleman.

209

The dog took them through the gate at the far end of the garden. She left the path almost immediately, plunging into trees to the right. The wood was long overdue for coppicing. Branches blocked their way; brambles caught at their clothing and tried to trip them; and the dying bracken brushed their legs, soaking their breeches and stockings.

'Are you sure she still has the scent?' Fournier said.

'Don't you worry, sir,' Mr Horton assured him. 'Bessie would follow a scent to hell and back if necessary.'

'I hope she won't take us that far.'

'I speak metaphorically,' the Vicar said, flushing a darker shade of red.

'Who owns the wood?' Savill asked.

'Mrs West, sir. Mr West used it for shooting for a year or two. But it's gone to wrack and ruin since he died.'

They marched on. Here, in this green, damp place, it was difficult to measure time. Savill guessed they had been walking for about fifteen or twenty minutes when the ground began to rise and they heard the sound of a stream growing steadily louder. Bessie led Mr Horton to the top of a small mound encrusted with a tangle of trees and bushes. A beech tree towered over everything.

Bessie was sniffing the ground inside a thicket of yew beside the beech, her tail wagging violently from side to side.

'There!' said the Vicar. 'Another print – and it's fresh.'

'But where's he gone now?' Fournier demanded.

The dog cast about, searching for the scent.

The old yew and the bushes around it made a natural shelter, a green cave, protected by the great branches of the beech. Savill stooped and entered. The rear of the shelter was formed by the beech's massive trunk. One of its branches had fallen. It now lay rotting in the gloom. Beside it was a small footprint. He bent to look more closely at it. The movement brought him closer to the branch, closer to what lay behind it. He swore under his breath.

'What is it, sir?' Fournier was just behind him.

A boy was lying there, wedged behind the fallen branch, his body partly covered with leaves and twigs, the face strangely discoloured and eaten away.

Savill broke out into a cold sweat.

But the boy was too small to be Charles. The face belonged to someone else, long dead, long gone.

'Charles?' Fournier said, with an edge of excitement to his voice.

'No,' Savill said. 'The other one.'

# Chapter Thirty-Four

When Savill called at the Vicarage just before midday, the servant told him that Mr Horton was still in church with the christening party. The man asked if Savill wished him to enquire whether Miss Horton was at home.

In the literal sense of the question, there wasn't much doubt on that score, for someone was fingering scales on the piano in the sitting room, and the sound had been perfectly audible as Savill was walking up the drive.

Even as the servant was speaking, the scales came to a stop. Miss Horton herself appeared in the doorway.

'Good day, sir – I thought I recognized your voice. Are you come to see my father?'

He bowed. 'Yes, madam.'

'We expect him at any moment. Come and wait in the sitting room with me. There's a fire in here.'

Savill followed her into the room. She closed the piano. He began to apologize for the intrusion but she interrupted him.

'Is there any news of Charles, sir?' she said, taking a seat.

'No. I mean to ask your father to pursue enquiries throughout the neighbourhood. In his capacity as a justice, that is.'

'A larger search party, perhaps? Sending to neighbouring villages?'

'Indeed. The odds are that he has simply strayed too far, and cannot find his way home.'

'Or even ask for directions,' she said.

He nodded.

'There is another possibility, I collect,' she went on, colouring slightly. 'Absurd, perhaps, but one hears these things. That Charles was kidnapped – by gypsies or tinkers, I mean. Or . . .'

'Or what, ma'am?'

'Or by someone else,' she said in a rush.

'By whom?'

She bit her lip, which made her look younger, like a girl caught out in a misdemeanour, not a woman of thirty. Rather a fetching girl at that, Savill thought. They both knew that the only other person who had an interest in Charles was the Count de Quillon. But this was not something that needed to be said.

'Anyone,' she said. 'Who knows? Did you hear there was a stranger about the other day? Well, a stranger to me, at least.'

'Where?'

'On the path from the Garden of Neptune – by the stile that leads to the woods. I was in the garden with Charles, you see.'

'When was this?'

'Tuesday afternoon, I think. It was the day before we met at Mrs West's. A man in a blue travelling coat. I couldn't see his face clearly – but it was no one from Norbury. He was talking to the gardener's boy – the one who complained to Papa when the Count thrashed him. He has red hair, and he's old Mrs White's grandson. His name's George.'

'Did you talk to the man?'

Miss Horton shook her head. 'He slipped away. But I asked George, and he said he was a traveller who had lost his way and desired to know the nearest road to Bath. There's a lane over the hills – he must have come from there.'

There were footsteps on the drive.

'You saw him,' Savill said quickly. 'And so he saw Charles?'

213

'Of course – he must have done. I don't know if I believe George, by the way. He's always been a liar. But I couldn't ask him more because Charles ran off.'

The Vicar's voice sounded in the hall. The door handle rattled.

'Charles is scared of George, you know,' said Miss Horton. 'I don't know quite why, but he is.'

Savill's commission lay on the table in the Justice Room. Mr Horton flicked it with his forefinger.

'I thought you were the father of that wretched boy. This puts quite a different complexion on it. What are you? A police spy?'

'No, sir. But – as you see – I am authorized to act as the magistrate's agent or deputy by Mr Ford under the terms of the Police Act. You are familiar with it, no doubt. It has particular reference to preserving the safety of the realm from sedition. The Government believes that the émigrés at Charnwood form a possible threat under the terms of the Act.'

'I am the authority here, sir,' Horton said.

'Of course you are, sir,' Savill said. 'Which is why you should direct the investigation in all things.'

'While you tell me what to do?'

'All I ask is that you permit me to act as an observer, and that you delay informing the world of what has happened until we know what we are dealing with.'

Horton drew out a chair and sat down. He was still carrying his prayer book. He stared at it, frowning, as if wondering how he came to be holding it, and then laid it gently on the table beside the magistrate's warrant.

'Tell me, sir,' he said wearily, 'what is going on? Since you and the French party have come to Charnwood, the village has turned itself upside down. And what has this poor dumb boy to do with it?'

\* \* \*

214

Mr Horton knew the value of theatre. He ordered his groom to ride to Charnwood, with orders to bring George White to the Vicarage immediately.

Wrenched from his natural habitat and transplanted to the awful surroundings of the Justice Room, the boy was already terrified. Mrs West might own most of Norbury but, since her husband's death, Mr Horton united in his plump person the principal powers of both Church and State. The sanctions at his command ranged from earthly imprisonment to eternal damnation.

He hammered the flat of his hand on the table. 'Empty your pockets, boy.'

The freckles on George's face glowed, given unnatural prominence by the pallor of the surrounding skin. One by one he removed the items in his pocket. A half-eaten apple. A penknife with a wooden handle and a broken blade. A length of twine. A twist of tobacco. A short-stemmed clay pipe. When he had finished, he stood motionless, hands by his side, looking at the floor.

'Ha!' the Vicar said. 'Shoes.'

The gardener's boy looked up. Savill saw the muscles twitching below his eyes and around his mouth. He slipped off his shoes. Horton gestured, silently ordering him to shake them out.

One shoe disgorged a length of brass wire, with loops tied in both ends. The other a scrap of folded paper that fell with a clunk on the table.

'A snare, eh? Poaching in the Park covers, no doubt. An offence against God and man.'

The boy stared at him. How old was the lad, Savill wondered? Ten or twelve? Charles's age, give or take a year, but much heavier in build. His skull tapered from a broad chin to a small forehead, almost invisible beneath the ragged fringe of ginger hair.

'Unfold the paper. On the table, where I can see you.'

George's hands were shaking. The paper had been torn from a newspaper. It contained two shilling-pieces.

'Where did you get that money?'

'My granny gave it me, your honour, I swear it.'

'Don't add perjury to your crimes, you wretched youth.' Horton leaned across the table. 'Where?'

'Gentleman gave it me, sir. He was lost. I told Miss Horton, sir, I told her.'

'What was he like, this gentleman of yours?'

'Face like a gypsy's, sir, for all he was a gentleman. A big black hat. He rode over by the back way, from the common. He was looking for the way to Bath.'

'What else?'

'Nothing, sir. That was all. Then Miss Horton came, and he went.'

The Vicar sighed and shook his head. 'You'll have to do better than that, George.' He pointed at the snare and money. 'I'll have to commit you. Perhaps it'll be the Assizes for you, perhaps not. But you'll lose your position in any case.'

George's eyes darted from Mr Horton to Savill and then back again.

'I wonder what Mrs White will have to say. She's not getting any younger, is she? Mrs West might have to put her out of the lodge cottage if she's by herself. I suppose she'll have to go on the parish. You know what that means. The workhouse.'

'Please, your honour.' George shifted his weight from one leg to the other. 'He wanted to know if I'd seen the French boy who can't speak. I said yes, he was here at Charnwood. The man asked if he ever came into the woods.' He hesitated. 'And I said he did, but he wasn't meant to leave the gardens so sometimes it was early, before breakfast.'

'Was that the only time you saw him?'

'No, your honour.' The boy wiped his nose with his sleeve. 'He was there yesterday too. Missed seeing the Frenchy by a whisker – he was in the woods early that day – I saw him coming through the gardens on the way to the house.'

'Did you tell the man we were leaving for London today?' Savill snapped. 'Did you?'

George looked away. 'Yes, sir.' He was trembling now, waiting for a blow or a kick. 'I'm sorry. I ask your pardon, sirs, I didn't know.'

Savill glanced at the clock on the wall. 'Listen to me. Where did Charles go in the woods?'

'He has a little place, sir.' The boy looked at Savill. 'Keeps things there. Food and stuff.'

'I know. There's nothing there now.'

'He must have taken them.'

'Or you did,' Savill said, and watched the terror return to George's face.

Horton chipped away at the story, testing it, trying without success to extract more details. At last he gave up.

'Wait in the kitchen yard.'

'By your leave, sir,' Savill said. 'One more question. George, you say the man rode over. Did you see his horse?'

'Yes, your honour. Not at first – but I followed him and I saw him riding up the lane. Piebald pony, sir. Too small for him.'

'So he couldn't have come far on it?'

'No, sir. But he wouldn't have, would he?'

'Don't be impudent, you scoundrel,' Horton roared. 'Or it will go even worse with you.'

Savill said, 'What do you mean?'

'It was Mr Fenner's pony, sir. So he must have come from there.'

# Chapter Thirty-Five

In the end they went together in single file, the Vicar on his grey gelding and Savill on the worn-out mare from Charnwood. They took the sunken road, hardly more than a path, that climbed up the valley and wound over the hills.

'Can't we go faster?' Savill said.

Mr Horton turned in his saddle. 'You can't go fast here. Not unless you want a broken neck. The going's easier when the lane levels out. Another half-mile and we'll be there.'

At last they emerged on to a windswept heath with long views to a blue horizon to the south-west. They rode side by side now and urged the horses to a trot. Twenty minutes later they came to a made-up road in poor repair. They followed it to an inn. A sign swung from a post at the front but the paint was so decayed it was impossible to make out what was on it. The building was L-shaped, with stables and coach houses enclosing a rectangular yard at the rear. Behind it lay orchards and a paddock with a brown horse grazing at one end and a piebald pony at the other.

'So he was telling the truth,' Savill said.

The Vicar grunted. 'Unusual, with George White. But it does happen.'

They rode under the archway. The yard was cobbled and

strewn with the remains of the summer's weeds. No one was in sight, but smoke trickled from two of the chimneys.

'It's not the place it was,' Horton said. 'Not since they cut the new road lower down.'

The doors of the large, empty coach house were standing open. An elderly ostler hurried out to take their horses.

'Where's Mr Fenner?' Horton asked.

'He don't come downstairs much now, your honour. It's Mrs Fenner you'll want to see.'

A maid showed them to a private parlour at the front of the inn. The room was cold and the hearth was choked with ashes. The maid asked if the gentlemen would take something while they waited, but Horton refused.

They sat at a table in the bay window. Mrs Fenner kept them waiting for several minutes. When she appeared, her perfume came before her.

She paused for a moment in the doorway and surveyed her guests. She was a tall, stout woman, slow-moving in everything apart from her blue-green eyes, which roved rapidly to and fro. Her features were small and regular. When she was young, Savill thought, she had probably been accounted a beauty; but now, as she approached the further shores of middle age, the surrounding face had expanded, marooning her nose, eyes and mouth in a sea of doughy flesh.

'Mr Horton, sir, what a pleasure. Your servant, sir.' She advanced into the room and curtseyed, or rather lowered her entire body a couple of inches in a manner suggesting she had contrived briefly to shorten her legs by means of an invisible mechanism. 'My husband will be distressed to miss you. But poor Fenner hardly stirs from his bed nowadays, sir.'

'I'm sorry to hear that, ma'am. Now—'

'It's sorrow that's brought him low, sir. Look at what this place has become since the turnpike company stole our trade.'

'Madam, I am grieved by your situation, but I have not come to discuss that now.'

219

Anger sparked in her eyes but was instantly suppressed. 'Of course not, sir. You'll be wanting refreshment, no doubt. There's a couple of chickens ready for the oven. And while you wait, perhaps something to keep out the cold?'

'We are not here to dine, ma'am. I am come in my capacity as magistrate.'

Mrs Fenner drew herself up and seemed to swell with emotion. 'You'll find nothing wrong here, sir.'

'There is no need to distress yourself.' Horton's words were conciliatory but his tone was not. 'I merely wish to make some enquiries. But first, give me leave to introduce Mr Savill. A gentleman who has been staying in Norbury.'

She curtseyed again in her special way and ran her finger down her cheek, unconsciously mimicking the line of the scar on Savill's face. 'Your servant, sir.'

Savill bowed. There was more than one way to deal with an interrogation. So, turning to Horton, he said, 'Perhaps, sir, I might trouble Mrs Fenner for a biscuit and a glass of sherry before you begin? I breakfasted early and I'm famished.'

'Of course.' The Vicar began to frown but changed his mind. 'Yes, perhaps you're in the right of it, sir. We would be wise to recruit ourselves before the ride back.' He hesitated and then added, 'Will a biscuit be sufficient, do you think?'

'What about a mutton chop or two, sir?' Mrs Fenner suggested, her head on one side. 'There's a good fire in the kitchen. It wouldn't take much above five minutes. Ten at the outside.'

'An excellent plan, Mrs Fenner, thank you,' Savill said. 'With a touch of caper sauce, if you have it? And perhaps you will take a glass with us, ma'am, while we discuss our business beforehand?'

'With pleasure, sir.'

'But our business will not brook delay, Mrs Fenner,' Horton put in.

'Indeed, sir. If I might just ring the bell and tell them what you need and to make haste, we shall deal with it directly.'

'A stranger has been seen in Norbury, ma'am,' Horton said, when the refreshments had been ordered. 'I desire to question him on a matter of importance. We have intelligence that he was riding that pony of yours. The piebald.'

Mrs Fenner sipped her wine in a markedly genteel manner. Her doughy cheeks acquired a slight rosy glow. 'Ah.' She glanced from Horton to Savill. 'You mean Mr Irwin. The artistical gentleman.'

'Does he wear a blue travelling coat?'

'Yes, sir. A very quiet gentleman. Out of the ordinary way, perhaps, but a lady in my position learns to be broad-minded. So long as a gentleman pays his way and gives no trouble.'

'Is he in the house?'

'Oh no – he paid his bill and left several hours ago. Or rather, his servant did, on his behalf.'

Savill leaned forward. 'But did Mr Irwin lodge with you?'

'Of course. Where else would he stay?'

'But why on earth did he want to put up here?' Horton said.

Mrs Fenner bridled. 'Why shouldn't he? I've had the Duke of Marlborough himself under my roof. Well, my father-in-law did, which comes to the same thing.'

'I'm sure you made His Grace very comfortable, ma'am,' Savill said. 'I think the Vicar meant to ask whether Mr Irwin had a particular reason to come to this locality.'

'His servant said his master thought the country around here was particularly fine. "A place of inspiration," he said. It's all very well, I'm sure, but it's only fields and woods when all's said and done, and far too much mud. And there's no society at all. "If I wanted inspiration," I told Mr Fenner, "I'd be off to Bath or Bristol in a flash. Whoever heard of a painting of a tree or a bit of mud or a cloud in the sky? He won't find much else around here." Anyway, Mr Irwin was out at all hours, making his sketches. To tell the truth, I think the poor man's wits were mazed. Indeed, his servant as good as told me so. He said artists are often peculiar folk.'

221

'Irwin?' Horton sniffed. 'I cannot recall an artist of that name.'

'There are artists and artists,' Savill said. 'Some hide their light under a bushel and perhaps they are wise to do so. But tell me, ma'am, was this Mr Irwin a young man?'

'Oh no, sir. He must have been thirty or more, if he was a day. Not that I saw much of him, after that first day – he had a private parlour next to his bedchamber and stayed up there when he wasn't outside. His man waited on him.'

'What did he look like?'

'Well enough. Nearer the Vicar's height than yours. Lovely black hair, though, so fine and glossy, like a girl's.'

Gradually, with glass after glass of sherry, Mrs Fenner disgorged what she knew about Mr Irwin, and much else besides, including a wealth of speculation about a range of subjects from the state of His Majesty's health to the probable antecedents of Mr Fenner's late mother. The artistical gentleman had arrived over a week earlier, on the evening of 11 October. He had not written ahead, but simply arrived in his own chaise, driven by his servant, who was named Plimming. The horses had been hired from the post-house on the new road.

'Where did they come from?' Savill asked.

'I don't know. I did ask, but Mr Plimming said they were travelling all over the country because his master was on a sketching tour. Mr Irwin was a very open-handed gentleman – nothing but the best. He liked his glass – he didn't stint himself in that direction, I can tell you – but when he left he paid up very handsome, as a gentleman should, not quibbling about trifles or any such nonsense.'

'How did he seem when he left? In a hurry?'

'I told you, sir, I didn't see him then – it was Mr Plimming paid the reckoning.' She shivered with obvious pleasure. 'Highwaymen, were they?' Her voice sank to a whisper. 'Or worse? We could have been murdered in our beds.'

'Nothing like that, ma'am,' Mr Horton said. 'You have no reason to concern yourself.'

The investigation came to a natural pause when the maid brought the chops. They ordered more sherry to wash it down. Savill, whose mouth was still sore, was obliged to cut the meat up into very small pieces, which he tried to swallow without chewing. Mrs Fenner stayed with them while they ate and played the hostess.

'The first thing Mr Irwin did was hire the pony,' she told them. 'He was out on him at all hours. Off he went, at the crack of dawn sometimes, rain or shine.'

The Vicar examined a piece of fat and popped it into his mouth. A smile spread over his face.

'What about this morning?' Savill asked. 'Did you know he was leaving today?'

'Yes, sir – he ordered the bill to be made up last night. But he went out on the pony again this morning as usual. Not that I saw him. He used to rise so early he'd saddle the pony himself.'

'What about your ostler? He must have seen him when he brought the pony back.'

'Not today, sir. Mr Plimming brought it back. Mr Irwin waited in the chaise.'

Mr Horton swallowed the remains of the fat and belched. 'I don't understand, ma'am.'

It transpired that Plimming had taken an early breakfast and ordered the horses to be harnessed to the chaise. He had settled the bill and driven over the heath to meet his master. On the way down to the turnpike road that had stolen Mrs Fenner's trade, he had left the pony with the ostler.

'So no one has seen Mr Irwin today?' Savill said.

'No, sir. I did see the chaise though, when Mr Plimming brought the pony. I was in Mr Fenner's chamber and I just happened to glance out of the window. But there wasn't anything to see, really. The blinds were down. Then Mr Plimming led

223

the pony into the yard. A moment later he came back and they drove away.'

'Which direction is the turnpike road?'

She turned to the window and pointed to the left. 'That way, sir. A matter of five or six miles. And not a bad road, excepting in winter, though—' She broke off. Her eyes widened and she stared out of the bay window. 'Now there's something you don't often see. A gentleman on a donkey.'

Dr Gohlis was not a happy man. It was fair to say that the donkey was not a happy donkey, either. Between them, they had done their best to mar each other's day with a considerable degree of success on both sides.

In an attempt to keep the donkey moving, the doctor had lashed it mercilessly, drawing blood even from its thick, scarred hide. For its part, the donkey had contrived to stumble on its way up the pack road, choosing to do so at a point where the road doubled as the bed of a stream. Having stumbled, it had rolled over as if to sleep with Gohlis partly underneath its body. It had tried this trick on several occasions, only to be whipped and tugged back to its feet again.

Gohlis was bruised and soaked. His neat black suit of clothes was covered on one side by a layer of mud. He had lost his hat. He was also hungry and cold. His outraged feelings had festered on the ride, creating animosity directed equally towards the donkey and the Count de Quillon.

'The Count insisted I ride after you,' he said when Savill and Horton met him in the passage. 'And that beast of burden was the only mount available. He simply would not listen to reason.'

'Yes, yes,' Horton said. 'But what's happened? Has Bessie tracked the boy down?'

Mutton-flavoured bile rose in Savill's throat. 'Is he . . .?' *Dead*. He found he could not say the word. 'Is he safe now?'

'Alas no. But a man came forward, a cowman or some

224

such, he works for Mr Bradshaw. He was walking to the farm earlier this morning, and he saw a man riding over the hills—'

'You should go in the kitchen, sir,' Mrs Fenner cried, joining them in the passageway. 'Stand by the fire and have a glass of something warm.'

'Hold your tongue, madam,' said Horton. 'A rider, sir. Coming or going?'

'Going this way, sir. But the point is—'

'I beg your pardon, sir,' Mrs Fenner said in an awful whisper. 'My ears must have deceived me.'

'Indeed, madam,' Horton said. 'Well, Doctor?'

'Never in all my life have I—'

'He had a boy up in front of him,' Gohlis said, enunciating his words with precision. 'A man in a blue coat, on a piebald pony. There can be no doubt about it.'

'No doubt!' cried Mrs Fenner. 'I should say so! I heard it with my own ears. A man of the cloth, too.'

Savill wheeled round to her. 'Mrs Fenner, we most humbly beg your pardon.'

She blinked. 'That's all very well, sir—'

'Mr Horton and I are dealing with a matter of the utmost gravity and urgency. But we should not have forgotten our manners. May I present Dr Gohlis, the personal physician and confidential adviser of the Count de Quillon? The kitchen fire, you say? What an admirable idea, ma'am, and thank heaven you proposed it. Let us go there at once, before the doctor catches a chill.'

With Gohlis leaning on Savill's arm, the four of them set off for the kitchen. They were joined by the maid on the way.

'One other thing, sir,' Gohlis said. 'When Monsieur Fournier brought the intelligence, I was examining the ground near the place where we found my *écorché* figure this morning.'

'This way, sir,' cried Mrs Fenner. 'Out of the way, you silly girl. Stay, you'd better fetch the brandy. Here is the key. Mind you touch nothing else, and I shall uncork it myself.'

225

The kitchen door opened as they approached it. Savill had a confused picture of a crowd of servants, their faces turned towards the doorway. Gohlis fumbled in his pocket and stopped.

'I found this,' he said.

The servants stared blankly at him. The doctor held up a small, brass cylinder, four or five inches long.

'A spyglass,' he said.

# Chapter Thirty-Six

All he does is stand there in the stream with his mouth hanging open.

And the man in the blue coat steps into the water, which comes halfway up his boots, and takes Charles by the arm. He doesn't say anything. He doesn't even laugh. He merely tows Charles after him, out of the stream.

Charles stumbles as he climbs out and falls on the bank. The man turns. For the first time, they look at each other properly. The man has very black hair and a sunburned skin. His eyes are large, brown and moist – not unlike Bessie's, now Charles comes to think of it. His face is covered with dark bristles.

The man frowns. He lunges forward, seizes Charles under the arms and swings him up as if Charles is no more than a baby.

'Don't move and don't speak,' he says in English, which is the first thing Charles hears him say. His voice is high-pitched and sometimes it wavers as if someone is shaking him up and down. 'Or – or it'll be the worse for you.'

So, with Charles in his arms, he walks on, forcing himself to hurry. His breathing grows laboured.

'Good God, you're heavier than you look. You'll have to walk now.'

He drops Charles to the ground and seizes his wrist. He is not a tall man but he is broad and muscular. His fingers grip so tightly that needles of pain shoot up Charles's arm. Together they fight their way through the wood. Something scratches Charles's face and the blood trickles into his mouth. He licks it greedily, feeding on himself.

The blood drips on his left forearm. And he sees it.

When Charles sees the blood, he remembers everything. All he wants to do is scream and scream.

*Hush now.*

Charles struggles, trying to escape the man's grasp, trying to run from the slippery blood, just as he ran long ago on that hot night in Paris. But he cannot run from this blood any more than he can run from himself and what is trapped inside his head.

'Stop it, you little fool, or I'll have to hit you.'

The trees are thinning. On the edge of the wood, hard by the lane, they come to a roofless barn with walls of crumbling stone. The piebald pony waits, tethered to the branch of an elder tree, for the woods have begun to colonize the barn in its decay. The pony raises its head and looks at them with a complete absence of interest.

Still holding Charles's wrist, the man fumbles in the saddlebag and takes out a length of cord. He ties Charles's wrists together in front of him and, for good measure, circles his body twice with what remains of the cord, binding his arms just above the elbows to his body.

'There,' he says, smiling. 'Trussed like a chicken.' He screeches like a chicken. 'Time for a celebration.' He is speaking very quickly, the words tumbling on top of each other. 'Elevate our spirits before the journey? Just by the merest trifle. Yes, an admirable idea.'

Out comes the bottle for the first time. Afterwards, he places Charles on the pony and mounts behind him. They ride on to the lane and climb, up and up.

The pony sways. The poor beast is labouring beneath the double burden. They are ascending a steep, rocky path with sides so high that it's almost a tunnel.

It is still early. The lane twists and rises, and there is a rare glimpse of the narrow valley below. A mist clings to the invisible village. The pale stone of Norbury Park gleams on the far slope. Charles wonders whether the Charnwood servants are about yet, whether the water has been sent to boil on the kitchen fire and whether George White, the gardener's boy, has come into the garden.

A cock crows in the distance.

Charles is sitting directly in front of the man with the blue coat, and he feels every movement his captor makes. His arms are bound to his side so the man is obliged to support him to keep him upright on the pony. His feet and lower legs are very cold.

On and on they go, jolting and swaying up the lane. Charles is stiff and sore and cold. In a while, the misery converts itself to a waking doze.

When he returns to full consciousness, it is much brighter and there is a breeze on his face. They have stopped moving.

The man is speaking: '. . . can't take any risks. Must seem a trifle absurd, if you really are dumb. But perhaps you can grunt or squawk, or something of that nature, which might give the game away, eh? Just for a little. An hour or two at most.'

A finger and thumb squeeze Charles's face, finding a spot between the upper and lower teeth and then tightening like pincers, which forces his mouth open. A strap is passed round his face, forcing his mouth to stay open. The man fastens the buckle at the back of his neck at the base of the skull. Charles squirms.

'Is it uncomfortable? Tell me if it is.' There's a laugh, thin and high like a hen's screech. 'But you can't, of course. You'll have to nod, I suppose.'

Charles hears the soft explosion of the cork leaving the

neck of the bottle just behind his left ear. He smells the fruity acridity of spirits.

'Ah,' the man says, drawing out the syllable until it ends in a cough. 'Ah.' He returns the bottle to his pocket. 'And now this,' he says. 'Don't be afraid. You'll be able to breathe perfectly well, and it won't be for long.'

He pulls a bag of some coarsely woven material over Charles's head. It smells of earth and damp and decay. At first everything is black but then he sees there are specks of lights like stars.

'Less you see, the less you know, eh?'

They ride on. There's another laugh, another screeching hen.

'It's for your own good, you know,' the man says. 'I dare say you'll thank me for this one day.'

Is this my punishment for what I did to Louis, Charles wonders?

There's another screech in his ear, and another acrid breath that catches the back of his throat.

'Ah,' says the man. 'At last.'

The sound of hooves in the distance. The rattle of wheels on a road.

'You know what old Mother Fenner said about him, sir.'

Another man is there, invisible to Charles because of the bag over his head. But his voice is quite different from the voice of the man in the blue coat. It's sharper and harder, pregnant with mockery.

'The mad mute. He runs wild at night and bites the heads off cats and chickens.'

'Oh for God's sake, that's enough.' This is the man in the blue coat. 'Help me get him in the chaise.'

This is how it begins.

After this point, when they bundle Charles into the carriage,

230

his knowledge of events becomes increasingly fragmentary and increasingly unreliable. He is still gagged and hooded. He knows he is in a carriage of some sort and that it is in motion. He knows the man in the blue coat is with him, sitting opposite but with his feet up on the seat beside Charles.

The chaise stops briefly. Charles hears the sound of voices outside. Then, with a jerk, they move off again, more rapidly this time, and gathering speed. He hears the man muttering to himself. Once or twice he takes out his bottle.

Charles dozes again. A terrible thirst possesses him. He dreams of water, endless water. He has a pain at the bottom of his stomach.

What wakes him is the change in the sound of the wheels and in the quality of the vibration: they are now travelling on a smoother surface and moving even faster than before.

'Well,' says the man in the blue coat. 'You awake in there? Time to have a look at you.' He lifts the bag from Charles's head. 'Pale, aren't you?'

Charles blinks in the light. The inside of his mouth is like cracked leather. The pain bores into his stomach. His arms are still bound at the wrists and his hands feel strangely clumsy, as if they are no longer entirely his.

One of the blinds is down, but the other is at the halfway mark. The man is a shadow, facing him and leaning towards him.

'Hold still. I'll take off the gag. Don't cry, eh? Won't help.' The familiar chicken screech. 'I should know, damn it. I've wept enough tears to float a frigate in my time. And where's it got me? Precisely nowhere.'

He fumbles on the floor. Once again, a cork pops out. But it's a different cork from before. It makes a deeper, more melodious sound. The man holds up an earthenware bottle.

'Water. I'll hold it for you.'

The water is the most beautiful thing Charles has ever known. He gulps and gulps from the bottle until the water

231

flows from his mouth and pours over his chin and soaks his shirt.

The man sits back and studies him. 'Hungry? No, perhaps we'd better wait. But you'll need to piss soon, I'll be bound – we can't have you stinking out the chaise, can we?'

He glances out of the window and then raps on the roof. There is an answering knock. A moment later, the carriage rolls to a halt. Charles sees a belt of trees at the side of the road. Then he sees nothing but stars because the man drops the bag over his head again.

The door opens. There's a rattle as the steps are let down. The man descends first and then draws Charles out of the chaise. There's a breeze and a hint of rain in the air. The man leads him forward.

'I'll unbutton your breeches. Then you can manage by yourself, eh?'

As soon as the urine gushes out, Charles knows that this is the source of the pain low in his stomach. Afterwards the man buttons Charles's breeches and leads him back to the chaise.

Inside the chaise, the man pushes him on to the front seat and closes the door. He removes Charles's hood and grins at him. He digs his hand into the pocket of his blue coat and pulls out a silver teaspoon and a small brown bottle. This cork makes another sound as it comes out – much higher than the others. He measures half a dozen drops on to the spoon.

'Time to dose you,' he says.

The drops taste bitter. The man gives him a drink of water to wash the taste away. Afterwards he has a drink from his own bottle and then raps the roof to tell the man to drive on.

Off they go, the chaise rumbling and swaying down the road.

Three corks, Charles thinks, and each makes its own sound. That is a fact. He wonders whether the sound of a withdrawn cork varies with the size of the bottle.

Here is another fact. Since he has become mute, Charles

232

has discovered that there are two sorts of people in the world: those who are unkind because they are obliged to be so, and those who are unkind because it gives them pleasure.

The man in the blue coat is one of the former. That is a fact.

Inside his head, Charles begins to count up all the facts he knows. Somewhere between a hundred and two hundred he falls asleep.

The journey continues. Charles sleeps for most of the time or inhabits a twilight place on the borders of sleep. The man in the blue coat gives him more water and, once, after one of the stops when they change the horses, some soup.

He hears the servant talking to someone outside. 'Closed carriage – doctor's orders. Could be the Bengal plague, they reckon. Weeping pustules the size of saucers. Doctor in there with her – he has a sanatorium over Maidenhead way. It's the only hope for the poor young lady.'

Many hours pass. Perhaps days or nights. Charles wishes he could measure the time but there is no way to do so.

He wakes with a start to find himself alone in the carriage, which is no longer moving. But there are voices outside.

'But we're in the middle of nowhere,' the servant is saying. 'You'll get soaked.'

'Why should you care about that?' says the man in the blue coat. 'Just do as you're told.'

'I thought I was coming with you, sir.'

'You're wrong. Here. That's for the stables – and that's for you. There'll be the same again for you if you do as I say.'

'But when will I see you, sir? In the Blue Posts?'

'Perhaps. In a while. Now listen: go away for a month or two. Right away. Go down to the country and see your family.'

'I thought you said—'

'"Thought?"' The chicken screech of laughter. 'Don't think. Just do as I say.'

\*     \*     \*

233

When the carriage is gone, the man removes the bag from Charles's head. It is very cold and almost dark, though one side of the sky is beginning to lighten. They are standing in the shelter of a hedge.

'You won't try to bolt if I untie you? There's nowhere for you to run to.'

He fumbles with the knots. Then, cursing, he takes out his pocket knife and cuts the cord. Charles's hands are so painful that he moans. The man massages each hand, slowly restoring them to life.

'Now,' he says. 'We shall contrive to warm ourselves with some exercise. And then, by and by, we shall come to our lodging.'

Instead of taking the high road, the man leads Charles into the field on the other side of the hedge. Hand in hand, they cross the roughly mown grass, stumbling because the ground is uneven and marshy.

The light is growing steadily, spreading from one side of the sky. A line of widely spaced willows marks the further field boundary. Beyond the trees lies a broad, oily river, gliding sluggishly towards the rising sun.

The man is looking for something. Whistling under his breath, he peers up and down, taking a few steps one way and then retreating. All the while he tows Charles after him.

Charles is cold and wet and tired. He whimpers quietly.

'There we are,' the man says, his voice suddenly cheerful.

A boat is pulled up on the bank, almost entirely concealed by the trailing branches of the willow. The man puts down his portmanteau.

'This deserves a toast.' He releases Charles's hand and takes out his bottle. '*Un bon voyage*, hey?'

# Chapter Thirty-Seven

Vereker.

The word was engraved in the brass, the small, discreet lettering following the curve of the brass cylinder.

Leaning back in his chair, Savill pulled out the spyglass and held it to his eye. He twisted it and a tree sprang into sharp relief on the opposite side of the road to the inn.

'Not a powerful instrument, as these things go,' Dr Gohlis said. 'A naval officer would find it inadequate for longer range observations. And an astronomer would simply laugh at it. But it's something better than a toy. As one would expect. Vereker, you know.'

'What's that?' the Vicar said. 'Who?'

'The maker, sir. The name is on the barrel.'

Savill closed the spyglass. 'He is well known?'

'In his field, yes. Mr Vereker may not enjoy the reputation of Dollond or Martin, but his instruments are not to be despised. When I lived in London I heard him lecture on his improved aquatic microscope. There is an admirable attention to detail, particularly in the grinding of the lenses.'

Mrs Fenner had ordered the fire to be lit in the private parlour. Dr Gohlis was now dry, warm and perhaps slightly tipsy, which made him more expansive than he was inclined to be in company.

'His instruments are certainly not cheap,' he went on. 'Though that is not a consideration for many of his customers – I believe he has a considerable connection among gentlemen who dabble in natural philosophy, and even the nobility. When I was last in his shop, His Grace of Devonshire's carriage stopped outside, and a footman came in to collect a parcel. Of course Mr Vereker went out to attend His Grace in person, though it transpired that the carriage was empty.'

Meanwhile, Savill was turning the telescope over in his hands. 'Where precisely did you find this, sir?'

'Eh? Within a stone's throw of that mound where we found my poor figure. On the bank of a stream.'

'It's plain enough,' Mr Horton said. 'The kidnapper must have dropped it. Perhaps he was using it to observe the grounds from the wood.'

Savill laid the spyglass on the table and pointed. 'There's a number here, Doctor. On the barrel, just above the eyepiece. Eight, nine, one, four.'

'Mr Vereker's mark, no doubt,' Gohlis said, taking up his glass. 'Where's his shop?'

'Between Temple Bar and the river, sir. Arundel Street, I believe.'

The Vicar glanced out of the window at the sky. 'We should go back, sir. I should much prefer to reach Norbury before the light goes.'

'Indeed, sir,' Gohlis said. 'But must I ride that wretched animal again? Is there not a horse I might borrow?'

Horton glanced at Savill with a smile glimmering on his face. 'Mrs Fenner has a piebald pony for hire, I believe. It knows the way to Charnwood.'

Savill ignored them both. For a moment he wished he had kept the dice he had given Charles. A decision must be made, and how else could a man choose in a case like this where so little was known?

The man in the blue coat clearly existed – independent witnesses from Miss Horton to Mrs Fenner – confirmed that. But had he been acting for himself when he kidnapped Charles? Or for a third party?

The Count had been determined to keep Charles, and Fournier was his friend and ally. Was it they who had arranged for the boy to be taken? If so, Charles might be still in Norbury or even concealed at Charnwood itself, though it seemed unlikely that he could be kept hidden for long.

Or had some other person or persons taken him? The only other person known to have an interest in him was his uncle Rampton. But Rampton had sent Savill to fetch Charles. He had no reason to snatch away a boy he believed he was about to have by perfectly straightforward and legal means.

Who else, then? Someone connected with Charles's past life in Paris? With the murder of his mother by the mob?

'Let us ring the bell, sir,' the Vicar said. 'We must pay our reckoning and go back.'

'You go back, sir,' Savill said.

'What? Aren't you coming?'

'I shall ride to the turnpike road and try to find a scent of them there.'

'But they have six or seven hours' start of you. It will soon be dark. They could be anywhere by now.'

'I shall get a description of their chaise from the ostler here, and then I shall enquire at the turnpikes. If not there, then at the post-houses along the road. Someone must have seen them pass and, if they're going any distance, they will be obliged to change horses. I shall take the mare but send her back at the first opportunity. Pray make my excuses at Charnwood, Doctor.'

'But, sir,' Gohlis said, 'the Count will want to discuss with you what is best to be done.'

Savill closed the spyglass and dropped it in his pocket.

'And pardon me, sir,' Dr Gohlis said, 'I believe we shall need the glass as well.'

237

'Indeed,' the Vicar said. 'Almost certainly it is evidence material to the case. It may be of the highest importance.'

Savill stood up and bowed. 'You may well be in the right of it, sir. Which is why I shall take it. But let us not quarrel. I shall give a receipt for the glass, and return it to you at the first opportunity.'

Mr Horton's amiability vanished. 'This kidnapping was in Norbury, sir. The spyglass was found there. You must surrender it to my keeping. I insist.'

Savill slipped his hand in his pocket and took out the warrant he had shown the Vicar in the morning. He held it up but did not unfold it.

'You know it is not in your power to do that, sir.'

There was silence, too long for comfort. The doctor looked from Savill to Horton and then stared out of the window.

'If you're going, sir,' the Vicar said at last, 'then the sooner the better, I suppose.'

Horton and Gohlis came out with him to the stableyard, where they stood in silence while Savill talked to the old ostler. Afterwards, the three of them exchanged polite but wintry farewells.

'But your baggage, sir,' said Dr Gohlis, with sudden agitation. 'It is still at Charnwood. Surely you will need it on the road?'

'Thank you, I have everything I require.' Savill had his papers in one inside pocket of his coat and Mr Rampton's gold was weighing down the other, making him feel permanently lopsided. 'But would you be so good as to ask Monsieur Fournier to send it on to me? I will write to him with my direction in London.'

As he turned the mare's head towards the road, Savill looked down at the Vicar and, feeling a sudden awkwardness, said: 'One more thing, sir. Pray give my adieux to Miss Horton and thank her for her kindness to Charles.'

*     *     *

'A closed chaise,' Savill said two hours later. The light was already draining from a grey sky heavy with rain clouds. 'Black or dark brown. A pair of horses, both dun-coloured.'

The woman who kept the turnpike shrugged. 'Could be, sir. But we've had a score or so come through since morning, and after a while you can't tell one from another, so long as they pay their tuppences like good Christians.'

'The man who drove it had a brown topcoat.' He remembered suddenly what Mrs Fenner had said about Plimming. 'A servant with an eye for the ladies.'

'Oh – him!' She was a buxom woman with a baby on the crook of her arm. 'Londoner, I reckon. Full of impudence. Wanted to pay the toll in kisses.' She turned her head away and spat.

'What time was this?'

'I don't know, sir. After breakfast, before dinner. Baby was asleep until the chaise went through, I can tell you that, because the gate banged – which was that man's fault because he drove too close and the wheel knocked it.'

The baby was awake now and staring with calm curiosity at Savill.

'A charming child, ma'am. Pray, would you accept this to buy him a trinket of some sort?'

'Her, sir.' The woman took the shilling.

Savill bowed. 'I beg Miss's pardon. I suppose you couldn't hazard a guess where they might have been going?'

It was a long shot and he was not surprised when she shook her head. He was losing the woman's attention now. The baby was shifting on her arm, her mouth puckering in distress.

'Up to London, maybe? That's where they came from, the other day.'

The baby twisted against her and vomited milk over her shoulder. The shilling's worth of goodwill had run out. The woman turned away.

\*     \*     \*

239

At the next post-house, four miles further on, Savill made enquiries and spent Mr Rampton's money with a liberal hand. He learned that Irwin's chaise had stopped there nearly seven hours earlier to change horses.

It was raining hard and it would soon be completely dark. Savill's body ached, for he was not much accustomed to riding now, and he was starving, for he had eaten nothing since Mrs Fenner's mutton chop. He ordered supper. While he was eating, he decided to spend the night at the inn. He was dog-tired and, even on a post road, it would not be easy or indeed safe for a single horseman to ride through the night.

He made arrangements to return the grey mare to Charnwood in the morning. After a brief internal debate, he decided that it would be both prudent and comfortable to hire a chaise with the assistance of Mr Rampton's guineas, and to travel post up to London. Having settled on a light chaise and hired a man to drive him, he left orders to be called an hour before dawn.

Despite his weariness, he slept fitfully. The empty socket in his mouth was hurting, though not as badly as before. But he missed Dr Gohlis's drops, which he had left in his portmanteau at Charnwood. Their absence gnawed at him.

While he was trying to sleep, his attention drifted to Harriet Horton, immured in her father's vicarage. A handsome woman, he thought. It was curious that she had not married before. She must have had offers.

Intelligent, too. Younger than he was, which was no bad thing in a wife, but not a foolish girl, either, but a woman of sense. He wondered whether she had any money of her own.

For everything was different, now Augusta was dead.

There was a close-knit and close-lipped fraternity among the men who made their living travelling up and down the great roads that led to London. This worked to Savill's advantage, for the groom he hired to drive him proved an ally worth having.

He was a weathered man with stooping shoulders and an acquaintance at every inn, and in every stable. He knew who was to be trusted, who was a knave and who was a fool. He knew to a penny the price to pay for information, and when it was better to offer promises or even confidences in lieu of money. On foot, he seemed permanently tipsy, though this never proceeded to drunkenness. With reins in his hands, however, he became the model of sobriety.

Savill told him something that approximated the truth during their first hour together on the road: that he was in pursuit of his son, who, owing to a dispute about a legacy, had been taken by a thieving relative who had no love for the boy.

The groom spat an arc of glittering tobacco juice towards the verge. 'They took my son, too, sir.'

'What? I don't understand.'

'My son. Press gang took him.'

'That was cruel indeed.'

'A son needs his father,' the groom said. 'Father needs his son.'

At every halt they made, Savill worried that they would find they had lost the scent, that Irwin had turned off and gone north or south where he and Charles would soon vanish in the immensity of the country. But when they stopped at an inn along the road, the groom would sidle into the stable or the kitchen or the bar the ostlers used. In a while he would emerge with a slightly more unsteady gait, bringing news of Norbury's chaise. In this manner they traced him from Chippenham to Marlborough, from Newbury to Slough.

Here they had a piece of luck when they enquired about the chaise they were following. Irwin had changed horses here too and demanded brandy to be brought while he was waiting. One of the inn's ostlers had recognized the chaise by the door handles, which were of a curiously intricate design and were the very devil to clean.

Better than that, he knew where it came from. The chaise belonged to the Swan With Two Necks in Ladd Lane, where the man had worked until his marriage last year brought him to Slough.

They pressed on to London. It was nearly eight in the evening when they passed through the Hyde Park Gate and plunged into the roar of Piccadilly.

In the City, they made their way to St Paul's and then turned north towards Ladd Lane. The groom eased the chaise into the yard of the inn.

The establishment was thronged with travellers and their friends, with servants and horses and coaches. The people of the inn were reluctant to answer questions about their customers. Savill was obliged to show Rampton's warrant to the landlord, as well as to spend liberally while he was there.

At last, at about ten o'clock in the evening, he was able to inspect the chaise that Irwin had travelled in. It had been in the stable since nine o'clock that morning. In the meantime it had been cleaned, inside and out, and was now waiting to be hired. There was nothing to be learned from it whatsoever.

'A boy? Not that I recall,' said the clerk who had taken the ticket and paid back the deposit on the chaise. 'But God knows, there are enough boys around the place as it is, and what's one more?'

'Who did you pay the deposit to?'

The clerk had a sad face and watery eyes. He wore a grey coat made some years earlier with someone larger in mind. After a moment's consideration, he said: 'Just a man, sir.'

'A gentleman?'

'No.'

'Did you see him arrive?'

'As it happens, sir, I did. I chanced to be in the yard at the time. He was driving.'

242

Savill took out his purse.

'Who was with him?'

'No one, sir. The chaise was empty.'

'How can you be sure?'

'Because I am obliged to inspect the vehicles, inside and out, sir, when they are returned. No one got out in the yard. And there was no one inside.'

Savill placed a shilling on the table. He did not put the purse away.

'And were you there when the chaise was hired?'

'Oh yes, sir.' The clerk inserted a finger in his ear and rotated it. 'I'm always here.'

'Who made the booking? The same man?'

'No, sir. A gentleman. A Mr Irwin.'

'What was he like?'

'Not a young man, not old, either. He had black hair, I remember that.'

Savill laid another shilling on the table. 'Did he give you his direction in London?'

'Of course, sir. Henrietta Street, by Covent Garden. Number twenty-three, the first floor front.' The clerk smiled. 'Not that it signifies.'

Savill's patience slipped away. 'What the devil do you mean?'

'The chaise was late back, sir. And when I went to Henrietta Street to enquire after him, the woman that keeps the house had never heard of him.'

# Chapter Thirty-Eight

When Charles wakes, it is broad daylight. Stripes of sunlight cross the floor and march up the wall opposite the window. The shutters are closed but they are crudely made and warped. The sun finds its way around them.

Something nearby is scratching and rustling.

He is lying on the floor with a pile of blankets weighing him down. They smell mouldy. His clothes feel damp. He is thirsty and there is a painful vacancy inside him that he knows is hunger.

Most of all, he wants to piss. But he hasn't wet himself, he finds, and the discovery makes him briefly happy. He lifts his hand and lays it palm downwards on the nearest golden stripe. There's no warmth to it.

The scratching and rustling stop.

'Awake at last?'

Charles struggles into a sitting position. The man in the blue coat is sitting at a table by the window with a pen in his hand. His face is both blotchy and pale, like stained linen. He looks very tired.

'It won't be long now.' He holds up the paper. 'I shall send a letter. And then we shall wait.' A screech of laughter, swiftly muted. 'We shall entertain ourselves as best we can.'

\*　　\*　　\*

There are stale rolls to eat, water to drink and a pot to piss in. The sun goes in and Charles hears rain pattering on the roof, mingling with the cries of seagulls. Occasionally there are voices, men calling to one another, but too far away for him to make out the words.

The man eats at the table, adding brandy to his water. Charles squats on his blankets and watches.

He guesses that they are still beside the river. The man rowed them here at dawn. The boat itself is beneath them, for this room is perched above the water, with the mooring enclosed beneath them on all sides except that which faces the river. A door at the side leads to a flight of steps down to the water's edge.

After breakfast the man throws water on his face and makes an attempt to brush his blue coat. He opens the door of the cupboard built into the wall beside the fireplace. It is tall enough for him to walk into. There are empty shelves on either side of a central gangway and a rusting rat-trap in one corner.

He puts the water jug and the last of the rolls on one of the shelves. He turns, frowning, towards Charles but then changes his mind and dives down to the chamber pot. He opens a window overlooking the river and empties the pot into the river. He places the pot in the cupboard beside the rat-trap on the floor.

'Now you,' he says. 'In you go. Don't be afraid.'

He takes Charles by the shoulder and pushes him into the cupboard. He throws a blanket after him.

'I could tie you up and gag you,' he says. 'But I'm not a cruel man, you know that, don't you? Truly, on my word, I'm not.' He sounds worried that Charles might think him cruel. 'I wish you no harm, not in the slightest.' He stands back, hand on the door. 'This is better, isn't it? You'll manage famously. You're too old to mind the dark. You'll be quite comfortable. But don't make a noise, I beg you.' The chicken

245

screech of laughter bubbles out of his mouth. 'Not that anyone will hear you if you do.'

In the old days, when Maman was alive and they lived in Paris, Charles had been afraid of the dark. He liked to have a light burning as he slept. His mother had indulged him with a special candle that burned very dimly and very slowly. It was enclosed in a lantern with a heavy base so it could not be easily overturned, and placed on the mantelpiece in his chamber.

Nowadays, there is no one to light a candle for him at night. Besides, he is no longer afraid of the dark. There are so many other things that terrify him even more. The dark, his old enemy, has become almost a friend.

When the footsteps have faded away, Charles sits very still for as long as it takes to count two hundred breaths. Occasionally the building creaks. Gulls cry, their voices muffled by the walls. There is also a noise in the background, continuous, fluctuating, too faint to identify. Perhaps it is the wind or the river. There are no other sounds.

Draughts swirl up through the floorboards, bringing with them the smells of the river.

The cupboard is not entirely dark. A thin rectangle of light shows between the door and its frame. A thin vertical crack runs down the lower panel of the door, admitting a line of daylight. The keyhole glows. Charles squints between door and frame at the room beyond where they slept and ate. There is nothing to see but the corner of the table.

As the minutes pass, Charles's eyes adapt. He makes out the side of the water jug where its lustre catches the light and reflects it back. The chamber pot is a dark suggestion of itself upon the floor. Beside it is the rat-trap.

Charles gathers facts. The cupboard is approximately one and a half paces wide and two and a half paces long. The height is harder to estimate, especially in the near dark, but he guesses it must be three to four paces.

He examines the shelves, trailing his fingers over each one, covering every inch of the surface, moving from top to bottom and from left to right. He finds dust, fragments of plaster and tangles of spiders' webs that cling to his skin. He disturbs something that moves under his fingertips. Woodlice, perhaps. He wonders if he could bring himself to eat them if the man does not come back.

Finally he searches the floor. Under one shelf there is a knot-hole in the floorboard, which allows in some light. He lies on his belly and manages to get his eye to the knothole. He is looking into the boathouse itself, at the shimmer of water.

The skiff they came in is still there, rocking slowly up and down. The side of the boathouse towards the river is open, but fringed by alders, which have grown to make an arch over the water. Their leaves filter green light into the gloom below. He cannot see the river beyond the trees.

Last of all he comes to the chamber pot and the rat-trap. The trap is a crudely made thing of wire that rests on a heavy wooden base. He runs his finger along the side. The metal parts are rough to the touch because they have rusted. He cannot see anything inside but, just to be sure, he picks up the contraption and shakes it. It rattles slightly and something metallic falls to the floor.

He brushes his fingers through the grit until he finds what it is: a nail, about two inches long. At one end it curves into a right angle. It is something to play with, though Charles can barely see what he's doing with it. Using it as a pen, he scratches his name on one of the shelves.

This is not forbidden, this writing, for there is no one to read it.

Afterwards – idly, for something to do – he pokes the nail into the cracks in the door. He pushes the curved end of the nail into the keyhole. He twists it to and fro. He feels resistance and twists the nail harder. He feels movement within the lock but the bolt does not move.

He tugs the wire from the lock. The movement is violent enough to make the door shift a fraction in its frame. The damp from the river has made the door buckle, twisting it from the jamb on the side where the lock is. He hears a scrape. The door swings into the room beyond.

This is not liberation: it is another reason to be scared. What if the man with the blue coat returns and beats him for opening the cupboard door? Still in the cupboard, Charles draws the door towards him. The extended bolt of the lock touches the frame on the outside. Using the nail as a lever he pulls the door laterally towards its hinges. The tip of the bolt scrapes over the lip of the retaining socket and drops into place. The door is locked again.

Relief washes over him. He opens the door again and, alert for sounds outside, steps into the room beyond.

There are two windows, opposite one another. One looks over the wide, grey river to fields and a handful of houses on the further bank. The other window reveals a wild garden choked with saplings and overgrown bushes. Here and there are glimpses of flagged paths and raised beds.

He tries the outer door but it is locked. No amount of pulling and pushing will open it.

In one corner is a rusty stove with the remains of its flue propped in the corner behind it. The two chairs stand on either side of a small table, its top stained with patches of colour in faded crayon and paint, and pitted with scars.

The remains of their breakfast are still there. Charles breaks off a crust and eats it, not because he is hungry but because he can.

The blankets are huddled in the corner. The man has a velvet cushion as a pillow. It has left a trail of feathers on the floor beside it.

His portmanteau is half-concealed among the blankets. It's not locked. But there's nothing of interest inside, only two dirty shirts, a pair of stockings, an empty bottle and a razor with a handle of ivory, tipped with silver.

Charles is about to retreat to the safety of the cupboard when, on a whim, he opens the door of the stove. The interior is stuffed with a pile of papers and books. On top of them is a scattering of broken pens, pencils and fine paintbrushes still encrusted with paint.

He takes out the first paper. It is a sketch in pen and ink of a church with ladies and gentlemen, strolling past the railings in front. The paper is spotted brown with damp and curls at the edges. There are initials in the right-hand corner: RO.

Charles examines another sheet, a painting in watercolour of a building with pillars in a city street. It disintegrates at his touch and the initials RO crumble to nothing between his thumb and forefinger.

One of the books is next. The pages stick together. Charles prises two of them apart, tearing some of the paper. But enough remains to make out that these are pencil sketches: on one side is a man with heavy features reading a book by the light of a candle; on the other is a lady bent over an embroidery frame. The next page is blank and has detached itself from the binding. He pushes it in his pocket, and finds a stub of pencil to go with it.

He hears a noise outside. Two crows have perched on the handrail at the top of the steps. Bright-eyed and restless, they shift from leg to leg. Charles thrusts the mutilated sketchbook into the stove. He darts back to the safety of the cupboard where the crows can't see him.


When the man returns, Charles is dozing, trying to ignore the cold and the hunger. The man wraps him tightly in a blanket and rubs his arms and legs. Warmth returns slowly. Charles cries softly with the pain of it.

The man does not seem to mind. He dabs at Charles's cheeks with a handkerchief that smells of spirits and stale tobacco. 'Hush,' he says. 'Oh dear, dear, hush.'

Afterwards, he crouches beside Charles and feeds him as

if he were a baby: a mouthful of dry, coarse bread; a morsel of hard cheese that tastes so sour Charles nearly gags; and a drink of water to wash it down. Then again, and again. So it goes on until Charles can eat and drink no more.

The man sits back. He's still crouching and his bony knees are nearly on a level with his head. He is like a strange insect that Maman used to call, in English, a father-longlegs. He rocks himself slowly to and fro.

'That's better,' he says. 'I could not help wondering – well, not to put too fine a point on it – you were going blue at the edges. I was afraid that – anyway, all's well that ends well.' He stretches a long arm to the table, where his glass stands beside the loaf. 'No idea I'd be so long.' He frowns. 'Can't think why I was. Business, I suppose. Always business, eh? Takes longer than you think it will. And it's much colder than it was – I didn't expect that.'

Charles stares at the window, at the darkening sky.

The man drinks. 'Strange little thing, aren't you?' He belches softly and screeches for the first time since his return. 'All bones and eyes and ears. You need feeding up.'

They eat supper by candlelight. The man has brought more rolls, another piece of cheese and some slices of ham that taste of apples and cloves. The man watches him eat and nods sometimes, as if in approval of Charles or possibly of himself. But he himself hardly touches the food. Instead he applies himself to his bottle.

Afterwards they sit in silence, each of them with a blanket over their shoulders. The man's eyes close; his head falls forward with a jerk; and he's fully awake again, wide-eyed and on the edge of panic. He drags out his watch and screeches with alarm.

'Good God? Is that the time already?' He leaps to his feet. 'He will – that is to say, you must retire for the night. At once, do you hear? At once.'

The muscles in the man's face won't stay still. He pushes

Charles into the cupboard. He closes the door but immediately opens it again to pass in another blanket, the chamber pot and a jug of water.

'Be quiet,' he says. 'Go to sleep, there's a good lad. It won't be long now, I promise. Everything will be better tomorrow.'

Charles lies awake in the dark and listens to the sounds of the river, to the man moving about the room and to his own breathing. Faint lines of candlelight waver around the door. He wonders what the man meant.

*It won't be long now, I promise you. Everything will be better tomorrow.*

How could anything be better? On the contrary, things become worse. That is clear from what has happened to his own life. Other lives support this – consider the poor King in his prison, Maman in her grave and even the Count, who has lost all his money and his power that made him so grand and important. Everyone is unhappier than they were.

Things become worse: this is a fact, as unassailable in its way as the measurements of the Garden of Neptune.

He begins to list the facts he knows in his mind. The more facts he has, the safer he will be. By the time he reaches number 38 (the colour of Miss Horton's eyes, which are not quite brown and not quite green but something in between, depending on the light and the angle you see them from), his eyelids are drooping and he is finding it hard to concentrate. That is when the sound of knocking jolts him fully awake.

There are footsteps, then the sliding of bolts and the scrape of the outer door.

'It is so late I thought you would not come,' says the man in the blue coat.

Another voice replies, but so quietly even the sound of it is barely audible.

'An honour, of course . . . a pleasure . . . A glass of something to keep out the cold?'

The second voice speaks again. The words are lost in the sounds of the river.

'I give you my word we'll be there,' says the man in the blue coat. 'You may depend on it. So the carriage at midday . . .?'

More lost words.

'Inspect the merchandise, eh?' The familiar chicken screech of mirth erupts from him. 'A thousand pardons. But nothing will be easier. And very prudent, if I may say so . . . No, not a word. Mute as a stone, eh?'

Heavy footsteps approach the cupboard.

'You must prepare yourself, he's not looking his best. But wash his face, give him a good meal and a change of clothes and I dare say his own mother wouldn't know him . . . I beg your pardon, my tongue runs away with me sometimes . . .'

There are footsteps and the key turns in the lock. Charles cowers under the blankets. His eyes are open, just a crack so no one will know he is not asleep.

The door opens. The cupboard fills with the light of the candle in the hand of the man in the blue coat. Behind him, in the gloom of the room, is someone else, barely more than a shadow.

'There he is. Shall I rouse him up? No?'

The shadow says nothing. Nevertheless there are sounds.

*Tip-tap.* Like cracking a walnut.

Charles cannot breathe. His body tightens up, fixing him in his agony.

'I wish he'd say something,' says the man in the blue coat. 'Anything.' He gives one of his quieter screeches. 'But it's like trying to converse with a statue.'

*Tip-tap.*

# Chapter Thirty-Nine

The bells of Westminster were summoning worshippers. The morning air was keen, sharpened by an east wind that brought a hint of winter's approach.

The outer door of the house in Crown Street was closed. Savill rapped the knocker three times.

No one came. He looked up at the blank windows of the house. There were no signs of life. He knocked again, more loudly and for longer than before. A moment later, the shutter in the door slid aside and two small eyes inspected him.

'Closed, sir.'

'My name is Savill. I've business with Mr Rampton.'

'Come back tomorrow, ten o'clock.'

Savill put his hand on the shutter to prevent the porter closing it. 'Jarsdel? You'll remember me. Mr Malbourne made me known to you the other day when I called on Mr Rampton.'

There was a spark of recognition in the eyes.

'My business with Mr Rampton will not wait. Is he in the country? Or at his house in Westminster?'

'Don't know, sir.' The ruined nose made the man's voice sound as dense and greasy as a pot of lard. 'Come back Monday.'

'Then I'll try his house here first. Where is it?'

'Can't say, sir.'

'Can't? For God's sake, man.' Savill felt in his pocket for his purse. 'Or won't?'

The eyes flickered. 'Sorry, sir. I would if I could. But it's more than my place is worth.'

'Mr Malbourne, then. What's his direction?'

'Mr Malbourne, sir? Why didn't you say? I'll enquire if he's engaged.'

The shutter closed with a bang. There was silence on the other side of the door. Savill waited, surprised that Malbourne should be here on a Sunday. Minutes dragged by. The shutter opened again and the eyes reappeared.

'You're to come in, sir.'

The porter unbarred and opened the door. The clerks' office on the left of the passage was shuttered and dark. But daylight streamed through an oval skylight above the stairs. There were footsteps above and Malbourne himself appeared.

'Mr Savill, your servant, sir.' He bowed gracefully. 'And I am mortified that we should have kept you waiting. Jarsdel, you're a blockhead. Have you no memory at all? Do you not recognize this gentleman? He was here only the other day.'

'I beg your pardon for disturbing you,' Savill said, squeezing past Jarsdel. 'I was enquiring after Mr Rampton.'

'Then you must permit me to see if I can assist you. Pray come up to my room – there is a fire there and we shall be quite comfortable. Have you breakfasted? Shall I send Jarsdel for something?'

Savill climbed the stairs to the first-floor landing. A desperate urgency possessed him – every hour without any sign of Charles made the boy's return less likely – but he could not allow a trace of his anxiety to appear, not to Malbourne.

Malbourne's room was smaller than Rampton's, to which it served as an antechamber. A small fire burned briskly in the grate. The smell of the coal mingled with a sweet, delicate scent that seemed to come from Malbourne himself.

254

The table by the window was strewn with letters, some open, some still sealed. There was also a set of rectangular baskets, similar to those that Savill had seen in Rampton's room.

'You are obliged to work on Sunday, sir?' Savill said.

'Yes. Cruel, is it not? But the mails arrive on Sundays as often as any other day, and it is not convenient to let them remain unsorted.'

Malbourne indicated a chair by the fire for Savill. He himself sat down at his table, angling his own chair away from the piles of correspondence. The house did not have the usual air of a government office, any more than the elegant Mr Malbourne had the usual air of a government clerk.

Savill wondered again precisely what business was transacted in this place, what business was so urgent that it had to be transacted on a Sunday. Clearly it included the opening of letters addressed to other people, which could hardly be an agreeable employment for a man of Mr Malbourne's stamp.

'Did your affairs prosper in Somersetshire?'

'They did not go as I had hoped they would, sir.' Savill hesitated. 'Which is why I am anxious to discuss the matter with Mr Rampton.'

'We are expecting him on Monday morning. He is probably at Vardells, though I cannot say for certain.'

'Then I must hire a horse and ride out there.'

Malbourne looked sharply at him. 'May I be of service myself? I could arrange a messenger to take a letter, if you wish. Or, if you prefer to discuss the matter with me at once, I shall place myself entirely at your disposal. As you know, Mr Rampton honoured me with his confidence.'

For a moment Savill was tempted to unburden himself. Malbourne knew already that he had been down to Norbury to fetch Charles, and he was fully cognisant of the peculiar circumstances of the émigré household at Charnwood Court. But did he know everything? For example, did he know about the magistrate's warrant that Rampton had given Savill? Did he know that the boy had been struck dumb?

A memory stirred in Savill's mind: when he had called here before, when Rampton had talked confidentially to him in the inner office, Malbourne had not quite closed the door to the outer office, the room in which they were sitting now. Had that been by accident or design? If the latter, had Malbourne eavesdropped on their conversation? Was it possible that he knew that Mr Rampton intended to make Charles his heir?

'You do not look yourself, sir,' Malbourne said. 'I understand from Mr Rampton that you've been unwell.'

'I'm quite restored now,' Savill said. He could not prevent himself from running the tip of his tongue over the smooth skin that lined the socket where his tooth had been, from probing the slight swelling that lingered there.

'I'm rejoiced to hear it. And where have you left Charles?'

'There has been a difficulty. That is why it's so urgent that I should see Mr Rampton.'

Malbourne smiled slightly and his eyebrows rose. He leaned forward in his chair, waiting for Savill to explain. Instead, Savill listened to the sound of a carriage passing along the street and said nothing.

'Ah!' Malbourne tapped his table in mock irritation. 'I had nearly forgot – there is something for you.' He opened a portfolio on his table, took out a letter and handed it to Savill.

It was directed to him care of Mr Rampton's office. Savill recognized his sister's large, careful handwriting. He murmured an apology and broke the seal.

*My dear Brother,*
*I have received News from my Sister Ann, saying that my poor Husband's Mother is very ill, and is believed to be on her Deathbed. She is most Anxious to see Me, and I to see Her, for She was very good to me when I was first*

*Married, so I am obliged to go to Norwich. Lizzie does*
*not wish to accompany Me, saying she would be a*
*Burden to my Husband's Family at this Sad Time.*
*Besides, she wishes to be here in London for your*
*Return. I have shut up the house, and Lizzie has gone to*
*Stay with Mrs Pycroft and to help Mary with her*
*Preparations. I shall return as soon as I may. With*
*Heaven's Blessing, the Melancholy Event will be Delayed*
*until another Year at least.*

*In the Hope that your Business in the Country has*
*prospered, I am, dear Brother, your affect. Sister,*
*J. Ferguson*

'Not bad news, I hope?' Malbourne said with a slight smile.

Savill shook his head. It occurred to him that Malbourne and Rampton might already know the contents; and even that Malbourne might expect him to consider this possibility.

'My sister has been obliged to shut up the house in my absence.' He folded the letter and put it in his pocket. 'Did Mr Rampton leave any word for me?'

'Not with me, sir. Was he expecting you and Charles today?'

'No. Not in particular.' Savill stood up. 'I must not trespass further on your time.'

'But what will you do?'

'I shall go home, sir, in case Mr Rampton left a message there. Then I shall go to Vardells.'

Malbourne accompanied him down the stairs. 'Where do you stay tonight?'

'I left my bag at the Swan With Two Necks. I shall probably go there, as my house is shut up. Unless Mr Rampton keeps me with him at Vardells.'

'If he is not at Vardells, why not come here, sir?'

Savill stopped abruptly, his hand on the rail. 'Here?'

'We have an arrangement with the house over the way,' Malbourne said. 'We keep two apartments at our sole disposal

257

– our couriers and so on come and go, you see, often with very little warning. The bedchambers are not large but they are clean, and you may have food sent in, if you wish. I'm persuaded you would be much more comfortable there than at an inn. And of course you would be able to see Mr Rampton the very instant he arrives tomorrow morning.'

'I am much obliged, sir.'

'Then I will leave word with them. And with Jarsdel. They will do whatever you require. If you wish it, they will have your bags brought over from the Swan With Two Necks, and pay your bill there.' Malbourne was studying him with pale, clear eyes. 'Forgive me, sir, but you look fatigued. Wherever you go, I hope you find a good dinner and a good night's sleep.'

Is a home to a house what a soul is to a body?

Savill stared at the shuttered façade of his house in Nightingale Lane. From where he stood on the corner, he could see the tops of the tall chimneys of the kitchen and bakehouse. There was no trace of smoke. He had looked forward to this moment since he left London – the first sight of his own house; the foreknowledge of the welcome that awaited him within.

Without people inside it, though, the place was as forlorn as a corpse. He chided himself for his folly – he had known the house would be empty; it was irrational to feel melancholy to see proof of it with his own eyes. Yet his sensibilities obstinately refused to behave in a rational manner.

Savill decided against calling on Mrs Forster, the servant who acted as a caretaker when the family was away, though this would have been courteous and perhaps sensible as well. Once, however, Mrs Forster had been a housekeeper for a lawyer in Lincoln's Inn and with old age she had become garrulous about the glories and curiosities of her previous position – and, indeed, about any other subject under the sun that took her fancy, so long as it related to herself.

258

Mrs Forster was a good woman and wholly trustworthy; and Savill's sister depended on her for assistance with the management of the house; but it was almost impossible to stop her talking once she had begun. She was deaf, as well, and when she and Savill's sister talked together, their conversation was audible all over the house.

She did not live with them, a circumstance that Savill considered a merciful blessing from almighty God, but lodged in the smallest of the houses in the lane with her niece, an altogether unfortunate young person who was in fact widely believed to be her natural daughter by her previous employer.

That was the reason why Savill had entered Nightingale Lane not by the wider entrance where it passed directly in front of her parlour window, but by the footpath that communicated with one of the new roads north of Bedford Square.

He took a key from his pocket and unlocked a low door set in the wall by the side of the house. The door opened into the kitchen yard. To the left was the house; directly opposite him, and attached to the house, was the lower roofline of the stable and the loft above. Through an archway on his right was his garden and, beyond it, the trees of his orchard.

Savill passed into the house by the door to the scullery, whose key was concealed under a stone in the yard. The air inside was cool and damp, for none of the fires had been lit for days. The kitchen table was bare and newly scrubbed. The walls were thick. The only sound was the ticking of the clock in the hall.

The shutters covered the principal windows of the larger rooms, but enough light filtered through the cracks for him to be able to find his way. He looked into the downstairs apartments, knowing they were empty but driven by a desire to see them again. He went upstairs and found a clean shirt in the press in his own chamber.

He left to last the room where he transacted business and sat reading when he wished only for his own company. His sister referred to it with a certain pride as the bookroom.

On the table he found a pile of letters waiting for him – three bills, and a line from his tailor to say that the Sunday coat he had ordered was ready for him to try on at his convenience.

There was also a letter from his daughter. He tore it open and held it to the light from the window.

*Dearest Papa,*
*I shall be Mortified if you bring my Brother home while*
*I am at Mrs Pycroft's with Mary. Pray call on us with*
*him as soon as ever you may. I have a Particular Favour*
*to ask. May I not come Home and Keep house for you,*
*even before my Aunt returns? I do so wish to meet*
*Charles, and to see you of course, and Mary will get*
*along very Well with her Sewing without Me. You have*
*been Gone such an Age.*
*Your Loving Daughter,*
*E. Savill*

But there was nothing from Mr Rampton.

The afternoon was well advanced by the time Savill came up the drive to Vardells. The weather had improved during his ride from town, though now it was growing colder. The long windows of the new library reflected watery sunlight, more silver than gold. The sky was a very pale blue and partly veiled with high lace-like clouds.

At the house they said that Mr Rampton had sent word he would not come down yesterday and probably not today, either. It left Savill with no alternative but to ride back with the sour knowledge that this had been a wasted day.

Near the lodge, he stopped and took from his pocket the brass telescope that Dr Gohlis had found in the woods. The house was visible from here and he focused the glass on it. It was a well-made thing and the image was so sharp that the wall of the house seemed near enough to touch.

There was no trace of the swallows that had so irritated Mr Rampton. By this time of year, they would have departed, or hidden themselves away in the mysterious place where they spent the winters. Aristotle, Savill had read, believed that swallows, swifts and martins huddled together in groups, wrapped themselves in balls of mud and lay, snug and dry, at the bottom of ponds until spring. He did not think it likely himself, for surely someone would have found a ball of them by now. He hoped Charles was warm, wherever he was, for winter was coming.

The grounds were studded with young trees that would flourish as mature specimens in a hundred years' time. It occurred to Savill that Vardells, like Norbury Park, had been built for a posterity that did not exist: that Mr Rampton, like the late Mr West, was building a dream, not a country house. A dream that needed Charles to make it real.

# Chapter Forty

Waking and dozing, thinking and dreaming, Charles hears the sound all night long. *Tip-tap.* Tell no one. Tell no one that the black sky will soon rain blood.

On the other side of the cupboard door, the man in the blue coat is restless. He paces up and down, the floorboards creaking. Once he stumbles. A chair falls over and so, perhaps, does he, for he swears and stamps and then weeps. He also breaks a glass.

Later still, when the man has been snoring for some time, Charles rises to his feet very slowly and, with the blanket draped around his shoulders, he listens at the door. The regular rhythm of the breathing does not change.

*Tip-tap.* If it were not for that, the scales of fear would be equally balanced. To stay or to try to escape. At least there is no longer room for doubt. Not now.

Holding his breath, Charles pushes the wire in the lock and pulls the door away from it, while nudging the door outward with a gentle pressure from his knee. With a scrape that assaults the ears, the door swings away from him.

The snoring stops. Charles holds his breath. The rustle of the river filters into the silence. The room is very nearly dark. The window overlooking the garden is uncurtained. The sky beyond the glass is grey, though the trees of the garden are nothing but jagged black shadows.

The man sighs. His breathing resumes and so, in a moment, does his snoring, though now it is a more delicate and melodious sound than before, with an extra whistle at the very end of each in-breath.

Charles picks up his shoes and, still with the blanket around him, takes a step into the room. Then another. This brings him within reach of the table. His fingertips dance over the scarred surface. He feels the outline of a small piece of cheese. He puts it in the pocket of his breeches.

His eyes adjust to what light there is. The man in the blue coat sprawls on his blankets in the corner, with his head on the velvet cushion. Step by step, Charles edges towards the door beside the window. It is impossible to do this silently, no matter how hard he tries. The warped timbers of the boathouse are in league with his enemies. They groan and squeak like malevolent animals underneath the floor.

All this time, the snoring does not stop. At last Charles touches the door. He runs his hand over it until he finds the lock. The key is not there. He almost stamps with vexation. The key could be anywhere – on the table, on the floor or – worst of all – in the pocket of the man in the blue coat. The room is too dark to see anything clearly.

Perhaps this door is warped, as the cupboard door was. Charles lifts the heavy latch and tugs it away from the jamb beside it. With a sigh, the door swings into him with such force that he almost falls backwards into the room. It stops abruptly when the bottom of it catches a slightly raised board in the uneven floor.

There is a gap between door and jamb of about a foot. Charles slips through it and pulls the door shut. It is only then that his brain catches up with his reflexes, and he understands what has happened: the man in the blue coat has forgotten to lock the door.

*　　*　　*

263

The day is beginning. The ruined garden is silvered with dew. Charles descends the steps and turns to his right. The great grey river runs past the bottom of the garden. The further bank is a dark blur, apart from a handful of lights from early risers.

A wooden jetty runs alongside the boathouse and projects a few yards into the water. The door to the lower part of the boathouse stands ajar. Charles looks inside. The dinghy rocks at its moorings, audible as much as visible. He glances up at the ceiling, at the wooden planks that form the floor of the room above. The snores drift down and mingle with the heave and slap of the water.

For a moment he entertains a wild idea that he will sail away downstream until the river takes him out to sea: the gentle wind will guide him to a desert island where he may live in peace as a hermit and never see blood again or hear the sounds of cracking walnuts. But the practicalities of such a voyage are overwhelming. Besides, the river is a cold, grim thing and he does not want to trust himself to it.

But the dinghy?

He unties the painter. Hand over hand, he eases the boat along the jetty and pushes it into the river. The current catches it. It turns full circle in the water and slides away from the bank. It moves downstream. A mist is hanging on the water and soon it is out of sight.

Find the island, he thinks, find the island. If nothing else it will make the man in the blue coat think that Charles has escaped by the river.

Seagulls cry. He walks away from the water. A dog barks in the distance.

On the landward side, the boathouse is masked by the overgrown trees and bushes. Even the gravelled path is thick with tall weeds, drenched with moisture. But someone has beaten down a path of sorts among them.

The further Charles walks from the river, the clearer the

path comes and more light pours into the world. The silhouette of a house appears, its chimneys and roofs sharp against the brightening sky. He veers away from it and draws the blanket over his head like a shawl.

A wall looms. It is built of brick and is at least six feet high. A fox appears and darts away, seeming to evaporate in the air before Charles's very eyes.

The reason is that the upper part of the wall has collapsed, leaving a gap a yard wide. It offers an easy jump for a fox and an easy scramble for a boy.

Beyond the wall is a meadow. Charles has a crushing sense of the world's immensity, of his own insignificance. He wishes himself back among the half-known terrors of the boathouse.

Only a moment.

Weeping, he staggers across the uneven grass. A dark shadow stands in his way. It is the size and shape of a cottage. He is almost within touching distance before he realizes it is a laden haywain sheeted with canvas, not a house.

The tears are cold on his cheeks. There is a pain in his belly. Weariness weighs him down.

It seems the most natural thing in the world to scramble into the belly of the wain and to wriggle higher and deeper into the loose, sweet-smelling and slightly damp hay. Covering himself with the blanket, Charles cries himself to sleep.

At first he is at sea, going to his island. The ship is swaying from side to side. The rigging creaks and groans. A strange rumbling sends vibrations through the timbers.

The sailors are talking among themselves.

'Say what you like,' says one, 'it's not right.'

'Only day that's left,' says another.

'But it's Sunday.'

'No Sabbaths on a farm. You know that.'

'They'll have to stack it themselves.'

'What's that to us, Dick? Besides, horses don't care what

265

day of the week it is. Got to eat, don't they, even on Sundays, same as us.'

So Charles learns that he is not on a boat, not at sea. He is still embedded in hay and he is thirsty. On the other hand, he is warm and surprisingly comfortable. He feels happier – or at least less unhappy, less fearful – than he has since leaving Charnwood on the terrible morning when Louis was revealed as a false friend.

The wain moves very slowly along a road. The voices of the two men are different from the peasants' voices in Somersetshire, sharper and harder and faster. He makes a peephole in the straw but all he sees are muddy fields.

Charles eats the cheese, which is salty and makes him thirstier. He licks and then sucks some of the damper pieces of hay. After a while he dozes, lulled by the grinding of the great wheels and the rising and fall of the voices. He has no idea where the men are taking him. He does not care.

Hours drift between waking and sleeping in the sweet-smelling new-mown grass. Charles sucks hay and dreams.

At length he becomes aware that there is a change in the sounds that envelop him. The heavy iron clatter of the wheels is still there, and so too are the voices of the men. But around them and beyond them is a deep, rolling roar like a waterfall. People are shouting, too, and once he hears a child scream.

Charles burrows to the side of the load and makes a peephole in the hay. The air is so foul that he retches. He sees the first-floor windows of houses passing slowly by, and then two men on horseback. A woman in black sweeps a doorstep. They have come to a town, perhaps London itself.

The more deeply they penetrate the city, the more slowly the haywain goes; the more halts there are; and the more the realization grows on Charles that he must not stay here until the wagon reaches its destination. They will unload the hay and he cannot fail to be discovered.

266

He negotiates his way to the back. The sides of the wain splay out from the bed on which the hay rests. They are formed of vertical planks with spaces for the air between them. But the spaces are too narrow for Charles to squeeze through. He struggles up to the rail that connects the planks at the top. He misjudges the speed of his ascent, and his head pokes out in plain sight, just above the rail.

Directly in front of him is a cart drawn by a skinny pony. An old man is sitting in the cart, a pipe clenched between his teeth and a hat drawn over his eyes. But the reins are held by the boy who sits beside him.

In the same instant, the boy sees Charles and Charles sees the boy. The boy sticks out his tongue and wrinkles his nose. Before he can prevent himself, Charles does likewise. The boy grins. Charles grins.

The wain comes to a halt again. So does the cart. Somewhere ahead, drivers are arguing and growing angry. Charles clambers up and rolls over the rail.

He lands heavily on cobbles smeared with horse droppings. The impact drives the air from his lungs. He scrambles up. The boy on the cart is craning over to watch him. He pokes out his tongue at Charles. He puts his thumbs to his ears and he wiggles his fingers.

'Yah . . .' he says.

The traffic begins to move again.

Charles runs through the streets. It is Sunday, late afternoon, shading into early evening. Despite the holiness of the day, streams of people pass up and down the streets and the roadways are crowded with vehicles. Though some establishments are closed, there are many shoppers about. The air smells of sewage and smoke.

Already lamps and candles glow inside some of the shops. Instinct keeps him to the busier thoroughfares. Dangers lurk in dark, unfrequented places, not among crowds.

He steals a roll from a stall in a poorly lit doorway and runs on, his heart hammering with fear. The roll is stale but it tastes wonderful: 'Quite divine,' Maman would say when she was served a dish she liked, for she had an appetite for food and a keen appreciation of it. 'Fit for the gods.'

Afterwards, he wanders on. A sign in the window of a shirtmaker's reads: THE FINEST LINEN IN LONDON. AS PATRONIZED BY THE NOBILITY AND GENTRY. PRAY WALK IN AND INSPECT OUR MANY TESTIMONIALS. So at least he can be sure he is in London.

The food has steadied him. Charles knows that he cannot walk the streets for ever, that he must find shelter. He cannot ask a stranger for help, for who would listen to a boy who cannot speak?

His mysterious uncle Rampton must live in London but he has no idea where. So does Mr Savill, who lives in a place called Nightingale Lane, with his daughter, Lizzie, the girl who once looked like Charles himself.

Lizzie, Charles thinks, my sister.

All at once, she seems the obvious solution to his difficulty. She is grown up now. She will protect him. He does not have to stay with her if he does not like her. She will do for now, at least until Mr Savill returns.

Nightingale Lane is on the northern edge of the city. That is what Mr Savill said. It is near a place where they are building new houses for rich people. There is an alehouse called the Royal Oak nearby. Nightingale Lane and the Royal Oak belong in the country, and the new houses belong in the city. There is a walnut tree in Mr Savill's garden.

*Tip-tap.* Cracking a walnut. A walnut tree. What does the coincidence mean?

Charles is passing a churchyard crowded with memorials, some broken, others at drunken angles. The tower attached to the church is crumbling and a wooden paling has been erected around it.

Movement catches his eye. He glances up at the house on the corner. A maidservant carrying a lamp has entered an upper room. The light is dim, and filtered through thick, distorted glass; but as the woman moves to the window to draw the curtains across, the outline of a canopied bed appears briefly behind her.

A bed. Bedford. That is the name of the new houses. Bedford Square.

Charles slips inside the churchyard and takes the pencil and paper from his pocket. Using a gravestone as a writing slope, he prints six words in careful capitals:

OAK TREE
NIGHTINGALE-LANE
BEDFORD-SQUARE

He is in a quandary. He must not speak. *Say nothing. Not a word to anyone.*

Until now he has extended the prohibition to cover writing as well, for Father Viré taught him long ago in his other life that God does not split hairs, that the spirit of His commands should be considered and obeyed, not merely their literal meaning.

But surely God and Father Viré would not want him to wander the streets of London for ever? Will they pardon him if he uses those six words in his hour of need? Or will they bring down their most terrible vengeance on his head?

# Chapter Forty-One

The smell of the river hung in the air, mingling with the acrid smoke of the kitchen fires. The three houses were set back from the thoroughfare on the west side of Arundel Street, separated from the road by an area paved with granite setts slippery with rain.

Mr Vereker's establishment was open for business. As Savill went towards it, an apprentice laid aside his broom and rushed to hold the door for him. A young man was polishing a large set of scales that formed a centrepiece in the middle of the shop. He set aside his cloth and bowed.

'Good day, sir. How may I serve you?'

'I wish to see Mr Vereker.'

'He is at breakfast, sir. He will be down in five or ten minutes. But in the meantime, perhaps—'

'I have not leisure to wait,' Savill said, wishing that he himself had had time for breakfast before leaving the lodgings in Crown Street that Malbourne had procured for him. 'Pray tell him I must see him now. I come from the magistrates' office.' He patted his coat pocket. 'I have a warrant.'

The assistant retreated to a curtained doorway at the back of the shop, contriving to bow as he went. The apprentice stopped sweeping and stared at Savill with interest.

There were voices above and then heavy footsteps on the stairs. A thin man with hunched shoulders came into the shop. He had a napkin in his hand and there were crumbs on his coat. His wig was askew and his chin was thick with grey stubble.

'What's this, sir? A magistrate?'

'Mr Vereker? My name is Savill.' He took out his letter of authorization and waved it. 'As you see, Mr Ford of the Westminster Magistrates' Office appoints me to act as his agent or deputy.'

Frowning, the old man took the letter, unfolded it and glanced at its contents. Too agitated to read it carefully, he thrust it back towards Savill. 'But – what is this about, sir? I have not reported a robbery or—'

'A telescope bearing your name was found at the scene of a crime, sir. It is of the utmost urgency that we establish to whom it belongs. It may lead us to the perpetrator.'

'Dear me.' Mr Vereker sank into a chair. 'How very distressing. A glass of my manufacture?'

Savill took the telescope from his pocket and handed it to Vereker. When the old man held it, the signs of age and agitation dropped away from him. He extended the cylinder to its fullest extent, whipped out a cloth and polished the brass. He took a jeweller's glass from his waistcoat pocket and screwed it into his left eye. He examined the telescope minutely.

'Sims?' he said, without looking up. 'Bring me the ledger. No, not the current one. 'Eighty-one to eighty-four.'

'There is a number by the eyepiece,' Savill said. 'Eight, three, one, four.'

'Yes, yes,' Vereker said, almost snatching the ledger from his apprentice. He turned the pages rapidly, running his forefinger down the left-hand margin of the page. 'Ah. It is as I thought.'

'Eight and three signify the year eighty-three?' Savill said.

Vereker looked up. A flicker of disappointment passed over

271

his face. 'Yes. The first two figures denote the year of manu-facture, or rather the year it was made available for purchase. The rest of the number identifies the particular instrument. So this is nine years old.' He held it up to the light from the window. 'I pride myself that it represents a tolerable marriage of utility and convenience.'

Savill wanted to snatch the ledger from Vereker's hands. 'What happened to it, sir?'

'Eh? Oh yes.' The forefinger moved slowly across the page. 'Yes, I recall the transaction perfectly. As if it were yesterday.'

'Who bought it, sir?'

Vereker peered at the entry. 'Mr Ogden, sir. A lawyer. He's not a regular customer of mine, and I cannot say I'm sorry for that.'

'Why?' Savill said. 'Doesn't he pay his bills?'

'He did in the end. But it was not just that – half my customers do not find it convenient to pay their bills as promptly as they should, and one cannot object to them because of that or one would lose half one's connection. No, it was Mr Ogden himself – his manner, one might say. Not an easy man to do business with.'

On the way to Lincoln's Inn Fields, Savill turned into a tavern and ordered breakfast. He lingered over the meal, reading the newspapers and drinking tea, since it was early for a morning call on a private residence. But he could not stay too long, for he was due back at Westminster by ten o'clock.

It was still raining when he walked on. He knew he was clutching at straws but there was nothing else to hold on to. Besides, doing anything was better than doing nothing. If he allowed himself a moment's quiet reflection, all he could think of was Charles and where he might be. His fear for the boy coloured every thought he had.

Mr Ogden lived in a tall, thin house in a street to the north of the Fields. It was one of a terrace of some substance, set back from the street by its own carriage road, and served by its own mews.

The manservant who answered the door said that his master was not at home. But the sound of a harsh voice upstairs suggested that this was not be taken literally. Savill produced his warrant again.

The manservant left him in a dark room off the hall and went to find his master. He returned with instructions from his master that Mr Savill should send up a note stating his business.

Savill tore a page from his pocketbook and jotted down: 'Mr Savill, from Mr Ford, Westminster Magistrates' Office, Case of Abduction.' The servant took the note away.

While he waited, Savill prowled about the room, trying to distract himself. He fiddled with the candlesticks on the mantel. He stared at a gloomy engraving that portrayed the ruins of an indeterminate building of antiquity. He examined a pile of books on a side table – all novels of a sentimental nature, he was surprised to see, and borrowed from Mr Bell's British Library in the Strand. He pulled back the curtains and stared across the carriage drive to the street beyond.

About ten minutes later, an old man in a dressing gown entered the room. His face was pale, almost green in the gloom of the parlour.

'Mr Savill? My name is Ogden. Well?'

Savill bowed. 'Forgive me for—'

'Let's see this warrant of yours.'

Ogden put on a pair of glasses and studied the letter from Mr Ford. He handed it back to Savill. 'If you want me to answer questions, sir, I suggest you show this to a magistrate and beg him to ask them on your behalf. Assuming that this document is not a forgery. I can see no reason why I should trust it, or you, without supporting testimony.'

'Then I shall be obliged to return later, sir.'

Ogden shrugged. 'In that case, I hope you will write and make an appointment in the usual manner. My time is too valuable to waste.' He rang the bell. 'I won't detain you longer, sir.'

The servant came at once. Ogden followed Savill into the hall. He opened the door of another room and paused.

'Why do you want to see me, anyway?' he said. 'What's this about an abduction?'

'It involves a telescope that may have a bearing on it,' Savill said. 'It was purchased by you from Mr Vereker in Arundel Street.'

Ogden clutched the jamb of the door. He stared at Savill. 'What nonsense,' he said.

'Why, sir? Mr Vereker remembered you. And I have seen his sales ledger.'

'I lost the thing years ago. And it never gave me any satisfaction. Good day, sir.'

He went into the room and slammed the door. High above Savill's head came the sound of scurrying footsteps. He glanced up but saw no one.

'This way, sir,' said the servant.

The old woman burst out of the mews and blurted out: 'Sir, sir – have you news?'

Her grey hair had come adrift from her cap and straggled down to her shoulders. She wore a grey shawl over a day dress. She had slippers on her feet, not pattens. But what Savill noticed first was her ruined face.

A younger woman followed, almost at once – a servant who laid her hand on the first woman's arm. 'Ma'am, you'll catch your death out here, and if Master finds out—'

'No, no – go away.'

Savill might have walked on, for the streets of London were full of unhinged people and lost souls, had it not been for the evident respectability of the maidservant and the pathos

274

of the mistress's face. The rain had grown heavier and neither woman was wearing a cloak or a bonnet.

'News of what, madam?'

'My son, of course.'

'I'm afraid I don't have the honour of his acquaintance.'

'You were talking to my husband, sir. You mentioned the telescope.'

Savill took off his hat and bowed. 'I beg your pardon, ma'am. Am I addressing Mrs Ogden?'

'Yes, yes.' The lady had suffered a stroke that had caused the left side of her face to droop and become rigid, though it had not affected her speech. 'It must be his telescope. My husband does not care for such things himself, and I know he purchased one for Dick. From – from Mr Vereker, you said?'

'Yes, it was.' Savill studied her face, which was wet with rain and perhaps tears as well. She must have run from the back door and through the mews in the hope of cutting him off, with the maid in hot pursuit. 'Madam, the weather is not clement, you will—'

'It does not signify, sir, not in the slightest. You see, there was a time when Dick had a fancy to pursue the study of astronomy . . . But tell me, have you seen my son?'

'I'm afraid not. The glass was found in Somersetshire. There is reason to believe it may have been connected with a crime.'

Mrs Ogden gave a cry and clung to her maid, who scowled at Savill.

'Forgive me for startling you – I should say that there is no evidence to suggest your son is involved.' Not yet, Savill might have added, not yet. 'But pray tell me more about the young gentleman. Perhaps I may be able to help.'

As he was speaking there were running footsteps in the mews.

Mrs Ogden took a piece of paper from the pocket of her dress. She thrust it at Savill, who took it.

275

'Four o'clock, sir,' she whispered. 'Four o'clock. I am there almost every day.'

Mr Ogden's manservant appeared, followed by a short, burly youth who was almost as wide as he was tall. Mrs Ogden cowered against the wall. Savill screwed up the paper in his hand.

'You're to come home directly, ma'am,' the servant said, shouldering himself between her and Savill. 'Master's orders.'

He took Mrs Ogden's arm. The maid took her other arm. They marched the old woman into the mews, half dragging and half carrying her.

The youth stayed where he was. He glared at Savill and folded his arms across his chest. He waited, seeming to inflate himself still further, blocking the mouth of the mews; and Savill looked at the retreating back of Mrs Ogden and listened to the rainwater rustling in the gutter.

Afterwards, walking to the Strand, Savill unfolded the paper. It was a printed bill, a copy of the subscribers' conditions at the British Library.

# Chapter Forty-Two

'I cannot for the life of me understand how you permitted this to happen. First the delay occasioned by your damned tooth. And now this.'

Mr Rampton paced up and down his room. It was mid-morning now. He had arrived only a quarter of an hour ago and still wore his long travelling coat and mud-splashed boots. Age and weariness made him unsteady on his feet, but his agitation drove him to movement. There were blue pouches under his eyes.

'Why should you let a little toothache distract you from your business? I tell you plainly, I would not have expected it of you . . .' He pulled at his fingers and cracked his knuckles as if to emphasize his amazement. 'It beggars belief! Besides, you don't even know Charles has been brought to London. He could be anywhere. I am surrounded by fools.'

Savill let the angry words alone, allowing them to dwindle into petulance.

Rampton sat down at last. He lowered his voice. 'It was ill-luck that you arrived on Saturday, too.'

'Where were you?' Savill said. 'I went to Vardells yesterday but they said you had sent word not to expect you. But you weren't in town, either.'

'His Lordship called me down to the country on Saturday morning – he was most pressing, he had a sudden desire to confer with me in private – indeed, the business of this department weighs heavily on me. He relies on me entirely.'

'The chaise was hired in town, from the Swan With Two Necks,' Savill said after a moment, returning to the subject on hand now he was no longer the immediate target of Rampton's fury. 'And they returned it there on Saturday morning, about nine o'clock.'

'Not so loud, if you please. Irwin returned it?'

'No, the servant, Plimming, did. He must have set down Irwin and Charles on the road. It was somewhere in or near London because Irwin was seen at Slough. And it must have been near the main road – they drove like the devil to get there as soon as nine – they had no time to make diversions.'

'They might have handed Charles over to someone long before Slough.' Rampton had not put in his teeth. His words had no hard edges to them and too many sibilants. 'It was a closed carriage. No one would know.'

Savill nodded. 'Perhaps. But there's nothing to suggest they did. Whereas we do know that Irwin himself hired the chaise in London. In the absence of any other information, that suggests he came back here. The first thing to do, surely, is to establish whether there is a connection between Irwin and the Ogdens. Are there grounds for a magistrate to—'

'No. It's out of the question.'

'Why? Abduction is a crime, and—'

'You don't understand.' Calmer now, Rampton leaned across his empty desk. 'There are elements of this matter that you know nothing about, elements that have to do with the safety of the kingdom and the impending war with France. Why do you think I was obliged to wait on His Lordship so urgently?'

'Sir, this is a question of a kidnapped boy,' Savill said. 'Charles is important too.'

'I'm quite aware of that.'

278

'Shouldn't I – or someone – try to talk to the Ogdens? It is surely significant that their son once owned the perspective glass that Dr Gohlis found at Charnwood?'

Rampton waved the suggestion away. 'You must leave all that to me. It will be looked into, and by people better qualified than you. In the meantime, you must mention nothing of this to anyone, even Malbourne. Particularly not Malbourne. Have you told him anything?'

'Only that there has been a difficulty. I have not mentioned the abduction.'

'Good. It must go no further than us. We cannot afford for news of this to leak into the wider world, not before we know what we are dealing with. We must ask ourselves who is behind this. And why.'

'If we know the one, we'll probably know the other.'

'No one but you has any legitimate claim on the boy. And myself, of course, as his great-uncle, and also as one who will soon be his adoptive father.'

'The Count de Quillon does not agree.'

'Would he kidnap Charles? You have lived with him now. What is your impression?'

'He is imperious by nature, sir, and accustomed to his own way. It would not surprise me at all to learn that he and Monsieur Fournier were concealing a good deal from me. It is possible that he ordered me to be poisoned to prolong my illness. I believe they searched my belongings while I lay ill and went through my papers.'

'Is he attached to the boy?'

'I suspect it is more a question of pride. But I can believe he would go to almost any lengths to secure Charles. On the other hand, I do not think he has the resources or the subtlety to arrange what has happened.'

'Of course that scoundrel Fournier must be a part of it.'

Savill sat down without being offered a chair. 'If the Count is behind it, then yes, Monsieur Fournier would probably have managed the affair for him. Though that assumes he has considerable resources in this country. And I don't know why he would do it, why he would run the risk, unless he has his own reasons to oblige the Count.'

'It is possible that he has. The Count's faction may be discredited, here and in France, but he still has friends, and who knows what the future will bring? Who else?'

'My— Augusta may have had friends in France we know nothing of. Or there may be other men who think the boy is theirs. Or perhaps it is not who he is that matters, not in himself. Perhaps it is what he knows.'

'What do you mean?' Rampton said. 'You talk in riddles.'

'It is probable that he was there when Augusta died. When she was killed. He may know the identity of her murderer.'

'In which case . . .' Rampton's voice trembled. He cleared his throat. 'In which case . . .'

'In which case,' Savill said, 'it becomes more likely that Charles's own life is in danger.'

In which case, he thought, it becomes more likely that Charles is already dead.

There was a knock on the door and Malbourne came into the room, bearing a letter.

'Can't you see I'm engaged?' Rampton snapped.

'I beg your pardon, sir.' Malbourne seemed unruffled by the rudeness. 'But I believe you will wish to see this at once. It concerns the Charnwood party.'

Rampton took the letter, which was already open. He put his glasses on his nose and read it. When he had finished, he very carefully folded the letter.

'Have it resealed and sent on at once,' he said to Malbourne, pushing it across the desk. He looked at Savill. 'Mrs West has written to the people of the house in Green Street where she lodges when she comes to London. She orders her apartments to be prepared for her arrival, probably late this evening. She is bringing a young lady with her as her companion.' He tugged at his fingers. 'And she instructs them to bespeak lodgings in the same neighbourhood for three gentlemen who will be accompanying her.'

# Chapter Forty-Three

On Sunday night, Charles sleeps among the dead.

He is too exhausted to care where he is or who are his neighbours. He has spent the evening searching in vain for Bedford Square and Nightingale Lane and a tavern called the Royal Oak. Fear of retribution prevented him from showing his paper with the pencilled names.

*Tip-tap.*

So Charles has roamed the streets for hours, reading the signs on the buildings and the bills on the walls, and hoping for a miracle. The later the hour, the more the city is crowded with drunken people and flaring lights. The noise of the traffic is interminable and deafening.

He has no idea where he has gone and where he is going. But always his legs bring him back to the churchyard with the broken graves and the crumbling tower.

At last he has no more strength. There is a gap where the paling around the tower joins the wall of the church. It is just wide enough for him to wriggle through.

A shallow porch projects from the west wall of the tower, leading to a door that is black with age and bound with iron. Stone benches face each other across the porch. He huddles on one of these.

It is quieter here. By now it is too dark to see very much. He searches his breeches pockets with his fingers, delving deep into the seams, and is rewarded with two crumbs of hard, fluff-wrapped cheese. Rainwater has collected in a puddle on the ground. He goes down on hands and knees and laps it like a dog.

Charles draws his coat around him, curls himself up in a corner of the bench and sleeps. This sort of sleep is really another form of wakefulness crossed with bad dreams. However small he makes himself, hunger and cold find their way in. They gnaw at his body like a pair of foxes.

While he lies there, clocks chime, the watch calls the hour and people pass up and down the street, talking, shouting and singing. There are people nearer by: in the churchyard itself, grunting and groaning, though whether they are alive or dead Charles neither knows nor cares.

The two-legged and four-legged animals patter and squeak and cry out. In this half-world between sleeping and waking, even the tower is awake. It creaks and groans like a ship at sea when the wind rises. At one point a stone crashes to the ground a few feet away from where Charles lies. He feels the impact as well as hears it.

There comes a time when the noises drop away and he can no longer move. It is dark. He wonders idly if this is death and why it has taken so long to come.

A grating sound fills Charles's head. He feels a draught on his face. He tries to move but his limbs won't obey him.

'Have you been here all night? Oh dear, dear. This will never do. We must get you away from here at once. It is most unsafe.'

Charles opens his eyes. A grey light fills the world. An old man is looking down at him. He has a great, curving nose and white, bushy eyebrows like a creature from a fairy tale.

'Can you walk?' He tries to draw Charles to his feet, but

Charles's limbs do not cooperate. 'Quite blue with cold. Can you feel anything? I shall have to lift you.'

Despite his age, the man is surprisingly strong. He carries Charles into the tower, where the air is if anything colder than outside, and hurries through an archway to the nave, which is crammed with box pews like rows of enormous coffins. He walks the length of the nave to a pew that is larger than the rest and shrouded with curtains. The door to it stands open. Inside is a cushioned bench, on which he lays Charles.

'Stay there,' he commands, not that Charles would be able to move even if he should want to.

He returns with an armful of old curtains and cloaks that he drapes over Charles, who drifts into a doze while this is happening.

When Charles wakes again, his feet and hands are burning and pricking and terribly painful. The light is brighter.

'I have brought you a drink,' the old man says. 'I will help you to sit up. Oh dear, dear, dear.'

The contents of the earthenware cup smell so richly of meat that Charles gags. The man holds the cup to his mouth, and makes him sip the thin liquid. It glides into Charles's stomach, warming and nourishing in a way that is oddly painful.

Afterwards there is stale bread, dipped in the drink. When he has eaten, Charles falls asleep, but this time he is almost warm, almost content.

The man is still there when he wakes. 'What is your name, my boy?' he says. 'Where are you from?'

Charles's eyes fill with tears. He would like to oblige his benefactor.

'I am Mr Herrick. I am the sexton of the place, though to tell the truth my son does most of the work of it now. Will you tell me your name? I promise I will not harm you.'

A great three-decker pulpit towers above the curtained pew. Charles lets it take his eyes up and up to the sounding board, on top of which stands an angel silently blowing a trumpet.

'Are you lost?' The old man touches Charles's shirt, rubbing the material between finger and thumb. 'I do not think you come from a poor family. Or from an institution. But perhaps these clothes were given to you by your master when his son outgrew them?'

Charles lifts his hand to his face and makes a cross with his forefingers over his mouth.

'Ah – you are dumb, then?' The old man takes silence for assent. 'Poor boy. Have they abandoned you? Is that why you are here?'

The fingers remain.

'And what's this?' The sexton holds up the scrap of paper with the words of Mr Savill's address written in pencil on it. 'Forgive me, I searched your pockets when you lay in a swoon. Is this place where you come from, or perhaps where you are going?'

Charles lowers his hands. He smiles at the old man. Surely a smile is just a smile? It will not bring the wrath of God with it or the sound of cracking walnuts.

A smile means yes.

The cart passes slowly northwards. The sexton's son is a large young man with a mouth hanging permanently ajar. His name is Jeremiah. In the back of the cart, a canvas sheet covers a slab of marble.

The sexton says the marble is to go to the mason's in Well's Yard off Bainbridge Street, where it will be cut, polished and engraved. It will not take long for Jeremiah to drive on afterwards and drop the boy in the neighbourhood of Bedford Square.

No one gives them a second glance as they crawl through the streets. It's a grey day and it's still raining. At the mason's yard, the men assume he is like any other boy. They order him to take the canvas off and look sharp about it. Jeremiah tells him to fold up the sheet and put it under the seat.

It is easier to do as they say than to do nothing. Under the seat is a basket containing a letter. Before they left, the sexton reminded Jeremiah to be sure to give it to the foreman of the yard for it contains not only the dimensions the slab is to be, but also the inscription that is to go on it.

'You must not forget this time,' Mr Herrick told his son. 'You must remember. Tie a knot in your handkerchief.'

Charles jumps down and hands the letter to Jeremiah, who gives a start of surprise and runs after the foreman. When he returns, he holds up his handkerchief and tugs at the knot. He smiles very slowly at Charles, and it is like the sun coming out.

They leave the yard and nudge their way into the stream of vehicles in Bainbridge Street. The rain stops and a watery sun forces its way through the smog that hangs over the city.

The further they go, the less traffic there is. They turn into a great thoroughfare called Tottenham Court Road. The houses are built of pale, yellowish-brown brick.

Jeremiah pulls over and points across the road with the whip. 'See? Bedford Street there. And the Square beyond.' He touches Charles's shoulder, half push, half caress. 'All right, then?'

Charles knows he must go, though at this moment he would like to stay with Jeremiah and his father the sexton for ever. He jumps from the cart, stumbles and almost topples into the gutter.

'Steady, young 'un,' says Jeremiah. 'Steady does it.' He smiles again and raises his whip in farewell.

Charles smiles back.

A smile is only a smile.

The great houses of Bedford Square look down on him. Most are of brick but in the middle of each side is a larger house faced with stone and topped with a pediment. Everything is on the grand scale, from the width of the pavements to the size of the oval grass plat, enclosed by a heavy iron railing, in the centre of the square.

Children are playing on the grass, watched over by servants. Three are throwing a ball. One child hops solemnly to and fro on a hobbyhorse. Another bowls a hoop that keeps falling over.

Charles pauses to watch. The children are much younger than him.

A blow between his shoulder blades drives him against the railings. Two servants out of livery are standing over him. He knows they are footmen by the traces of powder and paste in their hair and on the shoulders of their coats.

'Be off, you son of a whore.'

One of them kicks him, and he cries out and falls back against the railings.

'Oh, Mr Peters,' cries a pretty young servant on the other side of the railings, who is exercising a toddler on leading strings. 'Pray do not hurt the poor beggar boy.'

'It's to protect you, miss. He'd rob you blind as soon as look at you. We don't want his sort here.'

Charles is already darting away. Despite the pain in his leg, he skims across the square to a road on the other side, followed by the laughter of the servants. A carriage is passing and nearly runs him down. The coachman shouts at him.

He runs up the road lined with houses, some still unfinished. He ducks round a dray and plunges into a side road, and then into another that is narrower.

To his horror he sees that it ends in a high wall.

He catches sight of a sign swinging from a building beside a warehouse. Crudely painted on it is an oak tree. Perched among its branches is a monkey-like man wearing a crown.

With a leap of apprehension, he knows it must be the alehouse that Mr Savill mentioned, the one that backs on to his garden where the walnut tree is.

Beside the Royal Oak, a footpath runs between two walls

of faded red brick. Charles takes the path. It swings to the right and then to the left. It is much quieter here because the walls block out much of the noise of the surrounding streets.

A bird sings. He glances up. A thrush sits on the overhanging branches of a tree on the other side of the wall to the right. Above the bird is a small green fruit.

Not a fruit. A walnut. It is the only one he can see on the tree, for the others have long since been shaken or picked from the tree. Beyond the tree is a door in the wall. He lifts the latch. The door will not open.

But he has found Mr Savill's garden. He follows the path to the point when it turns into a short lane, or close, with a pair of houses on either side. Their roofs are mossy with age, and their frontages are framed with great timbers. The largest house, which has the walnut tree in the garden behind it, must be Mr Savill's. The windows are shuttered, though it is the middle of the day. No smoke rises from the chimneys.

Tears fill his eyes. If the house is empty, where can he go now?

A door opens in one of the other houses. Charles draws back to the safety of the footpath. He waits a moment. Footsteps are coming towards him. He retreats further, past the door in the wall, as far as the nearest corner.

The footsteps come closer, and then stop. There is a faint, metallic rattle, followed by the scrape and clack of the latch.

He walks back to the door in the wall. His first thought is that Mr Savill has returned or, if not, someone of his household, someone who may know who Charles is.

Very slowly, he raises the latch on the door. He pushes it a few inches open.

In front of him is a yard. An old woman dressed in black is crouching by a pump. She has not heard him. He watches her lifting a stone and taking out a key. She rises with some difficulty to her full height and inserts the key in a door into the house. She opens the door and goes inside, leaving the door ajar behind her.

Charles has learned fear in the last two months and with it has come caution. Mr Savill mentioned a sister, but he cannot be sure if she is this woman. She is dressed like a servant.

He enters the yard and closes the door to the alley. He slips through an archway to the right, which leads into a garden. He runs past vegetable beds and bushes to an orchard at the end. Here is the walnut tree.

In one corner is a place where compost is heaped in an untidy pile. He crouches beside it, wrapping his arms around his knees, and feels the faint warmth it gives off. An old apple tree stands between him and the entrance into the orchard. He does not feel safe – he never feels safe – but no one will see him unless they come to this side of the orchard.

The smell of rotting vegetation fills his nostrils, not unpleasantly. He watches the chimneys of the house. There is still no sign of smoke from any of them.

He listens. The sounds of the city rise and fall. Sometimes it is so quiet that he might almost be in the country. Clocks chime at intervals. One hour passes. Then half an hour.

Charles stands up and stretches. He urinates against the compost heap. He moves warily towards the house.

At the archway he stops a moment. The back door is closed. He glances at the door in the wall. He can see from here that the lock is engaged.

Keeping to the shelter of the wall, he moves round the yard to the pump. The area around it is paved with stones, roughly squared. All the cracks around them are lined with moss and weeds. But one stone is clear. Resting on it is a rusty nail.

Charles inserts the nail under the edge of the stone and uses it as a lever. The stone rises and there, lying in a jar beneath, is the key to the back door of Mr Savill's house.

# Chapter Forty-Four

Savill watched the two women, the mistress and the maid, approaching the round table in the middle of Mr Bell's Library. Here were displayed the latest arrivals to anyone who cared to pay a guinea a year and abide by Mr Bell's regulations.

Mrs Ogden turned over the new books for a moment. Then she broke away from her maid and approached the counter where the middle-aged clerk sat behind his desk.

'Good afternoon, Mr Fisk,' she said, turning the sagging, left-hand side of her face away from him.

'Good afternoon, Mrs Ogden. I declare I could set my watch by you. Every afternoon, four o'clock, shine or rain, and here you are.'

She ignored the pleasantry. 'Do you have Mr Mackenzie's *A Man of Feeling* on the shelves, Mr Fisk? I dreamed about it last night, and I have a desire to look over it again.'

The clerk took up his ledger and turned the pages. 'Novels,' he murmured, '*Man*, yes, here we are, *Man of Feeling*. Number four-six-three-two. An old favourite, ma'am – very popular with the ladies.' He looked up and ducked his head in a sort of bow. 'One moment if you please. Permit me to enquire whether it is available.'

He jotted the number on a scrap of paper and beckoned one of the youths behind the counter. Mrs Ogden turned away and looked at a wall of calf-bound spines. Everything about her was entirely respectable – her dress, her manner, her maid. There was nothing to recall the distraught, dishevelled woman that Savill had seen earlier in the day. Nothing but the ruined face.

The subjects of each shelf was announced by a card label attached to them. Mrs Ogden stared at SERMONS for a moment, and then transferred her gaze if not her attention to VOYAGES & TRAVELS. The maid sidled away and eyed a footman who had just come in, attending a lady with a dog that scurried, yapping, about her feet.

Savill drew nearer. 'Have I the honour of addressing Mrs Ogden?'

She turned, her hand flying to her throat as if he had caught her in a shameful situation. He watched her eyes widen as she recognized him from this morning.

'Pray don't be agitated. It will draw attention.'

The servant had discreetly turned away and was talking in whispers to another lady's maid.

'I did not think you would come – it was a such a desperate stratagem this morning. I am ashamed that I should be obliged to resort to it. I must apologize.'

'It doesn't matter, ma'am.' He drew her aside to a corner where magazines were displayed on a table. 'How may I help you?'

'I am so anxious for news of my son, sir. Dick quarrelled with his father, you see, and I have not seen him these two years or more.'

'And the telescope was a present from your husband to your son?'

'Yes.' Her hands waved the question aside. 'Mr Ogden says you called in connection with a crime that he had committed. It cannot be true, sir. Dick is impulsive, I know, and perhaps a trifle wild on occasion. But he's good at heart, sir.'

291

'I'm sure he is.' Savill handed her to a chair. 'And, as far as I know, he is accused of nothing. I am employed on an enquiry for the Westminster Magistrates' Office, and it is true that a crime may have been committed, though we cannot be sure even of that. The more I know about him, the more likely it is I shall be able to set your mind at rest.'

'I blame myself.' Her voice fell into a monotonous rut, as though she were following a train of thought that she had followed many times before. 'If only I'd taken his side more firmly when he said he wanted to be an architect or even a painter. But my husband, Mr Ogden, is not a man who changes his mind once he has made it up. And he determined that after Dick left school, he should go up to the University and then follow him into the law. Dick was at fault, I own it, for a son owes a duty to his father, does he not, and he should not set his will in defiance to his elders and betters. He did not apply himself to his studies, and his tutor said he had fallen into bad company. The foolish boy ran up debts he could not pay, and his friends were idle and expensive young men, who led him into vicious ways.'

'He did not have a friend named Irwin, I suppose?'

She stared at him. 'No, sir. Not that I know of – and I would have remembered that, you know. Irwin was my mother's name. Mind you, when he went to Oxford, there were many of his acquaintance I did not know, and I dare say I would not care to know, either.'

It was a familiar story. The young man had indulged himself at the University, and he and his parents had paid the price at home. Sent down from Oxford, he was articled as a clerk to an attorney of his father's acquaintance; but he was idle and was sometimes drunk even at the office; at length he was discharged, and after a final quarrel with his father he was expelled from his home.

'I am forbidden to mention him,' Mrs Ogden said. 'Mr Ogden has scratched out his name in our Bible. I might have

292

been able to mend things between them had I not been so ill at the time.' Her hand touched her left cheek, and Savill wondered whether the final quarrel between father and son had brought on her apoplectic seizure. 'He went to live in Turner's Grove – our cottage near Chiswick, you know; it was my father's once – and he tried to make his living with his pencil. But when Mr Ogden learned of it, he threw him out, and had the house shut up.'

'So he did not know his son was there?'

'No. It was standing empty – we haven't been there for years. We used to go every summer when Dick was young. We'd idle away our time on the river, and Dick would draw, and at the end of the week my husband would fish and forget the cares of his employment.'

'How old is your son now, ma'am?' Savill said.

'Twenty-eight last birthday.' She smiled at him with half of her face. 'July the fifth. He was a summer baby.'

'Tell me what he looks like.'

'He's a good-looking boy.' She looked up at him. 'I know what you are thinking, sir. That any mother would say that about her son. I own I'm partial, but he has fine, noble features and the most lustrous black hair. And anyone will tell you he has the address of a gentleman. If only he would not drink so much and fly into a passion with his father, he might have done anything he wanted.'

Black hair, Savill thought. A taste for drawing. A cottage near Chiswick. He said, 'Tell me where to find the house, ma'am. If he's there, shall I give him a message from you?'

Mrs Ogden looked directly at him. 'Give him my best love,' she said. 'Tell him to come home. Tell him his father misses him, whatever he says, and so do I. And tell him that, with God's help, there is nothing that cannot be mended.'

After Savill had dined, he walked up to Oxford Street to call on his daughter at Mrs Pycroft's. Mrs Pycroft was the proprietor and principal instructress of the Beaufort Academy for Young Ladies, an establishment that occupied the ground floor of a house in Little Castle Street, east of Oxford Market. Mrs Pycroft and several youthful Pycrofts shared the upper floors with Mrs Pycroft's mother, who kept to her bed and was never seen.

Lizzie had spent two years at the school. According to the prospectus, she learned French and Italian from visiting masters, as well as dancing and drawing and a host of other skills deemed essential for young ladies destined to move in good society, or at least in what passed for it in the circles they adorned.

All these things cost extra, and Savill sometimes wondered what Mrs Pycroft's fees actually covered, apart from the occasional ramble among the foothills of arithmetic and the learning by rote of the kings and queens of England, together with the dates of their reigns. But the money had been well spent nonetheless, for Lizzie had mixed with girls of her own age and Mary Pycroft had become her best friend.

When Savill reached the house, most of the ground floor was in darkness. He knocked on the door and was admitted by the solitary manservant, a wall-eyed middle-aged man who lived in the basement behind the kitchen and who had been chosen partly because his ugliness could be relied upon not to lead the young ladies astray.

'Madam's at home, sir,' the servant said, pocketing the sixpence that Savill slipped into his hand. 'Or she will be to you. Thank you kindly.'

'Is all well, Troughton?' They were old friends, for there had been many sixpences in the past.

'Well enough, sir. But you wouldn't believe the fuss there's been, what with the mistress and Miss Mary and your young miss, buzzing about like a parcel of bees. You'd think no one had ever got wed before.'

Savill found Lizzie in the drawing room on the first floor,

which the Pycrofts used as the family sitting room. Mrs Pycroft, Mary and Lizzie were there, sitting in a line on the sofa with their heads bent over a pattern book. Lizzie leapt up when she saw him and, careless of the company they were in, flung her arms around his neck.

'I did not know you were back – you don't look well, Papa, indeed you don't – I must come home directly and look after you. Is my aunt returned?'

He kissed her. 'No, not yet.'

'And what about—'

'Hush. All in good time.'

Savill bowed to Mrs Pycroft and her daughter. 'Forgive me for arriving without warning, ma'am. To make matters worse, I see I have interrupted you.'

Mrs Pycroft was disposed to be gracious about this. Not only had Savill been a model parent, paying his daughter's fees on time and not asking unreasonable questions about the extent of her formal education, but there were rumours that he was, despite his modest lifestyle, richer than he seemed; added to this, he had the knack of making himself agreeable in any company; and she considered that he could look quite presentable, too, notwithstanding that unsightly scar, should a lady take the time and trouble to make him so; finally, there was the point that Mrs Pycroft believed him to be a widower, and she was not entirely averse to the idea of a second experiment in matrimony, if the right gentleman were to offer her his heart and hand.

He was aware of all this, at least in outline, for Lizzie had given him several hints, which derived in turn from hints she herself had received from Mary.

Mrs Pycroft rang the bell for tea. After they had talked in wearisome detail about Mary's forthcoming wedding, Savill drew Lizzie aside.

'Is he at home now?' she murmured, colouring as she spoke. 'My brother Charles? What is he like? When can I meet him?'

'I'm afraid he isn't at home. There's been a difficulty, my love. It will sound quite ludicrous, but at the moment he cannot be found. It is like something out of a bad farce, is it not?'

'But what do you mean? That cannot be so.'

'On the morning we were to leave Somersetshire he could not be found . . .' Savill hesitated only a moment. Better to know than to suspect even worse. 'There is a possibility that he has been abducted.'

Her face froze with surprise. He watched her grappling with the notion, trying to bring kidnapping out of the world of the novel and the theatre and into the everyday world of Mary Pycroft's wedding and Aunt Ferguson's tiresome notions of what was suitable for a young lady and what was not.

'You must tell no one, my dear, even Mary,' he said softly. 'Only that Charles's coming to London has been delayed.'

'But who would be so wicked?'

'I will tell you more later. You must promise me that you will tell no one. Promise me, Lizzie.'

'But have you been to Bow Street? We must hire a Runner. Is that not the correct thing to do in these situations?'

Her assumption of worldly wisdom made him want to hug her. So did her willingness to assume that this was her business as well as his. He said, 'Not in this case. It is not as simple as it might seem – there are other considerations. But your uncle Rampton has concerned himself in the matter. He will see to it that everything is done that can be. He will use his influence, and he has it in his power to do more than any Runner can.'

'May I not come home with you? We should be together at a time like this.'

'No. You must stay here and help Mrs Pycroft and Mary.'

'But, Papa, you—'

'No,' he said. 'Anyway I am not at Nightingale Lane at present. The house is empty.'

In his distress he spoke more loudly than was prudent. He

heard a pause in the conversation behind him, where Mrs Pycroft and Mary were dealing with the vexed question of the lace on the veil.

'Tell no one,' he repeated, aware that in his despair he was going round in circles and making matters worse between them. 'Even Mary. You must promise me that.'

Lizzie stared at him. She made a sound that was a sort of smothered cry and rushed from the room.

After a moment, Mrs Pycroft said in her warm, comfortable voice, 'Oh dear, I dare say Lizzie is overtired, sir. And the relief of seeing you has brought it all to the surface. You must not concern yourself. It is often the way with girls, as I know to my cost. Mary will go up to her in a moment and make it all right again. Now won't you come sit by me and take your tea with us?'

# Chapter Forty-Five

Savill had agreed to pass the night in Crown Street again, in the house opposite the Black Letter Office. Mr Rampton had been insistent, saying that it was important that Savill should be on hand in case there were intelligence of Charles; besides, he had gathered that there was no one to look after Savill at Nightingale Lane.

There were no messages during the night. He slept badly. If his mind did not run on his stupidity in allowing Charles to be stolen from under his nose, it turned to the clumsy way he had handled Lizzie, the person he loved most in the world. He seemed capable only of hurting those he had a duty to care for.

The next morning Savill rose early and slipped out of the house. Only the maid and the boy who cleaned the boots and carried the coals were about. He left word that he had to go out on an errand, and that he would return later in the day.

He had taken the precaution of hiring a horse for the day the previous evening when he returned from Mrs Pycroft's. He had supped at the Sun in Splendour in Rose Street, which had a connection with a neighbouring livery stable, and arranged the matter there.

After breakfast at the tavern, he rode westward out of town.

Two uncomfortable thoughts occupied his mind, taking turns to prey on him. He had not been able to make his peace with Lizzie last night, which made him unhappy as he knew it would her. Second, Charles had now been gone for three whole days and nights. He had not been seen since he left Charnwood. The longer the absence, the more likely that, if he were found at all, he would not be found alive.

The road was busy at this hour but most of the traffic was coming towards London. He made good speed, passing through the pretty village of Chiswick before ten o'clock. The house he was seeking, Turner's Grove, lay several miles beyond the village on a lane that ran parallel to the high road along the river.

The houses were now few and far between. Though one or two labourers' dwellings remained, many of the residences along this stretch were villas and large cottages owned by Londoners who took occasional refuge in them from the noise and polluted air of the city.

Turner's Grove stood in isolation, an L-shaped house consisting of a modest cottage of some antiquity with a modern wing of more substantial dimensions. The long garden stretched down to the river, and on either side of it were meadows. The windows were shuttered and the woodwork needed repainting. The ground at the front of the house was thick with weeds running to seed. Rose bushes had sprouted into monstrous shapes covered with deadheads.

Savill dismounted and tethered his horse at the wicket. Mrs Ogden had said that no one lived there now. The farmer who leased the meadows from Mr Ogden kept an eye on the house and made sure all was secure.

'Not that Mr Ogden cares for the place,' she had told Savill. 'I believe he would not care a straw if it burned to the ground and vanished from the earth.'

An ash sapling had grown up just inside the gate. Savill took out his pocket knife and cut a stick from it, which he

299

used to beat down the nettles and brambles on his progress around the house. He tried the doors and the shutters but none of them showed any evidence of having been recently opened. There was no smoke from any of the chimneys.

At the back of the house, however, he discovered signs that someone had been here. Apart from a yard and stable behind the older part, the land between the house and the river had been laid out as a pleasure ground in the formal manner popular a generation earlier. Neglect had allowed the shrubs to grow until the design was obscured and the paths almost impassable. But judging by broken branches and crushed vegetation, several of the alleys between the beds had been used in the recent past.

Savill forced his way up one of them and found it took him to an iron gate in the brick wall between the pleasure ground and the neighbouring meadow. The gate was locked but the wall itself was in a ruinous condition and in several places nearby had fallen down. From here, another path had been cleared in the direction of the river. It led Savill to a two-storey building of brick and timber standing on the bank.

A door in the side stood ajar. He kicked it open and found himself looking at the interior of a small boathouse or covered jetty, open to the river on one side. In the half-light, the dark green water was almost black. Nothing was moored there. Two ancient chairs of canvas and wood were leaning against the wall, with a wicker basket, green with mould, beside them. He raised the lid. The basket contained nothing but a broken glass and an empty bottle.

Savill went back into the open air, glad to be out of that dank place. At the rear of the boathouse, a staircase rose up to a door, with a window beside it. He climbed the steps with care, for the rain had made the wood slippery and he was not convinced they would take his weight.

The door at the top was locked or jammed. He glanced over his shoulder. No one was about. He raised the latch and put his shoulder to the door. At his third attempt it opened, throwing him forward into the room beyond.

It was empty, but there were signs of recent occupation. Savill glanced around it, taking in the blankets, the table and chairs, the remains of a meal, the bottles, the rusting stove and a further door in the far wall. There was an oblong book on the table, with a pencil and a broken crayon beside it. He opened the book at random. He found himself looking at a sketch of a stile shaded by a tree; the lines were hurried and smudged; and the paper was hard and wrinkled as if someone had spilled liquid on it and then the page had dried.

He moved across the room to the other door. It was locked. But it hung askew in the frame because the wood was warped. When he tugged the handle, the door flew open.

A cesspit stink rushed out to greet him. The odour was mingled with an acrid underlay that caught the back of Savill's throat and brought with it a host of unwanted memories.

Beyond the door was a floor-to-ceiling cupboard, lined with dusty shelves. The shelves were empty, though there was a chamber pot under the lowest one on the left.

The body of a man in a blue coat lay on the floor beside the chamber pot. He was on his back, his arms standing stiffly away from his body. His head was near the far end of the cupboard. It rested in a pool of dried blood mingled with fragments of bone and the grey matter of the brain. The eyes were open.

Savill swallowed his nausea and looked at the shelves beside the door. One of them, about four feet above the floor, was not quite empty. A rusty two-inch nail lay there. He touched it with his finger. It moved a fraction, revealing a single word scratched in sprawling, irregular letters underneath, the freshly scarred wood still pale yellow.

Charles.

Savill knelt by the body. There was a bullet hole under the jaw, and the skin was blackened with a powder burn. The

301

man had been shot at close range. The bullet must have ploughed its way up through the brain and punched a ragged hole in the back of the skull.

The face itself was undamaged. The features were delicate. Savill touched the disordered hair.

Fine, black hair.

# Chapter Forty-Six

Charles wanders through the house in Nightingale Lane, pausing to listen every few seconds. The only sounds are far away – the rumble of wheels on the paved roads, the blows of builders' hammers from the new houses.

The air is cold and damp, flavoured with the smell of dead fires. The ground-floor apartments are dark because the shutters are across the windows. At the back and upstairs, many of the windows have bars rather than shutters, and some of the smaller ones have neither.

At first he feels like a burglar. In one of the rooms downstairs is a pile of opened letters addressed to Savill. That removes the niggling fear that he has found his way into someone else's house.

In the larder a ham hangs in a sack suspended from the ceiling and several cheeses are enclosed behind fine wire grills. He brings a knife from the kitchen and hacks into one of the cheeses. In the pantry beside the larder are bins containing walnuts and covered racks with apples and pears.

Walnuts. *Say nothing*, he reminds himself. *Not a word to anyone. Whatever you see. Whatever you hear. Do you understand? Say nothing. Ever.*

*Tip-tap.*

In his mind, Charles says to reassure himself, 'I am safe now.'

He has food and shelter. Soon his English family will come.

He eats quickly, cramming food into his mouth with both hands and swallowing it half-chewed. He washes it down with sour-tasting water he finds in the scullery in a bucket by the pump.

Only then does he realize how stupid he has been: he has left the key in the back door. He runs into the scullery and retrieves it. He must find another way into the house, so he can lock the door and leave the key in its hiding place outside. He begins to cry. Dare he risk staying here and leaving the house unlocked?

Fighting panic, he checks the windows overlooking the yard. Either they are too small or they have bars that will not even let a skinny boy squeeze between them. All but one – set beneath a shelf in the pantry: it isn't really a window but an ironbound hatch secured by four great bolts, with a sill at floor level much marked by the passage of barrels. The bolts have recently been greased and, for all their size, they glide out of their sockets. Five minutes later the back door is locked, the key is returned to its hiding place in the yard and Charles is safe in the house again.

He continues his stealthy survey. This is not a place that has been planned, unlike the Hotel de Quillon or even Charnwood. The floors are uneven. Walls do not follow straight lines and rarely meet other walls at right angles. Passages wind back on themselves. Flights of stairs lead unexpectedly to solitary rooms. Some doors are locked. Many of the windows are leaded and their distorted green glass gives the outside world the appearance of being at the bottom of a pond.

A difficult house to measure, Charles thinks, a difficult house to reduce to facts.

He climbs the stairs and roams through bedchambers and closets and mysterious apartments that have no obvious function.

At the top of the house is a series of shadowy attics, partly boarded and lit by tiny windows set high in the gables of the building. Beams and rafters criss-cross the dusty spaces. Even a cursory glance is enough to show that this part of the house is home to bats, birds, wasps, rats and spiders, and no doubt a host of invisible creatures.

Once Charles would have recoiled at these traces of parasitic intruders or even feared them. Now they are almost welcome, as an omen, as evidence that this is a house that gives shelter to refugees.

He returns downstairs, taking his time, relishing the pleasure of possession. This, he thinks, is what it should have been like in the castle in the woods. But that reminds him at once that the castle was something he planned to share with Louis, and that Louis turned out to be nothing but a lifeless doll, not a person; and that in turn reminds him of his solitude.

Self-pity wells up inside him and he is attacked by a desire to weep. But he has learned something in the terrible weeks since the summer; he has learned that tears bring no comfort and make nothing happen. So he stamps his foot to drive them away, and the dull thud of his heel on the stair booms through the quiet house.

On the first floor, he hesitates a moment, thinking of the day ahead and then the night. Even if he can find candles and a tinderbox, he knows it will not be safe to show a light. When evening comes, he will have to try to sleep.

The next question is where. There are three bedrooms on this landing – Mr Savill's, to judge its lack of ornament and the razor strop on the washstand; Mr Savill's sister's, to judge by the black dress hanging on the door and the row of devotional tracts on the mantel; and his sister Lizzie's, which has a jug stuffed with wilting Michaelmas daisies on the windowsill.

'My sister, Lizzie,' Charles says in his mind, trying the words for size, to see how they feel in his mouth. 'Madam, may I present Elizabeth Savill, my sister.'

Something forbids him from choosing a bed that belongs to someone else. He may take the Savills' food and the shelter of their house, but a bed is different. There are also two other beds that he thinks must be for servants – one in a maid's room on the way to the attics, the other a straw pallet in an alcove off the kitchen – but he has still less right to take one of those, and besides they both smell strangely and, even after everything that has happened, he is sensitive to certain smells and textures.

There is a closet beside Lizzie's chamber that he decides will do for his own bedchamber because it seems to belong to no one in particular. The small window is barred, not shuttered, and it overlooks the yard and the garden. The closet has a curtained alcove containing old cloaks and coats.

He casts about for bedding, and finds a shelf of blankets at the bottom of a cupboard full of lavender-scented linen. He carries two of them into the closet and lays them neatly on the floor under the window. He fetches a third blanket and folds it so it will serve as a pillow.

Charles glances at the sky and wonders what o'clock it is and whether Mr Savill will come soon.

The time hangs heavily. There are books in the house and he goes in search of one to read, though he hasn't tried to read more than a few words in English before. He returns to Lizzie's room, where he notices a line of books on the table. He picks a volume at random and opens the title page.

THE
LIFE
And Strange Surprizing
ADVENTURES
of
ROBINSON CRUSOE
OF
YORK, MARINER

\* \* \*

306

Charles sleeps more soundly, and for longer, than he has done for months. When he wakes, green-grey light is struggling through the leaded lozenges of the window.

It is still very early in the morning. He goes downstairs and lets himself out into the yard, where he urinates in the earth closet. After breakfasting on cheese, ham and an apple, he returns to his room, taking with him a jar labelled quince jelly to sustain him through the morning.

By now it is light enough to sit in a nest of blankets on the window seat and continue with *Robinson Crusoe*. Miss Horton had left the narrative at the moment when Mr Crusoe discovered the print of a naked foot in the sand. Charles spent some hours puzzling over the book yesterday but made painfully slow progress because of the English language and because, he suspects, Miss Horton must have left out many of the duller passages when she read the book to him at Charnwood.

Today, however, his efforts are rewarded by Mr Crusoe's stumbling on the site of a cannibal dinner party on the beach, a discovery that quite understandably disgusts Mr Crusoe so much that nature obliges him to vomit. This occurs nearly eighteen years after his shipwreck and the start of his solitary life. Charles reads on and on and for a while entirely forgets that he is a fugitive concealed in a house where he has no right to be.

The interruption comes as Mr Crusoe stumbles on a cave that contains a groaning monster.

The click of the latch of the door in the wall from the alley.

Charles tumbles from the window seat. Wriggling on to his knees, he peers through the window, keeping well away from the glass. The old woman he saw yesterday is coming into the yard. Her head is turned over her shoulder. Two young ladies follow her, and then another woman dressed as a maid. He cannot see their faces because of their hats.

As they cross the yard, the sound of their voices reach him. One of the girls laughs.

*My sister?*

Charles does not wait to see more. He gathers up the blankets and bundles them into the alcove behind the curtain. Then he follows them. He squats on the blankets behind the cloaks.

The closet door is open. There are noises in the house below – the old woman talking about something in a voice that grates like a rusty hinge, a door banging and then running footsteps on the stairs.

'Pray do not trouble yourself, ma'am,' a young woman says. 'I know just where it is.'

That is when Charles discovers that he has left *Robinson Crusoe* on the window seat. And the jar of quince jelly, now half-eaten, is on the floor. But the floorboards will betray him if he tries to retrieve them.

Light, rapid footsteps cross the landing.

A door opens. The footsteps are in the next room, Lizzie's bedchamber. There is the scrape of a drawer being pulled out; after a pause it is closed. Then another drawer. Then a third.

More footsteps. A long pause. Footsteps again. A faint click.

The steps are on the landing.

Downstairs, the old woman's voice drones on, cutting into the quietness of the house like a saw.

The young woman enters the closet. A pause.

She has seen the book, Charles knows, lying where he left it, face down on the window seat at the very moment when Mr Crusoe enters the cave with a flaming torch held aloft. And the jar, with the wooden spoon standing in what's left of the jelly.

He prays to Father Viré's God. *Make her go away.*

God does not listen. As usual.

She sucks in a breath of air. A flurry of footsteps. She snatches back the curtain and light floods into the alcove.

308

Even then he cherishes the hope that she has not seen him, that the cloaks and blankets hide him from her eyes.

'Come out,' she whispers. 'Come out now. Come on, you silly boy.'

'Lizzie? Where are you?'

It is the voice of another young woman, calling up the stairs.

Lizzie pulls away the screen of cloaks. She holds her forefinger to her lips.

'Coming,' she calls back.

She stares down at him, her eyes widening. She is so fresh and clean. She has a piece of lace in her hand, as delicate as a cobweb.

All of a sudden, he sees himself as she must see him: the ragged clothes, the unkempt hair and the dirt.

'Are you – are you Charles? You are, aren't you?'

*Say nothing.*

My sister, he thinks.

'Are you? Why won't you answer?' She pauses and then rushes on: 'Oh, of course. You have lived in France. Perhaps you don't understand English.' She draws breath, pauses again and whispers very slowly and carefully: '*Je m'appelle Elizabeth Savill. Comment vous appellez-vous?*'

'Lizzie?' The voice comes up the stairs again. 'Where are you? Have you found it?'

'Yes, Mary,' she calls back. 'I shall be down directly.' She swallows. 'You must be Charles. Who else could you be? And your eyes – oh, please say something. *Je suis vôtre sœur. Monsieur Savill – mon père – il vous cherche. Je vais – je vais le—*' She pounces on *Robinson Crusoe*. 'But you do understand English. You must, if you read this.'

He raises his hands to his face and crosses his forefingers over his mouth.

She frowns. 'Oh – do you mean you're scared to speak?' The frown deepens. 'Or you can't?'

309

There are footsteps coming up the stairs.

'Quick,' she says, and he knows that she has made up her mind to be his friend.

She arranges the cloaks to cover most of him and draws the curtain across the alcove. A moment later there's a soft thud as *Robinson Crusoe* lands on the blanket by his feet. The jar of quince jelly slides under the hem of the curtain.

'I've got it, Mary,' Lizzie says. 'What do think?'

'Oh it's lovely,' says another voice, a young woman's. 'But is it large enough?'

'Your mother will know.'

Mary lowers her voice to a whisper. 'Does she ever stop talking?'

'Mrs Forster? No. She probably talks in her sleep as well.'

The two girls giggle.

'My father says she is to be pitied, and we should not laugh at her,' Lizzie goes on, with the ghost of the laugh still in her voice. 'But I fear it is very hard not to. It's better than hitting her over the head with a rolling pin to make her hold her tongue. But Father says she works hard, and is entirely to be trusted, and she is a good mother to her poor unfortunate daughter. Which is all very true, no doubt, but I do wish she would be quiet sometimes.' She raises her voice to its normal level. 'Come – we must not keep Mrs Forster waiting.' She lowers her voice again. 'And your poor maid. She's bearing the brunt of all this. She'll give your mother notice when she gets home.'

Mary suppresses a snort of laughter. The two of them leave the room and begin to go downstairs. Charles lets out his breath and fights a desire to sneeze.

'You go down,' he hears Lizzie say. 'I might as well get my other cloak while we're here. It's much colder, isn't it?'

She runs into the closet. The curtain slides back. She snatches at a dark blue cloak. She bends down, bringing her face to within a foot of his.

'Stay here, Charles,' she says. '*Restez ici, je vous en prie.* I will write to my father and he will come and take care of you.'

# Chapter Forty-Seven

The encounter with Mr Rampton did not go well.

'You did what, sir?' he said when Savill told him how he had spent yesterday afternoon. 'You saw Mrs Ogden? I told you expressly that you must leave all that to me, that I did not want you—'

'You do not have the right to forbid me to do anything. I'm not in your employment.'

'You will find that I have the power to compel you. Do not make me use it.'

'Young Ogden is Irwin. I have proof. And there's worse—'

'Hush.' Rampton rose from his desk. 'The damage is done, I suppose. It will be better if we talk this over elsewhere.' His voice was very quiet. 'Let us take a turn in the Park.'

'But may I not—'

Rampton cut him off with a chopping motion of his hand. 'Pray oblige me in this, sir.'

He rang the bell and ordered his greatcoat, hat and stick to be brought. 'I shall be gone for twenty minutes or less,' he told Malbourne. 'I am expecting His Lordship this afternoon but I do not know when. If he should call while I am out, pray make my excuses and ask him to be good enough to wait.'

When they went downstairs, Jarsdel came out of his box to usher them down to the street. Despite his usual surliness, he could not keep his eyes from Mr Rampton's face, as a whipped dog cannot ignore his master.

'Brush your coat and straighten your wig,' Rampton said to him in a soft, chilly voice. 'His Lordship may call this afternoon, and I do not wish him to think we have a scare-crow to guard our door.'

Jarsdel lowered his head and leaned forward, which was all he could manage in the way of a bow.

Neither Rampton nor Savill spoke on their way to the Park. The rain had stopped and there were patches of sunshine, enough to lend colour to the notion that the two of them were taking the air after a morning's work in their office. They walked west along the street, crossed the top of Duke Street and cut through the alley leading to the open space beyond. Rampton encountered two men who bowed to him, but he avoided conversation with them.

They passed beneath the trees that lined the border of the Park and walked in silence across the open ground between them and the canal. The weather was growing colder now, with occasional gusts of rain. There were few gentlemen about – it was chiefly the common sort of people at this hour, and not many of those.

When they reached the water, Rampton stopped. They were near the eastern end of the canal, as straight as a ruler could make it. It pointed at the Parade Ground, with the arch of the Horse Guards beyond.

'Well, sir,' Rampton said at last, poking his stick at a slug that had the temerity to be passing over the stone border of the water. 'You had better tell me the whole.'

Savill described his encounter with Mrs Ogden at the British Library, and how he had known she would be there. 'She and her husband have a son, Richard, who ran up debts, quar-relled with his father and was sent down from Oxford. He

313

refused to settle to the law and in the end his father cast him out. He lived for a while on the river at their cottage beyond Chiswick and tried to make his living with his pencil, but it did not answer. His mother is desperate to effect a reconciliation – that is why she talked so frankly to me. Her description of him answers in every particular the description of Irwin, the man who took Charles away from Charnwood. You will recall that Norbury's landlady in Somersetshire said he was "artistical". And, to cap it all, Irwin was Ogden's mother's maiden name.'

Rampton grunted. 'Very well. Let us walk on. I'm cold.'

They followed the bank of the canal. To the west, at the far end of the long vista of water choked with lilies under a grey sky was the Queen's residence, Buckingham House, with its quadrants and pavilions and its forest of smoking chimneys. As they walked, Savill's hand brushed the side of his coat and felt the outline of Ogden's sketchbook in his pocket. He couldn't hide the truth for ever.

'There's more,' he said.

'I thought there might be. When you decide to meddle, sir, you do it wholeheartedly. I must give you that. Where did you ride to?'

'How did you know I'd ridden anywhere?'

'When I enquired for you this morning, one of the clerks downstairs said he had seen you riding down Great George Street on one of the hacks from the Sun in Splendour.'

'I went out to the Ogdens' cottage.'

'Why?'

'Because it's not so far from the Bath road, sir.'

'I see. So you thought Irwin might have had himself and the boy set down nearby as they were approaching London? Young Ogden, that is.'

'Yes, sir.' Savill glanced at Rampton: the old man's body might be showing its age but there was nothing amiss with his intellectual faculties. 'And I was right.'

Rampton stopped. 'You found him?'

Savill nodded. 'In a boathouse on the riverbank. Someone had blown his brains out.'

'Good God! And Charles?'

'He wasn't there. No one was – the place was quite deserted. But he had been there. The body was in a closet. As soon as I opened the door, I knew by the smell that a firearm had been discharged. The name Charles was scratched on one of the shelves. It was no more than two feet away from the body.'

'But we can't necessarily infer from that it was our Charles who wrote it.'

'I think we can, sir. The mark had been made very recently.'

'God damn it.' Rampton swung his stick at a pebble and sent it skimming into the water. 'Then you understand what this means?'

'We've lost his scent again, but he can't be far. If you were to muster a search party and set them to—'

'No, no. You mistake my meaning.' He looked up at Savill, his face sombre. 'From what you've said, there must be a strong probability that it was Charles himself who killed young Ogden. Presumably with his own pistol.'

The two of them circled the canal for nearly half an hour, from the railings of Buckingham House to the immaculately gravelled surface of the Parade Ground.

'I cannot trust anyone,' Rampton said, when they reached the western end for the first time. He stopped and stared at a carriage approaching at a trot along the Mall. 'That's why I cannot afford to send out a search party along the river, at least not without careful consideration of how it may be done discreetly. And that's also why you must stay away from Mrs Ogden.'

'Is it also why we need to talk here, rather than in your room?'

'Perhaps.'

'I don't understand,' Savill said.

'There's much you don't understand,' Rampton said, with a flash of the cold arrogance Savill remembered from their days together at the American Department. 'The point is, young Ogden was clearly acting on behalf of someone else. We don't know who. The obvious suspect is the Count de Quillon. We must look into that – all the more so because he is now in London. I wonder – would you call on him this evening? No, stay – call at Mrs West's, that will be better.'

'Why me?'

'Because it would be perfectly natural for you to call at Green Street because you made Mrs West's acquaintance in the country and she was most obliging when she offered you the loan of her chaise. So it would be a very proper attention if you call on her. In any case, it's likely that the Count and Monsieur Fournier will be there because they cannot easily go anywhere else in London at present. I'm sure they will dine with her and probably sup there too.'

'Would it not be better if you or Mr Malbourne saw them?'

'No. If I were to call, or even send Malbourne in my place, it would put quite a different complexion on the visit. It would add an official tincture to it.' Rampton flexed his fingers. 'Furthermore, sir, if you are right, and if Charles killed Ogden—'

'No court in the country would condemn him for that.'

'Perhaps not. But consider the notoriety. Consider the ordeal it would be for the poor boy, this on top of everything else. No, until we know more, it is yet another reason for us to exercise the utmost discretion.'

They walked in silence for a moment. Savill sensed that Rampton wanted him to speak, if only to give Rampton himself the opportunity to say what he wanted to say next. But Savill had learned the value of silence.

'There is another difficulty,' said Rampton at last. 'It's possible that the Count has nothing to do with the kidnapping.

316

We don't know why Charles was kidnapped. Was it because somebody wants him? Or was it because of something he knows, whatever that might be?' He paused and then added, 'Charles was in Paris with his mother. He was there when she was murdered.'

'Well?' Savill said.

'The French thought she was a British spy,' Rampton said slowly, as if thinking aloud.

'You said she was not.'

'As far as I know. But I don't know everything.' Rampton walked on, this time following the northern side of the canal. 'Let us say she was a spy for us or for the royalists, or indeed for anyone. If she had been arrested, the authorities would have squeezed a confession from her. Then a carefully managed trial blazed abroad to all the world. Perhaps someone killed her to prevent that.'

'Sir, why would one of our own do such a thing? We are not at war with France yet. Our Embassy could have issued her with a passport, and she could simply have left the country.'

Rampton coughed and blew his nose. He said very carefully, 'It might not have been as straightforward as that. Augusta was not welcome at the Embassy. And, leaving aside the possibility that she was passing intelligence, it is not difficult to imagine circumstances which would have made her the cause of considerable embarrassment – to the British Government, for example, or even to individuals connected with it.'

'I don't follow you.'

'She was an attractive woman.' Rampton said nothing more until they reached the Parade Ground end of the canal. He glanced up at Savill. 'And she had few scruples where her comfort was concerned, as you must remember all too well. What if she had taken another lover, perhaps in connection with the passing of intelligence, and then tried to blackmail him?'

# Chapter Forty-Eight

Savill had an hour or two to fill before going to Green Street. He might as well pass the time by walking over to the Strand as by doing anything else.

What else was there for him to do? There was nothing for him in Nightingale Lane and not much more in Lower Castle Street – Lizzie would not make him welcome at present, not unless he brought news of Charles or announced he was reopening the house before her aunt's return. She was acting like a silly chit of a girl, he told himself with great sternness, though in another part of his mind he feared he had failed to guide her judgement as a father should; besides, how could he justly reprove a daughter whose only fault was a desire to care for his comfort and that of her brother?

Savill's real motive lay like an iceberg in his mind, with most of it concealed beneath the surface currents of his thoughts. He felt guilty. Absurdly so, yes. Irrationally. Quite inexplicably. Nevertheless, there it was: he was guilty because he had failed to inform Mrs Ogden that her son was lying dead in a boathouse beside the Thames. That was what drew him towards the Strand.

He tried telling himself that it would be a kindness to allow the poor lady to remain in uncertainty about the fate

318

of her son, for the hope of being reunited with him would be preferable to the knowledge that he was dead. But another part of himself pointed out that not to tell her of his death was the act of a coward and a churl, whereas to reveal it was at worst the act of a fool, for it would save her grief in the long run, however much distress it brought her at the time.

The crowds were thick around Charing Cross. Still arguing with himself, Savill pushed himself through the press and entered the Strand. Passers-by glanced at his face and made way for him, as if recognizing the urgency that possessed him. It was at this point in his deliberations that he realized that his lips were moving and that he was having an animated conversation with himself aloud.

He turned into Mr Bell's Library and, as he had done on the first occasion, bought a day ticket that enabled him to browse among the volumes and magazines but not to borrow them. According to the clock in the entrance hall, it wanted ten minutes to four o'clock. He went through to the principal gallery, picked up the latest copy of the *Bystander* and took a chair that commanded a view of the door to the hall.

Perhaps, he thought, she will not come today.

The minute hand of the clock above the clerks' desk reached the hour and began to descend on the other side. Five past, ten past, a quarter past.

With each lost minute, Savill's hopes began to rise. Mrs Ogden had said she came to the library on most days, he reminded himself. But not every day, and perhaps not always at four o'clock. Perhaps she had already called.

He threw down the *Bystander* and took Ogden's sketchbook from his pocket. He had glanced through it once before, searching for memoranda scattered among the drawings. This time he examined it more carefully, turning the pages from the back of the book towards the front.

Most of the sketches were of buildings, or details of them, but there were one or two of people, drawn with rapid, economical fluidity and yet extraordinarily lifelike. Among them was a rear elevation of a large woman stooping over a jug on a table; almost certainly it was Mrs Fenner, Ogden's landlady in Somersetshire. Another showed a child curled up asleep on a bench or perhaps an inside seat of a coach. The child was surrounded by shadows. Charles?

It was now twenty past the hour. He would give until half past, Savill decided, and then leave. His conscience could hardly object: for he could not call at the house or even write to her there without running the risk that Mr Ogden would discover that his wife had been communicating with Savill behind his back.

He turned over another page to reveal a charming scene showing the corner of a house with a tree beyond and birds fluttering in the sky. Again, there was little detail or precision: but instead a sense of motion, of swift and even joyous execution. It was a pity that Dick Ogden had not, for whatever reason, succeeded in pursuing a career with his pencil.

As he turned another page, a movement distracted his eye and he looked up: Mrs Ogden came through from the hall, with her maid following her and carrying a parcel of books. She was limping. The left side of her face seemed to droop lower, as if it had yielded further ground in its unequal struggle with gravity.

At the moment that Savill raised his head, she glanced across the room in his direction. Their eyes met, and she changed course towards him. The maid began to follow. Mrs Ogden waved her away, pointing at the clerks' desk, where books were returned as well as provided.

Savill slipped the sketchbook in his pocket, rose and bowed.

'You have news, sir?' Her hand touched her throat. 'Have you found Dick?'

'Madam—'

He could not bring himself to tell her. He knew then that he was indeed a coward and a churl.

She caught at his arm and stared up at his face, willing him to say the words she wanted to hear.

'Madam, I have not.'

'You will, sir, I am convinced of it.' The grip on his arm did not relax. 'I have a premonition that you will be a friend to my poor boy. That is all he needs, I am sure, a friend who will guide him wisely.'

He could not look away from her bisected face – one side living and feeling, the other fallen and decayed. 'I—' He stopped and cleared his throat. 'I will do anything in my power to help him.'

An expression of sweetness filled the living half. 'You are kindness itself, sir. Dick has always been easily led, you see, but that may be for good, as well as for ill. I often wonder what would have happened if he had fallen into other company at Oxford. He was so dreadfully unlucky there – he fell in with such a wild young fellow. They shared a set of rooms. His grandfather was a lord, and I fear he taught Dick to think himself above his station in life – aye, and to spend his father's money accordingly.'

'Madam, forgive me, I'm pressed for time,' Savill said. 'I must not linger—'

But Mrs Ogden was lost in a maze of memory. 'He taught Dick to follow his own wicked ways. Mr Ogden was so ashamed of him – of Dick, I mean – he himself is a man of the highest principles. He simply cannot comprehend how such folly could be possible in one on whom he had devoted the most tender paternal care. He went to Oxford himself, you know, that last time, to plead with Dick to mend his ways and shut his door to Mr Malbourne for ever. But no, my poor son was so caught up in his toils—'

'What was that?' Savill said, loudly enough for them to attract curious glances from other subscribers.

Mrs Ogden stared at him. 'Sir?'

'I beg your pardon. I believe you mentioned the name of your son's friend at Oxford.'

'I cannot call him a friend, sir,' she said, drawing herself up. There was no sweetness in her expression now. 'His evil genius would be more apt. I do believe the devil himself could not have done a better job.'

'But his name, madam?'

'Malbourne,' she said. 'Mr Horace Malbourne.'

# Chapter Forty-Nine

The day drags its way towards the evening.

Charles dares not run the risk of going outside. He reads *Robinson Crusoe* but even that diversion soon palls. He prowls through the house on his stockinged feet, peering cautiously from the windows and through the cracks between the shutters. He pecks at food – a mouthful of ham here, a spoonful of quince jelly there.

His head is full to bursting with the meeting with the young lady who is his sister. She will bring Mr Savill to him, and all will be well.

Except it won't be well, he reminds himself, for nothing can be well again.

Nevertheless Charles clings to the memory of Lizzie: she brings a wisp of hope into his life, a sense that, even if nothing can be well, at least something may be slightly less bad than it otherwise would be. She said she would write to Mr Savill. How long will the letter take to reach him? If he is still in the country, it may be days before he receives it, and a week before he reaches Nightingale Lane.

The house itself is silent. The building is holding its breath, waiting for what happens next. When Charles moves from room to room, from floor to floor, the silence is disturbed by

323

the clack of a raised latch or the creak of a stair: and these sounds are almost blasphemous, like a drunkard's oath in the middle of Mass.

If Charles listens at the window of the servant's chamber at the top of the stairs, he hears quite distinctly the sounds of the builders' hammers and saws, the incessant rumble of wagons and coaches, and the clatter of hooves. Perhaps some of those sounds come from Bedford Square itself, from the carriages gliding round the oval of grass where the children of the rich play in safety, guarded by railings and servants.

This window has a view of part of the garden behind the Royal Oak. In the early afternoon, workmen pace in and out of sight, with pipes in their mouths and tankards in their hands. In Mr Savill's orchard, the birds squabble among the branches and peck at rotten fruit on the ground.

Most of all, however, he looks down on Nightingale Lane from a barred first-floor window. This is partly because he reasons that anyone coming to Mr Savill's house will probably come by this way. But it is also because it offers the most interesting prospect at his disposal, far more diverting than the antics of birds in the garden, and far more productive of facts.

There are three houses in front of Mr Savill's house – one on the left, with a shop selling wicker baskets and the like on the ground floor, and two cottages on the right. The lane is little wider than a wagon between the houses but it opens up in front of Mr Savill's house and then narrows into the footpath along the side of the house and garden towards the Royal Oak.

Charles studies these houses and assembles facts about their occupants. The house on the left has seven windows over-looking the street and two of them have broken panes with the holes stuffed with rags. The shop attracts scarcely any custom. Sometimes an old man emerges from it into the lane. He wears a long apron over his waistcoat and sweeps the front of his shop with slow, dreamlike movements. At three o'clock a boy appears in the lane. He is carrying a tray with a jug and a covered plate on it, so Charles decides that he must be bringing the old man his dinner.

Opposite the house with the shop, the two cottages lean against one another. The ridges of their roofs dip and their tiles are thick with moss. Their windows are tiny. In the one further away from Mr Savill's house lives a young woman with five very small children. She sits in her doorway, hunched over her sewing, with her children playing and squabbling about her. Every now and then she clamps her baby to her breast, and sometimes she suckles the next youngest as well, who tugs incessantly at her skirt, clamouring for his mother's milk.

Mrs Forster, the woman who looks after Mr Savill's house, lives in the nearer cottage with a young woman who must be her daughter. Even when she is inside, Charles sometimes hears Mrs Forster's voice grinding away like a knife on a whetstone. The daughter is very tall and very thin. Her shoulders hunch forward. She kneels to scrub the doorstep and Charles sees the back of her calves and holes in her stockings. She goes out to fetch water from the pump at the end of the lane, and she takes the slops to the cesspit the houses share. When she accompanies her mother to the shops, she carries the baskets and walks two steps behind.

Charles watches these people. He counts them. He accumulates information about them. All these facts are good, for one can rely on them.

A fact is not like a person, who may be here one day and gone the next. Or kind at one moment and cruel at another.

Despite his watchfulness, the coach takes him by surprise. When he hears the rumble of wheels in Nightingale Lane, he is looking over the back of the house, standing on a chair in an attempt to see into the yard behind the Royal Oak, which is between the alehouse and its garden. Careless of noise, he runs to the window overlooking the lane, arriving just in time to see a shabby hackney coach swinging into the space in front of Mr Savill's house. Three children dart towards it from the house where the sewing woman lives. The old man appears in the doorway of his shop.

The driver climbs from his seat, lets down the steps and opens the door of the coach. Monsieur Fournier descends slowly, leaning on his stick. When he has reached the safety of the ground, he turns and helps out two ladies, Mrs West and Miss Horton. They stand in a row, looking up at the house.

Charles ducks away from the window. He hears their voices below. There is a knocking at the door.

The echoes of the knocking dwindle away, and into the void they leave behind comes the sound of Mrs Forster's voice. On and on it goes, grating and sawing. Charles summons his courage and edges nearer the window. Monsieur Fournier and Mrs West are listening to the old woman. Her daughter is looking at her mother. Miss Horton has turned away and is studying the outside of the house.

They have come to take him back to the Count.

Charles trembles at the thought. He does not want to go to the Count. He sees now what has happened, that Monsieur de Quillon has hired the man in the blue coat to kidnap him, and that Monsieur Fournier is his accomplice. Even Miss Horton is complicit in the plot, which goes to show that no one can be trusted, no one whatever, and the best policy is silence.

*Say nothing. Not a word to anyone.*

Who has told them to come here?

Only one person knows that he is at the house in Nightingale Lane. His sister, Lizzie.

Charles has found a new hiding place. It is in Lizzie's room, where the bed is pushed against the wall. The bed has two mattresses. He hollows out a place for him to lie in an irregular triangle formed by the mattresses and the wall. With the covers pulled over him he is hot, uncomfortable and, he hopes, entirely invisible.

Like Robinson Crusoe, he has made his preparations: he has cut pieces of ham and cheese, wrapped them in a cloth and put them in the hiding place, together with a knife he found in the kitchen.

He waits, but nothing happens. When at last he comes out of the hiding place, the coach is no longer in front of the house. He knows that the relief is only temporary, that Monsieur Fournier will return, probably with Monsieur de Quillon. They are not men who will be delayed for long by bolts and locks.

But it will not be safe to leave until it is quite dark.

Charles stands by the window that looks on to Nightingale Lane. The light is already fading. A pall of smoke hangs over the rooftops. The old man has lit a candle and placed it on the sill of his shop window. Evening is coming, and soon it will be night.

Panic is everywhere. It rises like vomit from Charles's stomach. He wonders whether he would be safer inside the house or outside. But when he leaves the house, where will he go? He opens his mouth and a thin wail emerges and fills the room where he stands.

*Say nothing.*

Almost at once, as if summoned by his wail, a figure appears at the far end of Nightingale Lane. It advances slowly through the gathering dusk, taking monstrous form as it draws nearer Mr Savill's house. The figure is that of an enormous man. As he approaches, he glances at the cottages on either side. There is no one to see him. The children are inside at this hour, and so are Mrs Forster and her daughter. The old shopkeeper has shut his outer door.

The man walks with a slow, rolling gait as if marching through a muddy field. His head, legs and arms belong to someone who is shorter and thinner than he is. As he walks, he leans on a large stick. Nevertheless, it is a wonder that he does not topple over under his own weight.

Not a man, Charles thinks, but a man-mountain.

The figure stops in front of Mr Savill's house and stares up at it. Charles is standing well back from the window and he knows the man below cannot see him. He knows that with his mind but not with his heart, and the panic rises higher.

The man sways to and fro, leaning on his stick, with his eyes on the house. With his free hand, he scratches his belly at the place where the halves of his waistcoat meet. When at last he moves off, he does not turn and retrace his steps. Instead he goes down the path along the side of the house and garden.

The man-mountain is looking for a way in.

# Chapter Fifty

At this time the streets were so crowded that walking was as fast as any other means of locomotion. Savill marched from the Strand to Westminster, revolving in his mind the information he had received from Mrs Ogden. With two words, she had given him the link that bound together the whole unhappy business.

*Horace Malbourne.*

Dick Ogden had abducted Charles from Norbury on the very morning that Savill was to take him up to London. Ogden had long since estranged himself from his family and those who wished him well; and at the time of his murder he had clearly been on the edge of destitution. And here came this new piece of information: that Ogden and Malbourne were old friends and, if Mrs Ogden was to be believed, partners in vice, with Malbourne the senior partner.

Poor Ogden had been a pliable young man, degenerate in his habits and clearly at the mercy of his own vices. Ripe, in other words, for a final descent into outright criminality if the temptation had been sufficiently alluring, particularly if it came from his old comrade, Malbourne.

As for Malbourne, he was one of the very few people who

had known that Savill was going to Charnwood to fetch Charles. He had provided Savill with information about the household at Charnwood and their connection with Mrs West at Norbury Park. He had known of Mr Rampton's connection to Augusta, and hence to her son.

Mr Rampton had not told Malbourne of his plans for the boy, that he was considering adopting him and making him his heir. In Whitehall, Savill paused before the busy crossing by the Privy Garden, remembering again how the lock on the door of Mr Rampton's private room had not been entirely engaged when he and Savill were talking confidentially before Savill went down to Somersetshire. So – perhaps Malbourne had known of that as well, though the circumstance could not affect him either way.

But what if Malbourne himself had had expectations from Rampton? Rampton was childless, after all, and Malbourne had been his ward and was now his protégé.

Savill set himself to play devil's advocate. Ogden had not arrived at Mrs Fenner's inn until Savill had been at Charnwood for some time. Why the delay? The question prompted an unexpected glimpse of something – not a possible reason but the merest hint of a line of enquiry that might in the end provide one.

At that moment, the crowd at the crossing perceived a gap in the traffic and surged forward, bearing Savill with them. When he reached the west side of Whitehall, even this fugitive hint had gone. However hard he tried to recall it, the hint refused to oblige him.

Savill continued along King Street and turned into Crown Street. The outer door of the Black Letter Office was closed. He rapped the knocker continuously until the shutter slid back.

'Mr Savill for Mr Rampton.'

The shutter closed and the door opened, disclosing not the familiar bulk of Jarsdel but the elderly clerk, thin to the point of emaciation, who had summoned Mr Malbourne on Savill's first visit to the office.

'I wish to see Mr Rampton at once,' Savill snapped.

'I will ascertain if he is available, sir. If you would care to take a seat—'

'At once,' Savill said. 'I shall show myself up.'

An expression of alarm sprang into the clerk's face. 'But, sir, that—'

'Who is it?' Mr Rampton called down. He appeared at the head of the stairs. 'Who was that knocking?'

Savill pushed the clerk aside. 'May I come up?'

Without waiting for an answer he took the stairs two at a time. Rampton stepped back, his hand to his throat.

'Pray, sir,' he said in a voice that seemed older and more tremulous than usual. 'Why this haste?'

He led the way into the outer office. Mr Malbourne was not at his desk. They went through to Mr Rampton's private room. Savill closed the door behind him.

'Where's Mr Malbourne?'

Rampton frowned. 'He was obliged to go out on private business. Something to do with Miss Woorgreen, I fancy. The lady to whom he's betrothed. You remember? I believe I mentioned her.'

'You allow him a good deal of latitude, sir, if I may say so.'

'I'm not sure you may say so,' Rampton said. 'Or not with propriety. I allow him more latitude than I would the other clerks because he is not like the other clerks. But that's my affair. I fail to see what business it is of yours.'

'Then I shall enlighten you directly, sir.' Savill was suddenly too angry, and too desperate, to approach the matter in any other way. 'Your Mr Malbourne was once a close friend of Dick Ogden's.'

Rampton, who had been lowering himself with the caution of his advanced years into the chair, sat down in a rush and slumped forward over his desk, supporting himself on his fore-arms. 'You – you must have been misinformed.'

'I see no reason to think so. Come, sir, we must find him at once.'

'One moment. Who told you?'

'Mrs Ogden.'

'I forbade you to see her again.'

'Be damned to that, sir. Her son and Malbourne were intimate friends at Oxford. She believes it was Malbourne who led her son astray.'

Rampton straightened his back. His lips were compressed and he looked both older and infinitely weary. 'You have no idea of the damage you may have done.'

'That's because you have kept me in the dark.'

'You must trust me.'

Savill stared down at him. 'But I don't. And I have reason not to, haven't I?'

Rampton knotted his fingers together, tugged them until they cracked and looked away from Savill, as if refusing to examine the unhappy history of their acquaintance. 'I am not always my own master,' he said. 'I have told you before, there are considerations you know nothing of, matters that touch on the security of the realm. It is as true now as it was then.'

'You cannot hide behind your office, not in this case. Charles was in my charge when he was kidnapped, and I owe a duty to him, not to His Majesty's Government. We cannot afford delay. We must find Malbourne.'

Rampton unlaced his fingers and held up his hands, palms towards Savill. 'A moment, I beg of you. *Festina lente*, eh? Let us be sure of our ground before we advance. And pray moderate your voice, my dear sir. You do not want to let the world know of your suspicions.'

For a moment, neither of them spoke. Savill discovered his fists were clenched and forced himself to relax them. He took a turn about the room, glancing at the dockets and letters piled in their baskets, at the smouldering coals in the grate, at the portrait above the fireplace of a plump gentleman richly dressed in the clothes of an earlier generation. He was aware that Rampton was watching him, and aware too that Rampton was waiting to let him make the next move; the old man's patience – his passivity – was unnerving.

Savill drew up a chair and sat down, facing Rampton across the desk. 'We must conclude that Ogden was acting on behalf of Malbourne,' he said. 'There can be no other explanation. You must grant me that.'

'No. Why in God's name should Malbourne wish to kidnap Charles? Your fancy is absurd enough in itself, but it falls down completely on the grounds of motive.'

'There must be a reason.' Savill felt his certainty ebbing away. 'The connection between them cannot be coincidental. That would be stretching it too far.'

'Would it? I wonder.' Rampton smiled without conviction, as if at a bad joke. 'It would not surprise me at all. When you get to my age you learn to accept that Providence plays strange tricks. Not all of them are pleasant, particularly where the operations of chance are concerned.'

Savill ignored this excursion to the wilder shores of philosophy. 'I wonder whether Mr Malbourne could have eavesdropped on the conversation we had in this room before I went to Somersetshire.'

Rampton raised his eyebrows but said nothing.

'He withdrew to his own office, leaving us here. He seemed to close the door. But I believe the lock did not quite engage.'

'Are you suggesting that Malbourne was listening at the keyhole? Like a prying servant? That is a preposterous notion.'

'Nevertheless, let us say he did. One thing he might have learned is that you contemplated making Charles your heir.' Savill hesitated. 'The circumstance would be of no importance

333

to him – unless of course he had previously had reason to believe that he himself was your heir. Or even that he entertained the hope that he might be.'

He knew instantly that he had found his target. Not that Rampton said anything at first. But a flash of emotion – fear? doubt? – passed rapidly over his face.

'How did you guess?' Rampton said at last.

'I didn't guess. I merely thought it possible – you and he have clearly known each other for many years. He has been your ward. You have a kindness for him – that much is obvious, even to me. And, until Charles appeared, you had no one else to make your heir.'

Except Lizzie, Savill added silently, for she shares your blood as much as Charles does. But Lizzie was different for she was Savill's child, with his blood in her veins, and he did not want Rampton's money for her.

Rampton stirred. He wetted his lips with his tongue. 'It is true that I have considered leaving Horace Malbourne a legacy – perhaps a substantial one. Indeed, at one time I even considered making him my principal heir. But – well, I have not settled the matter. I never drew up a will to that effect. Of course now he will have twelve hundred a year with Miss Woorgreen. But her father is a shrewd man, and I'm sure he will settle it on her and on any children of the union. Malbourne will not be able to touch the capital.' He hesitated and then added with painful reluctance, 'I know he has considerable debts already. Besides, if he wishes to enter Parliament, he will need more than twelve hundred a year at his disposal, particularly at first. A man cannot make his way there without money to smooth his path.'

'The question is, sir, did Malbourne know that you were contemplating this?' Savill knew the answer already, for he knew Rampton, and he knew from his own bitter experience that the old man had a history of managing other people by dangling the hope of future benefits in front of them. 'Of course he did. Perhaps he has borrowed against his expectations.'

The coals shifted in the grate and a shower of ash fell to the hearth. There was no need to say the rest aloud. Horace Malbourne had a motive for disposing of Charles as well as the means, through Dick Ogden, of carrying it out.

Savill smacked the desk with the palm of his hand. 'So where is Mr Malbourne now, sir, and what has he done with Charles?'

Rampton was still reluctant but Savill forced his hand. A clerk was sent to order a hackney to attend them at Crown Street. When it arrived they drove directly to Cavendish Square, where Mr Woorgreen, the father of Mr Malbourne's intended wife, lived in a house on the north side. But their journey was in vain, for Mr Woorgreen had gone into the City and was not expected home until much later, while the ladies had driven out to Hampstead to dine with Mrs Woorgreen's sister.

'A wild-goose chase,' Rampton said when they were in the hackney again. He had to raise his voice to be heard over the din of the wheels and hooves. 'But I tell you, Malbourne's absence is not suspicious in itself. No doubt the business he is transacting has something to do with his marriage – a conference with his attorney about the settlement, perhaps, or a visit to his broker.'

'Yes, but how do we find him now?'

'Our best plan is to wait at the office. He will have to return after dinner – he will need to go through the afternoon's letters – but not for an hour or two.' Rampton pulled out his watch and peered at it in the swaying gloom. 'There's no point in our hurrying back. You will have ample time to eat your dinner and then call at Green Street.'

Savill turned his head sharply. 'But to what purpose? Besides, suppose Malbourne returns early?'

'Why should he do that?' A sour note entered Rampton's voice. 'He is not a man who attends the office unless he is obliged to. He cultivates a wide acquaintance.'

They dined – if such a word could be used to describe the snatched meal – at Flavell's, a chophouse in Kingly Street where Mr Rampton was known. They occupied a private booth and could talk without fear of eavesdroppers.

Rampton grew confidential. 'I own this has shaken me, this news of Malbourne. If there was one man in the world whose loyalty I trusted, it was he. But we must not rush to judgement. That is always a cardinal error. Perhaps there is a perfectly innocent explanation. Perhaps you were misinformed. After all, from what you say, Mrs Ogden does not strike one as a particularly reliable witness. Her sorrows may have unseated her reason.'

Afterwards they went their separate ways. Rampton took another hackney coach and returned to Westminster, while Savill walked westwards into Mayfair. He made his way to 14 Green Street, where Mrs West had taken apartments. The tall windows on the first floor were blazing with light.

The porter admitted him and Savill sent up his card. On the back he wrote that, if Mrs West was at home, he begged the honour of paying his respects to her. While he waited for the footman, he listened to the raised voices and laughter above his head.

The footman returned and led him upstairs, past candles flickering in sconces. He threw open the door of the drawing room and announced the visitor. For an instant the occupants of the room were framed in the doorway, turning towards the visitor, their conversation dying.

Miss Horton had been laughing at something a slender gentleman had been telling her. Her eyes widened as they met Savill's over the shoulder of the gentleman's dark green coat. Beside them, on a sofa, was the Count, while Monsieur Fournier and Mrs West were seated together, as close to one another as decorum permitted, on another sofa opposite him. Behind the Count hovered Dr Gohlis, a book in his hand. His glasses reflected a candle flame, giving his eyes a golden gleam.

Savill entered the room. Mrs West held out her hand to him. The slender gentleman turned away from Miss Horton and bowed to Savill.

'Good evening, sir,' said Mr Malbourne.

# Chapter Fifty-One

Someone is in the yard below. A shadow moves from the garden towards the back door. It advances inch by inch – so slowly that unless you were watching for it you would hardly know it was moving at all.

It is too dark to make out anything but the outlines of things. The window is ajar. In the background is the singing from the Royal Oak and, further away still, the rumble of traffic in Bedford Square and Tottenham Court Road. Every now and then there comes a nearer sound, sharper and harder than the rest.

The shadow draws closer and vanishes beneath the lee of the scullery roof. Charles hears the scrape and click of a bolt sliding in a lock. The back door.

The man-mountain? How has he found his way into the yard?

Charles slips across the dark landing. Despite his care, a board creaks beneath him. The door of Lizzie's bedchamber is ajar. He passes into the room. He would like to shut the door behind him – for any barrier between him and the man-mountain is better than none – but he does not dare, in case the sound of the latch is audible downstairs.

Head cocked, he pauses by the bed. He hears no sounds

of movement below. A wild hope leaps within him: perhaps he imagined the shadow in the yard, imagined the scrape of the bolt.

Charles burrows between the wall and bed. He slithers into the crushing embrace of the mattresses. He pushes his hand between the wall and the upper mattress, trying to make a gap that will allow the passage of air.

His heart twitches and thumps inside his chest. An image of it, astonishingly vivid, grows in his mind: his heart is a small pink animal with short legs; it scurries to and fro, trying to escape from the prison of Charles's ribcage.

He strains to hear the slightest sound apart from his own laboured breathing. But there is nothing. The mattresses cut off sound as well as air.

Time passes. In a similar predicament, Mr Crusoe would shoot the man with one of his guns or run him through with a sword. Or, if he were obliged to hide, he would do so in order to contrive an ambush and use the advantage of surprise to overpower the intruder. Or, if he judged it wiser to retreat, he would do so by a route he had prepared in advance, for Mr Crusoe was both far-sighted and industrious; he always thought ahead to what the future might hold.

But Charles is not Robinson Crusoe. He is a small boy with neither family nor friends. He is without resources and without the power of speech in a city that is completely strange to him. But he has food, he reminds himself, and he has a knife. He investigates his hiding place until he finds the bundle of cheese and ham, which he contrives to push into his pocket. His fingers close around the handle of the knife.

The mattresses press him into a musty sandwich of horse-hair, squeezing him harder and harder. The temperature is rising. The sweat streams off him, soaking his shirt. The handle of the knife is slippery. The air is growing worse. He pants for breath. He moves slightly in the hope of encouraging a current of fresh air.

Worst of all, there is a tickle in the back of his throat.

The tickle grows. Charles rubs his upper lip with his forefinger, a trick his mother taught him when he began to sneeze while she was talking with a gentleman in the Palais Royal. 'Rub it harder, my love, rub it faster – it will make the naughty tickle go away.'

But this time the rubbing has the opposite effect. Or perhaps it is the thought of Maman, a distraction that unlocks a great hollowness within him. The tickle swells to a sensation of elephantine proportions.

Charles rubs his lip even harder.

The tickle dies.

It is a miracle. Charles relaxes. Air glides from his lungs in a long, soft sigh.

But the tickle returns. Charles sucks in a breath. A spasm runs through his body and a mighty sneeze erupts from him so quickly that he does not even know it is coming.

The ringing in his ears subsides. He wants to be sick.

Nothing happens. Charles waits. He allows himself the luxury of hope.

At that moment, and without any warning, the mattress shifts above him. Next, in one swift movement it is dragged from the bed. Fresh, cold air rushes over his sweating skin. The room is dark apart from a covered lantern held high, its feeble light playing over the lower mattress until it finds Charles's face.

The side of the lower mattress still pins Charles to the wall. He wriggles from its embrace. The bedchamber is filled with an immense shadow. In the lantern's light he glimpses the brim of a hat and hears stertorous breathing. A hand grips his leg.

'Ha!' a man says in a whisper as he drags Charles across the mattress towards him. 'Ha!'

Charles twists his body and curls his spine towards the shadow. He stabs the knife down on the hand.

The man screams. The hand relaxes its grip. Charles pulls his leg free and rolls off the bottom of the bed. The lantern clatters against the post at the end of the bed and the flame inside it sways and flickers.

Charles crawls through the doorway. On the landing he scrambles to his feet and takes the flight of stairs leading to the floor above.

He knows at once he has made a mistake. He should have run downstairs, to the back door or to the hatch from the cellar into the yard.

Too late. The light from the lantern has steadied and grown stronger. The man's heavy footsteps are already on the landing.

Charles has the advantage of knowing where he is going. The man behind him has the advantage of the lantern. Charles is nimbler. The man is stronger.

In the dark, the house in Nightingale Lane is a maze of doorways, passages and stairs, arranged without rhyme or reason. Landings lead nowhere – more than once, Charles is forced to double back and almost rushes into the intruder's arms.

It is as much by chance as intention that he rises higher and higher in the old house and at last bursts through a low, slanting door into the loft.

The man is following him up the last flight of stairs. He is breathing heavily like a wheezing pump.

They are in the attics, a series of tentlike spaces beneath the many gables of the house. Their arrival has set off the rats – Charles hears a scurrying of tiny paws, diminishing rapidly in volume.

Despite the panic, despite the haste, everything moves very slowly. There is time for him to register the presence of the rats, and time for him to feel that the air is cooler up here and to notice the windows in the gables, rectangles of faint radiance in the gloom. There is even time to consider the courses of action before him: to turn and attack the man with the knife; to hide, if he can find a hiding place; or—

341

Even as the idea is forming in his head, he has made his choice: he is running again, knife in hand, making for the far end of the attics where a projecting gable forms an alcove at right angles to the main pitch of the roof. He cannot see where he is going. He stumbles and falls. Behind him, the lantern sways and its light lurches among the rafters. The breathing is louder than ever and drawing closer.

Charles reaches the window and fumbles for the latch. The opening is about eighteen inches high and less than a foot in width. The casement swings out in a rush and the night air rushes into the attic. He pushes his head and shoulders through the opening and drags his body on to the sill.

The night is cloudy, but the faint radiance of the city fills the sky to the south. On the far side of the window, a leaded valley stretches away between two lower roofs, which belong to the kitchen wing and the outhouses at the back of the house. Charles's hands scrabble for purchase on the leads. He feels water, a slimy puddle. He touches spongy moss and dead leaves.

His hips are through. The sill digs into his thighs. No man could crawl through this space, let alone a man-monster.

A hand grasps his left ankle. Charles kicks out with his right foot, though he cannot do much because his legs are so tightly confined by the window frame.

He twists his body, trying to stab the man's hand again. But the blade catches on the side of the window frame, and the force of his own thrust wrenches it from his hand. The knife clatters down the tiles and comes to rest in a gully.

Another hand shackles his right ankle. An immense force drags him back into the house. There is nothing to hold on to. The fronts of his thighs are compressed against the sill. He fears the bones will snap.

Charles opens his mouth. He wants to scream. But he cannot.

# Chapter Fifty-Two

The drawing room stretched the width of the house. Despite the candles, it was a place of vast and ill-defined shadows. It held five people, six now Savill was here, but it was large enough for forty or fifty.

'Do you know Mr Malbourne?' Mrs West said in a low voice, releasing his hand.

'Yes,' he said. 'But not well. Have you known him long?'

'No – a few hours. He is an acquaintance of Monsieur de Quillon, and they encountered each other quite by chance in the street. He seems very agreeable and *très bien élevé*, as Monsieur Fournier says. But enough of that – sit beside me, sir. Tell me, have you news of the boy?'

He joined her on the sofa. 'No, ma'am, or rather nothing to the point.' He answered almost at random, for his mind was elsewhere, struggling to comprehend this new information about Malbourne. 'I believe he was brought to London. But where he is now, I have no idea.'

Mrs West patted his sleeve with her fan. 'You poor man. Forgive me if I speak plainly, but you do not look at all well. I see that this business has distressed you greatly.'

Monsieur Fournier, Savill noticed, had joined Malbourne and Miss Horton. But the Count approached the sofa.

343

'Mr Savill,' he said, 'have you found my son?' He waved imperiously. 'No, don't get up. No need to stand on ceremony, sir. All I want is Charles.'

Once again, Savill explained that he had followed the trail of Charles and the man in the blue coat to the outskirts of London but had been able to find no trace of him since then. He did not mention the boathouse in Chiswick and what he had found there. With a glance at Mr Malbourne, he added that the authorities were pursuing the matter.

'You disappoint me, sir,' the Count said. 'I had hoped for news by now. If this were France in the old days, I would have—'

'Ah – that lost paradise,' Monsieur Fournier interrupted, turning towards them. 'France before the Revolution. How desperate we were to remove its blemishes, were we not? But now we would give anything to have it back, blemishes and all.' He smiled down at Savill on the sofa. 'You must forgive us if we sound impatient – we are so anxious for intelligence of Charles. Why, we even drove to your house today in the hope of finding you there.'

'My house?' Savill stared stupidly at him. 'I was not aware you know where it is.'

'Miss Horton recalled you lived in a place called Nightingale Lane near Bedford Square. That was all we needed to know. The coachman did the rest.'

Savill remembered now. Miss Horton had quoted some poem or other when he mentioned the name, and he had been bearish in reply.

'The shutters were up,' Mrs West said. 'And a woman came out of the house nearby and said you were away and asked if she could take a message.'

'Where have you been staying?' Fournier said casually.

'In lodgings,' Savill said. 'My sister and my daughter are away, and there was no purpose in opening the house until their return. But I own I'm surprised that you have come to London at all.'

This was too blunt to be polite but Fournier smiled in response as if Savill had said something droll. 'Because the authorities have a foolish fear we might indulge in seditious activities? You are quite correct. But this is merely a short, private visit as dear Mrs West's guests. We shall not go to public places and call on our acquaintance. Why, we can hardly be said to be here at all.'

Mrs West laughed. After the mild witticism, Fournier entered into conversation with Miss Horton and Dr Gohlis. The Count began talking to Mr Malbourne, speaking loudly in French and with obvious relish.

'I had not hoped for the pleasure of seeing you again so soon,' Savill said to Mrs West. 'I thought you intended to stay longer in Norbury.'

'This business with Charles has unsettled us all, and Monsieur Fournier was anxious to come up to town to see his attorney before the weather worsened. All in all, there seemed no reason to delay the visit.' She smiled at him. 'Particularly as Harriet wished it.'

He glanced involuntarily at Miss Horton, and caught her looking at Malbourne. 'Had she a particular reason, ma'am?'

Mrs West raised her eyebrows. 'If she had, sir, she did not confide it to me.'

Savill heard the arch intonation in her voice and cursed his own stupidity in giving her such an opening. He felt his colour rising and looked away from Miss Horton. He pushed the thought aside and forced his mind to turn to the matter in hand.

Malbourne was already acquainted with the Count. Was Rampton aware of this? If so, why hadn't he mentioned it? Did Rampton know that Malbourne was here? Surely not, or he wouldn't have urged Savill to call at Green Street. Was it possible that Malbourne had arranged for Charles to be kidnapped not for his own reasons but to oblige Monsieur de Quillon?

'You mustn't waste your time on an old woman like me.'

Mrs West poked him in the ribs with her fan. 'Go and talk to Harriet. She will want to hear whatever you can tell her about Charles. She is grown very fond of the lad, you know. Curious, isn't it? The fact he doesn't speak, I mean. Or won't speak. It makes him rather like a dog or a baby, doesn't it? I've never had a baby, but one can certainly grow fond of a dog, and I imagine it's much of a muchness.'

'He is more than a dog or a baby, ma'am,' Savill said, his voice sharpening. 'He is perfectly capable of thought, and of feeling. It's merely that he's a prisoner. A prisoner in his own silence.'

She smiled at him. 'How very poetical, sir. Be sure to tell Harriet that.'

He rose and bowed. His jaw had begun to ache around the empty socket where the tooth had been.

Fournier waved to him to join them. As Savill crossed the room, his eyes met Malbourne's over the Count's shoulder. There was no expression in Malbourne's face.

'Miss Horton has a message for you, sir,' Fournier said to Savill. 'From her father.' He hooked his hand under Gohlis's elbow and went on, 'And now, Doctor – would you be so good as to assist me . . .?'

Savill was now alone with Miss Horton, who declined to look directly at him.

'My father begs to be remembered to you,' she said. 'He is as anxious for news of Charles as any of us.' She looked up at him at last. 'He feels what has happened reflects badly on all of us in Norbury – and particularly on him as Justice of the Peace. Is there really nothing more to tell?'

'Nothing of any importance. I wish there were.'

She questioned him minutely about his pursuit of Charles and the man in the blue coat, trying to wring every scrap of information from his narrative. She was so probing in her interrogation that he had to work hard to avoid revealing more than he wished.

346

Then she took him by surprise with another line of questioning.

'And how is Miss Elizabeth, sir?'

He stared stupidly at her, unsettled by the change of direction and caught off guard by the formality of 'Miss Elizabeth'. 'She is very well, thank you,' he said.

'She is happy to have you home, I dare say.'

'In fact no.' It was a relief not to have to guard his tongue on this subject at least. 'I haven't opened up the house. So she is still staying with friends.'

Miss Horton smiled and, in that flash of white teeth, the formality between them dissipated. 'She would rather be with you?'

'Yes. She said she desired to act as my housekeeper until my sister returns. Indeed, she had her heart set on it.'

'That is understandable.'

'She is staying with her best friend at present,' Savill said, abandoning all restraint on this subject. 'The friend is about to be married.'

'Ah. A mixed pleasure for Miss Elizabeth, perhaps.'

It was his turn to smile. 'It is sometimes agreeable to be the centre of attention oneself.'

She laughed. 'You are cynical about the fair sex, sir.'

'And about my own. To be fair, Lizzie is worried about Charles, too. She takes a great interest in him.'

'That is natural. He is her brother, after all, and to a girl of her age no doubt the circumstances of his life have an air of romance and mystery about them.'

Savill was ready to take offence: Miss Horton presumed a great deal on such a slight acquaintance.

'Is your daughter in London?' she said, distracting him.

'Yes. She's staying at her old school. It is the principal's daughter who is getting married.'

'Would you permit me to call on her? She must be so curious about Charles, and I could tell her what I know of him.'

'I could not possibly trespass on your good nature.'

347

'Why not? I should like it.'

'Perhaps when we are settled in our own home again, ma'am. Her friends do not know of Charles yet and she could not talk freely in their presence.'

'Of course.'

She began to say something else but broke off almost at once. Her eyes moved away from Savill's face and her expression changed. Savill turned. The Count was bearing down on them with Malbourne beside him.

Master and man?

'Well, sir,' the Count said, 'Mr Malbourne has a position in a government department. I have been telling him that he must use his utmost endeavours to find my son. He will know just how to set about it, eh?'

Savill bowed in acknowledgement. Miss Horton curtseyed and withdrew to Mrs West on the sofa.

'He has already promised to raise the matter with the Secretary of the Home Department,' the Count went on. 'You must hold yourself in readiness – he may wish to question you.'

Savill bowed again, suddenly conscious of his shabby coat and unshaven face.

Malbourne had brought with him a hint of perfume. From his neatly dressed hair to his gleaming shoes, he looked as if he were fresh from the attentions of his valet.

'A private gentleman can do very little in such matters.' The Count's face was flushed a darker colour than usual. 'I apprehend you are acquainted with Mr Malbourne. I cannot understand why you have not approached him yourself.'

'The acquaintance is by no means close, my lord,' Malbourne said. 'And I have been out of town a good deal. So it's not to be wondered at. But you may rest assured I shall do all I can.'

'I am much obliged to you, sir.' The Count had put on his grandest manner. 'The more I see of you, the more you remind me of your father. I greatly prized his friendship.'

Malbourne bowed.

The Count smiled condescendingly at him and glared at Savill. 'Pray assist Mr Malbourne in any way possible,' he commanded. 'For Charles's sake.'

He strode away and sat down heavily in an armchair beside Mrs West's sofa. Savill and Malbourne turned to face each other.

'Does Mr Rampton know of this?' Savill said quietly.

'That I'm here? No.'

'He cannot approve it.'

'You are at liberty to inform him of it. If you wish.' The right half of Malbourne's face was brightly lit by the candles burning in a wall sconce beside him. The left half was in shadow, almost black. 'On the other hand, sir, you might do well to reflect that there is more at issue here than you are aware of, and you would be wise to tread carefully.'

With that, Malbourne turned on his heel. His abrupt and unfriendly manner was sharply at odds with his customary suavity. Savill watched him approaching the sofa, bowing to Mrs West and Miss Horton, and venturing some pleasantry that made both ladies laugh. The Count, who had picked up a newspaper, looked up and smiled at him.

Everyone's favourite, Savill thought, and the rascal does it so naturally, damn him, so elegantly.

'And how are you, sir?' Dr Gohlis said, approaching Savill from the other direction with Monsieur Fournier in tow. 'Does the site of the extraction pain you still?'

Savill turned. 'Slightly, sir, if I am honest. But nothing like it did.'

'I am sure Mrs West would not object if I looked inside your mouth for a moment. Pray step this way.'

The doctor drew Savill towards the sconce and asked him to open his mouth. He tilted Savill's head to make the best use of the light. Fournier watched.

349

'Ah, that is much better. You must expect some soreness, even a little swelling. But keep it clean and it will soon heal completely. Rinse three times a day with salt water.'

Savill said he was much obliged.

'By the way, was the telescope I found of any use? Did you enquire about it at Mr Vereker's?'

'Indeed.' Savill was aware of Fournier hovering beside them. 'He confirmed that the glass came from his workshop. But it was some time ago. He could not put his hand on the record of the sale.'

'What a pity.'

'I shall write to Mr Horton,' Savill said, 'and enquire whether he wishes me to send the glass to him by way of Mrs West.'

The Count called Gohlis over to him, leaving Savill alone with Fournier.

'A charming young man,' Fournier said, glancing towards Malbourne and the ladies. 'He will go far. I understand he is betrothed to a fine heiress as well.' He smiled at Savill. 'You should cultivate him.'

'Have you known him long, sir?'

Fournier shook his head. 'Not until tonight. But Monsieur de Quillon was friendly with his father before the Revolution, and Mr Malbourne encountered him when he was last in Paris.' The smile was rueful. 'But it was not the best of times to pursue the pleasures of society and there was no opportunity to take the acquaintance further. I believe that he was obliged to leave the city almost immediately afterwards.'

'Why?'

'Lord Gower – the British Ambassador – judged it prudent, I assume, and ordered him to go. Whenever there is trouble, the citizens of Paris tend to think that the English have a hand in it.'

Savill looked sharply at him. 'When was this, pray?'

'In August.'

'This August?'

'Yes.' Fournier's handsome features twisted and became ugly. 'When the mob stormed the Tuileries and so many gallant people were slaughtered in the name of liberty. What a night that was. What a terrible night.'

# Chapter Fifty-Three

Charles has a headache. That is the first fact. The second is that he feels nauseous.

He has been sleeping. Or perhaps he fainted. He has an insubstantial memory of a dark, confined place, of swaying and bumping, and of an unyielding surface beneath him. When he tries to recall it, the memory dissolves.

There are smells now. Earth. Urine. Something stuffy and acrid, perhaps the bedding. The mustiness of damp, so familiar from Charnwood.

He listens. A distant sighing that might be the wind. His own breathing. A moment later, he realizes that something is missing. *London is never silent.* Even in Nightingale Lane, even at night, you hear the sounds of the city.

So that means . . .?

His fingers explore. Sheets. Some coarse material, not fine linen. A pillow. Blankets on top of him.

He extends his arm and finds more material. Heavier. Hanging. Yielding to his touch. A curtain.

He opens his eyes. It is dark, but that may be the curtain blocking the light. He pushes it again, trying to find the gap.

A draught of cold air brushes the skin of his hand and arm

and then touches his face. Still he sees nothing. His skin grows cold.

Night?

Charles lies back on the pillow and draws the bedclothes up to his neck. The nausea has gone, leaving thirst behind. The skin inside his mouth is rough on the tip of his tongue. One of his first memories is of how, when he was a baby, a cat sat in his cot and licked his face for what seemed like hours, an activity that pleased both of them immensely. The same roughness as the cat's tongue.

He is very weary. Fact. He does not know where he is. Fact.

It's happened again, he thinks. He has been snatched from one place and thrown into another, as helpless as a counter in a board game at the throw of the dice. A memory stirs: Mr Savill's dice. He feels the outline of them in the pocket of his breeches. Shake them and throw them, and the dots change. The dice have nothing to do with it.

There is nothing he can do. This is yet another fact, he supposes. He cannot even call for help. He is mute.

Charles shivers. Memories and facts and silence. He has had enough of them all. He closes his eyes and waits for sleep to return.

# Chapter Fifty-Four

'You have lost your wits,' Rampton said. 'This is a monstrous slander.'

'No, sir.' Savill stood in front of Rampton's desk. 'Consider these facts, one by one, and forget for a moment how I came by them. Quickly now, for time is precious. And forget your old friendship for him, for it must not colour your judgement.'

He had left Malbourne in Green Street and come directly to the Black Letter Office, where Mr Rampton was in his private room. The only other person in the building was the whippet-thin clerk who had opened the door to him.

'As you know, Mrs Ogden told me this afternoon that Mr Malbourne and her son were intimate friends at Oxford. Indeed, she blamed Mr Malbourne for her son's wildness there and his subsequent dissipation. It is no great leap from that to suspect that the connection between them continued. If Mr Malbourne had wanted an agent to act for him in an affair of this nature, then Dick Ogden would have been a natural choice.'

Rampton rubbed his cheeks, which looked baggier and more wrinkled because of the deep shadows thrown by the candlelight. 'We have discussed that, and I have considered it further. The thing falls down on the question of motive, for a man does not commit such a terrible crime in the hope of a legacy that has not even been promised.'

'Are you sure?'

'Of course I am. And whatever else he may be, Malbourne is not a fool. Where is he, in any case? He should be here by now.'

'The next point is this, sir,' Savill said. 'I found him at Green Street this evening.'

'What?'

'You did not sanction it?'

'I expressly forbade it.'

'The Count was making much of him. It appears that he was acquainted with Mr Malbourne's father, and they encountered one another by chance in the street, and Monsieur de Quillon brought him up to Mrs West's drawing room. A strange coincidence, is it not? And were you aware of the connection between them?'

'I don't know everything about Malbourne,' Rampton said. 'Besides, we should hear what he has to say before rushing to judgement.'

'How much has the Count told him about Charles? Is there some deeper connection between them, some more sinister motive for Malbourne's action? Something perhaps based on the old friendship between the Count and Mr Malbourne's father?'

Rampton took out his snuffbox and tapped it like a gavel on his desk. 'Speculation,' he said. 'Pure speculation.'

'But all this pales into insignificance beside this last fact: Malbourne was in Paris in August. According to Monsieur Fournier, he was there on the very night that Augusta was killed. Is that true? If he was, you must surely have known.'

Rampton took a pinch of snuff and sneezed into his handkerchief. 'Of course I knew. He was in Paris on official business.'

'Did the business concern Augusta in any way?'

'I cannot say.'

'Cannot or will not? I think she was an English spy. Perhaps Malbourne was her paymaster.'

Rampton left the snuffbox alone and toyed with his silver inkwell. 'Once again – speculation.'

'Which you can confirm or not, as you choose.'

'But why on earth should he kill her?'

'Was she blackmailing him? She was capable of that.'

'As a threat to the security of the realm? That's absurd.'

'Or as a threat to himself.' Savill felt the ghosts of old jealousies stirring inside him. 'She was a woman used to employing her charms for her own ends.'

'You suggest she was his mistress?'

'It's possible, isn't it? And now he's betrothed to an heiress. That makes him vulnerable, particularly if she held letters of his, perhaps containing promises he made.'

'Malbourne is not a man to make a fool of himself over a woman,' Rampton said.

Another jolt of memory stirred and twisted within Savill, for he had made a fool of himself over her. 'Augusta was not like other women. If it suited her purpose, she could make a man sit up on his hind legs and bark at the moon.'

'That is not something I am competent to judge, sir,' Rampton said primly. 'But I must remind you that you have no proof whatsoever of this.'

Savill switched his line of approach. 'Tell me, sir, who collected the letters I sent you from Charnwood? You remember? Addressed to Frederick Brown at the White Horse Cellar in Piccadilly?'

Rampton looked up. For a moment he said nothing. 'As it happened, I sent Malbourne to fetch them.'

'If he opened those letters before he gave them to you, or read their contents in some other way, he would have learned that Charles has been struck dumb and will not even communicate by writing. He would also have learned that Charles may well have been a witness to his mother's murder.'

The room was silent now, apart from the rattle of a carriage in the street below. Rampton took another pinch, which led to another sneeze. The old man's anger had vanished. He seemed to have shrunk physically, as if the news of Malbourne's treachery had deflated him. Savill sensed the battle was nearly won, if not the war.

'It explains the timing, sir,' he went on. 'I had wondered about that. That's why Malbourne didn't send Ogden down to Somerset earlier. Because – until he saw my letter to you – he didn't realize that Charles might have been a witness to the murder. But once he did know that, it was imperative that he should prevent Charles from reaching London. Because one day Charles may start to speak or write again.'

Rampton shook his head slowly. 'I – I cannot but acknowledge there is some sense in what you say. But Malbourne? I have known him since he was a boy . . . It beggars belief that he would commit a cold-blooded murder . . . And it is not just Augusta, either, is it? If you are correct, Malbourne must also have murdered Richard Ogden, his former friend.'

'A man will do anything to save his own skin,' Savill said. 'Mr Malbourne could not hope to avoid the boy once he was in London. Then Charles would come face to face with his mother's murderer. It would be strange indeed if Charles did not show some sign of it. Even if he were still mute.'

'I must have time to consider this. It is not—'

'Sir, every moment is important. He must know I suspect something. Can you not have a warrant made out for his arrest?'

'I concede that you are right, Mr Savill,' Rampton said slowly, 'at least in this: that there are grounds for suspicion. Whether they amount to enough to persuade a magistrate to issue a warrant is still not certain. I shall give Malbourne a chance to refute these accusations first. I owe him that.'

'But it would merely give him a chance to escape justice.'

'Why would he flee?' Rampton pulled at his fingers, wincing as if they pained him. 'That would be an admission of guilt

357

– assuming he is guilty of doing more than call on Mrs West when he knows I would not have wished it.'

'Mrs West told me that he met the Count and Monsieur Fournier on the street quite by chance. And they swept him into the house, presumably, and introduced him to her.'

'Then perhaps that is precisely what happened. Malbourne is the soul of politeness. He would not wish to offend the Count, his father's friend, especially now when he is little better than a penniless refugee.' Rampton consulted his watch. 'Anyway, Malbourne should be here within the half-hour. I shall put all this to him and see how he replies. One way or the other we shall get to the bottom of this. If you wish, I shall summon a constable and station him downstairs.'

Shortly after this, Savill went downstairs, intending to cross the road to his lodgings and change his shirt, which was sadly soiled. The duty clerk greeted him by name in the hall.

'I should have enquired when you came in, sir – did you receive your letter?'

Savill stopped. 'What letter?'

'It came this afternoon, sir – about two o'clock.'

'I've had no letter. Who brought it? A carrier?'

'A servant, sir.' The clerk was a bright fellow: when he saw Savill's expression he went on quickly: 'Ugly-faced fellow. Had a wall-eye.'

'The left eye?' Savill said. 'Streaked with white and seeming to look over your shoulder?'

'That's the man to the life.'

'What did you do with the letter?'

'Took it upstairs, sir, and gave it to Mr Malbourne. He said he'd make sure it reached you.'

Though the hour was growing late, it was fortunate that the proprietor of the Beaufort Academy for Young Ladies had not retired for the night, and nor had the two young ladies. Troughton admitted Savill into the house with a great rattling of bolts and bars. He was wearing a long brown apron and had clearly been engaged in cleaning the silver.

'You keep late hours,' Savill said.

The manservant pursed his lips and winked his wandering eye. 'Mrs P is not what you might call a restful lady, sir. Especially now, with the nuptials hanging over us.'

'I'm obliged to you,' Savill said, parting with a sixpence. 'I understand you delivered a letter for me to Crown Street in Westminster earlier today.'

'Yes, sir, Miss Elizabeth was most insistent. "Urgent" she said, and she wrote it on the outside. Madam said I could go – I hope everything's all right, sir?'

Savill chose his words with care: 'I'm not sure. The letter was mislaid after it was taken in.'

'The porter said you'd been there an hour or so earlier but he was sure you'd be back.'

The letter must have arrived either during or just after his conference with Rampton in the Park, Savill thought; while he was at Bell's Library. He said, 'Do you know why it was so urgent?'

'Young girls, sir.' The eye dipped and swooped like a swallow on the wing. 'At their age, everything is urgent. Full of fancies. Sometimes it's as good as a play in a theatre here.'

For an instant, the thought of swallows was a momentary distraction, tugging gently at Savill's attention. 'Pray let Mrs Pycroft know I'm here,' he said. 'Give her my compliments and my apologies for calling at this hour and beg her to allow me to speak to my daughter in private for a moment. Tell her it's family business that will not wait till the morning.'

The eyebrow drooped again. 'Seeing as it's you, sir.'

Troughton showed Savill into a dining room that smelled of old greens and forgotten roasts. He paced up and down by the light of a single candle until he heard Lizzie's hurried footsteps. He turned to face the door as she burst into the room.

'Have you found Charles?' she said.

She was breathing hard and her colour was up. He drew out a chair and made her sit. He sat beside her and took her hand.

'What is it, Papa? Is he hurt? Is he—'

'No, my love, not as far as I know. But I haven't found him. Listen – your letter went astray.'

'It can't have done. Troughton said he'd—'

'What did it say?' Savill interrupted.

'That I've seen Charles. I've talked to him. I said I'd write to you and you would come.'

It was as if she had thrown a bucket of water over him. When the shock subsided, he said, 'Where?'

'He's at home. Mary and I went there this morning to fetch the lace my aunt gave me.' She glanced up at him, and he guessed there had been a spark of rebellion in her decision to go to Nightingale Lane – a desire to assert her right to go home if she wished, despite his prohibition. 'It will work beautifully with her dress,' she added quickly. 'Mrs Forster let us in, and I went upstairs by myself to fetch the lace. You know the closet where we keep the winter cloaks? My *Robinson Crusoe* was open on the window seat and there was a jar of quince jelly on the floor. So I knew that someone must be—'

He took her hand. 'Slowly, my love. And lower your voice.'

Her fingers tightened around his. 'Papa,' she whispered, 'he was hiding in the alcove behind the curtain. And he looked so small, so frightened, so delicate, so . . . so *dirty*. He has big, big eyes, you know, and they stare at you, and they look right through.'

'I know they do,' Savill said. 'What then?'

'I knew he must be Charles – who else could he be? Besides, I think his eyes were like mine. So I talked to him.' A note of pride entered into her voice. 'In English and in French. I said I would write to you, and you would come and take care

360

of him. I'm sure he understood. I could see it in his face.' She was still holding his hand. 'Was I right to do that? Have I made things worse?'

'You were absolutely right,' he said, wishing to God that he had allowed her to keep house for him in Nightingale Lane in which case she would have been there when Charles arrived, however he contrived it. 'And you're right about its being him, too. He is very like you, you know – or rather how you were when you were younger.'

'He wouldn't say anything. Is he really . . .?'

'He is mute. He used not to be. But – but since he lost his mother – he has not spoken a word.'

'Why?'

'No one knows.'

'He can read.'

'Oh yes. There's nothing wrong with his mental faculties.' Savill released her hand and smiled at her. 'And a lady in Somerset was reading *Robinson Crusoe* to him.'

'That proves it was Charles, then. We must go there now and bring him here. Mrs Pycroft will not mind my going with you, I'm sure, not if you ask her yourself.'

'No,' he said. 'You must stay here.'

'No,' she said. 'I must come with you.'

# Chapter Fifty-Five

Nightingale Lane was as black as a coal pit. The gables of the old houses on either side craned towards each other. Above them the sky was stained with the faint glow from London at night.

The surface of the lane was paved unevenly with old stones. The coach rocked violently as it moved forward. There were three of them inside the hackney, for Savill had begged yet another favour from Mrs Pycroft and brought Troughton with them. Lizzie's hand was tucked under Savill's arm. He felt her rapid breathing rather than heard it.

The lane widened, and they drew up in the wider space outside his home. Savill lowered the glass and put his head out. It had started to rain. The coach lamps threw a feeble light over the front of the house. To the side was the mouth of the alley leading to the Oak Tree.

The coachman descended and let down the steps for them. 'Never been here before.' He sniffed and added, just low enough for Savill to be able to ignore it, 'Can't say I like it much, either.'

'We won't be long,' Savill said.

'I need to go, sir. You can pick up a hackney at the stand by Goodge Street.'

'Wait for us and there's a half-crown for you on top of the fare. A quarter of an hour, no more.'

The coachman twitched as if stung. 'All right, sir. But some gentlemen make promises they can't fulfil. I'd like to see the colour of your money.'

'You'll see nothing at all unless you wait,' Savill said, helping Lizzie down the steps.

Troughton had brought a lantern and a stick with him. They lit the lantern with the aid of the coach lamp. Savill led the way into the alley, with Lizzie behind him and Troughton bringing up the rear.

Savill stopped at the gate to the yard and felt in his pocket for the key. Lizzie pushed past him and raised the latch. The gate swung inwards. It had not been locked.

They entered the yard. The house door was ajar.

They lit candles in the kitchen. In the hall, Savill picked up a walking stick weighted with lead.

'Keep behind us,' he told Lizzie. 'Or you go back to the coach instantly.'

'Yes, sir,' she said meekly.

They went upstairs, with Savill and Lizzie calling Charles's name and telling him not to be afraid.

The house was cold and damp. A current of air swept down to greet them from the upper floors. They looked first in the closet where Lizzie had found Charles. *Robinson Crusoe* lay on the window seat and the quince jelly was behind the curtain in the alcove.

Lizzie broke away and threw open the door of her bedchamber. Savill heard her sharp intake of breath. He shouldered her out of the way.

The top mattress and the coverlets had been dragged from the bed. He trod on something yielding. He stooped, and the light shone on a fragment of cheese.

His stomach lurched when he saw a severed finger beside it. But at once he realized his eyes were playing tricks with

363

him: it was only a piece of ham hacked from the side of a joint and roughly fingerlike in shape.

'Where is he?' Lizzie wailed. 'What's happened?'

'Be quiet,' he said. 'And stay behind me, do you hear?'

They searched the rest of the house. They found only two things of interest – further signs that someone had been foraging in the larder and the pantry and, in one of the attics, a casement window thrown open.

It was raining steadily now. When Savill held up the lantern, the feeble light shone on mossy tiles sleek with moisture. He looked out over the roofs of his house, calling Charles's name and hoping against hope that the boy had taken refuge among the chimney stacks.

There was no answer. He began to close the window.

'Papa, no,' Lizzie said, touching his arm. 'Leave it open.'

'The rain will get in.'

'But suppose he's still out there. Suppose he's too scared to come inside while we're here.'

He left the window open, persuaded by the desperation in her voice rather than the logic of her argument.

'What now?' she said as they were leaving the house.

'I take you and Troughton back to Mrs Pycroft.'

None of them spoke until they were in the hackney and rattling slowly down the lane.

'There must be something we can do,' Lizzie said in a whisper, in deference to the presence of Troughton not two feet away from her.

'Not tonight,' Savill said.

'But he must be out there. Lost. Cold. Hungry. This is a foreign country to him.' Her voice rose to a wail. 'And he is dumb.'

'Hush,' he said sharply. 'I shall leave you at the school and go back to your uncle Rampton. He has it in his power to do more than we can.'

'But will he use his power?'

'I shall make sure he does,' Savill said with more confidence than he felt.

They did not speak for the rest of the journey. Once they reached Bedford Square, the coach picked up speed. They turned into Tottenham Court Road and then right into Oxford Street.

The rain was falling more heavily now and there were fewer people about. They pulled up outside the school in Little Castle Street. It took several minutes for them to gain admittance, for the door was heavily barred, and Mrs Pycroft's maid was not used to the bolts and locks that secured it. Mrs Pycroft herself, armed with a poker, greeted them in the hall.

'Well, sir,' she said, 'this is a fine business, I must say. I'd have you remember that this is a respectable establishment.'

The situation was delicate and called for all of Savill's powers of negotiation. Mrs Pycroft was aggrieved, and with some justification. But he needed her to look after Lizzie and he could not afford to upset her. On the other hand the hackney driver was in a hurry to be gone, as was Savill himself.

When at last he left the house, leaving behind him a shower of promises, regrets and apologies, the coach was still waiting for him, or rather for his money. The rain was falling more heavily than before. The drains had overflowed and the pavement was sheeted with water.

'Crown Street in Westminster,' he called up to the driver.

'No, sir. This is as far as I go. I'll thank you to settle up now if you please.'

Savill failed to change the coachman's mind. He would not even consent to drive Savill to the nearest hackney stand, for his own home lay in quite another direction.

As they were arguing, however, another coach turned into the road and drew up some way behind them. It was not a hackney but a private carriage, so Savill ignored it and

365

continued to work on his driver, who was by now taking a perverse pleasure in denying him what he wanted.

'No, sir. If you'll pay what you owe, I'm sure I'll be much obliged.'

'Damn it, I'll take down your number and report you.'

'Won't do you any good, sir. My money, if you please.'

In the end, there was no help for it. Savill paid his fare and the coach rolled away. He turned up the collar of his coat, wishing he had brought an umbrella, and began to walk towards the hackney stand. He drew level with the coach waiting near the corner. The glass in the door slid down. He turned automatically in the direction of the sound.

'Mr Savill, sir.'

It was too dark to see the face of the man inside the carriage. But the voice was as thick as porridge and instantly familiar.

'Come to fetch you, sir,' Jarsdel said.

# Chapter Fifty-Six

Charles wakes.

He drops into consciousness like a stone into a pool. The ripples spread.

He is in bed still, and in the same room as before, so far as he can tell. But he is no longer alone.

Automatically he pushes his hand over his belly and touches his crotch. It is still dry. His bladder is full.

There is light, too – vertical lines of it where the curtains meet. The lines fluctuate in strength. Not constant. A candle. It is still night.

Someone is moving on the other side of the bed-curtains. Footsteps pace up and down – very slowly; the gaps between the footfalls grow longer and longer. Charles closes his eyes and wills his breath to be soft and even.

He remembers when the Count came to look at him on his last night at Charnwood. The memory is remote, as if it happened long ago: more than that, it is as if it no longer belongs to him; it is drifting away.

On that occasion, he pretended to be asleep, just as he's doing now. He smelled the odour of brandy, he remembers that, and also he heard what the Count said.

'Oh, my son,' he whispered. 'Oh, my son.'

The footsteps stop. The sweat breaks out on Charles's forehead. Soon the curtains will move aside. Soon someone will look down on him.

He waits. Nothing happens. He might be alone in the room. In the distance, an owl hoots.

Then he hears it, the sound he fears most in all the world. *Tip-tap*. Like cracking a walnut. *Tip-tap*.

# Chapter Fifty-Seven

Savill woke with a headache that split his skull in two. He was very cold. His body ached.

*Where in God's name am I?*

The headache had its vicious centre at the back of his head. He touched the place gingerly and found a bruise the size of an egg. The hair covering the bruise was stiff with dried blood.

The next discovery was that he was lying on a floor of packed earth in a windowless building. It was not entirely dark, for daylight filtered through gaps between the roof and the wallplate, between the door and its frame, and between some of the tiles.

He pulled himself slowly into a sitting position and leaned against a wall. The exertion made him feel nauseous and lent extra savagery to the pain in his head.

He was in a small building of crumbling brick. Much of the floor was covered with pieces of bark, twigs and scraps of tinder. An old casement window frame was propped against a wall.

So, he thought, a woodstore with hardly any wood in it.

The headache retreated to a tolerable level. He had no memory of being brought here. He tried to recall what had happened. When that failed, he tried to remember anything at all of what lay behind the thick grey fog of the recent past.

An image floated up from the darkness. Lizzie's face, lit from below by a candle in her hand, her lips parted, her eyes fixed on him.

The sound of rain. A coach rattling and swaying; iron-rimmed wheels and iron-shod hooves on a paved street; the flicker of lights from passing shops and houses.

Troughton's wall-eye looking at something Savill couldn't see. A piece of ham on the floor: it had made his stomach turn over, just for a moment, because in the flickering light it had looked like a severed finger. Charles's finger.

What had Lizzie said? 'Lost. Cold. Hungry. This is a foreign country to him. And he is dumb.'

Savill struggled to his feet, using the wall as a support. His vision blurred. Once again, the nausea returned. He retched, but nothing came up. He staggered to the door, splashing through a puddle of rainwater.

Though it hung crookedly in its frame, the door was a solid barrier made of oak, with heavy iron reinforcements at the joints. There was no sign of a lock or handle on the inside but, when Savill pushed against the door, it moved a fraction of an inch and then stopped. He ran his eye around the frame and made out the horizontal line of the iron bar that held it in place on the outside.

If this is a woodshed, he thought, then there must surely be a house or cottage nearby.

He leaned against the door and listened. He heard his own breathing and a faint and sporadic rustling, perhaps dead leaves shifting on the ground in the wind. The rain must have stopped.

The memories were coming back now. The fruitless search for Charles in the house at Nightingale Lane. The journey to Mrs Pycroft's house in Little Castle Street. And the sound of a voice in the rain.

Then, here and now, he heard the footsteps.

*   *   *

There were two sets of footsteps, one of which was markedly heavier than the other.

'God damn you.' It was Malbourne's voice, sharp with anger. 'Can you not grasp your own stupidity?'

'Yes, sir, but I had to do something.' That was Jarsdel's voice, thick as ever, but now wheezy as well from the exercise of walking. 'You don't understand, sir.'

The footsteps were gone. In that instant Savill remembered the voice he had heard outside Mrs Pycroft's house. Thick as porridge and instantly familiar.

*'Come to fetch you, sir.'*

The voice in the rain.

Jarsdel had brought Savill to this place. And it had been on Malbourne's orders.

When they had gone, Savill threw himself against the door, again and again until his shoulder ached as well as his head. He examined the walls. The brick was old and crumbling. The lime mortar had been carelessly applied, probably two or three generations earlier. But the walls resisted him for all that. They were stronger than he was.

Malbourne, he thought, sobbing with frustration, Malbourne and Jarsdel in alliance: everything at the Black Letter Office passed by one or both of them.

One by one, in the back of Savill's mind, the pieces were slipping into place at extraordinary speed. Augusta had either been recruited or had offered herself as a spy for the British Government; no doubt Rampton had had a hand in that. She was perfectly placed to send information on the liberal monarchists and their allies, who so recently had dominated the government. Malbourne was equally well placed to act as a bridge between her and the British Government. Rampton trusted him . . .

The ground. Savill examined the earth, looking for rat holes, or signs of subsidence, anything that might promise a way out.

Augusta had been a woman who always played more than one game at once. She would have hoped for more than money from Malbourne. She would have been looking to the future, perhaps to a life in England; even for marriage, for Malbourne was the sort of man who could, if he wished, manage a divorce case . . .

Nothing on the ground, nothing that promised even the possibility of escape. It would take Savill years to tunnel through the earth with scraps of wood and his bare hands.

But the roof?

Augusta would have wanted more than security, more than money. 'I have an appetite,' she had said all those years ago as she sat astride Savill with Lizzie in her belly and squeezed his thighs with her heels. 'And you shall feed me.' Malbourne was personable enough, and had fine prospects; she had always liked a gentleman, after all, which was more than Savill was or could ever be. (He suspected now that Augusta's attachment to him had always been, as it were, provisional.)

But Malbourne was betrothed to Miss Woorgreen, with her £1200 a year and an uncle who was a great favourite of Mr Pitt, the Prime Minister. Even Augusta's charms must have had their limits, particularly for a man as shrewd as Malbourne. But if she had insisted on her claim on him . . .?

The tiles.

Savill looked up at the roof. The tie beams and the purlins were dark with age and showed the marks of the adze. The rafters sagged under the weight of the pantiles hanging from battens attached to the rafters. Several of the pantiles had either slipped or cracked; or the laths supporting them had given way to the infirmities of age.

He stood under one of the beams and stretched his arms towards it. He could touch the sides, but he could not hook his hands over the top of it to give him a grip that could sustain his weight.

The only chance was the window frame. When he lifted it,

one of its uprights fell away. But the rest of the frame seemed sound, the wood still firm and the corners holding. He propped it against the wall beneath one of the beams but slightly to one side.

He studied the brickwork above it. There were two rusting nails just within reach, sunk into the mortar. One was above the beam, the other several feet below.

Savill retreated to the opposite wall. He broke into a run and used the top of the frame as a step. He glimpsed the top of the beam and flung his right arm across it. His weight dragged him down, jarring his shoulder, and sending stabs of pain into his neck and his arm. His feet flailed wildly, scraping against the bricks. His left shoe knocked against a nail.

That was the turning point. The nail took much of his weight, easing the strain on his shoulder. He reached a hand to the upper nail, twisted his body and wriggled on to the beam. For a moment he hung there, breathing hard, head and shoulders one side, and legs and feet the other, his muscles screaming like a choir of banshees.

Damnation, he thought, I'm too old for this folly.

He manoeuvred himself along the beam and, with some difficulty, swung his arms and legs on to it. After that, the matter became relatively straightforward, as long as he did not look down and realize how precarious his situation on the beam really was. He stretched an arm to the purlin above him, twisted his body again, and managed to raise himself so that he was perching on the cross-beam.

A current of cold air brushed his cheek. He brought his eyes level with a chink in the tiles where one of them had slipped a few inches. He saw a roofless cottage and, beyond it, a scrubby meadow rising to a bedraggled hedgerow.

Where the devil was he? Not in London.

He pushed at the tile immediately below the hole and felt it lift away from the lath supporting it. The rattle of its sliding down the roof sounded inordinately loud. He froze, listening for running footsteps.

No one came. The only sound was birdsong in the distance. He made himself wait another minute, counting the seconds. Then he set to work.

First he removed the tiles around the hole he had made. The difficulty was the horizontal laths, which were nailed to the rafters at each of the points of intersection. Savill tried to push first one then the other with the heel of his hand. None of the nails would move.

When the skin of one hand began to bleed, Savill considered using one of the tiles as a hammer but abandoned the idea on the grounds that the sound of the blows would carry too easily in the early morning quiet.

It was only then, with a sense of his own stupidity, that he remembered the clasp-knife he usually carried in his coat pocket. He felt for it, only to discover it had gone. His purse and pocketbook had gone as well. Jarsdel must have taken them all.

A disproportionate anger, fuelled by his own helplessness, welled up inside him. He lashed out at the nearest lath with his clenched fist.

Two things happened at once: he cried out with pain, and the lath snapped. He had hit it midway between the rafters on either side, where it was at its weakest, and where a knot in the wood had further lessened its strength. The age of the lath had done the rest.

He licked his grazed knuckles. Then, with the sweat pouring off him, he worked at the two halves of the lath, using the extra leverage to prise up the nails on either side.

Once he had cleared a tier of tiles and its supporting lath between the pair of rafters, he stripped the tiles from the tier below, which allowed him to attack the lath that had supported them. He could exert more force this time, and it soon snapped in two places.

Light now poured into the shed. Savill poked his head through the hole in the roof and looked about him. A mass of inky clouds was approaching from the east, where the sun was just visible, veiled with moisture, close to the horizon. Immediately below him was a yard with a small open store to one side and the roofless cottage directly opposite. The yard and the floor of the store were choked with tall, dying weeds that glistened with last night's rain. Like the cottage, the store had lost its tiles – but not from neglect: by the look of it, they had been deliberately stripped off. The cottage's back door and its window frames had also been removed.

The birds were no longer singing. But there were other sounds in the distance: scuffling and groaning and shouts.

Savill scrambled through the hole and let himself down to the yard below. He landed awkwardly, wrenching his right ankle.

He wanted to run in the opposite direction from the sounds. What stopped him was the chance that they might lead him to Charles. His headache now made thinking almost impossible. But it seemed rational to suspect that Jarsdel had brought both Charles and Savill himself to the one place, and that now Malbourne had come to see what his hireling had brought him.

He moved toward the end of the cottage, where the remains of a gate linked the house with the open store. Beyond it, a muddy track, scarred with deep wheel-ruts, wound its way between gently sloping fields. Salvaged tiles had been stacked untidily on the verge.

The sounds had grown louder. Savill passed through the gateway and turned left, guided by the noises. He followed the blank gable wall of the cottage. At the next corner he hesitated and then slowly put his head round it.

Not ten yards away was the huge bulk of Jarsdel, standing with his back to Savill. Seen from the rear, he was almost egg-like in his proportions. He was kicking something on the

375

ground. He was so absorbed, and so energetic, in his exertions that his hat had fallen off, and he had trodden on it.

Each kick was accompanied with a grunt. His legs and feet looked too small to do much harm to anything but each kick produced an answering scream from its target.

Savill craned his head further round, trying to see the victim. At that moment, Jarsdel swivelled about. As part of the same movement, he stooped and stretched his arm towards his hat. There was something inherently comic in the manoeuvre, for his dimensions made picking up anything from the ground difficult for him.

His eyes met Savill's.

Neither of them moved for a moment. Jarsdel's face was red with exertion. His mouth opened in a pink O of surprise. His great chest heaved up and down.

Jarsdel straightened up. His hat was still on the ground. In his hand was a short, heavy stick.

Savill turned and bolted. At the gateway to the yard, he turned sharply to the left, away from the cottage and its yard. His instinct – it would have been inaccurate to call it a plan – was simply to put as much distance between himself and Jarsdel as possible, and the simplest way to do that was to follow the track away from the buildings.

But he had miscalculated. The mud that spread out from the gateway was much deeper than it looked. It sucked at his feet and trapped them.

Jarsdel lumbered towards him, blocking the access to the lane. He crowed wordlessly and plunged toward Savill, the stick upraised.

The mud caught him too. He sank to his ankles. His momentum drove him forward. He tripped, dragged down by his own weight, and fell, bellowing, to the ground.

Savill wrenched his feet free and jumped to the firmer surface of the verge. He staggered as he landed, colliding with the stack of tiles.

Jarsdel was on his hands and knees now, still bellowing, trying to raise his bulk out of the mud.

Savill seized the nearest tile in both hands and, raising his arms over his head, threw it at Jarsdel. It hit the man on his cheek. He shouted more loudly and canted over.

Without a moment's hesitation, Savill threw another tile. This one caught Jarsdel on the side on his head, just above the ear. He collapsed into the mud. His limbs twitched but the enormous body lay still.

Savill waited a few seconds, watching him. Then he lobbed a third tile and the arms and legs stopped moving.

# Chapter Fifty-Eight

Savill walked away without a backward glance. Jarsdel's victim was more important than the question of whether Jarsdel was dead or dying.

At the corner of the cottage, Savill paused. His headache was now so acute that it affected his vision, which was sometimes blurred. Jarsdel had hit him so hard last night that he must have been senseless for hours. Savill touched his skull, probing the swelling there, which had grown larger. He could feel nothing broken, thank God, but he did not like to press too hard.

But he could not afford to attend to his injuries. Everything now had to be reassessed in the light of the alliance between Malbourne and Jarsdel.

He glanced up. A buzzard circled high above his head. Every now and then its wings flapped with luxurious languor. A shiver ran through him – partly for the sake of the bird's intended victim and partly because he was so very cold.

He walked on. His limbs were heavy with tiredness. His clothes were damp and his fall in the lane had left the right side of his coat smeared with mud.

The other man was still lying spread-eagled on the ground at the front of the ruined cottage, with Jarsdel's ruined hat within a yard of him. He wore a riding coat and boots, both filthy. His upturned face was a mass of blood, streaked with mucous. His mouth was open and he had lost at least one tooth. His eyes were closed, and his chest was not moving.

Savill knelt beside him. He picked up the victim's left wrist and felt for a pulse. He couldn't find it. Jarsdel would hang for this murderous assault, Savill thought, if for nothing else.

There was a flutter of life beneath his fingertips.

The man was alive, after all. His cravat had come loose in the struggle. Savill eased it away from his neck, registering the fact that it was made of fine linen. He used it to dab gently at the ruined face. The man moaned softly. His eyelids twitched but did not open.

Both the boots and riding coat were well made. Savill felt the pockets of the coat, seeking a clue to the man's identity. He found nothing apart from a box pistol, small enough for a waistcoat or lady's muff, which he transferred to his own pocket.

The man moaned again and opened his eyes. He stared up at Savill, still kneeling beside him. Whether he saw him was another matter. His eyebrows arched, creating an illusion of astonishment.

The swollen lips moved. A wordless mumble emerged. The man broke off and swallowed. The eyelids fluttered down.

Savill bent closer to his face. 'What did you say?'

There was no reply.

'Let me help you, sir. I am your friend.'

The lips twitched. The mouth opened. Broken words emerged, one by one, shorn of their proper consonants and separated by gasps of breath. They might have been meaning-less, not words but random syllables dragged up from the depths of pain. Or they might have been a desperate attempt to say five or six short words.

'Say it again. I can't understand you.'

It was too late. The eyes had closed again. The breathing settled to a regular rhythm.

At that moment Savill knew who this was. It was something to do with the man's slim build and the quietly expensive clothes. Or even those arched eyebrows, which hinted not only at surprise but also at disdain.

So why the devil had Jarsdel done his best to kick Mr Malbourne to death? And what had Malbourne tried so hard to say?

Time drifted away. It began to rain again, more gently this time, the drops of water floating gently down.

Savill had no idea how long he spent there, crouching beside Horace Malbourne and nursing his aching head. He was aware in a remote province of his mind that he needed to think about what had happened, that there were implications that changed everything. But his rational faculty was paralysed.

Slowly the pain in his head diminished and turned into the question of what to do next. Malbourne needed help. Charles must be found. Everything else was secondary.

With concentration and much painful effort, Savill stood up. The movement made the blood roar in his head. He swayed like a drunken man. He stared down at Horace Malbourne.

What if he wakes when I'm gone? Savill wondered, his mind seizing on a lesser question because it could not cope with the greater ones.

Malbourne's plight was bad enough without his having to wonder what had happened to him. Savill decided to leave a note. His pocket book had gone, but Dick Ogden's sketchbook was still there, an oblong shape in his coat, together with a pencil which Savill kept in his waistcoat.

He took out the sketchbook and, shielding it from the rain, turned towards the back, looking for a blank page he could tear out. He chanced to open the book about two-thirds of the way through, at a page containing one of Ogden's drawings of buildings. He stopped, distracted from his search for a blank sheet.

380

There was something unexpectedly familiar about the sketch. The drawing was in ink. It showed a two-storey wing of a house. On the ground floor, long windows opened on to a path or terrace that terminated with a column holding an urn. Half a dozen birds skimmed to and fro above the roof-line, their rapid, apparently erratic movements captured with a few economical flicks of the pen.

Swallows perhaps, Savill thought, pushing the distraction aside and turning the pages over, or house martins or even swifts.

*Swallows? Those confounded swallows.*

The shock was so great that Savill staggered and almost fell. He steadied himself against the wall of the cottage. This was a sketch of Mr Rampton's new wing at Vardells, together with the defecating swallows that Rampton hated with such strange ardour. The long windows of the new library opened on to the terrace.

But what had Dick Ogden to do with Rampton? And why had he been at Vardells?

Savill flicked the pages until he came back to the sketch. The urn was not standing on a column, as he had first thought, but on the wall that Mr Rampton intended to mark the end of the terrace. The builders had been at work on the wall when Savill had last been to Vardells, midway in September.

Therefore, Savill thought, fighting to dispel the mist in his mind, Dick Ogden had been at Vardells afterwards, when the work had been finished. Since the wall was complete, and since the mortar was apparently firmly enough set to sustain the weight of an urn, the sketch must have been made at least a week or so after Savill's last visit.

The conclusion was inescapable: Ogden had called at Vardells after Savill had gone down to Charnwood.

Perhaps it was the distraction of another puzzle, of another line of thought. Or perhaps it was that the shock of this new discovery jolted another, quite separate train of thought into motion again, and changed its direction.

Whatever the reason, Savill suddenly had a possible inter-pretation of the sounds that Malbourne had made, of the five broken words he had tried so hard to say.

*'He – came – to – Paris – too.'*

But who came? Ogden?

# Chapter Fifty-Nine

Charles knows at once that dawn has come. The light is different, grey and steady. The air is colder, too. Finally – as if to put the question beyond doubt – a cock crows in the distance.

Strange to say, he has slept deeply. His last memory is of the terrible sound – *Tip-tap* – and what happened next. He remembers how he shut his eyes and pretended to be asleep. He remembers the air on his face as the curtain was moved aside and the glare of the candle flame beyond his lashes.

But then nothing.

He listens but hears nothing except the crowing cock and a slight rustling that is probably the rain. When the pressure to relieve himself grows intolerable, he sits up in bed. He is still wearing the clothes he wore in Nightingale Lane, apart from his coat and shoes. His fingers poke the line where the curtains meet. He pulls them apart.

The light is still uncertain. It has no more sheen to it than dulled pewter. It shows the outlines of a small room with a sloping roof. There is a dormer window, which has a bowed upper edge. His eyes, drawn to the light, go to the window, so he notices at once the three vertical bars that divide it.

Charles wriggles away from the bedclothes and, shivering,

climbs down from the bed. His shoes are waiting side by side for him. He slips them on and feels under the bed for the pot.

Afterwards he tiptoes to the window and looks out over a valley of slates between two pitched roofs, joined by a broad gutter lined with lead. The slates are wet with rain. Everything is grey, including the sky and a wisp of smoke that ascends towards it from a chimneystack to the left.

It is not a big window. The bars are set too close together for even a small and very skinny boy to slip between them.

Charles puts on his coat, drawing it close to him for warmth. His wrists poke out of the sleeves and the coat feels tight around his chest and armpits.

He makes a survey of the rest of the room. It is bare of furniture apart from the bed and a washstand. It measures ten and a half paces by seven and a quarter. There is no fireplace.

He turns the door knob. The door rattles in its frame but it doesn't open.

All these are facts, and may be relied upon.

Is he still in London? The question is almost meaningless. Where everything is strange, one place becomes much the same as another.

Nightingale Lane, though: that is a real place. The memories are coming back now. Someone betrayed him and sent the man-mountain to find him there.

Only Lizzie knew he was in Nightingale Lane. His sister.

Did she betray him? Is she even really his sister? There is no way of knowing. But if she told Mr Savill, then he knew that Charles was there too, and probably it was he who sent the man-mountain, not the girl who might or might not be Lizzie.

Charles squeezes his eyes closed until he sees only sparks of false light in the darkness. The man-mountain is an enemy. That is fact.

He is very hungry. That is another fact. If one knew enough facts, then—

A key is turning in the lock of the door.

All the facts in the world evaporate.

Charles back away until his shoulder bumps against the wall. He pushes himself into the corner by the bedhead.

The door swings slowly into the room.

On the threshold stands an old man, hunched over a stick. He is dressed in a morning gown and slippers, and on his head is a nightcap. He carries a lighted candle. His eyes slide into the room and come to rest on Charles.

He raises the candlestick and pinches out the flame. His face is a place of hollows and shadows.

'Good morning, Charles,' he says in English. He pauses and wrinkles his nose, as if to satisfy an itch. He tugs with his right hand at the fingers of his left. 'I see you're awake already. I hope you slept well?'

He tugs again. The finger joints pop.

*Tip-tap.*

The man stares at Charles. Charles stares at him.

'Breakfast,' the man says. 'Are you hungry?'

*Say nothing. Not a word to anyone. Whatever you see. Whatever you hear. Do you understand? Say nothing. Ever.*

The man frowns. He is still pulling at his fingers.

*Tip-tap.* Like cracking a walnut.

The man stretches out his hand and wraps chilly fingers around Charles's wrist.

'You're shivering,' he says. 'We must warm you, mustn't we?'

He draws Charles from the room and leads him along the landing to another door. They enter a room which also has a sloping ceiling. But this apartment is larger than the bedchamber and has two of the windows with bowed tops and vertical bars. A coal fire burns briskly in the fireplace.

'Sit at the table,' the man says, closing the door behind them. He has no teeth and his voice lacks hard edges. His eyes glisten with moisture.

Charles can smell the rolls but not see them. They are covered with a cloth. A jug of milk stands beside them on the table, together with a piece of cheese. His mouth waters so much he has to swallow. For the moment, his hunger is almost as great as his fear.

'Sit,' the man says again. 'Eat. Will that do? I did not know what to tell her to bring.'

Charles sits. The man whips the cloth away. Charles takes a roll, breaks off a piece and stuffs it into his mouth. The rolls are still warm.

The man pours milk into a cup and pushes it across the table. 'Perhaps coffee? Should you have liked coffee? That would have been more difficult, but I'm sure it could be managed . . .'

His voice diminishes into silence. His hands clasped together and still holding the cloth, he stands in front of Charles and watches him eat and drink.

'Remarkable,' he murmurs, 'quite remarkable.' He pauses. When he continues, it is as if he is answering a question that Charles has asked him: 'Yes, the coffee – you see the house is closed up at present. I've sent the indoor servants away, apart from Tabitha, or taken them to my other house. Tabitha's deaf now. Even if I ring for her, she won't hear me. One has to go down to the kitchen and talk very loudly in her ear. But perhaps later . . .?'

The voice trailed away. The man pulls out another chair and sits. He does this very carefully, as old people do, holding on to the edge of the table and then lowering himself inch by inch to the seat of the chair.

'This damp weather,' he murmurs. 'It makes my joints ache so.'

Charles finishes the rolls. He has drunk all of the milk and eaten two-thirds of the cheese.

The old man nods. 'Good. You look refreshed.' He sits back in the chair and he too looks refreshed. When he speaks his voice is firmer and less slurred. 'Now listen carefully, Charles. For the time being you will live up here, in these two rooms. You will see me sometimes, and Tabitha as well, so you will not be lonely. We shall get to know each other. You will have a suit of new clothes: you must dress in a manner fitting to your station. Besides, you cannot wear those stinking rags a moment longer than is necessary. And then, by and by, you will meet other people and go out, and see more of the world.'

Charles stares at him and wonders how old he is. Older than Monsieur de Quillon, probably, but younger than Father Viré.

'You will put the past behind you, and all the sad things that have happened. There are bad people in this world but I shall make sure they cannot harm you. We shall live together and be very happy.'

Probably everyone is younger than Father Viré. Charles decides with reluctance that, while this last belief is almost certainly true, it cannot be classed as a fact. It cannot be included among those things that can be relied upon.

'So is it true what they say then? You don't speak?'

Charles does not speak. He does not move.

The man shrugs. 'It doesn't matter, not now.' He fumbles inside his gown and takes out a watch. He angles the face towards the window, to catch the light, which has been growing rapidly while Charles ate his breakfast. 'I must leave you for a while. I have business to transact. But come – I wish to show you something first.'

The old man stands up. Charles does too because Maman made it clear that one should never remain seated when one's elders rise. They go on to the landing. The man grips Charles's shoulder.

'You will be my support as we go downstairs. That is your duty now, Charles. To be my support.'

Side by side, they march slowly down a flight of stairs to a long high landing with many doors opening off it. The next flight of stairs is L-shaped; the stairs are broad and shallow; the two of them descend to a square hall where statues of ancient heroes stand in arched alcoves, one on either side of the front door. There are tables muffled with brown Holland covers. The air is very cold and Charles cannot prevent himself from shivering.

'Come to the library,' the old man says. 'There's a fire there.'

He opens a door and leads Charles across an apartment where the shrouded shapes of furniture stand against the walls. Their footsteps clatter across the wooden floor, for the carpet has been rolled up.

They pass through another door. The library is still gloomy despite the candles. A dying fire smoulders in the grate. The old man opens the shutters on the three long windows, and daylight pours into the room.

'Perhaps a book would amuse you?' he says, while he is snuffing the pale flames of the candles. 'It would help pass the time. You might study something, perhaps, and turn this period of leisure to profit. Yes, I shall consult a bookseller on the subject of what would be suitable for a young gentleman of your age. Mark what I say: one cannot have too much useful knowledge. One day, perhaps, I shall send you to the University and you will become a perfect paragon of learning.'

He smiles at his own wit. He puts down the snuffer and runs a forefinger along one of the shelves. He hums quietly. Charles looks out of the nearest window. There is a terrace outside, with an urn on a wall and a sweep of grass beyond.

'*De Bello Gallico*, perhaps? No, Caesar should wait, I think, though the Latin could hardly be more straightforward. I may engage a tutor for you, by and by, when everything has settled down. Ah – I have it: *A Serious Call to a Devout and Holy Life*.' He pulls out a volume and lays it on the table beside the snuffer. 'We must start there. Nothing is more important than a firm grounding in religion. I fear your head has been stuffed with Papist nonsense in Paris, but we shall soon root it out, my boy, and plant something more wholesome in its place.'

Charles edges towards the door.

But the old man moves in front of him. He is filled with sudden vigour. 'Before I take you back upstairs, I shall show you something.'

The claw grips Charles's shoulder again and draws him towards a mirror that hangs over a pier table between two of the tall windows. The pair of them stand side by side in front of their reflections, with the man's hand still on Charles's shoulder. Their faces are grey and weary in the light of the early morning.

'Look. Is there not a likeness? I hoped there would be, and indeed there is. The set of the eyes, of course, and their colour. The nose and mouth are similar, even now, and when you are grown the similarities will be quite unmistakable. You will be the very image of myself as a young man.'

Charles looks at their reflections, at the smiling man and the boy he no longer recognizes. He remembers the stranger he saw shimmering in the mirror on the stairs at Charnwood on the evening that Mr Savill arrived, and how he and the stranger stretched their hands towards each other. But the glass with its patina of candle grease kept them for ever apart.

Everyone has another side to them. A side they cannot quite touch. That is a fact.

'This library. This house. The gardens, the farms. Everything.' The old man releases Charles's shoulder and smiles down at him with his toothless mouth stretched wide. 'One day, Charles, when I'm gone, it will be yours. As is right and fitting.'

His fingers grapple with each other, squeezing and pulling. The toothless smile grows wider and wider, a pink wound. His face splits apart.

'From father to son,' he says, and pulls at his fingers.

*Tip-tap.*

Charles runs.

Through the door, through the apartment with the ghostly furniture and into the cold, cold heart of the house.

# Chapter Sixty

Malbourne was breathing heavily through his mouth. Savill tried speaking to him again but had no response. He would have liked to drag him into the partial shelter of the cottage doorway but did not dare, in case there was internal damage.

As he was tucking the note into the pocket of Malbourne's waistcoat, he heard a sharp intake of breath. Savill turned.

Jarsdel was three paces away and looking straight at him.

Soaking wet, and without his wig and hat, he was almost unrecognizable with blood and mud. What could be seen of his face was purple with exertion and perhaps excitement, the broad veins standing out on his forehead. In one hand was his bludgeon. In the other was Savill's clasp-knife, the blade opened.

'Now, sir,' he said. 'Now, sir, we'll see how you like a bit of mud. A man can drown in mud. Or in his own blood. Did you know that?'

Savill pushed his hand in his pocket and took out Malbourne's pistol. It was a tiny thing, little better than a popgun. He cocked it, fumbling with the unfamiliar mechanism.

Jarsdel lunged forward. He swung his stick. Savill ducked.

The blade in his other hand flicked out. The speed of the movement caught Savill off guard. The tip of the blade snagged on the cuff of his coat. He took a step back and stumbled over Malbourne's body, falling backwards on to the ground.

Jarsdel came a step closer. Savill raised the pistol and, without taking aim, pulled the trigger.

The flint scraped down the frizzen. The pan opened to receive a shower of sparks. The priming powder ignited, giving off a puff of smoke.

And nothing happened. Damp?

Then the flame passed through the vent and set off the main charge. There was a dull crack. The pistol jerked in Savill's hand. Jarsdel stopped in his stride.

In the long, frozen moment as the smoke cleared, the two men looked at each other. Jarsdel's face looked puzzled.

Had the shot missed? Was the charge a blank?

Time began to move again. The bludgeon fell to the ground.

Savill rolled sideways and scrambled up.

Blood oozed from a spot below Jarsdel's jaw somewhere among the folds of flesh that masked the division between head and neck. First it was a trickle that ran down to his collar, and then a positive stream that spurted before him and fell in a glistening shower of red spots on the wet, dead leaves on the ground.

He frowned. He released his grip on the knife. His head snapped forward. His knees gave way. He crumpled to the ground. For a moment, he stared up at Savill. He spat out a mouthful of blood. He rolled on to his side and drew up his knees.

A monstrous, hairless baby lying down to rest.

Savill knelt beside him, avoiding the pooling blood, and took one of Jarsdel's hands in both of his. 'Jarsdel?' he said. 'Jarsdel? Can you hear me?'

There was no response. The eyes were open but if they saw anything there was no sign of it.

Savill stayed on his knees beside Jarsdel as the life ebbed

away. He said nothing, for there was nothing to say. But, when all was said and done, a man should not die alone.

Dew lingered on the grass and patches of mist clung to the hollows in the field in front of the cottage.

Savill waited with Malbourne only long enough to make sure he was breathing and no more uncomfortable than he had been before. His own head still hurt but the pain had retreated.

Jarsdel now lay in a pool of blood, for Savill's bullet had nicked a carotid artery. In death he was at best an inconvenience and at worst a threat to Savill, who had killed him and might, if all went badly, face a murder charge. Malbourne needed help as urgently as ever. Charles was still missing. The dark heart of this affair was still to be exposed. The consequences to all of them, when the truth was at last uncovered, were incalculable.

First things first, Savill told himself. He must find help. He did not even know where they were. But Malbourne and Jarsdel could not have dropped out of the sky, and nor could he. There must be horses, somewhere, and a conveyance of some sort.

He put his knife in his pocket and slipped Jarsdel's bludgeon under his arm. He walked round the far corner of the cottage to the side he had not yet seen. There was a paddock, empty of livestock, that sloped down to a belt of woodland beyond. He continued past the gable end of the cottage and along the rear wall of the woodshed where he had been held captive.

There was a gate at the end of the paddock. He climbed over it and found himself at the back of the yard behind the cottage. There were more fields on this side. Then came a swathe of grass, dotted with young trees among which several cows were grazing.

Beyond the grass were two lines of lime trees, outlined with inky precision against the grey sky. They bordered an avenue. Savill knew this for certain because at one end of the avenue he saw the chimneys of Vardells.

# Chapter Sixty-One

A chandelier in a bag hangs like a giant wasps' nest over the centre of the salon. Behind him come the old man's footsteps, moving with surprising rapidity over the stone slabs of the hall.

Charles bolts through a door at the far end, which opens into a dining room, the table swathed in covers. He hears a sound in the room behind him and glances over his shoulder towards it. His momentum continues to carry him blindly forward. He cannons into the edge of a sideboard. He clutches at it for support. He misses. Instead, his hand collides with a tall blue vase. The vase topples and rolls off the sideboard. It shatters into a thousand pieces on the bare boards of the floor.

'Charles, dear boy.' The old man is in the doorway of the salon. He switches from English to flawless French. 'Calm yourself. No one wishes to harm you. You are home at last, just as your dear mother would have wished.'

The voice is so gentle that Charles wants to believe what it says. For a moment. He looks at the old man, who smiles uncertainly and tugs at his fingers.

*Tip-tap.*

The cracking of the knuckles. His mother's blood.

He dances round the table and leaves the room by a second door, which leads to a passage that brings him back to the flagged hall by the front door.

The old man knows the house better than he does. He is already waiting there. As Charles appears, the old man takes up a walking stick from a tall jar that stands by the front door.

'Charles,' he says and, despite the slushing sound he makes when he speaks, his voice has grown sterner. 'Charles, I do not wish to chastise you, especially on our first day together. But I can't brook disobedience. Spare the rod and spoil the child, eh? That's what I used to tell your mother when she was your age.'

Charles swerves and runs upstairs. He pauses at the half-landing, where the stairs turn to the left, and looks back. The old man is following him.

'There is nowhere for you to go to,' he says. 'There is nowhere for you but here.'

Charles bounds up the rest of the stairs. The landing runs around three sides of the stairwell. All the doors are closed. He tries the nearest one. It is locked. So is the next.

That leaves the stairs to the attic, which lead out of an alcove at one end of the landing.

He turns towards the attic stairs in time to see a servant, a squat woman who looks even older than her master, coming from the alcove. At first she does not see him. She carries a tray with the remains of his breakfast on it.

She looks up and sees Charles at the head of the stairs.

'Stop him, Tabitha!' The old man is very close now, hauling himself up the stairs by the bannister rail. 'The boy's not himself.'

Still staring at Charles, she holds a hand to her ear. 'What, sir? Is that you there?'

'His wits are disordered. Stop him. The boy's mazed, I tell you.'

The woman seems to understand now. She advances along the landing.

'You must take your beating like a man,' cries the old man, his voice high and excited.

He lunges forward, swinging the stick. It catches Charles on his thigh. But the blow is feeble, almost petulant. Charles snatches at the stick and finds to his amazement that he has a grip on it. He tugs it towards him.

The old man is still holding on to the other end. 'Let go,' he cries. 'I will not brook insolence.' He pulls harder himself, dragging Charles down the upper flight of stairs almost as far as the half-landing.

A voice in the hall below shouts: 'Drop that stick, damn you.'

Three things happen at once.

The old man turns sharply in the direction of the interruption.

The old woman drops the tray she is carrying.

And Charles stops pulling the stick. He pushes instead.

The old man staggers back on to the half-landing and cannons into the newel post that marks the right-angle turn of the bannister rail. He cannot stop: either the stick or his own impetus pushes him further than he expected. His body twists. He takes a step backwards. For an instant, one slippered foot hangs in the air – not on the landing, but above the stair immediately below.

A cup from the old woman's tray slips through the bannisters of the landing and falls to the hall below, where it shatters.

Charles cannot remember what happens next. Does he reverse the motion of the stick and pull it again? Or does he continue to push? Or does the sound of the breaking cup surprise the old man so much that he releases his grip?

But this is a fact, if nothing else is: that the old man falls. He topples over on to the lower flight of stairs.

Charles lets go of the stick, which clatters on to the half-landing. He watches the old man rolling rapidly downwards, like a child on a grassy slope. His cap falls off. His

396

skull is shaven. As his body rolls over, he gasps and squeaks. He sounds like a tiny animal, not like a man.

Mr Savill is running from a doorway below towards the foot of the stairs. But he is too late.

The old man reaches the level of the hall. The back of his head hits the stone-flagged floor. He lies face upwards among the shards of broken china from the cup.

His eyes are still open.

So is his silent mouth. It looks more than ever like a pink wound.

*Hush now*, Charles thinks. *Say nothing.*

# Chapter Sixty-Two

At a little before two o'clock on the afternoon of Sunday, 13 January 1793, Mr Malbourne called by arrangement at Nightingale Lane. It was a moot point whether he came on pleasure or business.

Lizzie had spent much of the morning deciding on her clothes and watching the weather. Savill had found her on three separate occasions consulting the thermometer which he kept in the passage at the foot of the stairs. The winter so far had been abnormally mild, and the temperature had risen to 45 degrees by midday. The wind had dropped too – a brisk westerly had moderated during the morning to a gentle southerly breeze. True, it was cloudy, and there had been the occasional shower of rain. But nothing that signified, Lizzie decided, nothing that would force them to postpone the outing.

There were five of them in the party that left the house, for Miss Horton was spending the day with the Savills. She had come up to stay with Mrs West in Green Street again.

'He has grown prodigiously,' she murmured to Savill as they walked arm in arm down the lane. They had had little chance for conversation until now.

'My sister has seen to that,' he said. 'She feeds him at every opportunity.'

'His face has filled out, too. He doesn't look fearful any more.'

'Not in the day, ma'am. Sometimes at night he does. He has bad dreams. And I have not seen him laugh or even smile yet.'

Ahead of them, Lizzie was leaning more heavily than was perhaps necessary on the arm of Mr Malbourne. There was a hint of rain in the air, enough to justify his raising his umbrella over them.

Charles walked between the two couples, occasionally glancing over his shoulder at Savill and Miss Horton as if to make sure they were still there.

'Will you send him to school?' she said.

'I hope so. Eventually. He is able enough – he reads whatever he can lay his hands on.'

'He and I had a game of chess just now. He beat me with ease.'

'But he does not speak yet,' Savill said. 'I would not wish to expose him to the ridicule of his schoolfellows. I think I shall engage a tutor, and we shall see how we go.'

She glanced up at him from beneath the brim of her bonnet. 'But what if he never speaks?'

'He will, ma'am. He will.' He smiled at her. 'Lizzie has quite made up her mind about that.'

She smiled back and looked ahead at Lizzie and Malbourne. 'Lizzie usually knows her own mind, I think.'

He followed both the direction of her glance and the current of her thoughts. But he said nothing.

They strolled along Gower Street to Bedford Square. By a fortunate chance, Mr Malbourne had been able to obtain a key to the gate in the railings in the centre of the square. His great aunt lived in one of the smaller houses on the north side.

The garden was not crowded at this hour. Half a dozen nursemaids were exchanging gossip as they took the air with their charges. Three or four small boys were kicking a ball between them on the south side.

'Do you make a long stay in London, ma'am?'

'Three or four weeks, perhaps, unless my father desires me to return earlier. I hope he does not – Norbury will soon offer even less in the way of society than it did before. Did you know that the household at Charnwood is to be broken up?'

'No. When?'

'It is happening already. The Count has left for Switzerland. Monsieur Fournier and Dr Gohlis came up to London with us but they return to Norbury on Wednesday to settle things there. They talk of joining him in a week or so.'

'The news from France is so bad that we must be at war at any moment.'

'That is why they must go – they can do nothing here, Monsieur Fournier says. Besides, they are not welcome in England, as you know. But Mr Malbourne has been most helpful in arranging their papers. He says the Count is quite resigned to leaving Charles in the care of his English family, on the grounds that when war comes he will be safer here.'

They talked a little more and then separated, for it would not do to leave Lizzie too long beneath Mr Malbourne's conveniently large umbrella. Lizzie and Miss Horton walked on, while Charles played a complicated game with himself which involved jumping and skipping in a zigzag pattern across the path.

Malbourne fell into step beside Savill. He still wore a dressing on his face that masked most of his nose. It had been broken in two places and the surgeon had set it badly. His face would never be called handsome again.

He had changed in other ways since Savill had first met him. He looked older, haggard even, and though he still dressed with scrupulous care there was little of the dandy about him now. Jarsdel's attack had left him with scars of the mind as well as the body.

'I was in Crown Street this morning,' he said. 'The mails from Paris came in. Yesterday they found the King guilty.'

'Have they announced the verdict?'

'Not yet.'

'Surely they cannot execute him?'

Malbourne shrugged. 'Those devils can do anything they please.' He lowered his voice. 'And I have news that touches us both more closely. Mr Rampton's attorney forwarded another packet of Mr Rampton's papers to the Magistrates' Office. They included a document that related to Jarsdel. It appears that he was once a tenant farmer of Mr Rampton's. Not a good one – he was on the verge of bankruptcy. But he killed his wife in a fit of temper one night when he was in his cups. He hit her with a hot skillet. Did you ever mark that scar on his hand? He must have got it then. He would have hanged, but Rampton swore blind that he had been there, that it had been an accident, and of course he was believed. But he made Jarsdel sign a confession and gave him employment at Crown Street. So Jarsdel became his creature.'

'What will happen about . . .?'

'As little as possible. The Government has no desire to make this affair more public than it is. This confession simply makes it easier for their consciences. It confirms the wisdom of what they have already done.'

It had been put about that Jarsdel had run amok at Vardells. It was said that he had been infected with the insurrectionary spirit of the times, that he had nursed an inveterate hatred of his betters. The authorities had found illegal broadsheets at his lodgings, though who put them there, and when, was another matter. The story was that he had attempted to murder Malbourne and had probably caused Rampton's death as well, by throwing him down the stairs. Malbourne had been commended for shooting him dead in self-defence, despite the almost fatal injuries he had sustained from him.

Neither Savill nor Charles had figured in this account.

As for Tabitha, the old servant at Vardells, she proved to be half-blind as well as deaf. She obligingly made her mark at the foot of every document that Malbourne laid before her.

They walked in silence for a few minutes. Savill wondered whether he could have saved Rampton if he had run forward to break his fall rather than stood there like a moonstruck fool. That was better than wondering why Rampton had fallen in the first place: whether he had been distracted by Savill or, worst of all, whether Charles had pushed him in the course of that last desperate struggle for control of Rampton's stick.

'Was it Jarsdel who killed poor Ogden?' Savill asked, grasping at a distraction.

'Perhaps. Unless it was Rampton himself when he came to collect Charles, and found him gone. To shut his mouth. We found a pair of pistols at Vardells, and one of them had been recently fired.' Malbourne looked away. 'Poor Dick. I blame myself.'

'Blaming yourself is not rational,' Savill said. 'Ogden was a free agent. He did not have to accept Rampton's commission and kidnap Charles.'

'It's not that, sir. It is the fact that Mr Rampton would not have known Dick at all if it had not been for me. He and I were friends at Oxford and I led us into scrape after scrape. By our own stupidity, we became prey to a moneylender and I had to turn to Mr Rampton to extricate us. That's how he came to know Dick in the first place. Through me. Through my folly. And perhaps it was also because of me that Dick became what he was after he was sent down from the University, for he always followed where I led.'

'Come now. You should not blame yourself for consequences you could not possibly have envisaged.'

'But the mistake was—'

'Sir, we all make mistakes,' Savill said. 'I believed it was you that my wife was blackmailing. I believed it was you who killed her. If I had thought clearly about the matter, I should

402

have known it was Rampton. I imagine she threatened to expose him as a spy if he did not pay what she asked for. Then, when he read my letter from Charnwood, he found out not only that Charles had been struck dumb, but also that he had witnessed the murder of his mother and might well have seen the killer's face. That's why he sent Ogden when he did. And that's why he was so shaken when I guessed the significance of the letter when I was building my case against you.'

'But at the end he spared the boy.'

'Perhaps it was easier to plan the murder of a child than to execute it. Or perhaps he meant Jarsdel to do the deed. Or perhaps when he saw Charles, he thought he could make all right with his conscience, and get himself an heir into the bargain. God knows.'

'He was kind to me once,' Malbourne said.

They walked, looking at the two women strolling ahead, arm in arm.

After a while, Malbourne went on: 'We discount the desires of old men. But the fact is, they are much the same as ours.'

Savill smiled at him. 'Come now, sir. Let us call a truce with our inner critics.'

Miss Horton raised her arm to point out a carriage that was passing around the square. She turned to the two gentlemen. 'Isn't that Mrs West's?'

The carriage slowed as it came level with the five of them on the gravel walk. It was thirty or forty yards away but Savill saw, quite clearly, the face of Monsieur Fournier inside. It was hard to be sure, but he thought there was someone sitting beside him.

Fournier saw them too. But he did not lower the glass or command the coachman to stop. Instead he raised his hand in greeting, and the carriage rattled on.

'To be sure, he's pressed for time,' Miss Horton said. 'I know he has much to do while he is in town.'

'By the way,' Malbourne said in an undertone. 'There's something else I . . .'

He continued to speak but Savill was distracted by shrill shouts from the boys, whose ball was now rolling across the grass towards them. It was clear from their voices and gestures what they wanted. As Savill watched, Charles paused in his erratic progress along the path and watched the ball. He stepped towards it and, with perfect accuracy, kicked it to the nearest of the boys.

Mrs West's carriage left the square at its south-east corner.

Savill turned to Malbourne. 'I beg your pardon, sir. I did not catch what you were saying.'

'Mr Rampton's attorney asked if I was acquainted with you,' Malbourne said. 'When I said I was, he asked me for your direction.'

# Chapter Sixty-Three

When Charles goes to bed, either Lizzie or Aunt Ferguson hears him say his prayers and blows out his candle.

Not that he says the prayers aloud: it is understood that he kneels while one or other of the ladies prays on his behalf. These are different prayers from the ones that Jeanne and Father Viré used long ago in that other life, because now he is Protestant.

He prefers it when Lizzie is there. Aunt Ferguson is not unkind but she is a bustling, practical woman, always with her mind on the next task. That is what looking after him is to her, he thinks: a task, like many others.

It is Sunday evening after the walk in Bedford Square where the boys were playing football. Lizzie comes upstairs. After they have finished the prayers, she lingers, as she does sometimes, wrapped in a shawl and perching on the edge of the bed.

'Do you like Mr Malbourne?' she asks, which is a question she has asked before, not that she requires an answer. 'Now that we have seen more of him, I mean.'

He smiles at her, which he sometimes does when they are alone together.

'I think he is a kind man,' she says. 'But he looks so sad, doesn't he, with his poor nose?' She lowers her voice to a whisper. 'But it's not just that. Have you heard? He's not betrothed to Miss Woorgreen any more. She jilted him. Mary told me when I went to Mrs Pycroft's yesterday. The news is all over town. Isn't it truly *heart-rending* for him?'

Lizzie sighs. But there is quite enough light from the two candles, his and hers, to see that she is smiling.

'It is so cruel,' she goes on. 'It's because he's not handsome any more, I think, and because he's not going to be Uncle Rampton's heir. These grand folk are not like us, you see – they can be very hard, very unkind.' She falls silent. She plaits her fingers together and stares at them. 'The trouble is, he is one of them too. He – he is quite different from us.'

He touches her hand. She looks up and smiles.

'But I think Father likes him. Don't you?'

She kisses him and slides off the bed. She blows out his candle, takes up her own and leaves the bedchamber. He listens to her footsteps on the stairs and the opening and closing of the sitting-room door.

The old house moans and sighs and creaks. Charles thinks about the boys in Bedford Square and about the way he kicked the football so neatly back to them. He sleeps.

# Chapter Sixty-Four

Five days later, Savill entered Lincoln's Inn from Chancery Lane and walked briskly through the maze of buildings to the great expanse of New Square. It was a fine morning, colder than it had been but still unseasonably warm.

Mr Rowsell's chambers were on the west side, a well-appointed first-floor set in the middle of the range. Savill was before his time but he mounted the stair and stated his business to a soberly dressed clerk in the outer office.

While he waited, he glanced about him, noting the portraits on the wall, the smell of beeswax and the neatly labelled shelves of files and boxes. Mr Rowsell was, according to his letter, an attorney, so he must be a tenant, rather than a Member of the Inn, as indeed were many of the occupants of these chambers. Everything suggested that he was successful in his profession and eminently respectable to boot.

Exactly at the appointed hour, an invisible bell jangled on the other side of one of the doors beyond the clerk's desk. The clerk climbed from his stool, bowed to Savill and ushered him into the presence of his employer.

The private room was bright with watery winter sunlight. In every respect but one it matched the comfortable respectability of the outer office. The exception was Mr Rowsell himself, who now was in the act of rising to greet Savill while allowing ink drops to fall from his pen to the leather surface of his desk.

He was much younger than his apparently prosperous circumstances had implied, no more than five-and-twenty. He was a large, untidy man, already putting on surplus weight. He wore his own hair, which displayed an unruly tendency to rise in tufts above his florid face. He had an ink stain on his forefinger.

'Mr Savill, sir – your servant.' He bowed awkwardly, revealing in the process that he had lost one of the buttons from the cuff on his coat. 'I hope you have not been waiting long?'

When they were seated, he twirled the pen between his fingers. 'It's very good of you to call so promptly, sir.'

'I am naturally curious about what you have to tell me.'

'Of course, of course.' Rowsell stared at the pen as if wondering how it had come to be in his hand. He laid it on the pen rack. It promptly fell off. 'May I offer you a glass of wine?'

'No, thank you, sir. I understand from Mr Malbourne that you act for the late Mr Rampton.'

'Yes. Or rather no.' Rowsell looked up. 'Allow me to explain. My principal, Mr Veale, was Mr Rampton's attorney for many years. Unfortunately, Mr Veale's health has obliged him to go abroad for a time, leaving me to represent him. Which is why – not to beat about the bush, sir – I'm afraid an apology is due to you. You see, Mr Malbourne's enquiries to us went to Mr Veale's private address, and the people there are at sixes and sevens at present, so a number of letters were put aside to wait Mr Veale's return which should have been directed here.'

'I am here now, at all events,' Savill said. 'But why do you wish to see me?'

'Because Mr Rampton did us the honour of lodging his will with us, sir, among other papers and deeds.' Rowsell opened a drawer of his desk and took out a file of papers. 'Now that the circumstances of his death have been resolved, the will must be executed. I may tell you that just before his death Mr Rampton wished to discuss his testamentary intentions – he wrote to Mr Veale to that effect in September – but he did not do so.'

The words tumbled out of the young man in a torrent, creating an impression of youth and nervousness. Savill was wary of him, nonetheless. He was not disposed to take for granted a lawyer employed, even indirectly, by the late Mr Rampton.

'We do not know whether he desired to draw up a new will or merely to add a codicil to the old,' Rowsell went on. 'I instituted a search for a new one, if it ever existed, or even a memorandum concerning his wishes, but we found nothing of that nature at Vardells or his house in Westminster. Mr Malbourne assures me there is nothing at the office, either – not that Mr Rampton was in the habit of keeping private papers there. So the will we have here will almost certainly be accepted as valid.'

'When was it drawn up?' Savill asked.

Rowsell did not need to refer to the document. 'The fourteenth of December, 1781. Mr Veale has appended a note that Mr Rampton desired to have the will drawn up and signed before he went abroad. He spent nearly a year in Germany and Italy.'

Savill knew the significance of the date. After Yorktown, in October 1781, the Government had fallen; the new Whig administration had wound up the American Department. There had been little to keep Mr Rampton in London then, and much to drive him elsewhere for a time.

Mr Rowsell took out the will and unfolded it. 'Apart from one or two small legacies – to servants and so on – he wills his estate in its entirety to your wife – his niece, Mrs Augusta Savill.'

The information took Savill by surprise, though he tried

409

not to show it. Mr Rampton had never greatly approved of his niece; and her scandalous elopement with a Bavarian adventurer during Savill's New York mission had put her altogether beyond the pale. But now it seemed that – not two years later – he had drawn up a will making her his principal heir.

Savill said: 'My wife died last August, sir.'

'I am sorry to hear it. But Mr Rampton – or perhaps Mr Veale – foresaw that possibility. In the eventuality of Mrs Savill's predeceasing him, then he willed his estate to her children living at the time of his death.' Mr Rowsell glanced at the paper. 'To be precise, "to the heirs of her body". It is rather a curious phrase, but entirely unambiguous. Are there children still living, sir? Mr Rampton mentions two in a letter to Mr Veale. Charles and Elizabeth.'

'Yes,' Savill said. 'They are both living with me now.'

Rowsell looked up. 'But not earlier?'

'That's partly correct. At the time of her death, my wife and I were estranged. She resided in Paris with Charles, while Elizabeth was here with me in London.'

'I see.' Rowsell's eyes were small and very blue; they looked as they might see further than most but only if it were prudent or necessary to do so. 'Well, we need not trouble ourselves with that. No other children alive at the time of Mr Rampton's decease?'

'Not that I am aware of.'

'I should add that there is one condition. The will stipulates that, in order to inherit, a child must adopt the name of Rampton. Unless the child is a girl and already married, in which case her firstborn son must bear the name. That's not unusual in these cases. A man wishes his name to live on after he is gone.'

'The estate, sir.' Savill hesitated. 'What does it consist of?'

'I cannot be precise at this time, I'm afraid. There is the country house in Stanmore, which is freehold, as is the house in Westminster. There are a number of small farms in Hertfordshire – good arable land, I'm told, about four or five hundred acres

410

altogether, perhaps more. None of these is encumbered with a mortgage, so far as I know. Mr Rampton derived a considerable income from various positions he held, but that of course will have ceased with his death. He banked at Wavenhoe's – they will be able to tell you what they hold in deposit for him there. Mr Veale handled the purchase of various bonds and securities for him, too. They will be at Wavenhoe's as well.'

'So you cannot estimate the approximate value of it all?'

'Not yet, sir. Though I should be surprised if it did not amount to a comfortable sum. I—' Rowsell broke off from what he was saying, distracted by the sound of laughter from the outer office. 'I beg your pardon. Before we continue, I should mention that Mr Rampton made one other provision. In the event of Mrs Savill's predeceasing him, he wished his estate to be transferred into a trust to be administered for the benefit of any surviving children by two trustees until they had reached the age of twenty-five. He appointed Mr Veale, or his successor, as one trustee; and he desired you to be the other.'

Savill looked up sharply. 'Are you sure?'

Rowsell peered at him 'Quite sure. There is no possiblity of error or even doubt about it. But I should warn you, it will take time for the will to be proved. Still, I cannot think there will be any difficulty about the matter. The dispositions are entirely straightforward. I understand there are no other living relatives. And there is no evidence whatsoever that the testator desired to change his mind.'

They talked the matter over for a few minutes more. Savill agreed that Mr Veale, or rather Mr Rowsell as his deputy, should continue to act for the estate. Rowsell asked Savill to provide attested certificates of his marriage, the children's baptismal records and their mother's death.

These were straightforward matters, and Savill listened and talked as if he were in a dream, paying hardly any attention to what either of them said.

411

Rampton had disliked Savill and destroyed his career in the American Department when it had been expedient to do so. He had spurned Augusta after her elopement and killed her when she tried to blackmail him. He had ignored Lizzie, his great niece. His interest in Charles had seemed, at best, purely dynastic, a rich man's obsession. At worst, he had seen Charles as a danger to him, an obstacle to be removed.

And yet. Did the will hint at another story?

*The heirs of her body.*

There was another burst of laughter from the next room.

Mr Rowsell coughed in a way designed politely to attract attention rather than to clear the throat. 'You will need time to consider all this, I am sure. There is no great haste, sir, after all. It is always the tortoise who reaches the end in matters of the law, not the hare.' He laughed at his own wit, and then blushed.

'I must talk to the children,' Savill said. *The heirs of her body.*

'That will be as you see fit, of course. Shall we make an appointment for next week? If you were able to look out the certificates in the interim, or at least those you have to hand, that would be of great assistance.'

Rowsell escorted Savill to the door. In the outer office, the staid clerk was smiling broadly, leaning forward over his desk. Before him, sitting at his ease in the visitor's chair and dressed from head to toe in black, was Monsieur Fournier.

# Chapter Sixty-Five

The house was in an alley north of Long Acre, where it clung
to respectability like a martyr to his faith. The lodgings were
up two pairs of stairs and at the back: they consisted of two
apartments, the one opening from the other.

Savill and Fournier stood in the outer room. It had a window
that admitted a dull green-grey light from a greasy court hemmed
in by the backs of houses.

'We could afford little better,' Fournier said, with a hint of
apology in his voice. 'But it was not merely a matter of money.
This is a discreet neighbourhood. No one asks questions in
case the answers are inconvenient.'

'When?' Savill said.

'When did we take the apartments? Late September, though
they weren't occupied until October – while you were with
us at Charnwood, in fact. Dr Gohlis made all the arrangements. Not just for this. For the journey from France. The
nurse. And of course the treatment.'

The room was furnished with a table, three chairs, a wall
cupboard and a battered travelling trunk. It was perfectly tidy.
The floor was swept. The window glass was cracked but it
had recently been cleaned. A coal fire in the grate had dwindled
to ashes.

'The Count paid for everything,' Fournier said. 'Though God knows he can ill afford to do so.'

'Why did he bother?'

'He felt it was his duty. It is quite absurd, I know. One might even say Quixotic. He's not a fool – he is perfectly well aware that there were others, both before him and afterwards.'

'Thank you for the reminder.'

'Pray forgive me, sir. I spoke without thinking. Won't you sit down?'

Savill shook his head, wondering whether Fournier ever spoke without thinking. They waited in silence on either side of the window until at long last the door to the inner room opened.

Dr Gohlis stood in the doorway. He bowed to Savill. 'You may enter now, sir, if you wish.'

Now, when at last the time had come, he wanted to put the clock back, to set the hands whirling in reverse through the hours, the days and nights, the weeks, the months, the years until he reached a time when everything could be made new. When everything was innocent.

*For are we not innocent when we dream?*

The draught from the cracked window touched his cheek. He felt the weight of his solitude. He could talk of this to no one – not Lizzie or Charles or Miss Horton (always supposing he ever saw her again). He would have to be careful with his sister Ferguson, for she would undoubtedly interrogate him at dinner in an attempt to discover why that charming Monsieur Fournier had called at Nightingale Lane this morning in search of Savill, when she had obligingly told him where to find her brother at Lincoln's Inn.

*He came to give me a lesson in morality, dear sister.*

Dr Gohlis stood aside to let him pass.

'You must prepare yourself,' Fournier murmured.

Savill walked through the doorway of the inner room.

\*    \*    \*

His wife lay in bed with the curtains tied back. The window was open. It was very cold. The air brought the hard tang of coal smoke with it, but it could not quite disguise the odours that lay beneath.

The nurse stood at the head of the bed. She curtseyed as the gentlemen entered. She was a respectable-looking woman in a grey dress, with a black shawl about her shoulders and draped over her hair that gave her the appearance of a secular nun. She waited with her head bowed and with her hands clasped before her.

The shroud was folded over the back of the chair. There was a washstand, with a bundle of soiled linen placed beside it on the floor and pushed against the wall. The only other furniture was a chest of drawers, a close-stool and a press with a shelf fixed to the wall above it. A crucifix hung from a nail in the wall opposite the bed.

The body had been washed but the jaw had not been tied up.

'Why?' Savill said. 'Why did she not come to me? Why did you hide her away?'

Fournier glanced at Gohlis. 'Doctor? Pray have the goodness to wait next door a moment, and take the nurse with you.'

Savill turned aside. He stared at the crucifix. He found he was trembling.

'It was by her own desire,' Fournier said gently.

'Because she'd wronged me?'

'Perhaps that was part of it. But she was a proud woman, and she had been beautiful. I think she did not want you to see what she had become. Not you, and not the world, either. Look closely at her.'

Savill approached the bed. Augusta lay on her back, looking up at him with blank eyes, dulled with death. He doubted he would have recognized her if they had passed in the street. Her complexion was already waxen, apart from the left cheek, which was an angry red, the smoothness of the skin disfigured by miniature mounds and craters. The eyelid was damaged too, and the orb itself was cloudy.

He said: 'What in God's name happened?'

'Oil of vitriol,' Fournier said.

Savill stared at him. 'Who did it?'

Fournier said nothing.

'Rampton? Surely not . . .?'

Fournier limped to the door and made sure it was firmly closed. 'I will tell you what I know – that will be better in the end, rather than leave unnecessary doubt. One's own disordered fancy can be one's worst enemy, I find.'

'The truth,' Savill said, gripping Fournier's arm. 'The truth, sir. You owe me that at least.'

Fournier was a small man. He looked calmly at Savill but said nothing.

In a moment, Savill removed his hand and stepped back. 'Forgive me.'

'It does not matter. But pray moderate your voice. You came into this affair at an angle, as it were, so you have never seen its true dimensions. The heart of it is not Charles. It is this poor lady lying here. You remember when she left London for the Continent?'

'How could I not?'

'*I have an appetite,*' she had said all those years ago as she sat astride him, her belly already swollen with Lizzie. '*And you shall feed me.*' And if he were not there to provide nourishment, then naturally she would have looked for it elsewhere.

'It was the summer of seventy-nine,' Savill said. 'I was in New York for the Government, and my commission lasted longer than either of us thought it would.'

'That, I suppose, was part of the trouble. I wonder if Rampton had a hand in prolonging your stay?'

Augusta had not eloped with her Bavarian adventurer solely for love of him, Fournier explained: she had also thrown her reputation to the winds in order to escape the

416

attentions of her uncle Rampton. 'He was making love to her, and pressing her hard, but she resisted, time and time again. A woman in her position is so very vulnerable. When von Streicher came along, he offered a way of escape. I dare say he was a handsome devil too, and very plausible.'

'But Rampton?' Savill protested. 'An old man. And her uncle.'

'He was younger then. As for the near relationship, well, these things happen every night in peasants' cottages – so why should they not happen in the houses of their betters? Lust is a matter of opportunity, sir, not morality.'

When Rampton had lost his position as under secretary in the American Department, he had gone abroad for six months, partly to escape the attentions of his political enemies. He had travelled first to Germany and then to Italy, where he had found his niece in Rome.

'Von Streicher had abandoned her by then. She was living in a precarious manner, dependent on her beauty. When her uncle laid siege to her again, she no longer had a refuge. In exchange for her favours, he set her up in a modest establishment before he left and remitted funds to her for a year or two.' He hesitated. 'That was when Charles was born.'

'Are you saying that Charles is the son of Mr Rampton, as well as his great-nephew?'

Fournier spread his hands. 'It is possible. On the other hand, other gentlemen paid court to her. Monsieur de Quillon's advances certainly met with success, and for a time, just after Mr Rampton left, she was his principal mistress. That's why she came to Paris, to try to rekindle his ardour.'

Savill looked at the woman lying on the bed, her passions spent, her desires set aside and her needs cancelled. 'So the Count may be right?'

'There is simply no way of knowing.'

'Did she see her uncle again?'

'Not until last year. After he left Rome, he had no wish to

prolong the connection between them and indeed every reason to end it. But then' – Fournier gestured gracefully at the window as if there were another country on the far side of the glass – 'the situation in France worsened, and Mr Rampton found employment with another branch of the British Government. I don't know how far you are acquainted with the secret activities of the Black Letter Office?'

'I believe I can hazard a guess as to some of them, sir.'

'Then you may understand why Mrs Savill and Mr Rampton had something in common again. Mrs Savill had the ear of Monsieur de Quillon and his party, and she was in a position to supply valuable intelligence of their activities and plans. She was also in need of money, and Mr Rampton was able to provide her with some. That's why he came to Paris in August.'

'And Mr Malbourne?' Savill said, thinking of Lizzie. 'Was he privy to this?'

'I believe not. He was in Paris to arrange courier routes and ciphers for the British Embassy. His role in this has been entirely innocent. Mr Rampton kept his connection with Mrs Savill to himself. Understandably.'

By this time, the political situation had altered, and it was clear to everyone that the liberal monarchists had had their day. The Count's party had contrived not only to lose the confidence of the King and the royalist party but also to gain the enmity of the Republicans who now held sway in Paris. Mr Rampton was no longer willing to spend his government's gold for information about them.

Fournier wiped his mouth with a handkerchief. 'That was when Mrs Savill made her fatal mistake. She had letters in her possession, letters from Mr Rampton dating back to her years in Rome. According to her, they revealed her uncle's passion for her, and the fact that it had been consummated.'

So Augusta, Savill thought, had been greedy. He said: 'What did she want?'

'A lifetime interest in a lease on a house in Dublin or York, because too many people might remember her here in London.' Fournier spoke with a marked lack of expression, as if reading from a list. 'An annuity of five hundred pounds; Charles to be educated as a gentleman; and, when he came to maturity, to be set up in a position befitting his rank in life.'

'She always knew what she desired.'

'But not what she could have.'

'Did she make her demands in person?'

'Yes,' Fournier said. 'On the night they stormed the Tuileries. Rampton met her by arrangement. She was living in hiding in a little cottage near the Rue de Richelieu. He refused her demands. She threatened to expose him. He tried to seize the letters. There was a struggle.' Fournier stopped and swallowed. 'Forgive me. This must be inexpressibly painful for you. There was a struggle, in the course of which he threw oil of vitriol in her face.'

Savill grappled with the detail, a distraction: 'How did he come by it?'

'In Paris, several gentlemen of my acquaintance have taken to carrying phials of it in their waistcoat pockets. The streets are not safe. Nowhere is. In this case, the vitriol, though agonizing, was not dangerous to life. But immediately afterwards, Mr Rampton stabbed her in three places, puncturing a lung. Then he took the letters and left her bleeding to death, as he thought, with the mob baying at the door.'

'Were you there? You are very well informed.'

'I knew of the meeting, though not about what she intended to discuss with her uncle.' For the first time, Fournier showed a trace of awkwardness. 'There was a possibility that she might have acted as an intermediary between me and the Black Letter Office. In, as it were, a private capacity.'

He waved away this delicate, stillborn idea.

Savill stared at the crucifix and wondered who had put it there. 'Who found her?'

419

'It was I. She was unconscious. After that, there's little more to say. The Count insisted that we bring her to England. His sense of *noblesse* is so very strong. We could not make arrangements to get her out of Paris until late September – and in any case she wasn't well enough to travel until then.'

'Was she at Charnwood? While I was there?'

Fournier shook his head. 'We could hardly have concealed her in Norbury. We brought her here. Not that it has answered, I'm afraid – she grew worse, not better; and then, like so many people in this warm winter, she fell ill with a fever of a putrid tendency. It proved fatal in her weakened state.'

'And Charles? Where was he when Rampton attacked his mother?'

'Augusta told Rampton that the boy was with his old nurse in the country. In fact he was sleeping in a cupboard nearby. She'd told the boy that if he chanced to wake, he must not disturb her, that there was important business she had to transact, a matter of life and death. She said he must promise never to speak of it to anyone, that it would endanger both their lives if he did.'

'But he saw,' Savill said.

'Certainly he heard. And probably he saw something too. At all events, he fled. Poor child.'

'And he has kept his word.'

Fournier's crooked eyebrows rose. 'I don't follow you.'

'Charles has said nothing,' Savill said. 'To anyone. Nothing at all.'

Savill drew out his purse and removed two ha'pence. He stooped and kissed his wife's forehead. It felt like cold leather.

Her eyes looked up at nothing. He closed the lids, one by one, with his forefinger, and weighted each with a ha'penny. He turned the copper discs so Britannia was uppermost, not the King's head. He drew the sheet over his wife's face.

420

He straightened and looked down at her. He wondered if he should pray. But he felt nothing whatsoever, and to pray for nothing seemed in itself a form of blasphemy.

'You almost saw her, you know,' Fournier said.

He turned to him. 'My wife? When?'

'On Sunday. Mrs West lent me her carriage. I knew you projected an expedition to Bedford Square if the weather was tolerably fine – Miss Horton told me. Mrs Savill was very ill, but she made herself worse by demanding to be taken to see you. In the end, Dr Gohlis said it might well kill her if she did not go, and it could not make matters much worse if she did.'

Savill thought about the carriage they had seen driving slowly along the railings. 'Yes. You waved.'

'Indeed. That was the third time we had been around the square. She wore a veil and sat well back. There was no danger of her being recognized.'

'She wanted to see Charles for one last time,' Savill said. 'That was natural. And perhaps Lizzie, too.'

'Oh yes, both of them. She said they were fine children. But she wanted to see you as well.'

Savill shrugged and turned away.

But Fournier would not let him go so easily. 'She said that she wished she could make time run backwards. So when she came back to you, she might change its course.'

Fournier accompanied him downstairs and, at the street door, offered Savill his hand.

'Thank you,' Savill said, raising his voice to be heard over the din of the street. 'If I can serve you in any way, pray let me know.' He released Fournier's hand and was about to go when a thought struck him. 'I had quite forgot. What about the burial?'

'It's in hand, sir. The doctor and I have already made the arrangements. She was received into the Catholic Church as

421

Madame von Streicher, and it would be simpler if she were buried under that name and according to those rites.'

Savill drew closer and lowered his voice. 'And the documents I have?'

'Concerning her death in Paris under the name of Augusta Savill? They are perfectly valid.' Fournier nodded, as if he followed the current of Savill's thoughts as well as Savill did himself. 'You will have no difficulty in establishing her death in a court of law, should you wish to, particularly in the absence of anyone to challenge you. We found another body, you see, Gohlis and I. There was no shortage of them at the time, and the city could not cope with their disposal.'

'I shall pay for the interment, of course, and any other costs,' Savill said. 'Pray have them direct their bills to me at Nightingale Lane.'

'That will not be necessary. Monsieur de Quillon will defray the expenses.'

'No, sir. I shall. It is my right.'

'The Count insists.'

'There is no need for him to play Don Quixote any more. Convey my compliments to him, sir, thank him for his generosity, and say that it is no longer required.'

'It occurs to me, sir,' Fournier said, 'that you and he are two of a kind.' He paused, and then added softly: 'Let him pay for the burial, my dear sir, I beg of you. After all, you have the boy.'

# Chapter Sixty-Six

They are playing a game in the parlour, Charles and Lizzie.
It is a very childish game.

There is a fire in the grate but they have moved away from
it, away from the firelight to the darkest corner of the room.
They have a solitary candle on the table and they are taking it
in turns to make shadow shapes with their hands on the wall
behind it. The game is that you have to guess what the shape is.

Charles does an elephant first, and that is easy for Lizzie
to guess because of the trunk. She does a bird with a big beak
that opens and shuts. It is perfectly recognizable as a bird but
Charles cannot say what it is. So – just this once, and because
it is only Lizzie – he forms the letter B with his finger on the
wall by the shadow.

'B,' she cries.

He makes an I and then an R, after which she says 'bird'
aloud, saying it cannot be anything other.

Now it is his turn to make the shadow, and he does a boar's
head with tusks. It is a remarkably lifelike creation, he thinks,
but for all that Lizzie cannot work out what it is. She tries
dog, cat, cow, and even rhinoceros.

Each time, he shakes his head. It is only Lizzie, after all,
his sister, and shaking one's head is not like speaking.

'Oh – it's so provoking,' she cries. 'Can you not give me a hint?'

A devil of mischief possesses him. He snuffles and snorts.

'A pig!' she cries, and he nods, though in point of fact it is a wild boar, and then she starts to laugh because the snuffling and snorting is so unspeakably droll.

So does he. Together they snuffle and snort and laugh as if they were children still in leading strings.

The parlour door opens.

The laughter dies, his and Lizzie's.

There is Mr Savill on the threshold. He must have come in by the yard, or they would have heard him knock, and heard the servant sliding the bars and bolts. He is late home, much later than expected.

Mr Savill holds on to the jamb of the door. Even in this light, his face looks flushed. He is in liquor, Charles suspects, for it is a fact that many gentlemen sometimes are.

Lizzie runs to him, and he kisses her cheek.

He looks over her head at Charles. 'Come here,' he says.

Charles obeys. He smells the wine on Mr Savill's breath.

Mr Savill drapes his arm across Charles's shoulder.

'Come,' he says. 'I find I'm a trifle unsteady on my feet this evening, and you must support me into the dining room. Your aunt says you may stay up late tonight and join us for supper.'